TRUE CRIME STORY

Also by Joseph Knox

Sirens
The Smiling Man
The Sleepwalker

For more information on Joseph Knox and his books,
see his website at www.josephknox.co.uk

TRUE CRIME STORY

A NOVEL

JOSEPH KNOX

doubleday

TRANSWORLD PUBLISHERS
Penguin Random House, One Embassy Gardens,
8 Viaduct Gardens, London SW11 7BW
www.penguin.co.uk

Transworld is part of the Penguin Random House group of companies
whose addresses can be found at global.penguinrandomhouse.com

Penguin
Random House
UK

First published in Great Britain in 2021 by Doubleday
an imprint of Transworld Publishers

A CIP catalogue record for this book
is available from the British Library.

ISBNs
9780857527707 (hb)
9780857527714 (tpb)

Set in 11.25/17 pt Palatino LT Pro
Text design by Couper Street Type Co.
Typeset by Jouve (UK), Milton Keynes
Printed and bound in Great Britain by Clays Ltd, Elcograf S.p.A.

The authorized representative in the EEA is Penguin Random House Ireland,
Morrison Chambers, 32 Nassau Street, Dublin D02 YH68.

Penguin Random House is committed to a sustainable
future for our business, our readers and our planet. This book
is made from Forest Stewardship Council® certified paper.

'Will you miss me when I'm gone?'
Mogwai, 'R U Still in 2 It?'

PUBLISHER'S NOTE

This amended second edition of True Crime Story *includes wider context on the previously undisclosed role of Joseph Knox in the narrative, as well as his response to various allegations raised in the press and online. Further, Penguin Random House can confirm that they and Mr Knox have mutually agreed to conclude their business dealings and have no plans to undertake any future projects.*

Please see below for a brief statement from Knox concerning this second edition.

When Penguin Random House suggested a second edition of *True Crime Story* to clarify my position, I just about bit their hands off. Legitimate questions have been raised about the validity of my participation in this project, questions which I will be only too happy to answer in due course. Unfortunately, there have also been libellous accusations, gross misrepresentations of my character and threats made against my family. These threats are completely out of line. Contrary to reports, I have not objected to any addition that Penguin Random House have made to the text, asking only for a right to reply.

I continue to be moved by reader interest in this story and, although at times personally painful, I consider this edition to be an improvement upon the first. It's my hope that these amendments will allow us to shift focus from salacious, peripheral details, and on to the true instigators and true victims of this crime.

Joseph Knox, 2020

In the early hours of Saturday, 17 December 2011, Zoe Nolan, a nineteen-year-old Manchester University student, walked out of a party taking place in the shared accommodation where she had been living for three months.

She was never seen again.

On the surface, Zoe had everything in the world going for her. In September of that year, she'd travelled from Stoke-on-Trent to Manchester, realizing a long-held ambition to live in the city. She moved into a high-rise student apartment with her twin sister, Kimberly, and two other girls who quickly became her closest friends. Singing had always been the great passion of Zoe's life, and she'd moved to Manchester to more seriously study music, finding herself unexpectedly popular with course mates and around campus. Her contemporaries found her talent and dedication impressive and she soon met the young man who would become her first serious boyfriend. She passed three seemingly happy months in this state, right up until 17 December, the day her parents arrived to take her home for the Christmas holidays, only to find that she had vanished without a trace.

I'd never heard of Zoe Nolan, or if I had I'd forgotten all about her. In 2011, the year she went missing, I would have been twenty-five years old, and myself living in Manchester. If you could really call it living. I certainly wasn't making my dreams come true, I was making minimum wage plus tips in a basement dive bar, and putting every penny I earned back into the business. Manchester had made me, for better or worse. It was the first place I'd ever had my heart broken, the first place I'd ever had my nose broken, and somehow that encapsulated so much of what I loved about the city. There was a kind of toughness on one hand and a kind of romance on the other. It was like a man with 'LOVE' and 'HATE' tattooed on to his knuckles – you never knew which one he might hit you with next. I was always more like a lover than a fighter, more like a punching bag than a slugger, so I just tried to keep my guard up and weather the blows when they came. The city always struck me as a lot of different things, some of them were good and some of them were bad, but make no mistake about it, the city always struck me. As a result, so much of it's a blur now. There are whole years I don't really remember, whole jobs, whole people, whole places, much less news broadcasts, much less front-page headlines.

Much less police appeals for information.

So when I looked Zoe Nolan up some six years after her disappearance at the insistence of a new friend, I found that all I really remembered was her image, the picture that had been briefly ubiquitous in the city for a few days half a dozen years before, the face I'd never quite put a name to. Zoe was an almost iconic *missing person* blonde – almost iconic, but not quite. I skimmed the story, muttered something to myself like, 'Oh yeah,' then got on with my day, because, from what I read, not much had happened since she walked out of that party. She'd never been found, and I couldn't see why my new friend was so interested in her, why she was suddenly so obsessed. And anyway, I was a busy man. By 2017, my own life had finally started, and I didn't have time for people who'd been careless enough to lose theirs. I was a published author now, an important person – going places, if only in my own mind. I had no idea what lay behind Zoe's frozen smile, and no idea what lay behind her disappearance. I had no idea that she'd go on to keep me up at night over the next few years, and no idea that she'd go on to put a good friend of mine in mortal danger.

Her story was sad, certainly, but hardly sensational.

Because in my experience – both fictional and factual – girls went missing all the time. As a crime writer, missing girls were more or less my stock-in-trade. Morbidly, I suppose I still expected Zoe to turn up somewhere, even all those years on, not alive necessarily, but at least as a dead body. Perhaps there'd be an almost-iconic death to match her almost-iconic missing-person picture. She'd be discovered in a shallow woodland grave, I thought, in a discarded roadside suitcase, or submerged, sunken, somewhere along Manchester's thirty-six-mile shipping canal. I expected the mysteries of her life and disappearance to be untangled and normalized, if not today, then at least tomorrow. I expected her to be rendered mundane by the great villain of our age – a man – a man who had watched her too closely, a man who had taken things too far, a man who had transformed his dark fantasies into a sad and disturbing reality.

If I hadn't met Evelyn Mitchell, I wouldn't have given the story any more thought than that. Hers was the first hand in the air at the Manchester Q&A for my debut novel, *Sirens*. She asked me about the provenance of serial killers in crime fiction, and the genre's tendency to focus more on its murderers than its victims. At the time I didn't know I was being tested, and I answered honestly, that I agreed with her to some extent. There were no serial killers in *Sirens*, and I said I didn't think there'd be any serial killers in my future novels either, simply because their motives so often seemed superfluous to me. I worried that these increasingly grotesque supervillains FedExing body parts back and forth across the country minimized victims, and occasionally just read as ridiculous. We talked a little more when I signed her book, and exchanged email addresses after she told me that she was a writer as well. Evelyn Mitchell, it turned out, was the author of *Exitlessness*, a scathing first novel about male excess that had been well reviewed but arrived too soon, selling so little that her publisher stopped returning her calls. A few years had passed and she was no longer the bright young thing who'd been touted for success by the likes of the *Observer* and the *London Review of Books*. Now she was standing in line waiting for me, just as in a few years I'd be standing in line waiting for someone else.

What Evelyn didn't tell me at the time, what she would, perhaps, have never told the world, was that her career had been waylaid by an unexpected and cruelly unfair breast cancer diagnosis in her late twenties. She had undergone a double mastectomy and suffered countless rounds of chemotherapy, losing crucial writing years and irreplaceable self-confidence. These losses had left her haunted somewhat by the idea, the statistical likelihood, of her own early demise, and she was hungry to make up for lost time on a larger project, one that might leave her mark on the world. Fiction held no more interest for her, she said, real life was terrifying enough. Her new worldview came with a kind of life-affirming fatalism and a surfeit of gallows humour. When she finally told me about her medical history, she smiled across the table and said:

'So, how does it feel?'

'How does what feel?' I asked.

'How does it feel to be the only tit left in my life?'

In the spring of 2017, when the buzz for my first book died down, I started to meet Evelyn for coffee, sometimes for drinks, and inevitably talk would turn towards what we were both working on. For me that meant *The Smiling Man*, my second novel, with which I was determined to improve upon the first. For Evelyn, it meant something else entirely. She had struggled, she said, to find the right project for her second book, struggled with what she saw as her own slow fade into obscurity, until one day she'd found herself thinking, idly, *Well, what happens to those girls who go missing? What happens to the Zoe Nolans of the world?* I encouraged her because I could sense her desperation, because I wanted to be kind, but as my focus shifted on to my own work I increasingly found cause to break our dates, excuses not to meet up for coffee or for drinks. When I was writing intensively I could comfortably go whole weeks without speaking to friends and family, whole months without opening my emails. I routinely lost track of time and people, but perhaps that's letting myself off the hook too easily. In Evelyn's one-room squat, in her frayed clothes and stalled projects, I felt like I could see the dim outline of my own future. A future with no more successes and no more highs, just unanswered calls and rejection letters, just limitless, endless lows. Writers can get superstitious about failure, they think it's contagious. Our conversation cooled and the basis for our friendship devolved into emails where we'd occasionally say hi and not much else. These emails went from weekly occurrences to monthly ones, from quarterly to almost nothing at all. Then, on 25 June 2018 an email arrived into my inbox with an intriguing subject.

True Crime Story.

Evelyn had, she said, taken the extraordinary step of contacting Zoe Nolan's immediate family, speaking to them first as a human being and later as a writer. With their consent, she'd spent almost twelve months talking with a wider range of Zoe's friends and acquaintances, interviewing everyone she could find, anyone who'd speak to her on the record. And as she did, a complex, contradictory picture began to emerge. Where some versions of events overlapped, aligning perfectly with one another, others stood in stark contrast, giving rise to troubling inconsistencies. There were the bitter disappointments that had led Zoe to the degree course where she was, in fact, struggling. There was the criminal boyfriend who refused to leave Zoe alone but admittedly never loved her. There was the unrelenting pressure from Zoe's parents and the strained, destructive relationship she shared with her twin sister. And then there was the so-called 'Shadow Man' who stalked Zoe through the city, tracking her every move . . .

What there clearly was *not* was any kind of conclusion.

Dwelling on Evelyn's physical and mental well-being, I felt guilty for having encouraged her down this path in the first place, encouraging her to invest precious time in some unfulfilling and unanswerable mystery. So, to my shame, the email marked *True Crime Story* went unanswered and the attachment which Evelyn hoped to use as the first third of this book went unread.

When a stunning new development threw much of the established narrative of the Zoe Nolan case into question some six months later, I got back in touch with Evelyn, suggesting that perhaps she'd been right all along. She responded quickly, telling me not to read her original file yet, telling me that this new information had shaken loose an important and previously obscured element of her story – that she had *finally* found the perfect opening for her book . . .

As I requested and then read this new opening, as I greedily started to work my way through Evelyn's original chapters, I began to see what she had. That even those closest to Zoe Nolan hadn't known her empirical truth, or, perhaps, that they had each known only their own part of it. I began to understand how Zoe had been forced to keep secrets from those she loved, and, perhaps, how she could ultimately even disappear into thin air. Some of the interviewees tended old grudges like garden plots, some of them saw events in a harsh new light. Evelyn argued that the full story, the real truth about Zoe Nolan, could only be assembled from these disparate threads. That in all the ink spilled during the coverage of the case, so much of that truth had been written between the lines, so much of it had been lost entirely. Evelyn argued for a book that would lay everything bare using the unvarnished words of those involved, contradictions and all, the full story unfolding for readers as it had unfolded for her, one revelation on top of another. She believed in a better world, one where a missing girl might actually mean something, but as I read on, I realized that I didn't.

I saw that in spite of the corkscrew twists and revelations in Evelyn's story there was still no conclusion in sight, and it fell to me to tell her the truth. That all of the inconsistencies, all of the affairs, all of the sex-tapes, secrets and lies would mean nothing without an ending. As long as Zoe Nolan was unaccounted for, there was no book. In publishing, as in the world, we're drowning in dead girls, and I'm afraid that missing ones just don't cut it. Evelyn had been right that first time we met. Our interests revolve around killers, not victims – 'What are you going to do,' I asked her, 'change human nature?' It was my opinion that with a mere missing person, without a dead body, without even a verifiable crime, there was no story. I didn't want to see Evelyn waste what might be precious years of her life researching a doomed, unresolvable narrative, so I said as much. As a result, by mid-February of 2019, our exchanges had grown terse, with Evelyn's in particular becoming paranoid, cynical and at times even disturbing.

So, sadly, I didn't believe her when she told me she was getting close to something, and I didn't believe her when her own shadow man came knocking at the door. When Evelyn finally found her proof, when she finally went to confront the person she believed to be responsible for Zoe's disappearance – when she told me that she no longer felt physically well – I was preoccupied, slow to act. Cynically, I'd warned her that this story needed a dead body at the end if it was ever to be told. By the close of 25 March 2019, there were two of them.

My thanks to the Mitchell family, who forwarded the notes, tapes and documents that Evelyn had collected, and who kindly trusted me with their editing and publication. Some chapters were already in finished form, just as she would have liked them to be read, others I had to pore through and assemble myself from her rough outlines. I sought out additional testimony where necessary, in some cases from experts, in some cases from people who Evelyn had never got around to interviewing, adding them to the established flow of her story.

As I worked, I saw that what had at first seemed like a digressive route through the secret lives of others was actually a menacing roadmap leading directly to the destruction of something good, a destruction that neither Evelyn nor I saw coming. Perhaps you can read these interviews differently, though. Perhaps you'll see the danger sooner than we did. Perhaps you're the person who could have done what I didn't, and prevented another useless death.

This book is dedicated to Evelyn Mitchell – to Zoe Nolan – and to everyone else who never came home.

Jfnox, 2019

From: evelynidamitchell@gmail.com

Sent: 10/01/19 18:04

To: you

Hey stinker

So here's what I'm NOW proposing to open the book with. Don't read what I sent before until you've read this prologue.

What follows actually happened BEFORE Zoe went missing, and is more to do with her twin sister, Kim (and no, I don't think they fucking swapped places). It's one of many unbelievable stories that takes place within this larger one – and in some ways it feels like the key to a lot of things that come later. I've tried to set it up as some kind of introduction to who all these people are, and to hint at the relationships/grievances that shape a lot of the story.

And oh boy are there grievances. I've only had a handful of people from Zoe's life who were unable or unavailable to speak, only one or two who've resisted my charms and refused to go on the record. Most of them feel like they HAVE to say something because they're scared of what the others might say about them.

Early on, I saw there was so much cross-talk and contention that I'd have to share statements between interviewees. In most cases that provided what illumination I was looking for, but in others it led to these spirited responses, withering put-downs, rebuttals, etc. I think it gives the text a nice back-and-forth conversational style, but each interview was conducted in STRICT isolation. Mainly because most of them aren't speaking to each other any more . . .

Funny how that happens to people (eh Knoxy?)

I'm going old school with this one – no digital recordings: everything's going down on tape. If you fancy hearing voices, I'm afraid you'll have to come round. ██ ████████*

Anyway, let me know what you think. If you're intrigued then by all means carry on and read through the chapters I sent you SIX MONTHS AGO.

Ex

*Evelyn never intended for her email correspondence to be made public. As a result, some small redactions have been made to protect her privacy. – J.K.

--0--

'Exposed Foundations'

8 Nov. 2011 – 40 days before Zoe's disappearance

In late 2018 Kimberly Nolan, Zoe's twin sister, claimed in a rare interview given to the Mail on Sunday *that she had herself once been kidnapped. She claimed that this kidnapping occurred roughly one month prior to Zoe's disappearance, while on a night out with her sister and three other friends.*

KIMBERLY NOLAN, *Zoe's sister*:
I feel like my *Mail* interview covered all this. There are just more interesting things we could talk about. We could go back into Zoe as a little girl, work out if there were any warning signs we all missed. Or we could cut right back to the good stuff, our move out to Manchester. First time in a new city, first time doing a lot of things. We could even rehash the night Zoe went missing – I mean, that's why we're here, I can take you through all that with my eyes closed. Midnight fire alarms, people I shouldn't have slept with, psychotic men standing in the shadows . . .

I know all of it, all of that, by heart.

But here you are asking me about my weakest subject, Kimberly Nolan. What can I tell you? I hardly know the girl.

FINTAN MURPHY, *Zoe's course mate, friend***:**
Right, Kimberly's kidnapping, this sad story. Would you like my opinion? I mean, let's put ourselves in poor Kimberly's position for a moment. Born a girl, an almost identical twin, but with a sister who was simply more attractive than she was, simply more intelligent. A sister who was outgoing and prodigiously gifted musically. Someone who effortlessly charmed everyone she met. I think we all might struggle if we were up against that.

Okay, so, remaining in Kimberly's shoes. You go away to university to get out from under your sister's shadow, but owing to an unfortunate series of events you end up studying at the same place, living in the same flat, even. Your physical resemblance is such that people routinely double-take at you around town, seem visibly disappointed when they realize you're Kimberly and not Zoe.

So you lose a load of weight and start wearing black. You cut your hair short and go Goth. Your sister is reserved in some senses, so you act out and start sleeping around. She drinks sensibly, so you drink like an open hole in the floor. She goes missing and becomes front-page news, so you generate this harrowing, incredible tale of how *you* were kidnapped once, too. I'd say in some senses that's perfectly understandable. It's one of the few things about Kimberly that really is.

JAI MAHMOOD, *Zoe's friend*:

I don't remember much, but I'm fairly sure Fintan wasn't even there that night.

LIU WAI, *Zoe's flatmate, friend*:

I think what probably happened was that Zoe and I decided to go out? I know it was a Tuesday, which is like a *big* student night in Manchester. Kim always tried to involve herself in mine and Zoe's plans, so I generally expected her to try and tag along. And she did, in that kind of dour way where it's clear she thinks she's doing you a massive favour. This was before she dyed her hair black and stuff, but she always had that kind of personality. And then, because it was the three of us, the boys ended up coming too. So that made for an eventful evening . . .

JAI MAHMOOD:

Y'know how some people drink so much of something they can never go near it again? They have to hold their nose while your Jim Beam's being poured because of that night they drank a whole bottle of the stuff and spent six hours blowing it out both ends? *[Laughs]* That's basically how I got sober, bro. One brand at a time, pushing everything so far over the line that I could never touch it again. I think the only thing I haven't had a bad night on by now's Babycham and, being honest, that's just so I've got something saved for the deathbed.

ANDREW FLOWERS, *Zoe's boyfriend*:

The Kimnapping? I mean, I know I shouldn't laugh, but we did go to Fifth Avenue. If you don't know it, it's the ten or eleventh circle of hell, this grotesque indie disco warehouse where girls are generally assured of a cheap night out. That's because they order one drink and some pale-faced northern boy called Gaz or Trev or something spikes it with Rohypnol. The girls are legless before they can even request Adele from the DJ. From some angles, that's the only good thing about the place.

JAI MAHMOOD:

Point being, I was fully in that phase of my life back then, yeah? Not just embracing disaster, but taking it home and really giving it one. I'd had my head kicked in a few weeks before, so I thought I had a good excuse for being a fuck-up. It was only over the next few years I started running low on excuses. So anyway, I know it's criminal to say, but I don't remember much about that night. It's not one where I can scroll through the viewfinder and see some stills or shaky handheld footage, it's just not there at all. Like, file missing, y'know? But if Fintan's saying he was there then he's full of it.

KIMBERLY NOLAN:

Looking back, I'm Bruce Springsteen. I wanna change my clothes, my hair, my face. Just please not the dress I was wearing that night. I was starting to experiment, trying to put some of my real self on display. I'd found this cool kind of Wednesday Addams outfit at Affleck's Palace and it made me feel more like myself than I had before, less like a second-rate Zoe and something more like Kim. It was the only time we ever went out as a group, which is strange when you read the papers from back then. You'd think we were thick as thieves when really we were just thick as kids. And everyone was acting invincible, no idea what was coming round the corner.

Jai had taken something, which he usually had. Andrew was in a bad mood, which he usually was. Him and Zoe were arguing, so the rest of us all had to suffer. Saying that, I'm not sure Zoe even really noticed. She was the most invincible of us all, everything-proof and stunning, wearing this luminescent red jacket, ultra-hot red all over. Matching red lipstick and a slightly visible red bra. Zoe was busy *being* noticed.

ANDREW FLOWERS:
After Zoe went missing the police became oddly fixated on that night, so certain details stuck. Yes, Zoe had on some red thing that they could probably see in outer space. If she'd still been wearing it when she went missing they'd have picked her up in five seconds flat. And if Kim says we were fighting, then I'm sure that we were, it was more or less our default setting. Once we started in on each other neither one of us could ever find the off switch.

JAI MAHMOOD:
They told me afterwards that I lit up and started blazing on the dancefloor. Like I say, that night's a blank slate for me, but it wouldn't be completely out of character. I know the bouncers wouldn't let me in when I went back a week later so, yeah, if they say I got kicked out, I probably got kicked out.

LIU WAI:
It's sad to say but I think even then Jai was a really troubled soul? I think he always felt like a bit of an outsider. Where I'm one of those people who feels comfortable talking to anyone at any level, quite

Virgo, Jai kind of wore his brown-ness? Like, he really *wore* his race. He felt like he had to be kind of street and smoke weed and listen to rap songs, where, I don't know. I've always seemed to fit in much more naturally?

ANDREW FLOWERS:

I thought Jai getting kicked out was the best thing about that night. He was so out of it he started smoking on the dancefloor, offering cigarettes to girls and stuff. Then something painful started playing, 'Sex on Fire' or whatever, and suddenly we were surrounded on all sides, just Midlanders, just Waynes and Janes as far as the eye could see. He offered this little blonde number a light and she accepted. They were laughing, getting close, then this cinderblock-headed prick started pushing him around, speaking fluent fucking caveman. 'Hands off my girl,' etcetera, etcetera. As I recall, Jai tried to apologize but ended up coughing two lungs full of smoke into the guy's face by accident. He went apeshit.

KIMBERLY NOLAN:

With Jai, people saw his slacker image and stopped looking, but there was more to him than that. He took these pictures, just tuned out the world and found amazing things that we were all looking at but none of us could see. The bouncers didn't know that, though, they just saw trouble. This wasted Asian boy who'd walked in with two black eyes. They were going overboard, pulling him out by the hair and stuff, so I guess there was some racism in it, too. I started to follow them so I could explain and check he was okay, but I'd just been *Exorcist*-sick in the toilets. The floor was like jelly under my feet so I stopped when I

17

got to the stairs. I thought if I was leaving I'd better find Zoe first and tell her. Something was wrong with me. I felt dizzy and sick, which was weird because I hadn't even really been drinking.

FINTAN MURPHY:
If Kimberly says she hadn't been drinking, then I suppose we have to take her word for it. There's a first time for everything, after all.

LIU WAI:
Kim was plastered.

ANDREW FLOWERS:
No, I wasn't counting Kim's drinks, and no, I wasn't spiking them either, if that's what you're asking me. She'd been gone for some time so I just assumed she'd left when Jai got kicked out. Zoe and I weren't getting along, and I could never quite stand Liu Wai, so I politely excused myself.

LIU WAI:
I think I was just saying that Jai *had* broken the rules, like, the club *is* No Smoking. Andrew told me I could wank him off with a pair of chopsticks and stormed out. I mean, aside from being a low-level hate crime, doesn't that imply to you that he's got a small penis?

ANDREW FLOWERS:
I'm sure she remembers better than I do. I'm afraid I didn't necessarily see Liu Wai as a person back then, she was just some strange Chinese tumour attached to my girlfriend.

LIU WAI:

I'm from fucking Essex.

FINTAN MURPHY:

Yes, Andrew and Zoe, the famous loving couple . . .

LIU WAI:

Andrew and Zoe *were* always challenging to be around. Nowadays I think we'd call their relationship quite toxic? Just a kind of unsafe chemical spill of a couple. Like, the only possible solution for both parties was extraction. I'm sure Zoe was upset to see him go – she blamed herself when things were bad. It was just that most of the time Andrew looked visibly uncomfortable around her? You'd see him sort of itching to get away.

But then he'd always be dropping in, always hanging around, always inviting himself out. A lot like Kim when you think about it. Given what happened between them all later, it's one of those things you can't help but torture yourself about afterwards. I mean, let's get it straight. He never loved Zoe.

ANDREW FLOWERS:

Perhaps it might seem circumspect from the vantage point of years passed, but I truly couldn't stand Fifth and I'm sure that's why I left. In nightclubs, as in life, it's my opinion that too many cocks ruin the broth. And Jai couldn't even remember his own name, he couldn't even remember his own PIN number – believe me, I tried to get it for the cab fare. So, monstrously, yes, I decided to take him home rather than let him sleep it off in the gutter. If I'd known Kim was struggling that night, I'd have taken her home too, that's just the kind of guy I am.

FINTAN MURPHY:

A selfless act from Andrew Flowers? Another first. After recent events I'd say we all know for certain what kind of *guy* he is . . .

LIU WAI:

I want to be fair but, honestly? I don't know what Zoe ever saw in him. I consider Andrew Flowers to be one of the most unpleasant human beings I've ever encountered.

KIMBERLY NOLAN:

Well, Liu lives to judge people. I'm not saying she's wrong on Andrew, but being cynical about everything doesn't make you Nostradamus.

JAI MAHMOOD:

If Andrew really did take me home, it's probably because it suited whatever was happening in Flowers-land.

KIMBERLY NOLAN:

We all scattered and when I got back to the booth where I'd left them, the only thing I could find of Zoe's was her bright red jacket. I was feeling so weird I couldn't tell how long I'd been gone, so I think I assumed they'd all left without me. They were probably just on the dancefloor or something. Fifth's this typical Manchester nightclub, a sweatbox that never drops below boiling point.

I was shivering, though.

My teeth were chattering and I was breaking out in goose bumps, so I grabbed Zoe's jacket and put it on. The room's this wide-open mezzanine-type space, like the Roman Colosseum or something, you can see the top floor from the bottom and everything just surrounds you. There was a song playing, 'Flux' by Bloc Party, the part where the singer starts screaming: 'We need to talk,' over and over again. And I knew then, from the way I was frozen stiff and the room was looming down on me, from the way everyone had vanished and this song kept insisting, *'We need to talk, we need to talk,'* I knew something bad was happening to us.

FINTAN MURPHY:

Jai's absolutely correct, I wasn't out that night, and I've never claimed otherwise, I don't drink for a start. I'm sure Zoe invited me, but I suppose I was busy or not in the mood. The reason I can discuss those events with some certainty is that I went there the following day, looking for Zoe's missing jacket. She'd emailed me mentioning how upset she was to have misplaced it, so I thought I'd see if it was in the lost property to surprise her.

In the event, it was me who ended up being surprised.

The club was closed during the day, but I badgered my way in and pleaded my case. The jacket hadn't been handed over, but Zoe had mentioned where she'd been sitting, so I asked if they'd let me watch the CCTV covering that booth. I came up with some spiel on data protection law, saying people have the right to request footage they've appeared in, and I was doing so on Zoe's behalf. Either I'm a gifted liar or they just got bored of me, because on the twentieth time of asking, the manager marched us back to the office and handed me over to a security guy. He got things running and we watched the booth on fast forward until Zoe, Kim, Liu, Andrew and Jai all arrived. We sped through their various comings and goings then slowed down when we saw the booth had been left vacant. Then Kim staggered back looking absolutely trashed, and I suppose an alarm bell started going off for me then. She checked there was no one around then put Zoe's jacket on and walked away.

We were able to follow her on camera after that, we saw her leaving the club in her sister's red jacket, as she said in her recent *Mail* interview. Then there were a couple of other things she never quite got round to mentioning. She was certainly confused, certainly disorientated. In fact, in this apparent search for her sister, she stopped in the doorway to check out a guy, even made a grab and shouted something after him. He kept on going. Perhaps her disorientation was also the reason why, when she began persistently calling someone outside, waiting for the phone to be answered, she never once dialled her sister's number, despite telling the *Mail* that's why she left the club in the first place. I have Zoe's phone records from her parents. No incoming calls that night or the next morning. Of course, I'd be interested to see Kimberly's records . . .

KIMBERLY NOLAN:
Could *you* find a phone bill from seven fucking years ago?

FINTAN MURPHY:
Look, what I saw on that tape was a young woman undergoing some kind of internal crisis, one exacerbated by drugs or alcohol.

She was walking with hunched shoulders, crossed arms, constantly picking at her nails and moving strands of hair, clearly in some kind of emotional distress, but also clearly on the pull. Whatever Kimberly's problem was, she walked into that building with it.

But once she exited the club and tried to make a couple of calls, it all seemed to fall away. I remember she was looking quite closely at the people gathered in the street outside, she even approached one or two of them. What's interesting is that everyone she looked at or approached was a man. I remember thinking, *Who's she looking for?* The impression I got was that she was searching for someone in particular, and she was confused not to find him out there.

KIMBERLY NOLAN:

There was a hand on my back and I was being pushed into this filthy white rust-bucket van. Someone had used their finger to write on the door in grime – *clean me* – and I was half-laughing at that when everything went black.

FINTAN MURPHY:

Now, because Kimberly never mentioned anything about this assault to anyone, not in the wake of her sister's disappearance, not for seven years afterwards, there was no cause for authorities to check cameras in the surrounding area at the time. Conveniently for Kimberly's story, there's no way for us to confirm the existence of this white van now, but I can tell you for damn sure I never saw it on the club's camera. I mean, not to state things too bluntly, but my dealings with Kimberly Nolan have *all* been characterized by tall tales.

KIMBERLY NOLAN:

When I was thirteen years old I got run down on a zebra crossing. They could never find the car – it was just one of those things. I didn't see anything and no one ever came forward. The driver was going too fast but, honestly, I walked out without looking. And the second it hit me, the word *IDIOT* just flashed through my mind in capital letters. It was so clear I thought, *This must be the last thing people think when they die in an accident,* and I used to tell my friends that when we'd talk about it. How lucky I was to have come so close, to have got this glimpse of the other side, but still lived to remember it.

The van was the same thing again, like a near-death experience.

There was a hand on me, I was in the back and then the door slammed shut, like it was all happening in one moment. Someone put a bag on my head, this thick fabric with a drawstring tight round my neck, then they ripped off Zoe's jacket and put cable ties round my wrists. I heard the plastic teeth when they pulled them on, so tight I thought my hands might fall off. And my whole brain's flashing *IDIOT, IDIOT, IDIOT* in mile-high capital letters, just like when I got hit by the car, only now I know what I learned from that. That it must be the last conscious thought a lot of people have.

LIU WAI:

I'm not a judgemental person, I say, 'Live and let live.' You know, a lot of girls have that one drink too many and find themselves in the wrong place at the wrong time. It's just that Kim seems to *frequently* have that one drink too many? She seems to *frequently* find herself in the wrong place at the wrong time.

KIMBERLY NOLAN:

When they started driving I couldn't speak, I don't think I could even cry. We'd been going a few minutes before it even occurred to me to try and remember the turns or work out where we'd gone. My head was spinning so much it wouldn't have mattered anyway. I was on my knees, leaning into the wall to stay upright. And I knew there were men in the van because I could *feel* their eyes on me, I could smell them through the bag on my head.

ANDREW FLOWERS:

So, we're talking gone midnight? Unfortunately, I was in possession of the world's most knackered Rolex back then. I couldn't tell you where I was for sure, even if I remembered. My guess would be that I was pouring Jai into bed.

JAI MAHMOOD:

Yeah, I'd have to go along with that. I was probably in bed or on my way there. I am sure I woke up back at ours the next day, I mean, I'd remember if I hadn't.

LIU WAI:

I think Zoe and me just enjoyed the rest of our night? I was probably quite happy that everyone had left us to it. She was definitely annoyed we couldn't find her jacket, though. I had to wait for Kim's

Mail on Sunday interview seven years after the fact to get some closure on that.

KIMBERLY NOLAN:

I was told that this bag on my head was the only thing keeping me alive, and if I tried to look at them when they rolled it up to check something, they'd have to hurt me. Only one of them really talked. He sounded northern but I couldn't be sure. He rolled the bag up to my nose and told me to open my mouth. You can guess what was going through my mind by that point, but I did it. And even though the bag was still over my eyes, I could see torchlight. I could tell he was looking into my mouth like a dentist, checking me for something. He grunted and I felt another guy come closer. It felt like they were both leaning in and looking at me. Then they started asking me about my teeth. Seriously, asking me about fillings and stuff while they'd got me tied up in the back of a van.

ANDREW FLOWERS:

The old cavity search? Right, I think I read about that, too. Is there a reason we're going over things I wasn't around for?

KIMBERLY NOLAN:

Well, I didn't have any fillings, which I just about managed to tell them. They said that was good then started feeling along my arms. I don't think it was sexual, but only because it felt worse than that to me at the time. It was like the way you'd handle meat or something. Turn it over, press it and check it for imperfections. I was so cold I could hardly feel their hands, and the cable ties were making my arms go numb. And at the same time we were still driving, turning, stopping, starting, I couldn't see anything. Then they picked me up and started feeling along my legs in the same way, checking for something. They got halfway down my right leg and stopped, still gripping me by the knee.

ROBERT NOLAN, *Kimberly and Zoe's father*:
Well, whatever we might think about Kimberly's gift for invention, the road accident thing's true, I can vouch for that. Music was a big part of our lives at home, I was a professional musician myself for a time, but she always went for different stuff, like, than the rest of us. Punk and whatnot. Some of what she listened to you'd struggle to call music at all. That's partly why we got her the iPod for Christmas, so we wouldn't have to hear it. I don't think she took her headphones off again until she went under that car. She broke her right knee and she was lucky that's all.

SALLY NOLAN, *Kimberly and Zoe's mother*:
That's when Kim and Zoe drifted a bit. Parents of twins, you know, they do the matching hair and toys and clothes. We never went in for all that, but I suppose you do expect girls to be close. It just didn't happen with ours, they were always their own people. Then around there, thirteen or fourteen, after Kim got knocked down, Zoe started going out more. She was already singing and getting paid and being hired for shows, it just got more. It's probably a chicken-and-egg thing, but the hit and run made them more different. After it, Zoe was always going out further and further into the world, and Kim was always going back, further inside herself.

KIMBERLY NOLAN:

Everything stopped. I mean, the van was still going but everything else stopped. And this man's still gripping me by my knee, not moving, making it clear that something's wrong with my leg. It doesn't reach his fucking leg standards or whatever. So when he asked me about the scar from the accident my brain went into overdrive trying to work out what to say, how to let him down gently.

I told him there was a flaw in my knee, like a birth defect.

From the way they'd been feeling me, and I know this sounds gross, but I thought they might want to *breed* me or something. It was late 2011, so the Rochdale grooming scandal was going on in the background, this child sex ring that had gone under the radar for years, and there were all these insane stories about sex trafficking round Manchester.

So I was trying to suggest I wasn't the right candidate if that's what they had in mind. I was trying to suggest there was stuff wrong with my body, that I was more trouble than I was worth. They made a big deal about my knee, they asked about it, so I started telling them how useless it was. I said I'd been forced to have surgery, I'd been forced to have steel pins implanted and stuff. I said I had to do an hour's physio a day just so I could walk on it, I said I'd probably lose my leg at some point in the future. I said anything I could think of to make me sound defective, just laying it on as thick as I thought it could go.

FINTAN MURPHY:

I must say, I personally find it difficult to stomach this story of hardened sex traffickers releasing a young woman because she had a bad knee. I think men of that stripe are usually preoccupied with other parts of the anatomy.

KIMBERLY NOLAN:

The whole atmosphere changed. The engine was still going and there were still bumps in the road, but it was like these men who I knew for a fact were inches away from me had disappeared.

Like, something I said had ruined the party.

One of them banged on the partition to the driver, the van pulled up and they all got out. I wondered if it was stolen. I thought they might leave me there, even torch it with me inside or something, but then I heard them talking, like, arguing. I couldn't make it out because I was too scared to take the bag off my head. I just stood there holding my breath, I didn't move a muscle.

ROBERT NOLAN:

If I've got one regret in my life, and I mean, obviously, I've got more than that now, but if I could fix one thing, I'd go back and pick Kim up on her lying. I know how that sounds, said of your own daughter, but I really would.

KIMBERLY NOLAN:

When they got back into the van they were all cheering. Laughing, joking, asking if I was okay. The talker said they were sorry, it had been a fresher dare or something. I remember thinking he sounded too old to be a student. One of them helped me sit down and said they'd drop me near to where they'd picked me up. I tried to laugh along, like, 'Oh, yeah, just drop me anywhere,' trying not to be sick through gritted teeth.

LIU WAI:
Well, I heard something supposedly *happened* inside that van . . .

KIMBERLY NOLAN:
Someone was drawing the bag back down fully over my face, then the driver started up and we jolted forwards. The bag got ripped off my head and there was a second, like a split second where I could see, where I half-saw this blur around me, these two shapes, then I screwed my eyes shut. I put my hands up in front of my face, looked at the floor, the wall. Tried to show them that I hadn't seen anything, I was still good for a laugh and they could still let me go.

LIU WAI:
. . . I probably shouldn't say what it was, though. I mean, Kim never came out and said it in her *Mail on Sunday* interview . . .

KIMBERLY NOLAN:
One of them pushed my face into the wall. He put the bag back on my head, pulled the cord so tight round my neck I could hardly breathe, then everything went quiet. And I knew then the prank stuff was bullshit, I mean, I always did, but even the pretence of it was gone, we were just driving in this dead silence. I could hear them breathing heavier, feel the driver driving differently, more abrupt, speeding up and stopping at the last second, making us fall

around in the back. I knew they'd seen me with my eyes open, they thought I'd seen their faces.

When we stopped a few minutes later someone got out of the back and – it sounded like – opened a gate. We reversed into something – it felt like wet ground, soft under the tyres – and when the engine stopped I couldn't hear any traffic or city or street sounds. One of them picked me up, opened the doors and threw me out on the ground, and I was just saying, 'No, please.' It was muddy and I was trying to talk and get up, but my wrists were still tied together, the bag was still on my head, I couldn't see or breathe.

LIU WAI:

. . . No, I shouldn't say, I was, like, *sworn* to secrecy . . .

KIMBERLY NOLAN:

They started to pour something on me. At first I thought it was petrol, then I realized it was vodka. One of them held my face up and they just poured the whole bottle over my head. I was coughing and choking but they kept on going until I was sick inside the bag. They dropped the bottle on to my face, it smashed my fucking front teeth and I still didn't move, I still didn't dare.

Then I heard the zips on their trousers and definitely two of them, maybe all three, pissed on me. It was so cold that the heat from it was scorching, like, searing to the skin. It went all over my hands and arms, all over my body, and all over the bag and in my face and in my eyes and in my mouth. I was just trying to breathe through my fucking ears or something until they finally stopped and I heard footsteps going away. I heard the driver's door close, then one of them leaned down to cut the cable ties round my wrists.

LIU WAI:

. . . Well, I heard that she actually *did* see something inside that van . . .

KIMBERLY NOLAN:

He leaned into my ear and said: *'Tell anyone about this and you'll get it in every hole, sweetheart.'* He picked me up and turned me facing the breeze. I felt the air sticking the wet bag to my face, all the piss and vodka and sick. He draped Zoe's jacket back over my shoulders and told me to walk two hundred steps straight ahead, said they'd be gone when I got there. If I took the bag off or turned round they'd have to use me like a village bike and then they'd have to kill me.

So I started walking, shaking, mainly trying not to be sick again. I had my hands out in front of me to stop myself from going into a wall or something. I couldn't have been ten steps in when I heard a loud bang and dropped to the floor, thinking I'd been shot. Then the van started up and I realized it had been the back door slamming shut. They were driving out and away, so I peeled the bag off my head – I couldn't breathe – and saw tail lights disappearing over my shoulder. Nothing else because my eyes were streaming and burning, hurting so much.

LIU WAI:

. . . Well, this is all according to Jai so I suppose you might have to take it with a grain of salt, but apparently she told Andrew what she saw inside the van.

JAI MAHMOOD:

Look, I mean, nah. What would I know? I was out cold.

KIMBERLY NOLAN:

I just held on to the ground and let my eyes stop stinging, adjust to the dark. When I did look up I saw I was on a building site, the abandoned one off Canal Street in town. It was meant to be luxury apartments like everything else, but the money had gone wrong so it was just a hole in the ground with a fence round it. The centre was this pit, this twenty-foot drop into exposed foundations, and I was about two steps away from walking into it when I took the bag off my head. They'd wanted me to fall into it blindfolded and drunk, covered in piss and sick.

FINTAN MURPHY:

My questions are just the obvious ones. Why did she take Zoe's jacket from the club? Why does she say she called Zoe when we can prove that she didn't? Who was she actually looking for outside? How come she didn't tell the police about her abduction? I mean, she makes it all sound fairly serious.

KIMBERLY NOLAN:

I'm sure Fintan would have reacted much more rationally. I'm sure Fintan does still have his fucking phone records from seven years ago, but I don't know. I didn't recognize their voices, I didn't think I knew them. And I knew how it looked. It was a running joke between us all at the time when we'd had too much – 'Oh, someone must have spiked my drink again last night.' But I think I would have said something, I think I would have found the right time or the words, but then Zoe went missing a month later. Nothing made sense to me after that. When I tried to say it, when I even tried to run it through my head, it just sounded pathetic and attention-seeking. Like I was making it up to compete with my glamorous missing sister.

FINTAN MURPHY:
Competing with her glamorous missing sister, I couldn't put it better myself. Funny she was brave enough to tell the story for a five-figure sum, seven years on.

KIMBERLY NOLAN:
I sold it to the *Mail* to defend myself, which I think Fintan knows.

FINTAN MURPHY:
Mainly, I'd ask what happened to the clothes she was wearing that night. They should have been a veritable goldmine of DNA evidence.

KIMBERLY NOLAN:
I walked home, I had a shower, I went to bed. I was frozen, I had to try and unthaw. I slept for about twelve hours and I don't remember seeing the clothes again. He knows someone was stealing stuff from the tower. Clothes from out of our rooms, Zoe's as well. That's all on record.

FINTAN MURPHY:
Yes, someone was stealing things from the tower, Zoe's too, but what a thief would want with urine-sodden, vomit-encrusted clothes I

don't know. Look, I say none of this to be cruel. Sometimes I think this story we're stuck in has messed with our heads. When people go through this kind of trauma they don't get closer to each other. Sadly, they just tear apart. The least we can do is try to be decent, and if I'm falling short of that with Kimberly then I apologize to her here, of course I do. But Zoe, my best friend in the world, is still missing all these years later, and this is what Kimberly wants to talk about? It's nothing, it's a footnote.

ANDREW FLOWERS:
Liu says that I know what Kim saw inside the van?

KIMBERLY NOLAN:
No, I *[inaudible]*. Look, I closed my eyes like I said.

ANDREW FLOWERS:
She did say something like that, as it happens. She told me she saw a face.

KIMBERLY NOLAN:
An illustrated face. Well, a tattoo on the back of one of their hands. This ghoulish, laughing clown face, a great big horrible grin. Look, I never thought I'd say it but I think I agree with Fintan. I mean, aren't we here to talk about Zoe?

on Fri, Jan 11, 2019, Evie Mitchell evelynidamitchell@gmail.com wrote:

Hey JK, just wondering if you'd had a chance to read the prologue?

Ex

---

on Sat, Jan 12, 2019, Evie Mitchell evelynidamitchell@gmail.com wrote:

Nudge . . .

Ex

---

on Sat, Jan 12, 2019, Joseph Knox joeknoxxxx@gmail.com wrote:

Argh, sorry – can't find the original email w/ attachment. Would you mind re-sending?

J

---

on Sat, Jan 12, 2019, Evie Mitchell evelynidamitchell@gmail.com wrote:

Sure. Here. (You're the worst btw)

E

---

on Sun, Jan 13, 2019, Joseph Knox joeknoxxxx@gmail.com wrote:

EVEning – apologies for my lateness (but never for my puns). Yes, sorry, I'm shit. Buried in writing. It's interesting stuff. I guess the question is, does the rest of it add up to a book? You said what you sent me before is the first third? How long have you been interviewing these people? Not sure I have a total grip on the main players atm (except that Andrew = sleazebag), though I'm sure I will. Do you think you'll keep going? Not being a dick but, w/ my commercial hat on, you might want to consider just starting with Zoe's disappearance . . .

J

Finally! Okay, so Zoe's dad was the first person I got hold of in late 2017. This was obviously before the recent allegations against him, and he opened a lot of doors in terms of access to the others. From him I got Fintan and Sally Nolan, from Fintan I got Jai and Liu, and from Sally I got Kim. No one was speaking to Andrew so I found him through Facebook. Kim was the toughest nut to crack, which I guess makes sense considering what she's been through. We talked on the phone (off the record) for weeks and weeks, then started meeting in early 2018. I've spent most of the last year interviewing them all and assembling the story, but Kim's really the backbone. Obviously she was always gonna have some unique insights into her twin sister, but there was WEIRDNESS between them and it went to some insane places. Some you'll have seen already in the press, but some, I'm afraid, are gonna cost you the price of a hardback book ;)

I have at least half the book done plus a lot more recorded material, but things are STILL happening. Most of the taped conversations were done in person over multiple meetings and then assembled into the best order afterwards. Some of them, like Zoe's parents, can be quite rigid. They've gone over it so many times in their heads and with the press that it's all a bit rote. The others are much more at pains to argue a point, or try and say it how they saw it, and I think that's where the truth starts to come out.

You've got someone like Andrew, a man with a BAG of chips on his shoulder, who says whatever sounds good to him at the time and constantly gets tripped up by it after. I wouldn't agree that he's sleazy necessarily (u jealous?), he has his charms, a gorgeous public school accent for one, but he had no compunction asking me out for a drink while I was interviewing him about the missing girl a lot of people think he murdered . . .

(I let him down gently.)

Jai's a sad story. A hotty when he was 18, artistic but ballsy and just how I like 'em, now missing most of his teeth(!) and looking about ten years older than he actually is. He's had a sad life, I think. They all have, in different ways, but where the rest of them just have emotional scars, Jai's are physical as well. Weirdly, he seems like the most well adjusted now. I guess you need some inner peace if you're gonna kick junk. Mos' def has an axe to grind against Andrew though . . .

Liu Wai's a funny one. Made up to the hilt and trying to give ME advice on which Max Factor Facefinity three-in-one foundation would 'go with' my eyes. Can be a bit performative, slips into these mundane conversations forgetting she's supposed to be crying her eyes out, but I think she has a good heart. You'd like her, she fans herself with one hand when she gets emotional.

Fintan seems to think about it, and about everyone else, the most seriously. It'll be clearer going forwards, but he's very dedicated, he's basically given his life up for Zoe's cause. He'd never say it but I'm not sure he always pats himself on the back about that now. He's not bitter, I'm not sure he knows the meaning of the word, maybe just rueful? Like, he wonders what could have been? He speaks very slowly and usually for a long time. I can listen to an Irish accent all day but I do wonder if he might be lonely.

Anyway, the idea now is that I'll start the book off with what you just read and generally introduce the key players. Kim's van stuff coming out has clarified a few things and has ramifications through the rest of the text. I didn't even know about it until she sold the story.

Then in part one I give some background on Kim and Zoe's childhood (troubling, infuriating, RELEVANT). From there I work my way forward to their first term in Manchester and the events leading up to Zoe's disappearance. I knew, *knew, KNEW* you'd say I should just open with the night she went missing, but cool your crime writing jets, Knoxy. Weird shit was happening WAY before December 17th, and I'm sitting on a pile of it.

You have to see it play out to properly understand, but it's as much about them as it is about Zoe. It's as much about prejudices, ours and theirs. You have to SEE why Zoe could never be the 'perfect' victim for the press to latch on to and turn into a big story. She was too messy, too complicated.

I'd say there were four or five DIFFERENT dark forces circling her before she even went missing, and those are just the ones we know about. I don't believe in victim blaming but I do think some people are like shit-magnets through no fault of their own. Sometimes I think I even know the feeling (*a lone violin plays*). But cancer can't compare to going missing, I don't think. I mean, obviously it's a fucker, but at least we understand it on some level.

My goal is that by the end of this book you'll understand Zoe. I don't want to wince away from what made her too messy for the press.

Let me know if I need to re-send the first third again. It's all from interviews conducted last year but like I said, I'm still talking to them.

You could even take me for a drink and blow some royalties if you want to hear about it first hand. I could be your muse, Knoxy. I've read your stuff and believe me you need one . . .

(KIDDING, love to ██████. Hope to see you soon.)

Ex

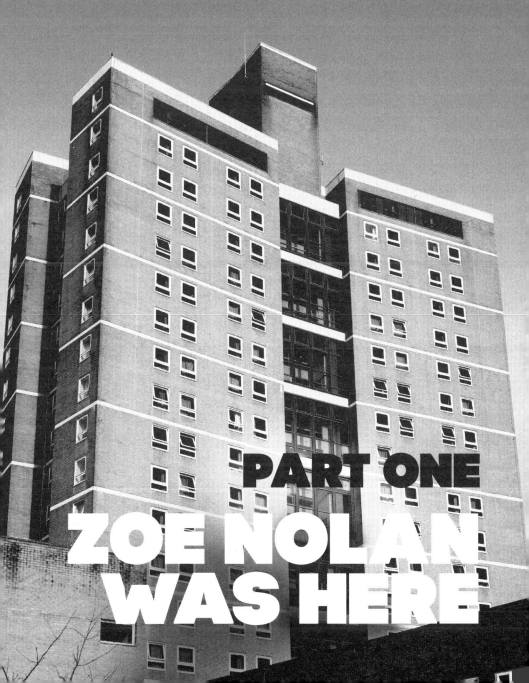

PART ONE
ZOE NOLAN WAS HERE

--1--

'Separate Ways'

Zoe originally intended to specialize at the School of Vocal Studies and Opera at the Royal Northern College of Music. Kim, meanwhile, was eager to strike out on her own, studying English at the nearby University of Manchester. An unfortunate event, however, would permanently alter the course of both their lives.

LIU WAI:

The first thing that really struck me about Zoe was her voice. I'll never forget the sound of her singing on our first night living at Owens Park. Manchester felt like a long way from Essex and, I think, where a lot of people my age were dying to break out and get into trouble – to find themselves or whatever – that was all quite alien to me? I always felt like I already knew who I was. Who else would I be? And I didn't *want* to get into trouble. So, sitting in my room on my own, yet to make a new friend – wondering if I even could – to hear this voice was really comforting. I actually moved my chair so it was closer to the wall, and I left it there for the whole term. That probably sums up my friendship with Zoe at first. She was just there, and I got as close to her as I could.

FINTAN MURPHY:

Growing up in Ballymena, just this knock-kneed waif kind of grappling with his sexuality, I learned early on how to hide inside myself. My family's quite religious and as you may have noticed, I'm slightly gay. Adolescence is a slightly different experience for someone like me because, until the day you come out, you are essentially this walking secret, and depending on who you tell, you might be a dark secret or you might be a bright one, you might be welcome or you might be unwelcome. I still wasn't out when I met Zoe, still nowhere near it in all honesty, and think I saw something similar in her, somehow, as though she was carrying something extra.

When we met at the Choir and Orchestra Society we were both eighteen years old, but I felt, in some sense, as though I was meeting an old friend. It felt like we understood each other immediately.

LIU WAI:

At first I struggled to connect this quite self-possessed voice with the shy, skinny blonde girl who could hardly meet my eye in the kitchen. I mean, sometimes you had to kind of smile and nod at Zoe because she talked *so* quietly. Then I hear her in the next room just summoning this song up from nowhere, something I could never do. And where most girls our age might have been singing 'Someone Like You' or whatever, this was classical, sung in Italian.

And it sort of confirmed something I thought I'd picked up on . . .

Zoe had obviously arrived at university with her sister, but her and Kim seemed so wary of each other. Like, my first impression of Zoe was that she was lonely. Why was she singing alone in her room when her twin sister was just down the hall? It seemed so strange.

KIMBERLY NOLAN:

My relationship with Zoe was always complicated. Basically, I struggled with feelings of inadequacy, and I take my share of the blame for that. So much of it came from the way we were raised, though. We were never really allowed to function as a unit, we were always pitted against each other, and I think that's really sad for two twin girls. Whenever one of us would try and voice it, or resist it in any way, Dad just shut us down, said, 'You'll thank me when you're famous.'

ROBERT NOLAN:

Well, you'll always see parents in our position saying how special their kids are, but in our case, with Zoe certainly, it was true, it really was. She just had this gift, this voice that felt like it had the power to change the course of someone's day. It was like she gave the unspoken some physical presence. I think if she'd been allowed to reach her full potential, her voice could have changed the course of whole lives.

SALLY NOLAN:

Rob was musical when we met. One of the things I liked about him. He was singing at a wedding, I forget whose. Suit and back-up band, though – the works. There was something different in him from the boys my age. No drinking after he'd played – saving his throat, he said – then he spent all night talking to me, which can't have helped it. Then life happened and we were pregnant with two kids. And full credit, he put his dreams aside. Worked in factories, on assembly lines, at construction sites. Nights and days and continental shifts. He wanted something better for them, and he thought the way was to pass on his music. He started them both, Kim and Zoe, on piano lessons and singing lessons and dancing lessons. They were happy for a time. But Kim didn't want it. Or, in fairness, she didn't have it. She just didn't have it in her.

KIMBERLY NOLAN:

People think of self-harm in a really simple way, teenage girls cutting themselves as a coping mechanism, taking one kind of pain and making it into something more manageable. Then there's self-harm as a cry for attention or help, making spiritual scars physical because you can't articulate what you're really going through, which is what Zoe went on to do. For me it was effective, for me self-harm was like an evasive measure. I wasn't interested in transferring my pain from one account to another, I just wanted it to stop.

So I tried to wreck my voice.

That's probably why I still sound like I smoke a pack a day. Dad didn't understand what music was supposed to be about. The idea of expression or creativity was just anathema to him. He wanted the same notes sung in the same order, day in, day out, no fun and games, no heart and soul. So I'd walk out into the back fields at night and do these low black-metal roars until I was on my knees, retching. Or I'd switch the shower on full blast and then scream as hard as I could into a towel, until I couldn't do it any more, just so my voice would be shredded enough that he'd leave me the fuck alone. I think I even got a knife back there once or twice. And I know that sounds insane, but otherwise it was endless.

He had this programme of exercises we had to do before school. Vocal warm-ups, high octaves, scales, dancing. Then at night we'd move into actual songs. Hits from when he was young but with his idea of *real* classics thrown in. My dad likes to tell people he was a professional musician, but he was a wedding singer. I think Zoe believed it all for a long time, this idea that she was special or chosen, that she was going on to fame and fortune. I just saw how stupid it all was. And I don't mean it was stupid for Dad to have a dream, I mean it was stupid for him to push it on someone else.

SALLY NOLAN:

Well, Rob held Zoe up as a good example, he treated her and made a show of her, he tried to motivate Kim. Or at least it started that way. It turned into him just treating them differently. And look, I'm not slinging blame, we're long past all that. Zoe was taking off. She was performing in public and being paid and sought after and wanted by specialist schools. Kim just had to wait, she just had to sit there in second place.

LIU WAI:

I think with social media and stuff, things have changed for the better now, but back then it was weird. I'm not sure young women would always necessarily take each other's side? I think for a lot of people when they saw Zoe, this kind of quite strikingly beautiful girl, then went on to learn that she was incredibly talented, their first instinct was to try and tear her down? And I mean the boys as much as the girls. Some of the shit she had to endure at university was *beyond* ridiculous. I've never really understood that impulse, and I wonder if it's because I was home-schooled, like, I wasn't raised in competition with anyone. What I'm saying is I always saw Kim as one of those people who never actually enjoys anything, someone who just tears other people down. But I guess her and Zoe were *born* in competition with each other and that must be hard if you're always the loser. Not to speak out of turn, but even meeting them both at eighteen, you could tell how much Kim struggled with Zoe's talent.

KIMBERLY NOLAN:

I wouldn't say we were born in competition with each other, it was more something that was thrust upon us. We were still sisters first. And I don't struggle in any way to say that Zoe had a nice singing voice. All this stuff you see and hear about me being jealous of her, it's not true. Fintan, Liu, Andrew, Jai – they knew Zoe for *three months*. I knew her for nineteen years. I'm not saying they weren't her friends, but they're not the authority on my relationship with my sister.

What made things complicated was my guilt.

Guilt about not shouldering my share at home, not absorbing as much of Dad's madness as she did. Once I got out of the singing for good I always felt like Zoe was suffering for me, on my behalf, like she was carrying my weight as well as hers. When your dad makes it clear to you that you'll be a disappointment to him unless you fulfil his dreams, when he forces you to define yourself by this thing you just *aren't* that spectacular at, he's setting you up to fail, whether he knows it or not. And that's what he did with Zoe. That's what the Royal Northern stuff was all about – it flowed completely out of his madness.

LIU WAI:

Right, yes, Zoe almost went to the Royal Northern College of Music *instead* of Manchester University. Or something?

KIMBERLY NOLAN:

I was the cautionary tale to Zoe's success story. The failed project who couldn't have time and money invested in her because she didn't indulge her dad's fantasies. Zoe was more of a go-along girl, so that's what she tried to do. And she really did try, even when it was killing her. Her weight and body issues, her paranoia about her throat.

ANDREW FLOWERS:

Yes, the low-talking thing. Truthfully, I could never hear what Zoe was saying. At the time I used to tell people that was the key to our relationship.

JAI MAHMOOD:

She could be quiet at times, yeah, but I think that says as much about the people round her as it does about Zoe. Why talk when no one's listening?

KIMBERLY NOLAN:

Everyone always had to lean in to talk to her because she was so, *so* quiet. And they used to think it was this ego thing, like those people who speak in tiny voices so everyone has to stand close and listen carefully. But really she was just terrified of damaging her throat like I had. Dad had drummed it into her that her voice and her body were the sum total of her worth. Without those things she was just like her talentless twin sister who he couldn't really be bothered with. I never once heard her raise her voice except to sing.

SALLY NOLAN:

The Royal Northern was too much, but we thought it was what they wanted. Kim at Manchester and Zoe a mile down the road. They'd still have each other but get their own space. And space from us as much as anything. There was this fault growing, all that pressure was pushing them apart.

ROBERT NOLAN:

Artists aren't like the rest of us. They're sensitive people. Their antennae are finely tuned from years of training, they'll pick up on the slightest emotional signals from people around them. That was Zoe. She was learning how to take everything in, like, and in time, she'd have learned how to use it all, too. But negative forces are like viruses for that kind of mind. You see it time and time again, these great artists overwhelmed by their own talent, by the burden of all the bad energies round them. They pick up on these negative wavelengths and they get infected. I can speak with some personal experience on that.

KIMBERLY NOLAN:

Negative forces? I think that's Dad's polite way of referring to me. The negative forces I saw in Zoe's life were all men. That was what he really trained her for without even knowing it. To be a doormat to some older man, and to isolate herself from anyone who saw things differently. Without all that in her head, without where it eventually led her, would we even be sitting here?

He'd always use one of us as a stick to beat the other, that's what made me and Zoe keep secrets from each other, and that was a slippery slope. She'd always attracted a certain kind of male attention, even as a kid. Not always flirtation at first, but fascination, and that turned into flirtation as we got older. And I mean, it was almost always one-sided, most of the time she didn't even notice. Grown men standing too close to her, teachers leaning in over her shoulder and stuff. When we had pay-as-you-go phones we used to top them up at a corner shop near school. You'd put, like, a fiver on and get a receipt out of the till, only the guy serving Zoe started keeping her receipts, and back then it printed your phone number on there.

He started sending her dirty messages – we're, like, thirteen, fourteen at the time – and Zoe would politely ask him to stop because she had no equipment to push back and say, 'Hey, dickhead, fuck off.' Which was what I did as soon as she told me. It got so bad I had to tell Mum, she had to call the police. What I'm saying is, me and Zoe used to talk about this kind of stuff, she'd tell me things, I'd tell her things. She helped me with my anxiety and I helped her work out what she actually wanted, instead of just doing what she was told. We were the yin and yang, we needed each other to fully function. But because Dad saw that as him losing his grip, losing his dream, he just pushed her harder and harder, and that ended up pushing us apart. So getting older, fifteen, sixteen, seventeen, she stopped talking to me that way, she turned secretive.

And I remember it because there were things in her life I really was jealous of. She had this whole other world through her music stuff, a way out of that house. Sometimes she'd be travelling, performing with ensembles or choirs, private functions at weekends, whole groups of people in her life I had no idea about. At home, she'd get calls and I'd go, 'Who shall I say's calling?' Then get a name back I'd never heard before. Or you'd hear her whispering on her mobile in the bathroom with the tap running, trying to cover up whatever she was saying. Or her phone would go off while we were eating and she'd disappear for twenty minutes. This was all stuff she would have shared with me once, but that impulse had been beaten out of her. If it hadn't been, she might not have been such a mystery to us when she went missing.

One thing that really sticks out in my mind now, for obvious reasons, is when we were getting ready for college one day and she left her phone on the dresser. It went off, and when I looked at the screen it was a withheld number. I don't know why I did it, maybe a joke, maybe just to feel like someone exciting for a second, but I picked up and said, 'Zoe speaking.' Silence. Then breathing, then a man's voice, not a boy, not someone our age.

He said: 'Are you still into it?'

SALLY NOLAN:
Yes, I think we were all tense before Zoe's audition, all out of sorts.

KIMBERLY NOLAN:

The phone went clammy in my hand because I knew this was out of my league, way too adult. I heard someone coming so I just said, 'Yes,' hung up and put her phone back on the dresser.

ROBERT NOLAN:

Now, I can say with some certainty I should have got her out of there, out of that house. Got her away from that bloody environment, all that negativity. I'll always blame myself that I didn't. I got to see Zoe in her prime, but the world never did, the world never will.

KIMBERLY NOLAN:

One way that call fucked me up was that sometimes after, I'd hear Zoe's phone go off, then she'd answer, listen for a second and say, 'Yes.' I'd ask who it was but she'd already backed too far away from me by then, she'd always just say, 'Oh, no one.' And all I could think was, *Are you still into it?* Like, are you still into *what*?

LIU WAI:

I only ever met her after the fact, but from what I remember she said her audition had gone well? She just preferred the idea of Manchester University.

KIMBERLY NOLAN:

So, with all Dad's dreams in her head, she applied to the School of Vocal Studies and Opera at the Royal Northern College of Music. You know, this isn't belting out golden oldies to your parents' friends after dinner. It's not small-town amateur-dramatic stuff. These kids have been raised for it. They show up singing arias out of their arses, references from private schools, known names, the lot. They speak three languages and still have nannies at seventeen years old. It wasn't fair forcing Zoe to compete against them.

SALLY NOLAN:

We could have handled it better.

KIMBERLY NOLAN:

She wasn't good enough, and that should have been fine. There's no shame in it. But to be at home around then you'd think there'd been a death in the family. I mean, for Dad, for *Rob*, there clearly had been. He went into this kind of tailspin. Finding phone numbers of professors and people on the board of the college, calling them at all hours. Mum just mute and terrified. You'd think Zoe had been diagnosed with a terminal illness or something, like, *There must be some mistake.*

PROFESSOR MICHAEL ANDERSON, *Head of Vocal Studies, RNCM*:

I must confess that although I was a part of the panel which assessed Miss Nolan's audition, I don't have any personal recollection of her performance per se. I do recall a rather regrettable phone call I received from Mr Nolan on the subject afterwards. It's probably not helpful to dwell on the substance of that conversation, but he was certainly upset with the outcome, he cared passionately about Zoe's future.

When I look at my notes now, her scores and comments, everything seems perfectly standard. Each audition lasts around twenty minutes with a ten-minute vocal warm-up. Prospective students are asked to prepare three songs of contrasting styles, to perform them from memory. Although there's a short written test and a slightly longer multiple-choice examination, the performance is what we're really looking at. And, to restate, Miss Nolan's results across all these tests showed a fine student with a demonstrable understanding of some aspects of musical theory. What I suspect she was missing was the natural talent and curiosity it takes to truly dedicate oneself to this level of training. We're talking about an incredibly competitive course, one where it would be unfair to award places to people without those instincts. Unfair, I should add, for the prospective students themselves. There's nothing worse than seeing someone flounder through no fault of their own.

KIMBERLY NOLAN:

So while Dad was losing it and Mum was busy being a rug he could walk up and down on, my sister got in the bath, unnoticed, and cut both her wrists.

SALLY NOLAN:

Kim found her in time. It was the worst thing I could think of. Up until then it was the worst day of my life. Zoe kept saying, 'I'm sorry, I'm sorry.' And what killed me was she wasn't saying sorry for her wrists. She was saying sorry for this stupid audition and for this stupid school, like it even mattered next to her life.

ANDREW FLOWERS:

Well, of course I didn't know her until later, but I certainly saw the scars when we got together in Manchester. I suppose I thought it best not to ask. I boarded at Harrow when I was a boy and found my room-mate hanged at fourteen. There was a family member who had something similar.

Those incidents just jaded me, made me afraid to talk about it.

When Zoe did spill the goods about her suicide attempt, I don't think it even occurred to me to ask why she'd done it. I was at a low point myself, I suspect that my feeling at the time was, 'Well, of course you'd try and kill yourself, who wouldn't?' I'm sure it looked like a lack of interest but it was really just a door I couldn't walk through, a place I couldn't find myself in again. I carry some guilt from that. If I'd shown the slightest curiosity in her life we might have known more about what she was going through, why everything happened the way it did.

KIMBERLY NOLAN:

It was a strange time because I'd had my troubles, I'd spent my life in the background, but I was growing up, into something different. Being a twin can be a headfuck. I mean, it always had been for me, but I felt like Zoe only really experienced that confusion at seventeen, after she'd hurt herself.

When I was young I was looking for an identity anywhere, in books and bands and films and everything, but I struggled because I kept being confronted with my own double every day. You know, I'd look in the mirror and see my sister instead of myself. And because she seemed to handle things so much better than I did, I never really felt like the finished article, just a defective one.

But my body was changing, my mind, too. I'd already been through what she was only just starting, and I was excited to put it behind me, to get out into the world. For Zoe, though, for a few months anyway, it was like her life was ending. Dad was heartbroken, Mum didn't understand. And all the texts and calls Zoe had been getting before her audition stopped dead.

I think that was really hard for her.

You'd see her constantly picking up her phone, checking the screen, then putting it back down again, disappointed. Music people falling away, I guess. I tried to be there for her, but in a way we were like strangers by then. And I couldn't hide my excitement, either. I'd been accepted for English at MU. I wanted to strike out on my own and find out who I could be without my sister.

SALLY NOLAN:

The doctors agreed it was a cry for help. We thought she'd stay home, recuperate, work out what she wanted to do while Kim went away to do English. She didn't like it, though. I think she started to see how Kim had it all those years, feeling second best. We'd made her think she couldn't be weak, so she forced herself to go.

ROBERT NOLAN:

They were both growing up, both needing their own space, like, but at the same time they were still just kids, they didn't know what they wanted. So when Zoe was turned down by the Royal Northern, when they were both accepted into Manchester, it seemed meant to be. I called student housing and explained my situation. You know, 'One of my girls is struggling, I want them close together, can you do anything?' I suppose I thought whoever I spoke to might house them in the same area, but they ended up in the same block, same flat even.

KIMBERLY NOLAN:

When you grow up in Stoke, Manchester might as well be New York. It's Joy Division, New Order, The Smiths, you know. *Definitely Maybe*. It's bookshops and Burgess and bars and *boys* and cafés.

It's culture and life.

But like that, this dream I'd been holding on to of stepping out from under Zoe's shadow just fizzled and died. Except it was worse now. I was expected to be her minder as well. It felt like everything was ending before it had even started. And once we moved into halls as well, we just snapped back to our old dynamic. She made friends and met boys, and I didn't. There were two of us, and one version was more smiley and outgoing, so what did I expect? Neither of us had even had a boyfriend before, not properly, so when she struck up with Andrew, who I actually met first, who I'd really liked, it was hard for me.

ANDREW FLOWERS:

Look, I won't sit here and insult Zoe's memory by pretending that we were particularly close. If she hadn't gone missing I doubt I'd have given her much thought in the intervening years. But she was a person, a kid really when she went missing, and of course it's a tragedy. She never got the chance to let her childhood and her pretensions fall away. And you could argue that's useful for the role that she's been cast in by the likes of her father, the likes of

Fintan Murphy and Liu Wai. A victim is apparently the best thing you can be in this day and age, so they just built their own. This eternal spotless victim. I suppose they must look back and see her that way, sort of immaculate, guileless and pure. Unfortunately, some of us actually knew her and can more easily locate the artifice in all that. The girl ate and shat, she slept and dreamed, she had sex and laughed at inappropriate things. She also trotted out dull, reheated opinions from her parents, she lacked identity, she faked that pained smile you see in all her pictures. In short, she was just like everyone else at that age. I'm not saying all of the above is necessarily who she was, I'm not saying it's necessarily who she always would have been. I'm saying she never got the chance to grow out of it. She certainly wasn't some saint, and it erases her, it erases the messy real-life truth of Zoe Nolan to suggest otherwise.

How did I get into all of this?

Yes, right, the music. I mean, there's the fundamental rose-tinted example in my view because, quite honestly, Zoe was no great shakes when it came to singing. Mannered, over-rehearsed, nothing real going on at all. She might make you cry in the pub after five pints, but in the cold light of day? Nothing special. She'd always sing 'Ombra mai fu' – that was her party piece after the music stopped – and I just found it intensely embarrassing. She couldn't even speak Italian, the song might have been about raw sewage for all she knew, but her dad had her believing it was the zenith of class and refinement. Perhaps in Stoke-on-Trent that was true. To me, I'm afraid it was as tiresome as an open-mic rendition of fucking 'Wonderwall' or something.

LIU WAI:

I'd never heard that, about Zoe's suicide attempt, I mean, obviously I met her after. It explains some things, though, and I suppose it makes others a lot sadder. You start to understand some of Kim's resentment, too.

KIMBERLY NOLAN:

Oh, fucking Liu Wai. I didn't resent her. I just felt like my life was being put on hold. Like, 'Okay, well, now my life won't start at eighteen, either. I guess it won't start until Zoe and me go our separate ways, somehow.'

From: evelynidamitchell@gmail.com

Sent: 17/01/19 10:17

To: you

on Thu, Jan 17, 2019, Joseph Knox joeknoxxxxx@gmail.com wrote:

Evelyn. Sorry this took me so long to get to, and that I missed your messages from earlier. Haven't read the whole first part yet but did just rattle through the first chapter.

Strange calls: check.

Overbearing father: check.

Thwarted dreams: check.

'Go our separate ways somehow'

Murderous sisterly resentment . . . ?

J

That cheque's in the mail. I told you, that's the whole story. You're just getting to Manchester and all the good stuff. ▓▓▓▓▓▓▓▓▓▓
▓▓▓▓▓▓▓▓▓▓▓▓▓▓▓▓▓▓▓▓▓▓▓▓▓▓▓▓▓▓
▓▓▓▓▓▓▓

Are you still into it?

Ex

--2--

'Relationship Status'

Some of the people who would become vital to the investigation into Zoe's disappearance were new in her life, with many of them having met her only recently, as they began their first term of university.

JAI MAHMOOD:
Well, I wouldn't even say I was her friend, and I don't mean that in a shitty way, either. Zoe was nice, we bonded a bit, but I'm not one of these guys going, 'Yeah, we were super close,' just because of what happened to her. I was more like a friend of a friend, whatever the papers say. Without my face on the fucking news, the accusations and stuff, you'd never have seen my name next to hers. One thing I have got that sets me apart from the rest of them, yeah, is a very visual memory. I took pictures most of my life and I've still got that muscle trained. I see things, I retain them and then they don't change. So I'll always cop to it when I can't remember shit because I want you to know that when I can, it's accurate.

Maybe it's because my skin colour kept me at a distance, maybe it's because my brain was always composing shots, but I saw Zoe

64

clearly. When you're a brown boy in Manchester, you can't help being an outsider, so that's what I was. The rest of them were kids, though, yeah. They had no reason to think that the world *didn't* revolve around them. What I'm saying is, they all saw Zoe through the lens of whatever their own issues were. She reflected them back at themselves, they thought *her* story was actually theirs. And her story's like this epic HBO crime drama, so it makes their stories into crime dramas, too. Her story's heart-breaking, a tragedy, so ditto, it makes them less boring, it feeds their egos, they can't live without it. That's why they all had her wrong at the time and that's why they haven't changed their tune since, it's why they're all stuck in the past, man. If they moved on, they'd have to actually take a look at themselves, and I'm not sure they'd survive it.

Like, in rehab we did Rorschach cards, the black ink blots on white backgrounds, and that was Zoe. Everyone who looked at her saw something different. Some of them saw what they wanted to, some of them saw their worst nightmares. So, for Kim? For Kim, Zoe was her exact opposite, a rival, this burden. She built her sister up into this massive thing she was forced to orbit.

KIMBERLY NOLAN:

Half the bookcase at home's stuff on bereavement. Loss, grief, coping, not exactly beach-read material. If I ever get a man back, he usually takes one look at the shelves and starts telling me how early he has to get up in the morning. Anyway, one thing that repeats through those books is this feeling the bereaved have of being 'defined' by their loss. I can't sit here and say I'm some great exception because I've just told you about my tragic bookcase.

I am defined by losing Zoe, absolutely.

I just think it's more accurate to say I was always defined by her, even before she went missing. You know, kids can seem cruel because they can put their fingers on things about yourself that you can't. On our first day in high school, eleven years old, a boy in our form called me the 'pound shop' version of Zoe. Just nailed my deepest fear in life within one hour of knowing me. What made it worse was that Zoe's relationship with me was never strained because of that stuff. As far as I could tell, the feeling only ever went one way – she never had any reason to be jealous of me.

The three months we were at Manchester were the closest I ever came to breaking free and striking out. We were away from home, spending more time apart, and I felt like I was finding my feet. Then, with her disappearance, all that work got undone, everything got put on pause and because we've never had any kind of resolution, everything's stayed that way. For a few months there, it felt like I had a chance to work out who Kimberly Nolan was, who she could be, then all of this happened instead. So now I just have the world's most miserable bookcase. Now I'm just Zoe Nolan's sister.

JAI MAHMOOD:

. . . Then you've got Andrew, yeah. And Andrew's gonna say, 'Zoe was just a body, just sex.' He was looking at her through the male gaze, simple as. But is that really what it was like at the time, or has that picture warped a bit in the years since? Seems to me like it must have, man, because I saw things different. I remember Andrew's stuff with Zoe being more fucked than anyone else's, but I think that picture's too painful for him to look at now. He kept it too close to his heart and it sounds like his heart's gone rotten. All you'll get are puns and wordplay, world-class bullshit.

ANDREW FLOWERS:

I think by the time she went missing, Zoe would have changed our relationship status on Facebook to 'It's Complicated'. I probably would have changed mine to 'I'm Single'. Funnily enough, after you called last week I looked her up on there and her profile still says that we're together, even now, seven years later. That's not actually funny, is it? It's actually wretched – I'm sorry, sometimes I can't spot the difference. You can probably tell from talking to me why we were never described as 'love's young dream'. Call us 'love's young wet dream' and you're probably getting close.

JAI MAHMOOD:

You've got Fintan, who's another thing entirely. Basically, he saw Zoe in the exact opposite way to Kim. Zoe made everything harder for her, she obstructed things. But for Fintan, yeah, Zoe was like this amazing promise. The rest of them were kids, but he seemed old, like he'd lived one life already and been a bit disappointed by it. To hear him talk, Zoe changed all that. She made everything seem possible for him, she was like a thousand green lights in a row.

FINTAN MURPHY:

Truthfully, I feel as though I've come to know Zoe more since she went missing. I was only eighteen years old when we met and so was she. We only knew each other for three months, I don't even have a picture of the two of us together. I suppose you'd define us as new friends, but it felt much more vital than that to me at the time. And I don't mean romantically – obviously nothing like that was on the cards between us. I think that helped. It can be nice to not have the sex question always rearing its head, especially at that age. Not to sound painfully naïve, but I'd characterize our relationship as one of hope. We each had hopes for the other. To me, that was the same thing as acknowledging that we each had hopes for the world, for life. I don't think Zoe necessarily had that kind of relationship with anyone else. Of course her parents supported her, thought she'd be famous and stuff, but a lot of that was more about material success than real hope. I just saw this inexhaustible well of goodness that perhaps I'd be lucky enough to draw from for the rest of my life. The world had given us both a bit of a kicking, quite literally in my case, so to me having hope felt *audacious*, it felt like a secret that we didn't dare say to each other. It was like we had this flickering flame between us, and we both had to keep it safe so that it could grow and burn brighter.

And I got into this trying not to sound naïve . . .

Although, sadly, it seems I'll never realize those hopes with Zoe, I still try to keep the spark alive through my work with the charity we founded in her name, the Nolan Foundation. I basically try to put good things and good thoughts into the world on her behalf, because I think that's what she'd be doing if she were here. In that sense, you could say that my relationship with her is still one of hope.

JAI MAHMOOD:
And then there's Liu Wai . . .

LIU WAI:

I just saw Zoe as this sort of perfect flawless angel?

JAI MAHMOOD:

. . . *[Laughs]* Liu Wai idolized her. Think Nazi propaganda posters from World War Two. She looked at Zoe and saw things that weren't even there, bro. This aspirational saviour figure with anatomically impossible proportions and sunbeams shining out of her arse. The Über-womensch.

LIU WAI:

I should probably point out that I was really close with her at the time, like, we always had a lot in common. We only lived together for a few months but we just completely connected. I'm not one of these spiritual people. Not superstitious or woo-woo in any way whatsoever, but I *did* always get this sense that we'd met in a past life, perhaps even past lives *plural*? And it was clear to me that Kim, who I think would have been much less popular than her sister even in Tudor times, was really threatened by that.

JAI MAHMOOD:

And then there was one. It'd be funny if it weren't so fucking true, but if I hadn't met Zoe I probably wouldn't have ended up sleeping rough. I mean, I might still be talking to my family, my sister. She had kids a couple of years ago. Didn't even want me to meet them. But whatever. That wasn't Zoe's fault. It was just a shituation that the press and the world made worse.

Everyone wanted someone to blame, and there I was, man.

And honestly, as well, it was me, wasn't it? I made a fuck-up of my life and then I found a reason for it after. I would have found a reason even if I'd never met her, and it's probably the same for the rest of them. Like, maybe Kim would have always found a reason to back away from taking that big chance in life? Maybe she'd always find something to blame for not quite becoming that great person she could have been? Andrew definitely would have found a reason to treat people like shit. I met him before he laid eyes on Zoe and believe me, he was a natural. Fintan would have found a good cause and something to believe in because he had to replace God, didn't he? And Liu would have found another hero, another supergirl who looked like she wanted to, or whatever that was all about. Zoe's parents would have found a different reason to get divorced, *Daily Mail* readers would have found a different reason to hate Pakis, and on and on.

Maybe I'm talking shit, yeah, and everything would have been different. Maybe we all could have been somebody, but I doubt it. And anyway, this is the world we ended up with.

--3--

'Melting Pot'

Zoe and Kim make the move to Manchester, where they meet their three new flatmates, and fatefully cross paths with Andrew and Jai.

LIU WAI:

That actually happened in our first week of living together. Zoe walked into my room, which she never normally did without knocking, closed the door and sat down on my bed. I could see she was really shaken up about something so I asked, 'What's wrong?' She looked at me and said, 'I think someone might be stealing my clothes.'

KIMBERLY NOLAN:

We moved to Manchester in mid-September, 2011. We were eighteen years old and we'd never lived away from home before, so it was great, whatever drama we'd both been through. There was something new in the air. It was six months after Zoe's incident, her suicide attempt, and three months before she went missing. I see pictures from that time now and can't believe how happy we all look, I can't believe that none of us know what's coming. We lived in Tower Block, which was a tower block – their imaginations must have exploded when they named it – on Owens Park in Fallowfield, the same one she went missing from.

JAI MAHMOOD:

You'll say I'm a sadist, man, but I'd actually called ahead and asked to be assigned to the tower. For whatever reason, I ended up in one of the normal buildings instead, Tree Court. The tower's just this fuck-ugly brutalist block. Looks like it was picked up in Soviet Russia and dropped into Owens Park, like a leftover prop from the film of *1984* or something. Falling down for decades, always about to be demolished, always petitions and protests to save it. I saw it for the first time when I went on my open day, before I actually moved to Manchester. I was studying photography and, because everyone else was so obsessed with taking pretty pictures, I'd always try and find the ugliest things I could. That's how I originally came to the tower. Destination ugliness. And I'd heard the inside was even worse so I was dying to get through the doors.

ANDREW FLOWERS:

Even before Zoe went missing I thought there was something a little bit *Heart of Darkness* about the tower. A little bit Lovecraftian or *Apocalypse Now*. Rumour was that people used to go mad in there for some reason, I mean *actually* mad. They dropped out or they disappeared, and the fail rate was something like 40 per cent – way, way above average. I didn't live there but whenever I visited it felt like such a novelty to me. After Zoe went missing the press went arse over tit to suggest I'd been born with a silver spoon in my mouth. Frankly, I'd say my father stuck it in a different orifice altogether, but I suppose the point still stands . . .

The tower was unlike anywhere I'd ever been before. It stuck in my mind. The thing had been up since the mid-sixties so the walls were just cobwebbed with jail-cell scratches from down through the years. You'd find initials in love hearts, carved into obscure places with dates from decades before and find yourself thinking, *I wonder if J and M 1993 are still together now?*

LIU WAI:

My first response to being placed in the tower was to *immediately* try and get out of it. I was actually working my way through the complaints process, I was trying to get moved, when I met Zoe and decided that maybe it was worth staying. I think I was scared of all the mythology around it more than anything? Like, people said it was haunted or had this weird psychosomatic effect on occupants. The fail rate was through the roof, too, which people seemed weirdly proud about for some reason.

I just remember being on edge there.

Noises, people skulking through corridors, strange men moving between rooms. There was something else, though. Like I say, I'm not a believer in 'the other side', but I *have* always had these feelings of intuition that are hard to explain. Like, if my mind was a compass that usually shows true north, then it would have been spinning like a tornado in the tower. There was just something wrong about it. The lift never took you where you actually wanted to go, the doors would just open on to random floors, sometimes on to pitch-black darkness. You'd constantly find yourself saying, like, 'Where the hell am I?' Basically, Zoe aside, I thought the only good thing about living inside the tower was that I couldn't see it when I looked out of the window.

KIMBERLY NOLAN:

The fail rate was sky high because there were so many parties going on. There were strange noises in the night because some boys invented a drinking game called the Leaning Tower, where they had to do a shot on each of the eighteen floors. The lift took you to places you didn't ask for because it dated back to Beatlemania and needed replacing. It's true that there were floors where the lights would just cut out for days on end, but I don't think it ever actually happened to us. Zoe and me were placed on fifteenth, sharing communal space with three other girls. Liu Wai, you obviously know about, then there was Alex Wilson.

LIU WAI:

I'm not into armchair diagnosis, I think it's cheap and limiting and judgemental and insulting, but if you'd put a gun to my head at the time, I'd have said Alex only really makes sense when you acknowledge that there's some kind of *severe* mental bipolarity going on there. She was always extremely one thing or extremely another, but never what you would have necessarily called 'chill'.

How to describe her . . .

She was kind of quite painfully thin? Sometimes she'd eat junk food all day and sometimes she'd go, like, forty-eight hours on water alone. She was definitely pretty, but in a kind of damaged way that can attract really scummy men. By the end of the first week she had *two* different boyfriends to suit whatever mood she happened to be in, which totally scandalized me. One of them, Sam, was this sweetheart who always helped her, then the other, who I only ever saw once, was this sort of dark, drunken loser who only came out at night. Like, she had a good guy and a bad guy depending on how she saw herself at the time. Real split-personality stuff.

KIMBERLY NOLAN:

Poor Alex. She was two years older than the rest of us, she'd had to get a job after college and save up because her mum didn't want her to leave home. We thought that meant her mum must be a control freak or something, but I think Alex had problems. There'd been a bad experience with a boy, some body issues, and she just couldn't quite see her own worth. She was lovely, though, and that's not hindsight talking. She was the only one of us who ever tried to keep things tidy or do some decorating. She bought potted plants for the communal space, put pictures up on the walls that none of us even noticed. Liu Wai immediately gravitated towards Zoe, they both had pink clothes and hearts in their eyes, and I think Alex and me drifted closer as a result. Alex wore black and listened to *Psychocandy* by The Jesus and Mary Chain, which I thought was really cool, because it really, *really* was. I don't know about a second boyfriend, I only ever met Sam, but Alex definitely moved in mysterious ways.

LIU WAI:

There was a guy on third who'd hacked into the housing records or something and could give you all the previous occupants of your room? It was like a really shit map to the stars – you know, 'Here's the grotty seven-by-ten where a member of Radiohead was wetting his bed for a year, here's where the Chemical Brothers rehearsed before their first gig.' So I looked at ours but they were all fairly unexceptional, all except for Alex's. A girl who'd been in Alex's room two years before had committed suicide over the Christmas break, then only been found by her flatmates in January. I'd have been straight out of there, but she didn't even seem to mind.

I couldn't tell if she was joking or not, but she said she was *glad* to have a ghost for a room-mate. That kind of made a chill run up my spine. Like I said, Alex could run hot and cold, but I remember thinking at the time that this dark side, like, this sort of alter-ego she sometimes had, could easily be the result of being possessed or something. Obviously in light of what we know now, her 'room-mate' comment is just incredibly upsetting.

KIMBERLY NOLAN:
Then the only other person was Lois Best. Except, Lois realized quite quickly that she didn't really want to stay there.

LIU WAI:
Afterwards we called her Lois *Worst*. I think she only lasted for less than a week? She was definitely gone before term started. After the first night she wouldn't even sleep in her room, like, she'd hardly even go in there. You'd walk into the kitchen in the morning and find her passed out at the table or lying on the sofa, or maybe – maybe – sleeping on her bedroom floor, but only then with the door wide open.

LOIS BEST, *Zoe's flatmate:*

Well, I was definitely homesick but mainly I hated that building. The situation with the others wasn't unstressful, either. The tower was really old, really badly soundproofed, so you could hear people through the walls and in the ceilings. It got to the point I couldn't sleep. There were strange noises and weird smells, things going missing then reappearing again. My room key got stolen on the first day. We came in after a fire alarm one night and found all our furniture had been moved around. At the time I thought it was one of the others playing a prank. Now we know Alex was right – something was haunting us.

FINTAN MURPHY:

Mercifully, I didn't live on Owens Park, I didn't actually get to know the others until later. I met Zoe early on, though, at the very first meeting of the Choir and Orchestra Society. My mother was big on God, but the singing was pretty much the only part of Catholicism I ever really warmed to, a typical fruit. Zoe looked sort of nervous, sort of vulnerable, and I probably looked about the same. So I don't know where I got the nerve, but I just went over, stuck out my hand and introduced myself. She must have sensed immediately that I was gay, because this defensiveness I thought I'd seen from afar sort of fell away. I think being a young, attractive woman is probably a strange experience. You're seen as a commodity in a sense, surrounded by the inarticulate desperation of young men – boys, I should say – all but sticking their dicks through letterboxes to try and get laid. So I'm sure she could see at a glance I wasn't looking at her that way, and I'm sure she was relieved. After the singing, we ended up walking round and talking all day. It was magic.

ANDREW FLOWERS:

I think up until that moment my father's greatest disappointment in life was that I'd chosen to study in Manchester. I've given him a few more body blows since then. I'd say I've even stepped into the role of world's greatest disappointment myself, but it was certainly the most strained that our relationship had been up until that point, and, well, not to get into it, but my mother was freshly off the scene. All that to say, I turned up a day or two late. And the whole time I'm in the housing office collecting my keys, I can just hear this alarm going off for what feels like miles around, like an air-raid siren or something. It's mid-September and the woman behind this plastic screen's just sweating intracellular fluid, asking me to *sign here*, as though none of it's happening. I asked for directions, you know, 'Where do I live?' and she sort of just wearily waved me out, like, 'Follow the noise.'

KIMBERLY NOLAN:

For the first few days the fire alarms were going off constantly. Even if we'd been evacuated and gone back in five minutes before, we could never just ignore it. I think for people in the lower blocks it was all fun and games. They walked out of their front doors into these massive gatherings, but for us, coming from the tower, it was fifteen floors down, slowly, with the staircase rammed, then the same again going back in, but now trudging all the way up. All it did was make me realize how slowly we'd be leaving if there ever was an actual fire.

LIU WAI:
It got old fast.

ANDREW FLOWERS:
So Owens Park is this gated, leafy green area in Fallowfield where I suppose the main halls are. Five or six houses, each containing a few hundred people, then the tower block in the middle with a thousand or so more. And I arrive as every single one of them is being evacuated out on to the lawn on this baking-hot day. Just this melting pot of chaos en masse, hundreds of clueless kids and girls in towels, all wandering round stunned like they've just found out that they're adopted or something.

JAI MAHMOOD:
Yeah, Andrew got there on like the fourth or fifth fire alarm of that day. I'm standing outside Tree Court taking pictures and this public-school boy starts asking me what's going on, looking like Paddington Bear or something, still holding a suitcase in each hand. We realized we lived in the same flat and I started filling him in, essentially saying, 'Fuck knows what's happening,' when some guy from housing with a loudspeaker starts talking over us. He says there's some fault in the system, so when one alarm goes off in one block it trips all of the others. They were trying to fix it but in the meantime, like, 'Stop burning bacon.'

FINTAN MURPHY:
There was this brilliant sun that day, an anomaly in Manchester, everything felt like promise and light to me, and I thought I might

even have made a friend. I felt as though I learned a lot about Zoe on our walk, some of it from what she told me and some of it from what she didn't. I was already starting to see that you had to meet her more than halfway on some subjects. The way she was polite but reserved when speaking about her twin sister surprised me – they didn't sound particularly close. And of course the way that she skirted round her musical experience and aspirations. I'd seen her singing in the church, I knew she meant business, but I could sense that there was some pain there as well.

During the course of our walk we happened to pass the Royal Northern College of Music and she actually blanched, I've never seen anything like it. I sort of mentioned how I'd idly considered studying there at some point myself and she immediately changed the subject. Kind of physically changed direction and almost got mown down in a bike lane. I noticed it, I remembered it, because I could see that I'd upset her, and I was careful not to bring it up again.

JAI MAHMOOD:
So, I don't know how we got talking about it, but I do know it was that day. A surprise blast of Mancunian sunshine, which was why the alarms didn't seem like such a big deal. I guess I must have been telling Andrew that I'd tried to get into the tower and he must have been asking me why. I said how weird and ugly it was, how it had this otherworldly vibe, and he seemed interested. We were talking while our housemates were busy being 'lads'. Like, starting drinking games and stuff. Andrew just looked at me and said, 'I bet I can get you inside that tower right now.' I was like, 'Go on, then. How?' He

just got up and broke the glass on our fire alarm. [Laughs] Evacuated the whole fucking place again.

ANDREW FLOWERS:

Once we were all outside, Jai and I just stood around with the blockies, then followed them into the tower twenty minutes later. We spent that whole night wandering between floors, going into people's rooms, introducing ourselves, gaining followers everywhere we went. By the time we got up to fifteenth there were probably ten or twelve of us. That's how we ended up meeting Kim, Alex and Liu Wai, that's how we nearly got ourselves arrested the following morning.

FINTAN MURPHY:

Geography wasn't Zoe's strong suit, and she was brand new in town, so after she'd had her funny turn over the Royal Northern, I offered to walk her home. We went almost all the rest of the way in silence. This was a lonely old time for me. Here I am in the gay capital of England, too scared to go and participate. Not drinking, not going out. I can't tell you how many nights I spent on my own in my room. Zoe was the first friend I'd made in a long time, and I treasured her, but I was really afraid that we might not speak again. I was afraid that I'd pushed a button somehow. So I walked her right to the door of her building, that awful tower in the centre of Owens Park, but I didn't go in when she invited me. I didn't want to overstep the mark.

LIU WAI:

There was this crazy racket, so I went out into the communal space to see Kim and Alex amongst all these strange boys in our kitchen, some of them drunk, all of them *weird*. I know Zoe definitely wasn't around at the time so I felt a little bit overfaced? The first person I spoke to was this quite tanned, posh-looking guy who told me his name was Andrew Flowers. I remember thinking at first, like, *Wow, Flowers, that's such a fun name?* He looked really smart and had this incredible accent, and I thought, *He must be so nice.*

ANDREW FLOWERS:
My first impressions of Liu Wai? Amazingly cynical about class but quite naïve with it. If you told her that piss was perfume, she'd rub it behind her ears.

LIU WAI:
Of course, I quickly realized he was dreadful. I was quite impressed with Jai, though. He was handsome in a sort of *I don't care* way, and he had a camera round his neck, which made him look somewhere between an artist and a war reporter. There was a misunderstanding between us, which of course everyone else found hilarious . . .

KIMBERLY NOLAN:
I remember something like that. Liu got it into her head that Jai was a barrister or something?

LIU WAI:
And he looked so young, and was dressed so street, and was kind of a little bit out of it, and I just thought, *Wow.*

JAI MAHMOOD:

I told Liu I was a barista and she started asking me all these questions about where I'd got my law degree, where my offices were and stuff.

LIU WAI:

And I was just saying, like, 'Oh, my cousin's a court reporter,' and everyone was gathering around us and starting to laugh. In the end I just pretended my phone was ringing and excused myself from the conversation. It was, like, two or three days later when I saw him working in the Caffè Nero on Oxford Road and the penny finally dropped. These days I'm in HR so my emotional intelligence is much more developed? But at the time I was a bit naïve.

KIMBERLY NOLAN:

I'd always had this sense that everyone my age was gliding ahead of me. They all knew something I didn't and I had to swim twice as hard just to tread water. But that night I felt like I'd finally, finally caught up. Life had arrived at our front door. Everyone was new there, everyone was starting from the same level.

I thought, *I can do this.*

And I'll admit it helped me that Zoe wasn't there for that, she'd been out singing. I'd texted to ask if she was okay and got a message back saying she was fine, with a friend, on her way home. So I picked my moment, said now or never. I saw someone I liked the look of, walked over and tapped him on the shoulder. I smiled, looked him in the eye and said, 'Big Hands, I know you're the one.'

ANDREW FLOWERS:

Well, I love that song. I think I laughed and said, 'My name's Andrew Flowers, what's yours?' And just as she was about to tell me, the fire alarm went off again. We both sort of rolled our eyes and headed for the door. There was a second where her hand brushed against mine, where we just ever so slightly linked little fingers. There was this electricity, this spark. I can't quite describe it because I never felt it again, not once in all the years since. Then we got separated in the crowd going down the stairwell and I couldn't find her down on the ground. But I thought, *Whatever*. I knew where she lived and I knew I'd remember her face. I knew I'd find her, I'd get that smile again and I'd pick up right where we left off.

Sadly, it hasn't happened yet . . .

JAI MAHMOOD:

Well, when the alarm went off again, so the seventh or eighth time that day, I knew it had dick-all to do with fire. We were still in the tower so I walked into the stairwell with everyone else, but I went the other way – *up* – to the next floor. I'd got my camera and I had the idea to go round shooting empty rooms while the alarm was going off. There was something extra about it, man, Chernobyl vibes. But when I got to the top there was a door open leading on to the roof. I didn't even know you could get out there, then all of a sudden I found myself walking through into this amazing electric-blue half-night sky.

I had my camera up taking a shot before I noticed there was someone else out there, this girl standing right on the edge of the building. I didn't dare move or say anything in case I made her jump.

She was lifting one foot off the ground and hanging it over thin air like she might step off into nothing. She always brought it in again but I was holding my breath until she backed off from the edge. And when she did I saw she was smiling, she was happy. I kind of leaned into one of the air-con units up there and she walked back inside and down the stairs. So I don't think she saw me, but that was the first time I saw Zoe. It's how I still see her now, one foot on the floor and the other one raised up, like, hanging out over the abyss.

LIU WAI:
We got back inside twenty minutes later and that was the last alarm of the night. I was quite glad it seemed to have got rid of all the lads who'd been milling around. It seemed like quite a big coincidence to me afterwards, though. We'd had all these quite *unsavoury* characters in our place for the first time, and the next morning Zoe was in my room telling me that her pants, like every single pair of knickers she'd brought with her, had been stolen. At the time I thought that was the darkest thing I could possibly imagine.

These days, I have something like seven people working under me, so, rest assured, my imagination's *much* richer. At the time, like I said, I was still a bit naïve.

From: evelynidamitchell@gmail.com

Sent: 19/01/19 18:27

To: you

Hey

Don't know if you're there yet – but a quick note about the tower block. Construction work started in 1964, the same year that the last ever execution was carried out in England(!)* and was fully complete by 1966. There were originally only fifteen floors, so Zoe and Kim's flat would have been right at the top. Four further floors were ADDED in 1974–75 to increase housing capacity. This might help explain certain irregularities later on . . .

I'm charging ahead, still interviewing, transcribing and assembling part two. Getting seriously dark. I think I might have come into this as naïve as Liu Wai was. Not any more.

PS –

Ex

* By chance, that execution took place a 20-minute drive down the road from the tower, at Strangeways Prison. The hanged man was a pathological liar named Gwynne Evans, who was seemingly incapable

of telling the truth. He'd killed someone he was maybe having an affair with, and he told mainly what they call 'prestige' lies, things to improve his standing in the eyes of others, all easily caught out and disproved. These days he could have pled diminished responsibility and got a reduced sentence because he literally couldn't help himself. Something about that really unsettles me though.

I sit with Kim, Liu, Andrew, Jai, Fintan, Robert, Sally, etc., sometimes for hours at a time, recording everything they say, transcribing it later, then printing it up, trying to get it published. What if one day it hits the shelves and I find out one of them was like Gwynne Evans?

Like, what if there was someone like him in Zoe's life? Someone who just couldn't help himself? That would mean he's in my life now, too . . .

Anyway, I digress, read the rest of my email.

--4--

'Dark Room'

The investigation into Zoe's missing underwear pulls certain people closer together and pushes others further apart.

KIMBERLY NOLAN:

I was awake early, watering Chihiro, my bonsai, my pride and joy. She was three years old and I'd grown her from this softwood cutting, so from literally two leaves into something resembling a tree. I got her when I was fifteen, when Dad told me I was no longer required in his vocal classes, when he basically decided I was no longer required at all. I didn't have many friends outside of Zoe, so I was lonely, and I liked the idea of these living things that only revealed themselves over years. They were all about patience and I guess that's how I thought of myself, a late bloomer. Or maybe just high maintenance. And I learned as I went that it wasn't really about patience anyway, it was more about contemplation, effort, ingenuity. I'd named her after the brave little girl in my favourite film, so she felt like my spirit guide or something. I'd usually find myself thinking about life while I worked on her, and that morning I felt good. I'd taken a chance the night before – I'd tried and I'd made, if not friends, then people who might become friends.

My room was right next to Lois's, and I could hear she was up early, too, murmuring something through the wall.

LIU WAI:

I think I felt violated on Zoe's behalf? If you see theft as a form of envy, then the theft of someone's most intimate personal possessions seems like a declaration to the world about what you'd *really* like to be stealing from them. I just thought it was psychotic behaviour, not cool, not a joke. Zoe seemed fine at the time, a little shaken maybe. I said something like, 'It's probably a stupid question, but you don't share clothes with Kim, do you?' She shook her head, she was distracted by something, and I could tell she hadn't spoken to Kim about it. I remember thinking it was strange that she was confiding this in me rather than her twin sister. But then of course it occurred to me that Kim had let all those people into our flat the night before . . .

JAI MAHMOOD:

I'd never be arsed now but I was really into developing my own prints back then. Just black-and-white 8x10s and stuff, but magic to see, like making gold out of nothing. Our place was perfect for it, man, no natural light in the bathroom, nothing to black out, and it had a pretty strong ventilator for all the fumes and stuff. I just swapped the bulb with a red one and wheeled everything else in. There was no room on the counter so I had this plywood base that sat on the rim of the bath, then I put my enlarger – this old Beseler

89

23c – on top of that. Drop your developing trays inside the tub and you're flying. I'd found this roll-around kitchen cart on the first night that everything fit into, so my set-up and take-down time was about ten minutes flat. I never forgot I was living with four lads, though. Like, I was up early to make sure I wasn't in anyone's way. And I was making prints from the night before. Life always started to feel real for me the next day, when I started developing it, seeing stuff for the second time around.

KIMBERLY NOLAN:

I don't remember what I would have been doing – pruning, watering – but Lois's voice started getting louder. I kind of called through the wall, 'Is everything okay?'

LOIS BEST:

I could hear a man in my room. And I don't mean through the walls and floorboards, like normal stuff. When I was in bed it sounded like someone was whispering through a traffic cone into my ear. And I knew it was probably just some eighteen-year-old boy from the next floor up, someone with no idea his voice was travelling so much, but I'd been awake half the night, I felt like I was losing it.

KIMBERLY NOLAN:

I knocked on but got no answer. We'd been there a couple of days by this point and Lois had really kept to herself. I think I wondered if she was struggling. Looking back, I was probably quite keen to find someone more socially awkward than I was, take them under my wing like a bonsai tree or something. So I opened the door and found her kind of staring at her wardrobe. I asked what was wrong and she said she'd woken up thinking there was someone inside it, someone in her room. We looked at each other for a second and I just started laughing. I didn't know she was serious – I mean, I didn't even know her – but she laughed back and I think I suggested breakfast as a way of getting her out of there. It honestly didn't occur to me to open the wardrobe or look in it.

LIU WAI:

As someone who's witnessed their own mother go through shock, like, be completely normal one moment and then break down in the spice aisle of Waitrose the next, I didn't feel comfortable letting it go? So while I brewed some coffee and sat Zoe down on the sofa I called the police to report the theft of her clothes. They clearly weren't interested, so I was in the middle of convincing them that this was serious when Lois and Kim came in.

KIMBERLY NOLAN:

Andrew told you some people cast Zoe as a victim after she went missing, but that's probably because he didn't know her that well. People had *always* cast her as a victim. And she knew it, too, she could really lean into that too-thin, too-quiet, too-delicate thing when it suited her. So I think wrapped up in Liu Wai's Zoe worship was this weird need to protect her at all costs.

Basically, I walked in on Liu reporting some missing clothes as a cross between armed robbery and sexual assault, hissing into the phone, demanding they send their 'best man' down to take a statement. And all this time Zoe, in her tiny voice, is saying, 'No, no, no, it's fine, it's not that big a deal,' just getting talked over. And it's all news to me, so I'm like, 'What's going on? Are you okay?'

We hadn't talked the night before because she came in so late. I was thinking, *fuck*, I really can't let her out of my sight. It hadn't occurred to me that Liu would be calling the police about the harmless ten-minute gathering in our kitchen the night before. Then she reeled off every name she could remember, including Jai Mahmood and Andrew Flowers, giving me this look like I'd sold my sister's virginity to them on eBay.

JANINE MORRIS, *Ex-student experience officer:*
Well, I was contacted by the authorities that morning. Managing student housing, you can imagine the kinds of calls I usually got. *[Laughs]* I was in my mid-thirties then but I'd long since lost my ability to be shocked. I'd long since lost the colour in my hair, let's put it that way.

This one stuck in the memory, though.

The police said they'd had a report of 'sexually motivated theft' in the tower block and needed assistance tracing possible culprits. I didn't want to know what 'sexually motivated theft' was, so when they gave me a list of names I looked them up. They were all students of ours so it didn't take long. Next thing you know the police are on site and I'm taking them round to knock on. Two of the boys, Flowers and Mahmood, lived together in Tree Court, so we went there first.

I've reported my share of robberies to Greater Manchester Police, but I don't think I've ever seen a quicker response. I remember thinking, *Next time the house gets broken into I'm telling them a teenage girl's knicker drawer got turned over, too.**

JAI MAHMOOD:

I heard the buzzer going but I was still working on my prints so I just left it for the others. I didn't really notice anything until a few minutes later, when Harry, one of the guys we lived with, started knocking on, saying there was someone there to talk to me. I walked into the hall still holding a dripping photo.

ANDREW FLOWERS:

I went into the communal space to find the police interrogating my flatmates. In a room containing four white boys and one brown one, the constables wore out their powers of deduction deciding which of us was Jai Mahmood. So when they asked who Andrew Flowers was I thought I'd better raise my hand and close the case for them. Look, I honestly thought it was all a joke, I thought they were male strippers or something. I was checking their IDs, expecting to see Officer Nasty and Sergeant Ticklish. And just when I think they're about to rip their shirts off and start playing Wham!, they ask the others to leave the room. Then me and Jai are looking at each other, like, 'What did you do?'

You have to remember, we'd only just met, we didn't really know each other. Then they started telling us why they were there and I lost all credulity. They said they'd received a 'serious complaint'

---

* This interview was conducted by Joseph Knox, and added to Evelyn's text in 2019.

about our behaviour from the night before. Was there anything we wanted to tell them?

JAI MAHMOOD:

So while Flowers, this walking definition of white privilege, is proving how funny he can be, I'm winding my neck all the way in. I can tell these guys don't like the look of me. And I can hear my mum in my head, saying I'm the first in the family to reach higher education, how she's killed herself to get me here, so I just go quiet, which is the worst thing you can do. Andrew's dickheadedness makes him look innocent. Cops understand hostility and being called pigs, but they don't understand fear, so I just look like I'm hiding something, I just look guilty as shit.

And at the same time, I'm racking my brains trying to work out what we've done. Y'know, is this because we were in the tower? Is this because I was on the roof? Is this because that girl thinks I'm a fucking barrister? But it's clearly something more serious than all that, and then they tell us that 'personal items' have been removed from a property we'd visited the night before. That we were trespassing in the tower block and the best thing we can do now is own up to it. I'm sitting there shitting it, staring at the floor memorizing my fucking Converse, when they say, 'Look, we know you've got priors for theft.' And that's confusing, man, because no I haven't. 'Course, I look up and realize they're talking to Flowers.

ANDREW FLOWERS:

A complicated story, a boring one. Not funny and not interesting. I just grew up estranged from the rest of my family. There was a nanny around in Surrey when I was a boy, Mrs Withers, then when I was of age I got packed off to boarding school. And you know who my father is? Right, correct, one of those men who owns things. Not just hedge funds and lobbies, but whatever he happens to be handling in any given moment, whatever falls within his sightline. People and places and you name it. So it wasn't theft, whatever the police might like to call it. He took something that belonged to me, so I took something that belonged to him. That's quid pro fucking quo as far as I'm concerned.

```
=====================================================
Case No: VT 08/03/11/3462
Reporting Officer: Constable Alice Hardy
Date of Report: 08 March 2011
=====================================================
```

At 1755hrs on 8 March 2011, I met with Mr. Richard Flowers at Ashwan House on Christchurch Rd. regarding a vehicle theft. Mr. Flowers said his son, Mr. Andrew Flowers, had stolen one of his cars, a vintage Jaguar, after an emotional argument in the family home at approx. 1600hrs. Mr. Flowers was concerned his son may have been under the influence of drink and/or drugs when he took the vehicle.

Mr. Flowers described his car as a burgundy-coloured, 1952, C-Type Jaguar, registered in the UK. The car registration is FLW3RS. He estimated

the value of the car at in excess of £450,000,
adding that it is a 'one of a kind' collector's
item and due to be sold at Sotheby's Auction
House in early April. He described no
distinguishing marks or items.

Mr. Flowers stressed that he had not given his
son permission to take the car, and that he was
concerned his son would intentionally damage the
vehicle as a result of their disagreement. He
stated further that his son was given to
dishonesty in discussing his father's business
dealings, relationships, morality and sex life.*
==

ANDREW FLOWERS:

Look, the short version is that my maternal grandfather, Charles Barclay, owned a merchant-shipping venture which went under, I think literally, and he basically sold off his daughter – my mother – to be married. She'd been around the world but, as with everything else in my grandfather's possession at the time, she was basically damaged goods. One bad marriage behind her, one burgeoning speed addiction in front. I was always embarrassed by her. Eyeliner that looked like it had been scrawled on with a Sharpie, smile painted a few millimetres away from where her mouth actually was. Always walking out of shops without paying, always crashing cars, always crying in the shower. Mainly I was away at school anyway, and when

---

* This police report was added to Evelyn's text by Joseph Knox in 2019.

I went home I spent most of my time with the daughter from next door, a seventeen-year-old half-Parisian princess called Élodie.

Anyway, I got a worrying phone call from Mother one day in term time, which was rare, and then I couldn't get hold of my dad, which was the norm. I travelled home to find he'd had her hauled off to the nuthouse a fortnight before and not told anyone. And, look, it's not like she shouldn't have been there, she was mad as a box of ballbags, but the fucker hadn't even been to see her. In fact, I found him busy making house with my girlfriend, Élodie, the half-Parisian princess from next door – forty-three fucking years his junior. So, I don't know. I suppose some days passed, Mum cut her wrists and killed herself, Dad and Élodie eloped, *yada-yada-yada*, I rolled his vintage half-a-million-pound ponce racer. I didn't mean to damage the car, I think I just wanted to stop. Stop everything. The fucker pressed charges, too.

FROM THE OFFICE OF RICHARD FLOWERS (CBE), DATED 08/09/19:

Mr Flowers does not wish to make any comment on his relationship with his estranged son, Andrew, at this time. Furthermore, Mr Flowers has no information on the disappearance of Zoe Nolan and no interest in the case beyond that of a citizen wishing to see justice done. He will make no further statements on this topic, nor on the subjects of his deceased wife, his current wife or his three other children. He would urge readers to address their attention to Andrew's criminal record and to disregard unverifiable and emotionally presented 'facts'. Finally, Mr Flowers requests that the press respect his privacy and that of his young family.*

ANDREW FLOWERS:

Clearly, with hindsight, I shouldn't have been at university a few months after all that, and I certainly shouldn't have been dating any young women, least of all ones as troubled as Zoe. I shouldn't have been allowed within fifty feet of anyone at all. It's funny to think that in all my protestations that Zoe and I had nothing in common, I was overlooking our two recent suicide attempts. Well, not funny *ha-ha* . . .

JAI MAHMOOD:

I'd never seen someone change like that before, fucking Jekyll and Hyde. Andrew goes from this swaggering kind of cocksure danger-man to this ice-psycho, literally at the mention of these charges. He stands up slowly, in this way that makes me think he's about to smack someone, then he storms down the hall to his room and slams *open* the door. He *demands* that they search it, which they do, but then they start asking about my room.

---

* This statement was added to Evelyn's text by Joseph Knox in 2019.

Well, I haven't hulked up and lost my shit, so I just say, 'Do I have to?' I didn't massively care but it seemed weird to let the cops go through my stuff based on nothing. Then they see the 'Do Not Enter' sign I've stuck up on the bathroom and want to go in there, too. I'm blocking the door, like, 'I'd rather you didn't,' telling them it's a dark room. So they go, 'Why, what kind of photos are you taking, anyway?' I kind of shrug and one of them snatches the picture I've got out of my hand. It was the one from the roof the night before, Zoe standing with one foot over the edge. At the time I didn't know this was anything to do with her – I mean, we'd been through a lot of rooms the night before – but their eyes start bulging, like, 'Anything you wanna tell us, son?'

KIMBERLY NOLAN:

To me, Liu calling the police felt over the top. I thought it might seem like the right thing if you'd read a textbook on how to live life, but it didn't consider the victim or the context we were living in. And it for damn sure didn't make Zoe safer. I mean, one of those policemen who came for a statement was cracking on to her, he gave her his number. 'If there's anything you need, day or night, even if it's just someone to talk to.' I cut in, like, 'Is this you laying the law down, pal?'

LIU WAI:

Listen, on the one hand I can be quite laid-back and analytical about these things. On the other hand, if pushed, I'm sorry, but that's when my Virgo comes out. You know, if pushed I can be critical, clinical, precise. I'm not saying anything radical here. Women shouldn't have to put up with this shit.

LOIS BEST:

Kim and Liu argued, Zoe shrank down. I thought it was bizarre. Twins and missing underwear and the police and everyone fighting. It felt like everyone's worst traits were coming out within three or four days of knowing each other. Mine, too. We were all just kids trying to adapt to our surroundings, except our surroundings seemed hostile towards us. Like, while I lived there, there was never a normal day. I never felt like myself, I don't think anyone else did, either.

ANDREW FLOWERS:

The police pushed Jai a bit about looking into his room, about looking at the rest of his pictures. They'd taken a photo of some girl from him, then started asking, 'Who's this? Who is it?' And Jai was like, 'I don't know, I didn't get her name.' To which they're saying, 'Oh, you like taking pictures of girls without their consent, do you?' Essentially calling him a pervert. I realized belatedly that I'd sort of set all this in motion by losing my rag, so I finally piped up and suggested that they come back with a warrant, which is funny because I didn't even know what a warrant was. They gave us their best hard-man stares and said it wasn't over. Then they walked out with the picture that Jai had developed, which I thought was pretty shit of them. I tried to apologize, but he just shrugged. He shrugged like I was the sort of person you expected to fuck you over. Then he went back into the bathroom, closed the door on me and carried on working.

KIMBERLY NOLAN:

It had been this high-stress day – the theft, the police, the fight about it all – then we got woken up, just after midnight. Screaming coming from one of our rooms. I realized it must be Lois sleepwalking, having her night terrors again. I got up and went into the hall, saw Liu, Alex and Zoe, then I opened Lois's door and turned on the light. She was standing up in her pyjamas, holding a glass bottle by the neck with one hand and holding her wardrobe door shut with the other. She kind of shouted for help and said she'd heard someone in there. I think I'd started to say something like, 'There's no one in there,' when the rest of us heard it as well.

LOIS BEST:

I didn't want to open it or look at it or anything, I wanted to get out and call the police, but Kim was trying to reassure me. And she was acting less scared than she was, which only made it worse. So I moved and stood back in the doorway while she looked.

She opened the wardrobe and there was no one in there, and nothing, I mean. And I didn't want to be right, so I was relieved – we all were. Then she pushed my clothes to one side and we saw this maintenance, or this service panel in the wall, right at the back. You wouldn't see it without opening the wardrobe and really looking for it. But that was where all these weird sounds were coming from. Kim basically touched that panel and it came off in her hands, like, no resistance. We all moved in and saw it opened on to piping, for repairs and stuff. It was a crawlspace so someone could get inside and follow the pipes and fix them. Someone, probably Liu Wai, said something like, 'I bet this goes through every apartment on our floor,' and that was it. That was my last night living there. I slept on the sofa and had my stuff packed the next morning.

KIMBERLY NOLAN:

Lois hugged me when she left the next day. She hugged me and looked at me and held my arms and said, 'Look after yourself,' really seriously. At first I thought she'd seen something in me, like some weakness, whatever it was she had. I thought she was saying I was the same as her, too fragile for this world or something. I remember it pissed me off at the time. The longer I stayed, the more I realized she'd been talking about the tower, that place. There was something wrong with it.

LOIS BEST:

Leaving there I just had this sad feeling for them all. Like, I knew something sad would happen. If it had been up to me I would have had them all moved too, but what could I do? I didn't know anything, I just felt it. I cried every day for a week when the news broke about Zoe.

KIMBERLY NOLAN:

We kept expecting Lois's room to get given to another student, but it never happened. In the end we just started using it for storage space, a spare bed. And actually, the only other person who stayed in there – a friend of Alex's – said basically the same thing: it sounded like there was someone in the room with her. I don't think any of us were curious about it. It was just a horrible, dark, cramped space that made noise. I know I'm flashing forward a bit, but just to say, Zoe hated that stuff, she wouldn't even look in it. She'd never have gone in there in a million years.

ANDREW FLOWERS:

I walked around all night feeling like shit, about the past and the present. You only really miss your mother when you know you'll never see her again. I wasn't speaking to my father at the time and I'd dropped Jai, the closest thing I had to a friend, right in the shit. It was one of those nights where you feel like there's nothing in front of you. Somehow I arrived at the tower, probably with half a bottle of bourbon in me. It was late, but I thought, *whatever,* and buzzed what I thought was the flat where we'd been the night before. I couldn't believe it when the girl I'd been speaking to actually picked up. I sort of said, 'Hi, me and a couple of friends were in your kitchen last night. I know things went south but I was wondering if I could see you again? I was wondering if we could talk?' I just wanted to explain, tell her it wasn't us who'd stolen her clothes and check that she was okay. And yes, I'll admit I wanted to see her, to see if I'd feel that same spark again.

KIMBERLY NOLAN:

Shit, I'd forgotten that. Yeah, we were all awake after Lois's scare, having a communal midnight hot chocolate with some rum or something, then the buzzer went off and I went to answer it. It was late but I would have been thrilled to think it was Andrew, this hot toff I'd met the night before. I wanted to see him again but I looked over my shoulder, saw us all bonding there for the first time, and told him I was sorry, I was busy. I think I said we should try another day.

ANDREW FLOWERS:

I said, 'Sure.' I wished her a good night and walked on. There were some corners of OP that got so dark you could convince yourself you didn't exist, so I went and stood in one for a while and finished whatever I was drinking, watching the occasional person walk by, none of them even knowing I was there.

What I'm saying is that, in my mind, there *was* no Zoe Nolan.

I'd met Kim that first night, I'd talked to her, so when the police snatched what looked like a picture of Kim from Jai, I assumed it was *her* clothes that had gone missing. I assumed it was *her* who must have called the cops, etcetera, etcetera. I didn't have her name yet, but that's what I thought. And absurdly, that misunderstanding, that mix-up, has more or less altered the course of my entire life. There are always moments when you look back, these weak spots you realize your entire existence hinged on. You could say that my arrest was one of those – I mean, after it, the relationship with my family was more or less irretrievable. And Zoe's disappearance was, of course, another low-water mark that would go on to define my future. But not getting Kimberly's name when I met her. That's the one that fucking haunts me.

JAI MAHMOOD:

I developed film all day in fits and starts. Obviously I couldn't use the bathroom uninterrupted, but everyone was sound about it at first. When I redid my shot of Zoe it came out even better the second time. Her on the ledge of the tower, looking like she's contemplating life more than contemplating suicide. It was black and white so the shadows really stuck out, *Touch of Evil*-vibes, pure noir. And then I noticed this shadow that shouldn't have been there, this shadow that had the same shape as a man.

Someone had been stood at the other side of the roof where I couldn't see, like he'd been watching her while she dangled her foot over the edge. I told the police this after Zoe went missing, but by then the picture and the negative had both disappeared, both nicked out of my room, so either I imagined it or someone really didn't want it to be seen.

From: evelynidamitchell@gmail.com

Sent: 22/01/19 23:33

To: you

Are you still reading the chapters, JK? Feel a bit like I'm talking into the void.

After Sirens came out, did you feel more confident as a writer? I don't know how I can feel MORE frustrated and confused but I really do. A second book should be like the 13th floor of a hotel. You just skip the fucker entirely.

Did I ever tell you that Curtis Brown tried to get me to write a cancer book? Mum died of breast cancer, so they thought it might be 'fun' to chart my progress against hers, like that's how either one of us would want to be remembered. It was before I'd even finished chemo, when it could still have gone either way. I replied suggesting some titles: *Almost Gone Girl*, *Infinite Tests*, *Remission Impossible*. They never got back to me.

Anyway, the reason I'm writing is that someone called my landline the other morning, at THREE in the morning. I didn't even know my landline still worked. There was no heavy breathing sadly, so I couldn't get myself off, just silence then the dial tone.

Too much to hope that it was you tryna remember my number after a few stiff ones, eh?

Thought so.

Ex

--5--

'Evil Eyes'

Zoe and Andrew meet each other on a night out, while a sinister presence begins to make itself known in Zoe's life, social circle and bedroom.

LIU WAI:

Personally, I never felt safe from that moment on. Once I knew someone had been in and stolen Zoe's stuff I felt like we were under some kind of surveillance. Someone actually set up a Facebook page posing as an appeal for information on the location of her underwear, invited half the student population to join, like, *hundreds* of people. At the time it seemed juvenile. Now, like everything else, it just looks sinister. We never found out who it was, but let's just say I was looking a little bit more closely at the people surrounding me at the time.

FINTAN MURPHY:

I'd guess that Zoe and I had only met two or three more times by this stage. There'd been a couple of choir practices at St Chrysostom's

Church and we'd taken a long stroll, walking and talking, after each one. I'm afraid she didn't tell me about the theft, no. My relationship with her was quite humorously chaste, almost old-fashioned. No off-colour jokes, both kind of focussing on music, positivity.

I suppose we both must have needed it.

I'd grown up in the old country, in an old family, and I think I was quite old-fashioned myself in some senses. I did, unfortunately, find out about it all *without* Zoe's consent. I was invited to join a Facebook group called 'Knickers with Attitude' which had been established to resemble an appeal for information on Zoe's missing underwear. I declined the request and blocked the page. To me it felt intensely childish. I can't imagine how it must have felt for her.

KIMBERLY NOLAN:

People nudged each other, they looked her way, word definitely got around. It could have been really distressing, but I think she sort of enjoyed it. She was recognizable for a few days – who wouldn't want to be the centre of attention at eighteen? It's what Dad had been priming her for her whole life. Suddenly she was getting smiles in the lobby, boys were buying her drinks . . .

That's actually how we found out Jai was the main suspect.

Two boys bought us a bottle of wine at the Friendship Inn and one of them said he'd heard 'that rag-head' took Zoe's pants from her room. I didn't know Jai outside of the night I'd seen him in our flat, and as far as I knew Zoe hadn't met him at all, but I guessed he was the person they were talking about. We left without finishing our drinks.

LIU WAI:

So, whoever set up the page had taken pictures from Zoe's *real* Facebook. Like, personal information and stuff from her wall. We realized it must have been someone who was actually friends with her on there, or someone who had access to her account, which I think made it even more disturbing? Zoe loved Facebook, she was always talking to ten people at once, putting up pictures, making comments, so to suddenly realize someone was monitoring her was dark.

KIMBERLY NOLAN:

I think what disturbed me more than the page itself – which was just stupid – was that none of us were talking about the theft outside of our group. Me, Zoe, Liu, Alex and Lois all knew about the robbery. Well, I didn't tell anyone. Zoe said she didn't, either. I think Fintan backs that up because she never said anything to him. Then you've got Liu Wai, who was scarily loyal, you've got Alex, who was busy with her own life, and Lois, who left immediately afterwards. I just couldn't see it coming from anyone in that group. So to me the most likely person to have started that page was whoever had actually stolen her pants, or maybe whoever the police had spoken to about it. No one else should have even known.

ANDREW FLOWERS:

I personally never saw the Facebook page, but you could tell something was in the air. Who knows if one thing was connected to the other, but what I remember were posters appearing around Owens Park warning of a predatory photographer. As I recall they specifically urged girls to 'Beware'. I mean, it could only have been directed at Jai, which was ridiculous, but he started getting shit for it pretty much immediately.

JAI MAHMOOD:
I wasn't even into pictures of people, man. The odd thing came along, but only when they weren't facing the camera. Maybe massive groups like the fire-alarm evacuations, stuff at a distance, but faces didn't really float my boat. Owens Park was ugly as shit, though, and that did. You'd see me around with my camera a lot at the time, I was always trying to get on roofs and in hallways and to hang out of windows, always trying to find new angles, man. And I started getting hassle. Shouted at and called a sex-pest and stuff. Yeah, I remember the posters.

HARRY FOWLES, *Andrew and Jai's flatmate*:
I think we were only a few weeks in by then, but there was already a rift between us. Like, Andrew and Jai one side and the rest of us – me, Chris and Lee – on the other. For one thing, Andrew would always refer to the rest of us as One Direction, like, really scornfully. More seriously, none of us had ever dealt with the police before, so it felt pretty real when they turned up questioning the two of them about something in our first week. You've got Andrew kind of shouting at them and Jai refusing to cooperate, being accused of this awful stuff.

It just felt like a lot.

What really made ears prick up and kind of stay that way was this mention of theft, things going missing. Because that had started at ours, too, gently at first, then sort of snowballing out of control. You couldn't leave anything in the fridge without it going missing. Y'know, if you left your wallet lying around for the day and then picked it up later, you'd find yourself saying, 'What happened to that twenty?' My house keys, the fob and my room key and everything went walkabout in the first week with no explanation.

It was only much, much later I put it all together.

After Zoe Nolan went missing and it was all over the news, I realized that the police had been talking to Andrew and Jai about things vanishing from her place. I suppose it always struck me as a kind of clue. Like, stuff was going missing from our building and stuff was going missing from theirs. And who went between both buildings? Andrew and Jai. We put our foot down about Jai doing his science-lab shit in the bathroom, too. Someone was going round taking pictures of girls against their will or something, so it seemed weird for him to be developing stuff in secret all the time.

KIMBERLY NOLAN:

I checked the Facebook page once or twice, just looking for clues of who might be running it. I stopped going on there when people started posting mad stuff – that wall was like a public toilet. People saying a perv was on the prowl, he needed reining in, attaching pictures of some posters that had been put up around Owens Park, all warning about a photographer who was stalking women.

LIU WAI:

And maybe it came from the Facebook thing, but someone kept pranking our door relentlessly. Like, they'd buzz up from the ground-floor entrance and then when you answered no one would say anything. Occasionally people would play knock-a-door-run and stuff. It's hard to tell what was sinister and what was the result of being surrounded by teenage boys. My main problem was more inside the flat, like, a feeling of not knowing who was coming and going? It sounds like hindsight talking, but I'm telling you I could feel it. I have quite bad allergies and certain things really set me off. *Every* time I stuck my head inside Zoe's room I'd come away sneezing.

KIMBERLY NOLAN:

I didn't live with Liu Wai for very long, but even just across those three months, she was quite sensitive to her surroundings, always noticing draughts or dust, quite often coughing or sick.

ANDREW FLOWERS:

If someone sneezed in Australia, Liu Wai caught a cold in Manchester.

LIU WAI:

I think it was because I grew up with just me and Mum, but men's aftershave has always really stood out to me? It's always just made my nose itch, and that was what I was getting from Zoe's room. And as far as I knew, she hadn't had any boys round at that time. When I mentioned it to her she'd say she couldn't smell it, but it was definitely, definitely there..Now, I want to go back and scream at her, at myself, like, 'Get out!' I wondered if whoever had taken her underwear was returning to the scene of the crime or something.

Another thing that meant nothing to me then was how I'd always come into the flat after a day of no one being there and sort of find myself saying, 'Wait, why is Lois's door wide open?' Like, that room was supposed to be empty.

JAI MAHMOOD:

I never made it out on the night Andrew met Zoe. If I had, I might have realized what was going on before he did and changed the course of history.

ANDREW FLOWERS:

Look, if I'm down on all fours in the confessional booth, then no, I cannot fully recall the night I met Zoe. If I'd known then that I'd end up having to discuss it for the rest of my life, I probably would have drunk some water or something. I can give you my movements, though, the vague sequence of events.

JAI MAHMOOD:

I was meant to meet him back at ours before he went out, but I never made it. At the time I was working on this project where I'd document the multistorey car parks of Manchester, all in black and white, then develop the pictures myself. I was starting with the ones nearest to us, yeah, Oxford Road, Salford, satellite towns, then thinking I'd work my way out, maybe even right to the airport. It came out of a story I'd read about the city's population growing so massively. The census said it was something like 20 per cent up in ten years, and I was buzzed off how that works. Where does everyone go? Where are their houses and rooms and cars? I wanted albums full of multistorey car parks and apartment blocks and sub-lets and things. The idea was to build this kind of bible about the margins and where we cram all the stuff we don't want seen. It probably would have ended with illegal squats and homeless shelters. That's ironic now I think about it, because I never finished the project, but I did end up living in those places.

Anyway, I was in the car park on Grafton Street, basically finished for the day but just walking up to the roof to see if there was a view. I wish I could say I saw something or sensed it coming, but my head was all the way into what I was doing. I was on my last roll of film with some shots saved just in case. The advance leaver on my SLR always stuck, so I think I'd stopped to jimmy it on when I heard footsteps, started to turn and got twatted on the back of the head. I hit the floor and a guy said, 'So you like stealing white girls' knickers, eh, Sinbad?' I tried to say something but he hit me again. Ripped my camera out of my hands and smashed it on the floor. Then he just kicked me, my face, body and back until I passed out.

LIU WAI:

I personally don't agree with violence in any circumstances, I think it usually says more about the attacker than the attacked. In an argument, anyone who has recourse to physicality automatically loses, in my opinion. But I would also observe that sometimes those who live by the sword die by the sword.

JAI MAHMOOD:

Bruised ribs, two black eyes, sprained ankle, a dislocated knee and a bloody nose, but the only thing he actually broke was my camera.

Things might have been better for me if he'd cracked my skull open instead, man, because that fucked me up. Maybe it was the hassle I'd been getting, the dirty looks round campus whenever I took a picture, but I think it was mainly that kicking. I've never owned a camera since. I just didn't see the world in the same way. The woman who called the ambulance had to pull a pair of piss-stained boxer shorts out of my mouth.

ANDREW FLOWERS:
I waited for Jai but he never showed, so I ended up on this misbegotten night out with our other flatmates, collectively known as One Direction, and yes, that's the night I met Zoe.

KIMBERLY NOLAN:
It was October 15th – I can tell you the date because it was mine and Zoe's birthday. The idea was this big night out, but as it got closer, as Liu Wai made more and more plans, I just found myself dreading it. Another night fielding no-brainer questions from boys about being a twin – 'Can you feel it when your sister gets hurt?' – or watching them just walk straight past me to Zoe.

Sometimes it happens that way with me. I get this urge to cut and run. So I came down with a mystery illness and stayed in with Chihiro. I've often wondered if things would have been different if I'd gone.

LIU WAI:
I thought it said a lot about their relationship that Kim wouldn't even spend their shared birthday together. Like, what kind of twin are you?

ANDREW FLOWERS:

We did the Great Central, the Deaf Institute, Font and Trof. It was one of those nights that feels like it goes on for days. We finally ended up in a club called Heaven. Not the worst place in the world, but if you were forced to spend eternity there, then I think you'd lose your faith fairly fast. The idea was to blast your brains out with drum and bass, but through all the Day-Glo dickheads and denim dungarees I saw this familiar face and thought, *Hey, isn't that the girl you met on your first night here?*

LIU WAI:

Zoe and me ended up in this *amazing* nightclub called Heaven and I ran into Andrew at the bar. It was the first time I'd seen him since he'd been holding forth in our kitchen a few weeks before. I started trying to talk to him but he didn't listen or actually engage, he was quite drunk. He was squinting at Zoe on the dancefloor.

ANDREW FLOWERS:

Yeah, I thought. It's the one whose pants went walkabout while you were in her flat. The one who said you could talk another time when you buzzed her door. *Well*, I thought, *this is another time. I should go over and buy her a drink, make my peace.* And I guess it must have worked because the next thing you know we were on the dancefloor, kissing like our flight was going down.

LIU WAI:

It was an incredibly disappointing end to the night. Andrew was dancing with Zoe, trying to scream into her ear over the music, but it was so loud. She was just laughing and nodding – I mean, there was no way you'd ever hear *her* in that place, either. Let's just say they weren't connecting intellectually.

ANDREW FLOWERS:

Listen, I freely acknowledge that I'm every shade of shit rolled into one for not noticing the difference between Zoe and Kim that night. I did think, somewhere right at the back of my brain, that this didn't *seem* like the funny, self-deprecating girl I'd met before. I couldn't feel that same spark that had almost lifted my feet off the floor the first time. But who thinks of twins? Who outside of fucking Poirot thinks of twins? I hadn't got Kim's name the first time we met. But I'd seen that same sneering Asian girl with her. The same one who was even then giving me the evils across the dancefloor. So in my head, in that moment, it all just clicked into place. When the girl I was dancing with told me her name was Zoe I thought, *Yeah, great, that must have been her name.*

KIMBERLY NOLAN:

I think I probably tried to stay awake for them, just to see Zoe and check in, but sometime after midnight I nodded off. I would have been in my room asleep when they got back.

ANDREW FLOWERS:

Zoe and I went back to hers. Not to air her dirty laundry, but she knew what she was doing. I only say this because I've seen stories online suggesting I was her 'first' or whatever, and I think we can probably put those to bed, so to speak. In the morning, while she was still out cold, I guess I had a chance to get a good look at her. And I guess some doubt was really starting to bubble up because I definitely recall thinking, *Wait, was this really the girl I met before? The one quoting 'Blister in the Sun'?* I couldn't see anything in the room that would verify things one way or the other, but what I could see was giving me an extremely bad feeling. We're talking Ed Sheeran posters, Harry Potter merchandise, the Twilight books. So I go out into the hall thinking I'll just double-check this is the same place I was in before . . .

KIMBERLY NOLAN:

I was the first one awake, as usual, watering Chihiro. I'd gone through into the kitchen to make some toast when Andrew walked in wearing basically the stupid look on his face and nothing else. We just looked at each other, both silently computing the situation. Then he nodded, sighed and went back into Zoe's room. I sat there for five minutes with the toast in my hand, then I think I left it and went back to bed. That was my first day of being nineteen.

ANDREW FLOWERS:

I see no reason why anyone would believe me, but at the time it broke my heart. Before that, even with all the shit I'd been through with Élodie and my father, I didn't even know the meaning of the phrase. After it, I couldn't believe that people were expected to walk around that way without medical intervention.

When I met Kim for the first time it just felt different. I felt different. Like another man, or the one I might have been. That evaporated when I saw her sitting there in the kitchen and realized I'd slept with her sister. I got dressed, kissed Zoe goodbye and I started to leave. She asked if we could see each other again and I suppose I must have said yes.

KIMBERLY NOLAN:

It wasn't the end of the world. Men always went for Zoe over me. *[Laughs]* Even though I had my own tree and everything. It was just confusing. Was I upset because a boy I fancied had slept with some-one else? Or was it because he'd slept with my sister? And I *liked* Andrew at the time. I think if it had been different, if he'd shagged Alex or Liu, maybe I'd have said something, I might have fought for him. But I was trying to be my own person. I was trying not to have issues with Zoe. So I never said anything to her about it, I swallowed the whole thing.

ANDREW FLOWERS:

When I got back that morning I saw Jai, of course. And I mean, he'd had the living shit kicked out of him. Plaster across his nose, black eyes, bald patches. Someone had ripped out clumps of his hair with their hands. I went straight into my room, found the card that the two police officers had given us and called them. It took them three days to get around to visiting and taking a statement.

Three fucking days.

And I knew then that this was all shit they'd put into play. They took that picture of Zoe from him, I'm sure they had something to do with the posters going up around campus, the rumours of a predator or whatever. They knew they couldn't get him one way so they got him another. I sat there and watched them and didn't say a word while Jai gave his statement. The fucker taking notes was just doodling, he didn't even try and hide it.

JAI MAHMOOD:

It wasn't the violence that sent me off the rails, man. I mean, it didn't help, but at the end of the day I could see it for what it was. Some cock-lump hit me because he had a hang-up about brown boys and white girls, yeah? Seeing the posters didn't change his mind or make him think that way, the posters just gave him permission to act like he wanted to. That shit's normal. What wasn't normal was getting back to my room the next day and finding it turned over. Like, someone had gotten in there and stolen stuff. I didn't tell Andrew, I didn't tell the others and I didn't tell the cops. At the time I thought it could have been any one of them, I was scared.

Every single picture I'd taken since I got there, either developed or on film, printed or framed, had been taken. Nothing else in my room was out of place, it hadn't been trashed – it was just like those pictures had never existed, man. It made my blood run cold.

--6--

'Shadow Man'

KIMBERLY NOLAN:

There was someone standing outside our building, night after night, the later the better, holding down the buzzer for our flat. This piercing, mechanical noise, constantly going off at two or three or four in the morning. That went on for most of October. You'd answer, you'd ask who it was, and no one would say anything. It might stop a few seconds, maybe a few minutes, then start up again.

Looking back, there were so many warning signs we missed. Like how much Zoe said she was enjoying her classes, how much extra time she was spending on them – she'd leave for the day saying she was workshopping, showcasing, auditioning, taking extra lectures, you name it. Just doing so much more than the rest of us combined. Then there was how close she seemed with her tutor, Hannah Docherty. I'd never even heard of lecturers taking that kind of interest in students before. I thought, *Maybe she really is special?* Like, she must have had this incredible talent all along, and I've just been too jealous to see. I worried about that a lot. We'd been drifting apart for years, but it was so undeniable there. I suppose her disappearance felt like the logical conclusion to that.

And then there was Andrew.

We never really talked about him, but she must have noticed me backing away from her once they got together. I worried about the way I felt for him, I didn't want to say or do anything stupid – I didn't want to ruin things. And, as well, I was busy. Unlike Zoe, who could go out all night and still point to this acclaim and incredible attention she was getting from tutors, I really had to put my head down to get the work done.

Anyway, that's all a long way of saying that, sifting through it all with hindsight, there was one thing, looking back, that I always felt sure about, and it was that buzzer going off in the night. It started after Zoe got with Andrew, although thinking about it, it never happened while he was around.

It was the last Sunday of October. I remember because I had to be up early on Monday morning, on Halloween, and it had got to the point where I was too annoyed to answer. The buzzer went, I got out of bed, opened the front door, went straight to the lift and pressed for ground. This is gone midnight and, for once, all the halls, the lift, everything, was deserted. I was shaking, wondering what the doors would open on to when I hit the ground floor, but it was just the empty lobby. The lights had gone out, which they always did, but there were lamp posts outside so I could see the shine across the plastic floor. I walked to the entrance and opened it and saw someone, just this shadow man, walking away. I shouted after him and he stopped and turned and looked at me. All I could see was the shape of him, but I knew he was looking right at me. It had been raining and I had bare feet so I didn't go outside. After a few seconds he just backed off into the dark and disappeared.

I've always been convinced that if I'd taken four or five steps into the light I would have seen him, this man who went on to take Zoe. And I've always been convinced that I annoyed him, like, I pissed him off by going down there that night, because after that all hell broke loose.

on Tue, Jan 22, 2019, Joseph Knox joeknoxxxx@gmail.com wrote:

Hey, yes, I am still reading, but it's definitely not me calling you at three in the morning (no matter how many stiff ones I might have had). Not enough hours in the day rn sorry.

And I think a lot of people feel that way about writing their second book. After the first, your talent's just a rumour, then with the second you've got to find a way to try and prove it. From what I've read so far, you ARE proving it, so keep going.

I've been through the stuff referring to the tower and the weird kind of presence in those rooms. I find it interesting that both Lois AND Harry mention their keys being stolen early on. Just read the Shadow Man chapter, which is v unsettling. Do you know who it was? Does she??

Maybe we should both unplug our phones tonight?

Jx

Hey – well thanks for that, Knoxy – sometimes I think the rumours of my talent have been greatly exaggerated.

Re: Shadow Man, no, I don't know who it was, Kim says she doesn't know either, but just wait until you see what the mad fucker did next.

Ex

--7--

'High Notes'

The below is an uncompleted, tampered-with assignment found on Zoe Nolan's laptop on 31 October 2011:

I have always been fascinated by popular music and its culture from a young age. Although I would like to think my interest is natural, I have also been encouraged by my family who are also musical. I have mostly been encouraged by my father, who was a professional musician himself for many years. I learned basic piano from him at a young age and was specially inclined to singing. I began to play the piano and sing at family gatherings, where I learned that I also enjoyed performance. This is because I believe that music is a "language" which exists to make people feel, and I enjoy watching these feelings take place as I perform.

Although I studied music at college and passed with a B+, I am less interested in theory than I am in practical music. I sing at a Grade 8 level and am now improving my piano skills, which are currently at a Grade 5 level. However, my main focus remains on performance. I have performed as part of choirs, ensembles and rock groups. I have accepted many offers of paid singing work in and around my local area. I feel that this has given me good insight into life as a musician and . . .

And . . . ?

And what, Zoe? You never quite finished your thought.

There are too many pronouns here, sweetheart – I this, I that, I the other – although I can understand the urge. You're Zoe Nolan, after all. I wonder if you realize quite how lucky that makes you? To look the way that you look and contain the gifts you contain. I'm inside your room as I write this, but I'd like to be so much closer to you than that, because I can never – I can *never* – get close enough. If I could, I'd be inside your brain and I'd be inside your body. I want to see you throw that head back with your mouth wide open, I want to hear you really hit those high notes. Because if it were up to me, sweetheart, I'd be wearing you. I'd peel you from top to bottom with my shiny then stitch myself into your skin. I'd go out into the world with your face on over mine. I want to see out of your skull. There's more but I think you might be coming. Well, you and me both, darling ;) xx

KIMBERLY NOLAN:

Liu Wai was suddenly sitting next to me in my room, eyes down, doing this stage whisper like she was taking my confession or something. 'Listen, I know how hard it can be to live in someone else's shadow, but you've scared your sister. I thought I'd give you the chance to explain.' I just got up and walked out, went into Zoe and asked what was wrong.

She showed me her laptop.

She'd left it open in her room while she'd been out, halfway through some personal statement, then come back to find this psychotic breakdown in its place. I was reading it, rereading it, when the intercom started buzzing and we both jumped. We went to it and asked who was there but got no answer. I double-locked the door. After that we always did.

LIU WAI:

Reading the essay, I'd just naturally assumed it had to have been written by Kim? She seemed the obvious person to me because she so *clearly* felt that way about Zoe. Like, there weren't that many suspects. Our flat was only me, Kim, Zoe and Alex. Obviously I hadn't written it. I'd been with Zoe for most of that day – we'd met after my last class and gone shopping for Halloween costumes in town – then when we got back I'd perched on her desk, still talking, and noticed how hot her laptop was, as if it had been on all day. She opened it to look and kind of went pale. So clearly *she* hadn't written it either – I mean, she'd hardly stalk herself. That left Alex, who'd been out with one of her boyfriends for most of the day, or Kim. And by the way, it's no coincidence that the 31st was a Monday that year.

Mondays were the only days when the flat was dependably empty. Everyone had classes. I thought, who else but one of us would know that? My suspicions were only raised more when I started calling the police and Kim ripped my phone out of my hand.

KIMBERLY NOLAN:

I was stressing the point that maybe we should talk to Zoe first, maybe we should see what *she* wanted to do? Maybe, since Liu had made her into a laughing stock the last time something like this happened, she should get some say in how we handled it . . .

LIU WAI:

Kim *totally* flipped. Like, I enjoy Drake's music as much as the next person, but I think outside of art there's not really a call for that kind of language? I'm convinced that Kim bullied Zoe out of calling the police that day, and I can't help but wonder why. And, I mean, I hate to say it, but I'm convinced that if I *had* called the police, Zoe would still be here now.

KIMBERLY NOLAN:

She might be right.

FINTAN MURPHY:

I met Zoe the next day for coffee. I think she was just glad to get out of the madhouse to be honest with you – that tower was no place to live. She'd often come to me when things got too much between Kim and Liu, or between her and Andrew. Anyway, she was in bits and pieces about the whole thing. I kept saying she should call the police, she should speak to the authorities – if you can't leave your flat empty for a few hours, what can you do? She just downplayed it all. Now I know that's at least partially because of the nonsense she'd gone through the last time – the police had only made matters worse. But another part of me wonders if she was afraid of who might have done it . . .

I'm certain that, at the time, Zoe had her eye on the people who were coming and going from that flat. When I saw the note itself I couldn't quite imagine Andrew Flowers articulating this chilling body-swap scenario. Whoever wrote it was a deeply disturbed individual. My dealings with Andrew have all been with a simple man who's trying hard to appear complex. If he'd been getting his rocks off in her room he'd have just spunked into the desk plant or something.

There *was* someone in that flat who had a rather more complex relationship with Zoe, though, someone who was studying English at the time and might have picked her up on her writing style. I know for a fact that Kimberly was the first one back in the flat that day, Zoe told me. It felt like neither one of us could just come out and say what we were both thinking, but when Zoe said she 'couldn't' call the police, I felt like she was telling me who she thought the most likely culprit was. I felt like she was telling me she had to protect Kimberly.

KIMBERLY NOLAN:

I've really tried to be honest about my hang-ups around Zoe. That's not because I'm proud of them, because I'm really not, it's a part of me I'd physically cut out of my body if I could. I've been honest because I know what's coming, I know what people think. I know I need to try and make them understand that I didn't want to be her, I didn't want to be inside her head or her body or her heart or whatever. I need people to understand that, whatever they see or hear to the contrary, that was someone else's fantasy, it wasn't mine.

ANDREW FLOWERS:

Yes, I had a key. And yes, I got some severely cock-eyed looks from the girls at the time. I knew some of them thought I'd written the thing on Zoe's computer. I was over there enough, had easy access, all that. So what's the idea? I was so mad with, what? Lust? That I wanted to, what? Take the girl I was consensually sleeping with by force? Rape seems like a strange fantasy for a boyfriend to have. You know, not to be crass, but there's no need to crack open a safe when you already know the combination. Zoe can't have given it much credence anyway, because our relationship didn't change a jot, even though I'm sure some people around her would have quite liked it to. She found the note on Halloween and we spent that night together, we even went out dressed up. I was the psycho killer from *Scream* and she was a bloodied Drew Barrymore, my first victim, so she clearly wasn't quaking in her boots about proximity to me.

And to anyone out there who still has their doubts, I'd point them to the text of the thing itself, which I feel quite clearly exonerates me. 'You are Zoe Nolan, after all'—well, I'm afraid that didn't mean so much to me. I didn't think Zoe was gifted or talented, not in any way whatsoever. That's not to say I consider myself some kind of hot shit by comparison. I just think, by and large, people aren't that special. You're lucky if you meet even one special person in your life. No, you should be looking for people who idolized her and thought she was the second coming of Christ. That's the substance of that essay. I'd look for a person who used to sit with her ear to the wall between their bedrooms, just so she could hear Zoe's every cough and fart.

LIU WAI:

I think what Andrew might be struggling with here is that I *loved* Zoe? Maybe you could drop a definition of the word into your book somewhere for him?

HARRY FOWLES:

That was when we had our one and only flat meeting. I know it was November 1st because Andrew was still hung over, still wearing the black gown from his Halloween costume, letting us all know how seriously he took it. None of us wanted to call the police, but stuff was going missing. Still. And not just from the fridge or the kitchen, either. Someone was going into our rooms and ripping us off left and right. And what was weird was that you never heard Andrew or Jai talk about it. We weren't blaming anyone, just trying to have the conversation.

JAI MAHMOOD:

Money had been tight for me, yeah. The rest of them had rich parents, but mine couldn't help me out like that, I'd always had to work. When I first moved to Manchester I transferred from the Caffè Nero I'd been working at in Birmingham, but got fired a few weeks in. I was never employee of the month, but the last straw was when this tweaker came through demanding the code for the toilet. There were people using it to shoot up in all the time, and I'd spent my whole morning cleaning up this modern art installation of diarrhoea. So I said, 'Sorry man, paying customers only.' While I was talking to the next person in line the guy got a chair, climbed up on to the counter and shit on it. They fired me the same day.

HARRY FOWLES:

It was impossible to talk to Andrew about money. He's the classic example of someone who'd believe a pint of milk costs a tenner. He was in our flat meeting wearing Dolce & Gabbana sunglasses, which he wouldn't take off. Jai was still bloodied and bruised. He'd been really wary of us ever since he got beat up, like it was us who'd done it or something. He was locking his bedroom door, cutting himself off. Anyway, at some point Andrew asked what time it was and then realized he couldn't find his ridiculous gold Rolex anywhere. There was this second where you could tell he wanted to ask Jai if he'd seen it, like, he'd just been lecturing us, saying we were all imagining things going missing, but he clearly suspected Jai of taking his watch. And who the fuck even *has* a gold Rolex at eighteen, anyway? In the end he just muttered something like, 'I must have left it at Zoe's,' and slunk out. He put the mask back on with his costume to walk over there.

ANDREW FLOWERS:

Look, if their things were going missing, then I'm sure some of mine were, too. I simply wasn't there a lot of the time. And I guess I didn't really care about my property either. The only thing that had any value to me whatsoever was my shitty gold Rolex, and only that because it had been my grandfather's, because it was given to me by my mother. My fidelity to that watch was a way of being close to her, it was literally the last surviving relic of my grandfather's largesse. Jai wasn't the last person to have it or anything, but he'd expressed interest in it from the off. He'd even taken it for a short period, an hour or so, to photograph.

JAI MAHMOOD:

I thought that watch was fucking hideous, man. Tasteless, tacky, boujee bling. It just went well with my portfolio of ugly objects. Course I said it looked cool, why would I tell him the truth?

ANDREW FLOWERS:

I couldn't quite put my finger on it, I just sensed something strange in Jai's interest. This half-smile would creep on to his face whenever he handled it. Anyway, I asked if he'd seen it and he said no, so I left to go and look at Zoe's.

JAI MAHMOOD:

Yeah, the boy band we were living with became convinced that either me or Andrew, or maybe me *and* Andrew, were stealing shit. I can't speak for him, but I'd grab stuff out of the fridge at worst. At *worst*. And I had money by then anyway, it just wasn't strictly legal.

After I got fired and after I got beat up, when I really was shitting it about the rent, I went limping into the Great Central, this Wetherspoon's pub in Fallowfield. I'd been taking my CV around bars and coffee shops, trying to scare something up. So I get there and find this fucking great Russian standing outside smoking, yeah, looking meaner than death. He makes some joke about me being Aladdin, says I must have fallen off my magic carpet mid-flight, and I just lose it. For a start, the guy was in worse nick than me. Someone had cut both his nostrils open, like, with scissors or a knife or something. They'd healed up but you could tell it had happened – he'd lived this knockabout life and he was giving *me* shit. So I'm just like, 'Suck me off, Igor. I hope those Marlboros turn your lungs black.' He must have been about three times my size, but instead of killing me he doubled up laughing. When he saw I'd really meant it, like, how pissed off and on edge I was, he offered to buy me a drink. I thought it might be all the nutrition I'd get that day so I said, 'Sure.'

He introduced himself as Vladimir but said that wasn't his real name. People just called him that because he'd snort anything: *Vlad the Inhaler*. He asked what had happened to me and I told him, then he asked if my bruises hurt and I told him that, too. Then he dug round in his pockets and found this vial of pills, alprazolam, and said they might help me. I thought alprazolam sounded like something Harry Potter might say. Told him I was grateful but I didn't take stuff I couldn't pronounce, and anyway, I couldn't pay him, I was on my arse. He asked if I could pronounce Xanax, which was the brand name, and I said I could. It wasn't around as much then, but I'd heard of it. Then he asked where I lived and when I told him I was over the road in Owens Park he offered me a job. Said he had a booming market for pills on campus. Nothing evil, just uppers for students doing late-night cram sessions, downers for ones who couldn't switch off, painkillers for people like me. That's what he called those Xans – painkillers – said they'd solve all my problems. He couldn't really walk around campus himself – he looked like a taller, fatter, more fucked Joe Stalin – but I could. He said all I'd be doing was making some deliveries, maybe fielding some phone calls. It paid more than Caffè Nero, and cash in hand. My phone wasn't exactly ringing with offers, so I said yes.

ANDREW FLOWERS:

I started spending more time at the tower just to get out of our home situation. One unintended consequence of the note on Zoe's laptop was that I didn't feel like I could break up with her. I knew if I did, people would think I'd been the one harassing her all that time so, strangely, the whole thing pushed us closer together. Physically, at least. She was a person who liked me when I was incapable of liking myself, and that was appealing, but there wasn't really an emotional connection.

It was already November by this point, so my plan was to limp on until the holidays and break up with her once we got back, to let her have a good Christmas and allow her to start the new year fresh. I just never got the chance. Technically, I suppose we're still together.

LIU WAI:

I've been thinking about what you said Andrew told you, like, how they're still 'technically' a couple. It got me going on all his weird abandonment issues. Like, his mum and his dad and his French ex or whatever. No matter what, his relationship with Zoe is *permanent* now. Nothing can ever break it off. When you think of it like that, it kind of makes you shudder, doesn't it?

From: evelynidamitchell@gmail.com
Sent: 24/01/19 20:56
To: you

From Andrew's Facebook.

FYI he says he wore this costume back to Zoe's flat after falling out with his housemates and then lost track of it. Unfortunately, it's reappeared in a bad way during one of the interviews I'm transcribing for part two . . .

E(!)

--8--

'Self-Harm'

One month before Zoe's disappearance, serious cracks emerge in her relationship with Andrew. Both Zoe and Kimberly begin acting wildly out of character.

LIU WAI:

I've found that a man's quality has a kind of cataclysmic half-life from the first date to the second, then from the second to the third, and, frankly, kind of just endlessly after that. People always start out on their best behaviour when you first meet them, then slide down into who they *really* are afterwards. I thought after the note on Zoe's laptop everyone was acting weird, but now I look back and wonder if they were just showing their true colours? Alex really darkened on me, went from this quite nice influence to totally negative overnight. She started spending less time with Sam and more time with this awful wannabe poet she was seeing on the side. She'd met him at an Interpol concert, which probably tells you everything you need to know. Any time the frontman for a band sings like he's phoning in sick, you can usually depend on his fans being pretentious. I can't remember this boy's name, but the one time I met him he had a second-hand copy of *The Stranger* sticking out the back pocket of his skinny jeans . . .

Zoe was up and down like a seesaw, unpredictable and jumpy in ways she hadn't been before. And I'm absolutely not one to judge in any way whatsoever, but Kim's drinking was out-of-control crazy. You'd think she was more upset about the note on Zoe's laptop than Zoe was.

KIMBERLY NOLAN:

November was a rough time for me, I had my own stuff going on. Yes, I was upset about Zoe and Andrew, yes, I was stressed out by someone stalking my sister, but there was more. There was a night out I'm not really ready to talk about, but just believe me when I say it was bad. After it, I got panic attacks every time I turned the light off. I guess being drunk just seemed like the simplest way around some shitty nights and some shitty feelings. I'm sorry if that made Liu Wai uncomfortable.*

FINTAN MURPHY:

Zoe met me for a coffee and turned up with this Casio keyboard under her arm. She told me she was worried about Kimberly. Not only the drinking in isolation, but everything that came with it. She'd started rolling in at all hours, sometimes in the company of strange

---

* This interview was transcribed by Evelyn in early 2018, before Kimberly had publicly told the story of her abduction from outside of Fifth Avenue nightclub. – JK

men. Zoe said they didn't know how to speak with one another any more, which just seemed bizarre for twin sisters.

And one other thing I should mention . . .

Once we'd finished talking it through, she tried to give me this keyboard that she'd turned up with. I must have said to her in passing that I was dying to have something I could play in my room, and she knew I wasn't worth a bean, so she wanted me to take it. I said I couldn't accept, but she insisted. She said she saw Kimberly's life of cheap thrills and no love, and she was afraid of that happening to her. I said, 'Oh, Zoe, you don't have to buy my friendship, not ever.' She became emotional – probably we both did – and in the end I think I agreed to take it on loan. I said I'd give it back to her once I'd saved up for my own.

Of course, I've never had that chance.

ANDREW FLOWERS:

Did Kim have a drinking problem? I think that's what most people go to university for in the first place, isn't it? I thought that stuff was always exaggerated by people afterwards, but maybe, sure, who knows? From what I saw she always spilt more than she actually drank. She certainly wasn't the sloppy, loud, messy wreck that the press made her out to be. She was sort of insular, she had that unfortunate thing of appearing more drunk than she was. She'd take a sip of something and her whole body slurred afterwards. I found it quite charming.

LIU WAI:

I remember one time we were going out to this nightclub, Fifth Avenue. It was a Tuesday, student night, maybe six or seven o'clock, and

I think we were all just in our own rooms getting ready. Then a full-blown domestic kicks off. I mean, being next door, I couldn't help but overhear that Andrew and Zoe were having this *apocalyptic* fight.

On one level it was quite normal? It was the kind of thing Andrew would initiate quite often. He sort of seethed and regenerated and then, once his rage reached full capacity, it just got unloaded on whoever or whatever happened to be in front of him at the time. Unfortunately, that was usually Zoe. Like, I thought he could be a real bully? Laughing if she didn't know where a certain country was or mispronounced a word. What was strange about this occasion was that *she* was the one shouting. I don't think I even knew she *could* shout.

ANDREW FLOWERS:

Oh, naturally, Liu Wai couldn't help but overhear. Conversations taking place in the next room are always so difficult to ignore when you've got your head pressed against the sodding wall listening to them. Look, you know what I was going through at the time. My mum did herself in, my dad was doing my ex and I almost did time for nicking his car.

For all intents and purposes, I'd been disowned.

I freely admit that I shouldn't have been dating at the time, I shouldn't have been around people full stop. They should have tied me to the mast of a ship and sent it out to sea for six months so I could scream it all off my chest. But I don't accept that I was a bully. Not of anyone but myself. Who knows why we were arguing? If this was that time we went to Fifth Avenue, then it was probably because Zoe had invited Liu Wai on a night I'd thought was supposed to be about the two of us. In fact, yes, I think once I heard that her friend was coming I insisted on bringing one along, too.

JAI MAHMOOD:

Yeah, man. He was trying to make some kind of point and didn't have any other friends to make it with, so he called me. I was pissed off with him for getting me in trouble with the cops, which I think indirectly led to everyone thinking I was a sex pest and having the shit kicked out of me, to getting my camera smashed. And he was pissed off with me because he thought I'd stolen his Rolex. Some days we were pals but some days it was like we didn't know each other.

ANDREW FLOWERS:

The Rolex was an heirloom, something my mother had given to me when I turned sixteen. About as accurate as looking up at the sky and guessing the time, but I loved it. The fucking thing had been around the world on my grandfather's wrist – there was probably sand from a thousand different shores clogging up the cogs. It didn't work and was rapidly depreciating in value, so in that sense it stood in handsomely for my family. Then it really became one of them by vanishing from my life completely. I was fucked if I knew where it went missing from, my room or Zoe's. I wasn't blaming anyone at that stage, I just couldn't help but wonder.

LIU WAI:

Andrew says him and Zoe fought because she invited me out? Interesting. I'm sure that's how he's spinning it now, but they definitely weren't arguing about the guest list. Listen, Zoe shouting was one thing. What made it *really* unusual was that she kept repeating one word. As if to say, *I can't believe this.* And what made it almost unique was that Andrew wasn't saying anything in response. Like, he was clearly speechless, which was unheard of. The word Zoe kept repeating to him was, '*Kim?*' And I'm talking very much with the question mark attached . . .

ANDREW FLOWERS:
Well, fine. I suppose we'll have to trust wonderful old Liu Wai's memory, then, won't we?

LIU WAI:
It's no mystery. Listen, I owe no loyalty to Andrew fucking Flowers. My loyalty's to Zoe, and I see no sense in protecting the feelings and reputations of people who might have had something to do with her disappearance. She was angry with him because he'd said Kim's name while they were being intimate, like, while they were having sex. He realized immediately, apparently, like, actually gasped. I think she was too shocked to even say anything at first, then she *totally* let him have it. This is about an hour before we were all due to hit the town together.

So . . .

Just something to keep in mind when he's banging on about how boring and stupid and beneath him his girlfriend was. At least she always got his ridiculous name right.

ANDREW FLOWERS:
Fine. I don't quite remember it that way, but fine.

KIMBERLY NOLAN:

What? No, Zoe never said anything like that to me. I remember that night for my own shitty reasons, though. She was acting really offhand, like she didn't want me to be there. I couldn't get her alone when we were in Fifth, she was always talking to Liu Wai in one corner or fighting with Andrew in another. Then I got separated from the others and had a bit of a crisis, ended up coming in really late. I always wondered why Zoe never checked on me the next day. She never asked me what happened or why I ghosted them. Until she went missing that was the shittest night of my life, and I kind of had to deal with it on my own.

I guess it's good to understand why, finally. Andrew never can say the right thing at the right time.

JAI MAHMOOD:

I was trashed that night. I was still a mess from the kicking I'd got in the car park but, really, I was starting to use the pills I was supposed to be selling for Vlad. So yeah, Andrew invited me out, but in a sense I wasn't really there.

LIU WAI:

Andrew didn't come back with us that night. Jai got into some fight on the dancefloor so they left together, and Kim just plain *vanished* on us. So it was just me and Zoe in the cab on our way back. She'd gone out in this bright red jacket that had been stolen from our table when we went to the dancefloor, but she was really cool about it, just shrugged and said she'd buy another. I tried talking to her, to broach the argument I'd overheard earlier, and that was when she

144

told me what Andrew had done, like, saying Kim's name while they were in bed. She seemed over it, she said the 'Andrew problem' would probably solve itself soon. That was music to my ears, and I asked if she had her eye on someone else. She just smiled and said, 'All in good time.'

Then she changed the subject, suggested we take a shopping trip the next day. I told her there was no way I could afford to, but I'd go along for moral support. She said it was okay, it would be her treat. I kind of smiled and said, 'Aw,' but I didn't think much more about it until she got me up the next morning and told me to get ready. We took a cab to the Trafford Centre, she bought me this gorgeous Ted Baker dress and then bought us both lunch as well. And that was the least of it, like, there was *steam* coming off her credit card by the end of that day. I didn't know much about her background, her family situation, but I came from a single-parent household and just thought, I guess this is how the other half live?

SAM LIMMOND, *Ex-boyfriend of Alex Wilson:*
Yeah, I was basically seeing Alex from the first week of the first term. We weren't always exclusive, but it was a real relationship – it was to me. I only met Zoe once because we tended to crash at my place. Al said there was always drama at hers, and the one time I stayed over that was true. We were sitting on the sofa talking when Zoe and their other flatmate – Liu – came in with all these shopping bags. I think we found it funny. Not in a mean way, but Alex and me were Nine Inch Nails kinds of kids. Tattoos and straight vodka, and suddenly this It-Girl satire started playing out in front of our eyes. Zoe disappeared while Liu made small talk and then came back with all

these clothes that she laid out at Alex's feet, telling her that they were hers if she wanted them. Al gently pointed out that they had quite different styles, but Zoe kept trying until Al had to quite forcefully say no, she didn't want them. Then, as if to make some kind of point, Zoe turned to Liu and said, 'Well, I want you to have my laptop.'

LIU WAI:

I had this busted-up old MacBook you could have heated an entire house with, I was forever cursing its existence. Zoe said she wanted me to have hers. I was like, 'No, really, that's too much,' but she insisted. She said after that note she'd found, it just didn't feel the same, that I'd be doing her a massive favour.

SAM LIMMOND:

When she went into her room to get it Alex leaned in and kind of quietly told Liu she should politely decline. Liu just shrugged and said we'd just watched her try to politely decline. Al insisted that Liu *actually* decline. Liu started to say maybe this wasn't any of our business, but we were trying to point out, like, 'Doesn't Zoe seem strange to you?' It just seemed so obvious to us she was going through some kind of manic episode. We'd both already been through one of those together, Alex and me, and there were a few more in our future. We knew the signs, and so I'm sure did Liu. It felt like she was taking advantage. When Zoe came back, Liu took that laptop without a fight.

So, yeah, when Zoe went missing it didn't come as a huge shock. I thought it was sad but that she'd done something to herself. And there was the other side of things as well. Alex told me this story after, the real reason she'd tried to get Liu Wai to turn down that laptop. Al could be really abrupt. Indecisive for a long time and then *very* suddenly decisive – she did a lot of turning on her heel. So she must have announced she was leaving their flat for the day with absolute certainty then an hour later had a typical change of heart and turned round. Only, she walked in on something that made her quite uncomfortable. She got inside, shouted hello and went down the corridor towards the kitchen. She said she found Andrew and Zoe pulling their clothes back on, both breathless, trying to style it out.

Their business, right?

Except, when they disappeared into a bedroom, Al said she saw Zoe's laptop set up on the bookcase facing the sofa. It was filming. No one said or explained anything, but she said Zoe was acting weird. She said she looked pale and sick, like she was scared of something. Alex basically came away thinking they'd been making a sex tape but, mainly, that Zoe was frightened of Andrew. You know, he did *not* want her to talk about whatever it was they'd been doing.

ANDREW FLOWERS:

I'm sorry, what is it that you're asking me? Did I say the wrong name once while I was sleeping with my girlfriend? Did I fuck once in front of a camera? Did I upset Zoe from time to time? Or are you asking me something else? Are you, perhaps, asking if I had something to do with her disappearance?

SAM LIMMOND:

Anyway, Alex knew there could be footage on that laptop. Footage Zoe might not want out there in the world. And she was concerned because Zoe had just given it to Liu Wai, who could be like the town gossip.

LIU WAI:

That night at Fifth seemed like a turning point in some senses, you know? Obviously Andrew and Zoe had their bust-up over Kim, Zoe told me she was moving on from Andrew, and Kim had some kind of ordeal that put her in a funk for a few days. Then she suddenly changed her image and went Goth. And I mean, overnight. She originally had this beautiful blonde hair just like Zoe. Then, coming up to Christmas, she got thinner and thinner, and suddenly the hair was just gone, down into this military brush cut or something. She dyed what was left of it black and started dressing really punk and stuff. Andrew called her 'The Girl *without* the Dragon Tattoo', which I had to admit was quite funny.

KIMBERLY NOLAN:

I couldn't believe it hadn't occurred to me before. There'd always been differences in style and hair between Zoe and me, I didn't think we looked that much alike, but people round campus always confused us, or hinted I was pulling off the look less well. I'd never felt comfortable in my own skin. But when I shaved my hair off I felt like I was on to something, something like the real me.

LIU WAI:

Well, I suppose that's one way of looking at it. The other is that her sister was *so* beautiful, *so* pure. When Kim changed her image it was like an act of self-harm? Like she was *refuting* everything that

Zoe was, like she was criticizing it. And then the next thing that happened was that Zoe went missing without a trace and no one ever saw her again. I'll leave your readers to draw their own conclusions from that.

From: evelynidamitchell@gmail.com

Sent: 28/01/19 19:27

To: you

on Sun, Jan 27, 2019, Joseph Knox joeknoxxxx@gmail.com wrote:

Right – finally got some free hours and am up to ch.8. My conclusions:

1. Kim wrote the message on Zoe's laptop but didn't mean it to go so far.

2. Andrew was the guy buzzing the door in the night, trying to get Kim's attention again. Trying to reignite the same 'spark' he got on the night that she actually answered him. This would also explain the 'shadow man' staring at Kim.

3. I also conclude that Fintan badly needs to get laid and Liu Wai doth protesteth too much. Did she really love Zoe or did she just love having money spent on her?? And why do I feel like the laptop has more relevance?

4. Alex thinking Zoe was scared of Andrew is very interesting too. I wish we could talk to her and work out what she actually meant by that. I hate that it comes second hand from this Sam guy.

5. And speaking of Sam's hands, he mentions loving tattoos – there wouldn't happen to be a ghoulish smiling face inked into his skin, would there? He also mentions vodka, which I think is what

got poured on Kim after her van ordeal. Something's weird there.
We only have HIS word for what Alex saw.

J

Well, you're the expert, but I feel like you're being quick to judge on
Kim, Andrew, Fintan and Liu. Re: Sam, that's something that had
never actually occurred to me. He's one of the few people I've had to
speak to over the phone because he lives in France now and his
involvement's so small. I've trawled Facebook for a picture but can't
get a close-up of his hands. A LOT of tattoos though . . .

Your spidey-sense is right on the laptop, it's coming back. And really
ALL of Zoe's drive to give her things away feels troubling. My police
contact says they really zoned in on that afterwards (alongside all the
money she was spending) because it's something suicidal people so
often do. It's considered a BIG warning sign.

Her mental health issues had reverberations through the whole case,
really. When she first went missing, I think the authorities just
assumed she was having an 'episode' or something, but as well, it
really put a glass ceiling on how invested the press ever got. She was
damaged goods – too working class, probably too old to fit the
missing blonde girl archetype (at 19!)

I know that sounds cynical, but when you look at stories like this that have blown up in our lifetime, you get the sense that people prefer their missing girls to be virgins, which is some sad shit. And yes, before you say it, I know that means no one would come looking for me. ███████████████████████████

The next chapter is Zoe's actual disappearance, so let me know what you think. I've taken your advice and unplugged the phone for the night – so if you were gonna call me you're OFF THE HOOK.

Ex

--9--

'Nowhere Girl'

On their last night in Manchester before the Christmas break, the occupants of the tower's fifteenth floor throw a party doomed to live in infamy. But the release of an illicit tape and a building-wide evacuation are only the start of their problems.

ANDREW FLOWERS:
Not my finest hour.

JAI MAHMOOD:
One of the worst nights of my life, man, and given how my life's actually gone since, that's saying something.

LIU WAI:
I don't know whose idea the party was, but not stopping it's obviously one of the greatest regrets of my life. I'm sure everyone feels roughly the same, though. Imagine the average stupid student night, just covered in cheap tinsel. Everyone far too lubricated, the music

far too loud. The girls all dressed beautifully and the boys wearing their best *Family Guy* T-shirts.

KIMBERLY NOLAN:

Well, there were six other apartments on fifteenth and the idea was that all the doors would be open between them so the party could spread across the whole floor. I can't say it was what I would have chosen to do on our last night, but there was no escape. Christmas songs and girls dressed as slutty elves. Shit music, shit people, a series of shit events and the last night I saw my sister.

FINTAN MURPHY:

I suppose in that case I must be one of the 'shit people' she's describing. It was the first time I met most of them – not quite the best circumstances. I think, given the way that Zoe and I interacted, discussing what might seem like quite juvenile concepts of nervousness and not fitting in, she was a bit embarrassed to have me around her stand-offish boyfriend and hard-drinking sister. She knew I didn't drink at all, of course, so when she brought me up there I could see she was hesitant. I remember saying, 'Hey, I'm not my family, you're not your friends.'

We got separated almost immediately, which is when I met Kimberly. I could just about see the resemblance to Zoe through all her black clothes and make-up, but she seemed in so many senses her opposite. She struck me at the time as kind of out of control, and I can't say as I liked her image. I've spent much more time around the gay community now – I understand burlesque, glam, punk and leather these days – but I think back then I could be quite judgemental. At the time I just thought, why would you do this to your appearance when you started out looking like Zoe? It was like drawing a moustache on the *Mona Lisa*.

KIMBERLY NOLAN:

I never really hit it off with Fintan. I think he came over to me talking about Zoe. What an amazing voice she had, her incredible stage presence. I thought he was weird, all wiry and pale. And I was hurt that Zoe hadn't introduced us. It was like when we were kids again. She clearly had this whole other life I didn't even know about. And I could sense this veiled criticism in what he was saying. He was making it clear that he loved all these things that I wasn't, and that he disapproved of the way I looked. I mean, he was probably drunk – I could smell the booze pouring off him.

FINTAN MURPHY:

I think Kim might be misremembering one crucial detail about the way that I was looking at her, and about the way I smelled. She'd just poured more or less an entire glass of wine all over me. She was turning round and I'm not sure she even noticed. I was trying to talk to her, but the music was so loud and she was so, so wasted.

ANDREW FLOWERS:

I had to keep putting Jai out that night, as in, extinguishing him. He was so out of it he kept putting lit cigarettes in his pockets. Everyone was throwing their coats into a pile on the landing and when his went down I saw it smouldering.

JAI MAHMOOD:

Well, never let it be said that Andrew Flowers isn't a world-class prick, but I was as much to blame for the bust-up as him. I was swallowing Oxys like they were spit, man. I'd climbed the ladder from Xans, which are just benzos, to opiates quite quickly, so sometimes he'd be talking to me while I was basically in orbit. When we got to the party there was some argument – I'd left a joint lit in my jacket or something. Yeah, I was a mess, I agree, but there was more to it than that. He was spoiling for a fight.

ANDREW FLOWERS:

Look, we fell out, we both said things we shouldn't have. We were kids and we were drunk. Jai had God knows what in his system. In any other circumstances we would have made up the following day and never thought of it again. We were just never afforded that chance – none of us got to return to our real lives, or even to progress as people afterwards. Call me a cunt, a racist, a sexist, whatever, but don't print that I didn't care about my friend, because I did. And I say that in spite of how I might have acted. I say it in spite of whatever he'll say back about me.

JAI MAHMOOD:

Suddenly we're in this fight about his fucking watch again. Andrew saw me taking a pill. I guess he remembered I was supposed to be broke and started doing the maths. It kicked off with him saying something like, 'If you've got it, I won't mind,' then rose up into him asking if I'd sold it, then shouting, *'Fucking give it to me!'* Next thing I know he's got me by the throat up against a wall.

ANDREW FLOWERS:

He denied having it, so I said, 'Let's see what you've got on you, then?' Obviously I regret that now. I let go of him and saw I'd ripped his collar. That should have been it right there, the warning sign that I'd lost all perspective, but of course I'd committed myself by then, so I pressed on. If I could have talked to him, if I could have just told him I'd watched my mother destroy herself with drugs . . .

Half the floor was watching us.

Suddenly the music cut out and girls in Santa hats were holding us back from each other, the full *EastEnders*. Jai turned out his pockets like a cartoon character, and of course they were empty. And he looked so innocent and sweet that I knew I had to double down. See, back home, I'd learned from the best. You don't let innocence stop you, you can't allow sweetness or lack of malice to slow you up. What you do is you go at innocence a hundred times harder. Because then the other person might blow their lid, blow up right back at you, a little mother–father action, and then it doesn't matter who was originally right and who was originally wrong. You're both down in the dirt together, covered in so much shit that no one can say for sure who threw it first.

JAI MAHMOOD:

He gets this superior look on his face, yeah. This curling, smug grin, and says, 'What about your jacket?' And I know what he's getting at. He thinks I won't turn out my pockets because of the pills. Then he can stomp off looking like he was right all along. We're surrounded by people, out on the edge of the landing, this audience he's playing to. So I go over to the pile of coats and dig through them for mine. I don't care who sees some pills in my pockets – half the people at the party are scoring from me by then anyway, and I know for fuck sure there's no gold Rolex in there, man. So I hold up my coat and turn everything out for the whole room, I don't even look. Not until I hear this sharp intake of breath.

LIU WAI:

I just saw Zoe gasp and put her hands over her mouth, you know, like *Oh my God.* Her pants, the ones that had been stolen three months before, were scattered *all* over the corridor.

ANDREW FLOWERS:

And everyone – fucking everyone – started cheering. Like, 'Yeah, we all knew what you were, Jai.' Everyone thought this was him admitting to stealing Zoe's underwear. People started jostling him, roughly mussing his hair and stuff. Dickheads picking thongs up off the floor and rubbing his face in them. He looked at me to say something in his defence. We both knew he had nothing to do with that and his eyes actually implored me, like, *Say something.* I didn't have the balls to back down, though, so I locked myself in a bathroom instead.

JAI MAHMOOD:

There was some rough stuff, some shit-talking, then some guys grabbed me by the arms and legs and threw me down the staircase. I must have rolled down a whole flight before I hit a wall. There were a couple of seconds where I stopped, where I remember concentrating on breathing, in, out, in, out, just to see if I could still do it. Then they all crashed down on top of me and kept kicking. Luckily I'd taken too much Oxy to really feel it.

FINTAN MURPHY:

I followed them down the staircase in mounting disbelief. I didn't know what Andrew and Jai's problem was with each other but I thought Andrew's behaviour was repulsive, he showed himself up as a real shitbag. The *lads* who threw Jai down the stairs were even worse. If that's a party, I'll stay home, thanks.

KIMBERLY NOLAN:

When I saw Andrew wasn't going to say or do anything, wasn't even going to defend Jai, I saw what a two-faced fucking coward he could be. I went outside for some air.

Like I said, Fintan's not my cup of tea, but at least he has the strength of his convictions. He threw himself on these guys and just started scattering them around. I couldn't believe it, this wiry, white Irish kid. And they actually backed off, they actually shit it. They were laughing at him and taking the piss, but they backed off.

LIU WAI:

I mean, teenage boys, am I right? The moment passed, people dispersed and I think Zoe wanted to get the music back on. Then the next thing I know, all these *lads* are looking at their phones, pointing at Zoe. This time it wasn't like with the underwear, where she was kind of the victim and in on it. It was cruel – they were all laughing at her. One of them came over with his phone and showed us what they were cracking up over. My mouth just fell open. I didn't know what to say.

SAM LIMMOND:

I'd already left and gone home for Christmas before the party, but

Alex called and told me what happened. She said, 'That fucking girl, that fucking laptop.' She was drunk, ranting. I said, 'What girl?' She told me the sex video of Zoe and Andrew that she walked in on had leaked, that it must have come from the laptop Zoe gave to Liu Wai.

LIU WAI:

Look, Zoe *clearly* didn't think I'd put it out there. When Andrew finally emerged from the bathroom she fully lost it with him. I'd never *once* seen that girl lose so much as her temper, but here she was scratching his face, and I mean badly. Slapping him, kicking him, calling him names, ripping his shirt. And he just stood there and took it, very un-Andrew. Almost like the guilty man he so clearly was. In the end, I grabbed her arm, like, for Zoe's sake as much as anything – I was scared she might kill him.

ANDREW FLOWERS:

Why did I stand there and take it if I didn't leak the video? Well, what should I have done, hit her back?

LIU WAI:

I said, 'Zoe, let's go somewhere and talk.' She looked around, dizzy, like she didn't remember where she was, then said she needed a minute. There were people everywhere, all through our flat, everyone staring at her, all laughing. She said, 'Meet me on the roof in five minutes.' I offered to go with her but she just said, 'Five minutes,' and walked up the stairs. That was the last time I ever saw her.

FINTAN MURPHY:

I guess I was helping Jai down the stairs while all this was going on. He lived in Owens Park, but I lived outside it, down Wilmslow Road. He was upset, annoyed with Andrew and insisting he wouldn't stay in their flat, so he asked me to wait a second while he got his stuff to go and stay with a friend. When he came back out he seemed shaken by something, he hardly seemed to notice I was there. We walked out, down the road together, but when I asked what was wrong he kind of shrugged it off. I don't think we even said goodnight when I got to mine, he just kept walking.

JAI MAHMOOD:

Man, I was too out of it to even notice Fintan. I went to my room for the only thing I had worth keeping, yeah, my stash, which had been hidden under the bed. It was an empty Ben and Jerry's tub filled with Xanax and Oxy, and it was gone. And just like that, man, I owed Vlad the Inhaler a grand I didn't have. He'd always been sound with me, but he was still built like a brick shithouse. They said he'd been a bank robber, like a safe-cracker back home, and if you saw him you'd believe it. If Fintan says we walked out together, I've got to take his word for it. I just remember looking back at the tower. All those lit windows, all those lives behind them. I felt banished. Not just from the building, man, from something way bigger. That night was the end of something for me.

KIMBERLY NOLAN:

When I got back up to fifteenth everything felt different. The

Christmas music had stopped and people were leaving, still rowdy but leaving. Some of the boys were looking at me, so I could tell something was wrong. They were crowding round the lift to get out or just tramping down the stairwell. Almost all of them laughing at something on their phones. Some guy came up to me like, 'Have you seen what your sister's getting up to?' That's when I saw the video.

LIU WAI:
I only saw it once, when I was standing there with Zoe. Even that felt like a betrayal.

SAM LIMMOND:
I asked Alex what was on the tape. She said it was five seconds long, if that. It just showed Andrew and Zoe having sex on a sofa. He kept saying her name, like, 'Zoe, Zoe, Zoe,' and apparently all the boys were doing impressions of him.

KIMBERLY NOLAN:
While I was watching it, trying to work out what I was being shown, the fire alarm went off, right on cue. I didn't know what to do so I followed everyone else down into the stairwell, kind of in shock. It was full of people, boys all dicking around and jostling each other, the girls with fingers in their ears against the alarm. It took us for ever, like, ten minutes to get down, so it was only once we all got out there that I could actually look for Zoe. Liu Wai was standing by the door gossiping with a group of girls. They all went quiet when I walked past.

LIU WAI:

Erm, I was waiting for Zoe? Like, maybe I was asking people if they'd seen her? I was hoping she'd heard the alarm on the roof and was coming down with everyone else.

KIMBERLY NOLAN:

I'd been through the crowd, I'd called her a few times, I'd asked people if they'd seen her. Everyone was just laughing, trying to show me the fucking video while I was just feeling sick. In the end I went back to Liu, who was still standing by the door. The girls she'd been talking to were doing vodka shots by this point. I asked if she'd seen Zoe, if she'd come out, and she told me she'd been standing there for twenty-five minutes, that as far as she could tell Zoe still hadn't left.

The building was basically empty by this point and I was just thinking, like, what could be going on in there? I looked around for another five minutes with Liu before she finally – *finally* – told me Zoe 'might' be on the roof. This is forty-five minutes after the fucking fire alarm went off.

LIU WAI:

When I told Kim that Zoe had gone up to the roof she *fully* freaked out. Everyone was evacuated by that point, then we started to see smoke coming from the building. Like, in student flats you're for-ever being evacuated because of faulty fire alarms so it felt like a shock to see that this was something real. It kind of started to sober everyone up.

KIMBERLY NOLAN:

I didn't know if you could hear the alarm on the roof so I ran back inside. People tried to stop me but I just ripped their hands off my arms and pushed past them, shouted that my sister was still in there. I tried the lift, which was probably stupid, but anyway, it had switched itself off with the alarm, so I went up the stairwell instead. I didn't see anyone else come down.

It took about ten minutes to get to the top, all eighteen floors, and with the alarm blasting the whole time. When I walked out on to the roof I was sweating and light-headed, my ears were ringing and it was so, so dark up there. It felt like walking into space or something. I thought I could see Zoe because I could see the glow of her phone right at the edge of the roof, but when I called out she didn't answer. It was only when I got closer that I saw she wasn't there – it was only the phone. I picked it up and saw she'd started writing a text to someone. And either she'd deleted the recipient or she'd never put one in. It just said:

How could you do this to me?

And that was it. As far as anyone can tell, she never walked out of that building. She was never found inside it, either. She went from being a person I spoke to every day of my life, to this sort of nowhere girl. We've never seen or heard from her since.

From: evelynidamitchell@gmail.com

Sent: 31/01/19 05:11

To: you

on Wed, Jan 30, 2019, Evie Mitchell evelynidamitchell@gmail.com wrote:

Hey JK – you around?

---

on Wed, Jan 30, 2019, Evie Mitchell evelynidamitchell@gmail.com wrote:

Are you awake? Need to talk. Don't worry about the time, there's no way I'll sleep.

Can you just call me?

When I'm assembling these chapters I fully transcribe one person at a time then start seeing how and where they cut together. If there's overlap I call up whoever's involved for responses or commentary so it all flows.

I'm towards the end of part two so I spent most of the day at a coffee shop editing. Around dinner time I realized I'd completely fucked up something Liu Wai said and made a note to double-check it when I got home. I went to the tape about an hour ago to try and confirm what I'd got wrong and it was blank. I thought I must have put the wrong one in, but I tried the next and the next and the next. I've tried both players, all my tapes.

Every single recording I've made is blank. It's ALL fucking GONE.

I'm fucking freaking out rn, can you call? It's 07.

Sending you part two of TCS now so I can be sure it's safe somewhere.

e

PART TWO
THE UNUSUAL SUSPECTS

--10--

'Half Midnight'

Difficult questions must be answered in the immediate aftermath of Zoe's disappearance, but as the police and her parents arrive on the scene, Andrew, Kimberly and Jai are nowhere to be found.

SARAH MANNING, *Former detective constable, Greater Manchester Police:*

I was assigned as FLO – Family Liaison Officer – to the Nolans on Saturday, December 17th. This is the day Zoe went missing, when we really didn't know much at all. There's a common misconception that FLOs are there to stand in the background of crime dramas making cups of tea, but really, at least at its most effective, the role should be investigative. It's true that you're the main point of contact for family members. You need to keep them in the loop and answer questions – to clarify what's happening during an investigation and offer support where necessary.

First and foremost, though, you're there to gather evidence.

In a case like this, nothing's more important than bringing that missing person home. I was twenty-six years old at the time and it was my first posting with a family.

SALLY NOLAN:

We were collecting them on the Saturday. The plan was bring them home and unpack and get dinner, then maybe watch a Christmas film while we decorated the tree. Rob had gone into town for a haircut, so I was on my own when I got the call. I thought it was a joke. I thought it had to be a joke until I called Rob and tried to tell him what they'd told me.

ROBERT NOLAN:

I ignored the first call, like. Just let it vibrate. I thought I'd ring back after I'd finished at the barber's, but it kept on and on, and when I saw it were Sally I picked up. I couldn't understand what she was saying to me. In the end I shouted something, like, 'Just tell me what you're trying to say!'

Then I honestly don't know. I think I more or less got out of the chair and drove home. I still had the bib on when Sal came out to the car. We were in Manchester before she noticed I only had half a haircut. I walked round like that for three days.

LIU WAI:

I probably wasn't the best person for them to talk to at eleven o'clock in the morning, but it felt like everyone had just *gone*. Like, Andrew, Kim and Jai *all* just disappeared around the same time as Zoe. I couldn't get Kim on the phone, I didn't have Andrew's number. I was panicking, talking to Mr and Mrs Nolan too fast, just overflowing with caffeine and fear. I'd hardly slept, I could *hear* myself going a million miles a second but I couldn't slow down. They kept asking me where their daughters were, and I had to keep telling them I didn't know.

FINTAN MURPHY:
This was the first time I'd met Zoe's parents, and I suppose I was in a slightly better state of mind than poor Liu. She'd known about Zoe's disappearance since almost the moment it happened, she'd been due to meet her on the roof of course, and I don't think she'd slept much in the interim. I'd gone home after Andrew and Jai's fight and not heard about Zoe until the next morning.

My flatmate, Connor, had lent out some speakers for the party in the tower, and I'd gone with him to Owens Park to help load them up. In the event, once I heard what was going on there, I left him to it and reported to the police so I could join the first search party. I tried to be strong and direct for Robert and Sally, but it seemed as though the news was all bad. Zoe hadn't been seen for something like eleven hours by this point, and her last known location was the high rooftop of a burning building while intoxicated.

To make matters worse, Kimberly had wandered off soon after giving a statement to the police. No one knew where she was and no one could get hold of her, not for the rest of that night or the following morning. We were worried sick. Even more so when we heard Kimberly was on her way back to Owens Park with the police, that she'd been arrested for something.

KIMBERLY NOLAN:

I thought Zoe had gone over the ledge of the building, she'd fallen or jumped. Everything was so dark up there that when I got to the edge myself I nearly stepped off it by accident. I could see cars and buses going up and down Oxford Road, lit windows all round me for miles, but not Zoe, not anywhere. I shouted her name, got down on my knees and leaned out over the side of the building, as far as I could go. On the ground, at the foot of the tower, I could see this mass of people, just shapes moving under the lights. I thought she must be down there, I thought she must be dead, and this voice in my head told me to follow her, to lean out a little further and let go.

For a second I think I did.

Then it all came crashing back and everything hit me at once. The smoke pouring out of the building, the smell of it, then the sound of the fire alarm and how high up I was. I edged back in until I was safe then pulled off my boots and went back inside, down the stairs as fast as I'd gone up them. It was unreal. Eighteen floors and not a single other person.

When I got to the bottom I was looking through the glass doors, expecting people to be screaming or gathered round, upset, in shock, but they were all just normal. They were all just like I'd left them. Still drinking, laughing, smoking, being kids, not taking anything seriously. I walked out wondering if I'd got it wrong, like when you wake up out of a dream where someone you love died.

LIU WAI:

While Kim was checking the roof I was going through the crowd, looking for Zoe, asking if anyone had seen her. Alex stayed by the door in case she came out, but of course she never did. The tower was still smouldering, so until the fire brigade arrived we were all just kind of powerless to do anything else. Speechless, arm in arm, staring at it. I think the natural assumption was that Zoe was somehow something to do with the fire? That she must be trapped inside or hurt or something.

JOHN MARBER, *Watch manager, Greater Manchester Fire and Rescue*:

Two crews were dispatched from Manchester Central in the early hours of December 17th in response to an automatic alarm from the Owens Park campus. On inspection the fire was fairly serious, even if the damage was minimal. A lit cigarette sent up a communal sofa on the seventh floor, then that had spread to the entire kitchen, then the entire flat. No one was hurt, though, and we'd arrived in time to contain it. We were satisfied there was no structural damage preventing most of these kids spending their last night in there before the Christmas break.

Once the space in question had been made safe, we were made aware of a resident from the fifteenth floor who was unaccounted for. We agreed to look for her while we conducted our own safety search of the premises. Six firefighters and, I think, four welfare officers from the university swept that tower from the ground up. Searches like those are fairly standard procedure for us before letting people back inside a reported structure. We didn't see anyone, and nothing stood out as unusual. In the end I think we concluded that if Zoe was missed during our sweep, then the students would have to see her when they went back in an hour later. All I can tell you's what I wrote in the call-out log. There was no one in any of the rooms and there was no one on the roof.*

KIMBERLY NOLAN:

When Zoe didn't turn up in the search, and when I told the people from housing that she'd last been seen heading for the roof, they called the police. I had to repeat everything to them and things started to ramp up. At the same time, all I could think about was the building site near Canal Street where I'd been dumped after those guys grabbed me from outside Fifth Avenue. I got this idea that Zoe must have been the one they'd wanted, I mean, I'd been wearing *her* jacket when they took me. I got this idea that they must have come back for her. People were already searching Owens Park, Liu Wai was going on and on, and at a certain point I just stepped back, out of the light. I heard someone shout after me but it was so dark I could be invisible. Then I just gravitated towards town, not even thinking. I was on the 142 up Oxford Road then standing outside the building site. I don't know what time it was by this point. If Zoe went missing around half midnight, then I'd guess it was three in the morning, maybe later.

I climbed over the fence and stood on the other side with my back to it for a few seconds, just shaking, like, shivering all over with fear. Then I thought about those men marching me towards the foundations and forced myself forward one step at a time. I got right to the edge of the pit and wavered there. I didn't have a torch so it was just this big, black, wide open space. And I could feel this magnetism,

---

* This interview was conducted by Joseph Knox, and added to Evelyn's text in 2019.

174

this thing inside pulling me down, like it was where I was meant to be. I shouted out for her, moved round the edges, listened back, but all I could hear was myself. Then I saw her, this pale, haunted face looking back at me from inside the foundations. She looked horrible, awful, in pain. When I shouted to her I realized it was just a puddle at the edge of the pit, I was just talking to myself. I slid down the bank to it anyway, down on my hands and knees until I was in it, rainwater up to my waist. I think I just cried and said I was sorry, either to my reflection or to Zoe, probably to us both. Then there were sounds and flashlights. I don't remember the police or security or whoever it was finding me there. That night was like getting hit by the car when I was a kid or getting taken from outside of Fifth. It felt like it was all happening in the same moment.

ANDREW FLOWERS:

I'd had this huge blow-out with my friend, this screaming row with the girl I was seeing, and – I don't know. It was like catching my reflection in a mirror and not liking what I saw. And I mean that literally as well as metaphorically – my face was still bleeding well into the next day from Zoe's attack. So I suppose I decided to go into this self-imposed exile for the night, I decided to walk it all off or something. I seem to recall Christmas lights but, look, I went over it and over it with the police afterwards. 'No, I didn't see anyone who could confirm my whereabouts. No, I don't particularly remember where I went. Yes, I have some idea of how that might sound.'

JAI MAHMOOD:

Once I clocked that the stuff had gone missing from under my bed,

I knew I had to get the fuck out, man. Questions about how and why just had to wait. I still had stitches from getting decked in the car park, so they'd ripped open in my fall down the stairs and the kicking I got at the bottom. I was a sight, hurting all over, and I mean inside as much as out. And yeah, I felt guilty as well, even of these things I hadn't done. All I had were the pills in my pocket so I decided I'd spend as long as possible out of my head, if I was careful I thought they'd last me a few days. My friend Tariq lived in a flat on Oxford Road and he'd gone home for Christmas. I knew where he kept his spare key, so I crashed there. I thought I'd get my head down, work out where I could get a grand to pay Vlad back with.

I turned my phone on once or twice to see a million and one missed calls from Andrew, but I thought, *Stuff him.* Part of me wondered if he'd nicked the pills as some kind of revenge for his watch. Everyone was going home for Christmas, which my family didn't celebrate, so I thought I'd stay put until I was sure the others had left Owens Park. I thought I'd let them worry about me for a week and then have it all blow over in the new year. I didn't know Zoe was missing, man.

SALLY NOLAN:
When they brought Kim back to Owens Park that morning I didn't recognize her. Stick-thin and screwed-up and black and white, this soaking-wet wraith getting out of a police car. She was all make-up-streaked and dead-eyed, I thought she looked like a murder victim.

LIU WAI:
In all of this I hadn't realized that Mr and Mrs Nolan were yet to see

Kim's new look, and I didn't properly prepare them for it. Her dad, who I think is kind of a bit old school, looked at her and said, 'What the fuck have you done to yourself?' I couldn't tell if he meant the way that she looked or the fact that she'd been arrested. It kind of covered both.

SARAH MANNING:

I reported for duty at nine o'clock that morning and I'd been assigned by ten. They told me the parents were already on the scene and understandably distressed, so I arrived at Owens Park roughly the same time that Kimberly did, around noon. Honestly, I thought she looked like she was in shock. Maybe people thought it was the make-up making her look so pale. But her pupils were huge, her breathing was irregular, her lips were blue. I couldn't believe the arresting officers had booked her at the station then brought her to the scene. She should have been in hospital. She was barefoot, bleeding, out of breath, shivering. We're talking about December in Manchester, cold as ice.

I remember thinking something else was wrong, though.

A family member going missing has to be the height of trauma, and I'd say especially so when it's your twin sister. But I felt like Kim was carrying more than that on her shoulders – and that's certainly the opinion I expressed to Detective Inspector James, who was onsite that day and went on to take the lead in the investigation. There was no body, no ransom note, no threat. No reason to suspect foul play so few hours after her disappearance. So why was Kim so agitated? Why was she so aggrieved? It felt like she wasn't telling us everything.

The other thing wrong was the scene itself. I can't point fingers because there were only a handful of officers onsite at that time. No one could have known how things would develop, but the tower was bad for us. We had eyewitnesses saying Zoe had never left the building, but it still hadn't been locked down twelve hours later. There were something like a thousand students all being collected by parents that day for the Christmas break, all leaving the building at the same time, all carrying large suitcases, holdalls, backpacks. It was a disaster.

Detective Inspector Gregory James declined to be interviewed for this book, reiterating Greater Manchester Police's statement that to do so could prejudice the ongoing investigation into Zoe's disappearance.

FINTAN MURPHY:

Kimberly arrived looking freezing cold, I think she had one of the police officers' UV jackets draped over her shoulders. DC Manning, Sarah, the Liaison Officer, the person we dealt with most, said that they'd spoken to security at the site where she was found, that given the circumstances, everyone had decided to let Kimberly's trespassing misadventure go. Somehow that had the strange effect of driving home the seriousness of Zoe's disappearance for me. Round my way, kids aren't just taxied about by the cops and let off with a warning.

SARAH MANNING:

I offered to help Kim, to get her inside, maybe find her a hot drink and a shower. I'd only just introduced myself to her parents, so that might be why they resisted the idea. They were still being briefed and, after all, they'd lost one daughter already that day. On the other hand, I thought they seemed worried by the prospect of Kim speaking to the police. I remember Sally pulling the high-vis jacket off her immediately, putting her own jacket round Kim's shoulders instead. It's not that I thought Kim had something to do with her sister's disappearance, it's more that her parents seemed to think it.

They acted like they didn't really know her.

That is, they seemed more comfortable with Zoe's friends, Fintan and Liu, these people they'd never met before. That feeling lingered for as long as I was around them. The family dynamic – Zoe and Kim's relationship especially – was anything but simple.

FINTAN MURPHY:

DC Manning took us all aside – this would be myself, Liu Wai, Sally and Robert – and asked if we had any idea what Kimberly might have been doing there, out on this building site in town. We were all at a loss and, quite honestly, still preoccupied with Zoe. Then I saw Kimberly smiling at something. She was sort of wavering off at the side while we talked, just a ghost of herself all in black, make-up streaming down her face. It's this terrible day and she's standing there like that, *smiling*. She wasn't wearing any shoes, her feet looked ripped to shreds, so I suggested I take her up to the flat before she face-planted on the lawn.

Mainly, I think I wanted to get her alone.

While we were walking towards the tower I said, 'So what's so funny?' She scowled at me then nodded over her shoulder at Robert, said, 'My dad's hair.' He had this half-finished haircut at the time. I couldn't imagine laughing in that moment, but I thought she was distressed. I wondered if, without the police and her parents and the weirdness of this situation all in her face, she might talk to me. Clearly she knew something, clearly something was going on. In the lift on the way up she didn't even look at me, she was just texting someone, like, furiously, furiously texting someone. The whole fifteenth floor was trashed, like a bomb had gone off at a Christmas market. Once we got to Kimberly's room and I'd asked if there was anything she needed, I sort of put it to her, you know, 'How did you end up at this building site? What's going on?' She looked at me then all right, and for a long time. I think she wanted me to leave but I wasn't going anywhere. So she started to undress in front of me. I kind of turned away, but I still waited. In the end she said, 'I met a guy, we just needed somewhere to go and fuck.' So I nodded at the wall and walked out.

KIMBERLY NOLAN:

Whatever I did or didn't say in the moment, obviously that isn't what happened. If I couldn't tell my sister about the van, and if I couldn't tell my friends, then how could I tell this boy I'd just met the night before? I thought Fintan was probably gay so I started undressing to try and make him feel awkward. I thought he'd leave or at least turn away so I wouldn't have to lie to his face. And I think I said I met someone, I might have said we got to talking or something, but I never would have said I was 'fucking' *some guy*.

FINTAN MURPHY:

Look, I come from a background of quite brutal honesty – emphasis on the word *brutal* there. So I suppose when I arrived in England, in Manchester, I was quite naïve in that sense. I thought grown-ups told the unvarnished truth – that's just what they did. No one had ever lied to me so brazenly, not about something so serious. In that sense I've always thought of Kimberly, perhaps unfairly, as this master, this originator, of dishonesty.

LIU WAI:

Andrew Flowers came crawling back while Fintan was with Kim, we were all standing outside. The police were organizing a second search of Owens Park – they hadn't found anything the first time. We were all stood vaguely at the main entrance when he kind of staggered in, still wearing a Santa Claus hat. His clothes were dirty, shirt all ripped and his face was just *livid* with scratch marks. I'd mentioned to the Nolans, to the police as well, that there'd been an argument, I mean, everyone from the party had seen it, there was no secret.

Even so . . .

To see his face was something else, you couldn't look at him without thinking, *He killed her, he fucking killed her.* I mean, Zoe's parents hadn't even met him at this point, didn't know him from Adam, but I could see they thought the same thing. Mrs Nolan let out this gasp and just kind of *fell* on her husband.

SARAH MANNING:

Myself and two officers were forced to restrain Rob Nolan when Andrew Flowers arrived back at Owens Park. Rob was swinging his arms, shouting, 'Where's my daughter?' I was still getting up to speed and had to be told that Andrew was Zoe's boyfriend. His appearance was certainly distressing, concerning even. We asked if we could speak to him somewhere more private and he just shrugged. He said, 'Am I under arrest, too?' I thought that was a strange thing to say, but it only occurred to me afterwards that it didn't make any sense. The word 'too' implied that he knew Kim had been arrested earlier, yet they both denied having spoken to anyone.

SALLY NOLAN:

The second I saw that boy my heart ripped in half. I knew something evil had happened. I remember feeling it, somewhere down in my bones. I thought, *We'll never see our Zoe again.*

LIU WAI:

Fintan had been so strong up until this point, we were just meeting for the first time that morning but he clearly had a good head on his shoulders. He seemed upset and shaken by something when he came back down from the tower, though. I was kind of belatedly worried about Kim – everything had been so hectic before – so I asked how she was. I remember what Fintan said, because at the time it didn't make much sense to me. He was looking out at the grass, like, at nothing, and went, 'That girl should get royalties every time someone lies.'

--11--

'Scratch Marks'

SARAH MANNING:

The operation, which began as a simple missing-person search, developed rapidly during the course of that day. There were the strange circumstances surrounding Zoe's disappearance, as well as Kim's arrest and Andrew's physical injuries, the unusual behaviour displayed by them both. There was the fact that several of Zoe's friends couldn't account for their movements that night, or, as in the case of Jai Mahmood, were literally uncontactable. There was the fact that the fingertip search of Zoe's room had turned up no evidence to suggest she'd been planning this – she'd left without her purse, without her phone, without a change of clothes – and that nothing had been found on the roof or in the building, or even in the wider Owens Park area. Nothing except for her phone, this unsent message that had clearly been meant for someone who'd hurt her.

It said: *How could you do this to me?*

I was present when DI James spoke to the parents. He asked if they had any idea who that message could have been meant for, if there was anything like this in Zoe's past. Mr Nolan told us absolutely not, kept emphasizing that Zoe was 'straight down the line normal', and that someone had to have taken her.

SALLY NOLAN:

I let Rob fill them in on the details. I was struggling to talk or think. But when they asked if Zoe had been acting strange lately, if she'd been under any pressure, when he shook his head I had to put in. You know, 'Well, hang on. She hurt herself six months ago, she was living with this disappointment.' Rob looked at me like I'd spat on her name.

LIU WAI:

When the police interviewed me they kept coming back to the text from Zoe's phone. *How could you do this to me?* I'd told them broadly what had happened at the party, how there'd been a set-to and Zoe had asked me to meet her on the roof. I immediately regretted that because they jumped on it, like, 'So the text message must have been meant for you.'

SAM LIMMOND:

I spoke to Alex that day on the phone. It sounded like there was a full-scale search underway by morning. She said she'd talked to the police and told them her worries about Zoe's old laptop. She thought it was the device used to film the sex tape, and emphasized how Liu Wai had recently come into ownership of it.

I wanted to see it Al's way, course I did, but she was so manic at the time, maybe even on something. I was worried how seriously the police would take her. Al was prescribed Seroxat for depression, but sometimes when I wasn't around she'd mix it with other things.

LIU WAI:

I never bore any ill will to Alex because she was *clearly* going through something, *clearly* not of her right mind. When it came to the police, I just said, 'Putting the sex tape itself to one side for a moment, why would Zoe write a text message to me if she thought I was on my way up the stairs to talk to her? Zoe was quiet, but she wasn't a *mime*. She didn't have to walk round with a blackboard, she didn't have to spell out what she wanted to say like a Victorian mute.'

So I told them what I thought.

You text people who *aren't* with you at the time. Your sister, for example. Maybe the same one who'd left the building seconds before an incriminating video of you was leaked into the world. I mean, who writes unaddressed texts? Clearly *someone* deleted the recipient . . .

KIMBERLY NOLAN:

I'd had a shower and maybe an hour's sleep when the police asked to see me again. They wanted to know about the text I'd found on Zoe's phone, if it could have been meant for me? They wanted to know if we'd been fighting, if we had problems. I asked why they'd think that and they said outright that 'several people' had approached them about tensions between us. They wouldn't say who, but that was the day she went missing, that was how long it took for us to start tearing each other down.

LIU WAI:

I've personally never understood those songs where rappers are upset about people talking to the police. If you haven't done anything wrong, you shouldn't have anything to be afraid of? So I was happy to tell them exactly what I'd seen and heard. And, frankly, Kim *was* long-suffering around Zoe. Anyone would have said the same. She didn't like Zoe's clothes or her music or her friends, and yet she was *always* hanging around us for some reason . . .

KIMBERLY NOLAN:

I had to start justifying myself to them, which always makes you sound guilty, and especially when you feel guilty, and especially when you've just been arrested. I said they could think what they wanted, but I never fucked with Zoe's text. If I'd wanted to avoid suspicion, I would have just deleted the entire message. I feel like it was left that way to raise as many questions as it could. Then, I guess there were a few hours between Zoe going missing from the tower and my arrest at the building site. They were obsessed with that window of time but I just couldn't say where I was or what I was doing. It was a blur. The other thing the police could never get their heads round was me and Zoe – twins – being two separate people. Some detective actually asked me which one of us was the evil one, and I knew he was joking, but Jesus.

I had to explain that we were both individuals, tell them about Zoe's music, her suicide attempt, the reasons why we were living together in the first place. I had to explain why I felt like I couldn't let her out of my sight and, yes, why that might have made things difficult between us. Then I saw the way they were looking at me and started to clarify, like, 'Wait, she didn't do this to herself, what happened before was a cry for help.' Then the lead officer, James, just looked at me and said, 'Okay, fair enough, so what was she crying about? What's wrong at home?'

SALLY NOLAN:
I think I'd been talking to them for all of five minutes before I stopped and said, 'Wait a minute, why are you asking me where Rob was?'

ROBERT NOLAN:
I'd been performing at a pub in Stockport, a Christmas party, about a fifteen-minute drive from Fallowfield, about a forty-five-minute drive from home. I got back around one, one thirty in the morning, which apparently would have given me time to get to Fallowfield and back the night she went missing. I'm not sure what I was sup-posed to have done with her, or why. It was offensive, and I'm talking to them bleary-eyed and with half a haircut, losing my rag. It makes me angry even now. They're wasting their time talking to me while my daughter's twelve hours gone? I said, 'Where's the prick with her scratch marks on his face? Why aren't we talking to him?'

LIU WAI:
Andrew has one of those great big upper-class English noses, like, you'd think he could smell around corners or something. And he was *always* looking down it at Zoe. Nothing was good enough. He'd correct her, mock her taste, all this. Sometimes you'd think he

didn't even like her. So why was he *always* hanging around us? I was like, 'He's in the stupid sex tape, he'd be more likely to leak it than me, probably more likely to leak it than anyone. Zoe was probably texting him, asking how he could have done that to her.'

SARAH MANNING:

We were made aware of the so-called sex tape that afternoon. Alex Wilson told me about it, but she was clearly under the influence of something, and I found it difficult to follow exactly what she was trying to say. When I spoke to Liu Wai she confirmed the broad strokes of the story. I actually saw the tape myself when I caught two students in the tower lobby sniggering, watching it on their phones. It was short, just a clip, but no doubt devastating for Zoe to see leak out into the wider world. One of the kids was doing an impression of Andrew, saying, 'Oh, Zoe, Zoe,' over and over again.

ANDREW FLOWERS:

Which I suppose is how I ended up in this fetid fucking police station, free to leave at any time, just with three or four shit-kickers between me and the door, explaining my sex life on a hangover and no sleep. More to the point, how I ended up hearing every word I'd ever spoken in Liu Wai's presence recited back to me verbatim but now helpfully context free. So I'm racist, I'm sexist, I fucking hate Zoe, blah, blah. It was no surprise to me that Liu Wai memorized every word I ever said around her, because her issues with Zoe were as profound as anyone else's. She had no life of her own whatsoever, no social skills whatsoever, and her only pleasures were attained vicariously. She was then, is now, a leech, and that's far more destructive in my book than a boyfriend who's only after one thing. Most importantly, returning to the matter at hand, when Zoe attacked me she never said anything about the damned tape, and there's a room full of people to back that up.

LIU WAI:
I'd say Zoe's reaction to the tape was *pretty* clear.

ANDREW FLOWERS:
The truth was, not only had I never seen the fucking thing, but I didn't even have a copy of it, I didn't have a file, I didn't have anything. Not on my phone, not on my laptop, not anywhere.

LIU WAI:
Let's meet Andrew halfway and say, hypothetically, that he didn't leak the tape, let's say someone else did. *Dozens* of people saw Zoe more or less rip his face off seconds after seeing it. Does he expect us to believe that those two things are unrelated? She wasn't thick, however much it might suit Andrew Flowers to keep suggesting she was.

ANDREW FLOWERS:
I've never *once* suggested that Zoe was any less intelligent than me, and certainly not thick. I resent those words being put into my mouth. Am I glib? Yes. Cynical? Sign me up. But don't call me a fucking snob just because I reject this sombre procession of grief that we're all supposed to lockstep into out of some misplaced notion of etiquette. We react – we think and we feel – in different ways. I

wouldn't think to delegitimize however Liu Wai wants to grieve – fucking incense and lanterns, Hello Kitty coffins, whatever, fine by me. But while her grotesque Saint Zoe shit might make her feel morally superior, it's been scientifically proven *not* to bring people back from the dead.

Oh, where was I?

Yes, well, I suppose the police considered the text important because they perceived some causality between the sex tape and it. They thought whoever leaked the tape was the intended recipient of Zoe's text. Once I agreed to hand over my phone, my laptop, my university log-in, for forensics – all of which came back clean, I might add – I thought they eased up on the idea of it being me. But of course their next questions were, 'Well, who do you think leaked the tape, then? Who do you think the text might have been intended for?'

KIMBERLY NOLAN:

We reached a point where I thought the questioning was over. They'd moved on to me, what I was going through, I thought they were sympathizing. They said that kind of responsibility, my sister's well-being, was a lot for someone my age, and I agreed. Then they started to turn it, said, 'You'd probably rather spend Christmas doing things you want to do, not babysitting your sister,' at which point I looked up. James leaned in and put his hand over mine. He said, 'Wouldn't your life be a lot easier if Zoe wasn't around?'

HARRY FOWLES:

When the police were doing their door-to-door stuff the morning she went missing, we all said how Andrew talked about Zoe.

Basically, he didn't like her very much. He'd say stuff like, 'Has anyone seen my earplugs? I'm going over to the tower.' One of us asked once why he was with her since he seemed to have such a problem. He said, and I promise this is true, he said, 'I won't be with her for much longer, count on it.'

ANDREW FLOWERS:

That's right, Harry, my housemate, told them I disliked Zoe. That I wanted to split up with her a month before but didn't have the balls to go through with it. They started to suggest that my life might be a lot easier if she just went out one day and never came back. I thought, *Right, that makes sense, doesn't it? I perceived some social awkwardness in splitting up with a girl who was being stalked, so obviously the simplest solution was to stave her head in and incinerate the body.* I said something like, 'Let's hope I don't get bored by these questions or I might have to murder my way out of the station, since that's apparently how I solve all my fucking problems.'

SARAH MANNING:

Andrew definitely didn't endear himself to the investigating officers.

LIU WAI:

Of course, I'd mentioned that the police had been called out in September when items of Zoe's underwear were stolen. And that they'd then been found in Jai's pockets all this time later at the party. So they started asking me if Zoe's text could have been meant for Jai? Maybe because of the thong thing, maybe because Zoe thought he'd leaked the tape.

ANDREW FLOWERS:

When they moved on to Jai I was relieved. 'What about your other flatmate, the one who kept stealing her pants? Could she have been texting him?'

LIU WAI:

Jai? I thought it wasn't the craziest idea in the world. He seemed to have some kind of one-sided obsession with her, and I thought maybe he could have even got the video from Andrew somehow? Like, he obviously enjoyed stealing from Zoe.

ANDREW FLOWERS:

I thought about it, then sort of explained that Jai and Zoe didn't really know each other.

LIU WAI:

I said, no, actually, hang on. Zoe and Jai weren't really that close. *How could you do this to me?* That's something you'd say to a person who's in your life, I think.

KIMBERLY NOLAN:

I said, no, Jai was more like a friend of a friend to Zoe, I wasn't sure they'd ever even spoken.

LIU WAI:

I said how we'd only ever had one night out with Jai and he'd been so wasted he got kicked out of the club. They were interested in that, like, '*Why did he get kicked out?*' So I said, 'Oh, you know – he got into a fight.' And I saw that they were super-interested in that so I said, 'You know, he didn't *start* the fight.' *'Oh, who did?'* And I said, 'Well, Jai was flirting with some guy's girlfriend on the dance-floor.' *'And the guy got annoyed?'* Well, I told them Jai actually blew smoke into the guy's face. Their eyes were getting wider and wider and I kind of wanted to back up. I kind of reiterated that Jai and Zoe didn't really know each other. As far as I knew, they'd never properly spoken.

At which point they said: *'So is there any reason why she might have his number saved in her phone?'*

KIMBERLY NOLAN:

'Is there any reason why Zoe called him three times last night?'

ANDREW FLOWERS:

'So how come your girlfriend's been meeting with this guy in secret once or twice a week?' There were texts and calls between them backing it all up. It was one of those rare moments where I was rendered speechless.

From: evelynidamitchell@gmail.com

Sent: 05/02/19 17:18

To: you

on Sat, Feb 04, 2019, Joseph Knox joeknoxxxxx@gmail.com wrote:

Well, that was a lot of fun. Great, great, great to see you. We must do it more often. ██████████████████ Thanks again for sending through P2. Don't have heaps of reading time right now, but rest assured it's safe.

I did just finish chapter 11.

Have you noticed Liu Wai says Andrew used to pick Zoe up on her English? If memory serves that was the theme of whoever messed with Zoe's essay too. It also feels weird to me that Rob Nolan had hair missing on the morning he arrived at Owens Park . . .

It would be really helpful to have a cheat sheet of who was where on the night Zoe went missing, if you have such a thing?

Stay well.

Jx

Hey, he████████████████████████████████

████████████████████████████████

████████████████████

Interesting catch re: Andrew correcting Zoe's English. The essay said: 'Too many pronouns' . . .

Alibi cheat sheet below:

Andrew Flowers: No alibi (says he was walking round the xmas lights).

Fintan Murphy: Left tower with Jai (Jai too wasted to remember). He stayed in with his flatmate Connor Sullivan that night then went back to Owens Park on the morning of the 17th to retrieve speakers from the party. (Connor confirmed Fintan's alibi at the time but would be good to speak to him.)

Jai Mahmood: No alibi (says he stayed at absent friend Tariq's place).

Kimberly Nolan: No alibi (says she left party after Andrew and Jai's fight. Then was in tower, apparently alone, looking for Zoe, then some missing hours before her arrest at the building site).

Liu Wai: Down in the crowd outside the tower.

Rob Nolan: No alibi (played xmas gig in Stockport. Got home after Sally was asleep, so could easily have been out longer than he said). Interesting thought on his missing hair . . .

Sally Nolan: I guess because Rob was away we need to mark her down as having no alibi too?

I'm working away on the next part. Feel like seeing you gave me a shot in the arm, though. ████████ Speak soon.

Ex

--12--

'Special Relationship'

As the investigation moves into its second day, evidence surfaces of multiple clandestine relationships in Zoe's life.

FINTAN MURPHY:

I think the main thing driving me on to campus that day was that I couldn't face another fruitless search of Owens Park. In my view, we already knew where Zoe wasn't. I was supposed to be going home for Christmas that night, I badly needed to see my ma, I just couldn't face the thought of leaving without being of some use. It was a Sunday, December 18th. I wasn't sure if Martin Harris, the building that houses the Music and Drama department, would even be open. And it seemed even less likely I'd find Zoe's course tutor, Hannah Docherty, sitting at her desk. When I saw her there it seemed like such a run of good luck that I thought I might step inside and see Zoe, too. But of course that's where one kind of streak ended and another one began.

KIMBERLY NOLAN:

One of the ways that Zoe and me backslid when we went to Manchester was academically. Basically, I turned up to my classes, frowned, did the reading and melted my brain trying to understand it all. I loved reading but I was never a classroom kind of person. I blended in – I doubt my teachers could have even told you my name. But Zoe's tutors seemed to really see something in her, and one of them especially. Zoe said they emailed each other all the time, met outside course hours, talked on the phone, all this.

ANDREW FLOWERS:

Miss Docherty, yes. I mean, on more than one occasion Zoe actually cancelled our plans to accommodate her. Dinners, drinks, even concerts and shows. My lecturers just told me to stop talking.

SALLY NOLAN:

When she called home, Zoe talked about Miss Docherty all the time. Rob had looked her up online, checking her credentials. I think he felt like her special interest in Zoe was a vindication of what he'd seen in her himself.

FINTAN MURPHY:

I found her young and friendly, in fact precisely as she'd been described to me. And her face actually lit up when I mentioned Zoe's name. She said something like, 'Oh, I've been waiting for this.'

Dr HANNAH DOCHERTY, *Zoe's course tutor*:

Well, Zoe Nolan was something of a fascination for me. You get perhaps two or three of them each year, these students who simply stand out from the crowd. Unfortunately, in Zoe's case she was standing out for all the wrong reasons. She'd never once made contact with me or attended any of our weekly meetings, which of course she was supposed to. So when this waifish Irish boy tiptoed into my office just before Christmas break, I thought, *Ah. This is the boyfriend and Miss Nolan's standing out in the corridor, too scared to come in.* Of course, as it turned out, that wasn't quite the case.*

ROBERT NOLAN:

When they told me about it, I said, 'She's lying.' I just said she was lying and then left the room. And I remember this feeling of massive, sky-scraping fear out in front of me. Because I couldn't work out why anyone – why a teacher especially – would lie about something like that.

FINTAN MURPHY:

I think I told her that she had to be mistaken. I took my phone out and started showing her pictures from Facebook, like, 'You don't know this girl?'

Dr HANNAH DOCHERTY:

And I assured him that I'd never seen her before in my life. I explained that the only reason I recognized her name was because she was one of my black marks – she had, as far as I knew, never attended a single

---

* All interviews with Dr Hannah Docherty were conducted by Joseph Knox and added to Evelyn's text in 2019.

lecture, class, workshop, anything. I'd been sending emails and letters trying to establish if she'd even arrived at the university. Of course, I'd learned from the housing department that she had. Her friend, Mr Murphy, was quite stunned. Quite impressive, though, in another sense. He seemed to be so much more mature than people usually are at that age. His diligence on Zoe's behalf made me warm to him.

He explained to me that she'd gone missing, then had me producing attendance records, correspondence – you name it. I think he even asked for the email addresses of other students from the course, to corroborate that Zoe hadn't been in class, but I gently explained there were privacy guidelines, and that I might be better off talking to the police.

KIMBERLY NOLAN:

The university cleared out another apartment on the fifteenth floor for my parents, somewhere they could stay over the Christmas break until we heard something about Zoe. I didn't get a say, but it would have been the last thing I ever suggested. We always ended up congregating in one kitchen or another, just watching the paint peel off the walls. Alex was still around for another couple of days, still coming down from whatever she'd taken at the party, so there were five of us for a while. Me, my parents, Alex and Liu, all kind of waiting, when Fintan and DC Manning burst in.

SARAH MANNING:

Fintan arrived back at the tower out of breath, telling me to call Zoe's tutor to confirm what I couldn't even understand he was saying. Once I did, once Dr Docherty more fully explained the situation, it was clear we needed to talk to the family and friends. When I mentioned Hannah Docherty's name to them it was nods all round, as if to say, 'Of course, they're close.'

So I was watching everyone when I told them that Zoe and Hannah Docherty had never actually met. Either it really was news to them or they were very good actors. Rob Nolan called her a liar and stormed out. Kim started pointing at Fintan before she could even put what she was trying to say into words. She shouted something like, 'But you're her course mate, you met her in class.'

FINTAN MURPHY:

I'd met Zoe at orientation, and after that we'd attended meetings of the Choir and Orchestra Society together. They were off campus, at St Chrysostom's Church, we weren't actually in the same modules for anything. And while everyone's trying to process the Hannah Docherty situation, Sarah, the Family Liaison Officer, was quite sensibly trying to establish *how* we'd all come under such a grave misapprehension. Specifically, she kept asking, 'So, what was Zoe doing with her time? Where did she spend her days? Was she staying in the flat?'

KIMBERLY NOLAN:

But it was the opposite of that. She got ready and went in most mornings, more than the rest of us, more than anyone else I knew. Afternoons as well, even weekends, even days when she didn't have to.

LIU WAI:

As far as I knew, Zoe *lived* for her studies. I'd never met anyone my age who was more motivated.

KIMBERLY NOLAN:

And now we're all looking at each other. Me, my parents, Fintan, Liu and Alex. I don't even remember who said it, but we were all thinking the same thing. So where was she? Where had she been going all this time?

ANDREW FLOWERS:

Yes, well, the police were very touching when it came to the scratch marks, very concerned for my well-being. They made sure I saw a doctor and got treated and everything. *After* they'd taken pictures of the wounds, of course, as if they were going anywhere any time soon. Then they just returned to their new favourite subject. Jai and Zoe, sitting in a tree, F-U-C-K-I-N-G.

The special relationship.

Their take-away was that they'd been doing the dirty behind my back for weeks, calling, texting, meeting, screwing. I reiterated that, *obviously*, I didn't know anything about it. They asked me why that should be obvious, and I said, 'Because if I'd known, I'd have done something about it, wouldn't I?' Then I realized they were looking at me differently. They said, 'Oh yeah, you'd have done something like what?'

SARAH MANNING:

Detective James, the team and me were in close contact. We all agreed that Andrew causing Zoe's disappearance because he was struggling to end their relationship seemed unlikely, so I think we closed that door early on. But he did have a temper, he could be arrogant and project these feelings of entitlement, and it was looking more and more likely that his girlfriend had been having an affair with his best friend. I think his potential anger at finding that out seemed like a much more compelling motive to us.

ANDREW FLOWERS:
I told them that if I'd known of an affair, I'd have had my ticket out of there, wouldn't I? It would have solved all my sodding problems.

SARAH MANNING:
Alex Wilson told us an interesting story, about walking in on Andrew and Zoe filming the leaked video. Alex, in my experience, could be quite up and down, but she was obviously incredibly concerned, and I remember struggling to get my colleagues to take her seriously. Once they did, they had to sit up and listen.

She said she'd got the sense that Zoe was scared to death of Andrew in the moment where she'd walked in on them. Partners are always high on the list of suspects in cases like these, but I'd say Andrew's name got underlined as a result of that. I'd say in some police notebooks it's still underlined today.

ROBERT NOLAN:
I'd been pressing from the word go, from the minute we first got there. Let's get on the news, let's get in the papers, let's get an appeal going. Let's put some pressure on the pig who's got her and keep it up.

SARAH MANNING:

Mr Nolan was essentially trying to organize a press conference on the first afternoon he arrived, but DI James was able to talk him out of it. Within the first twenty-four hours we couldn't be absolutely certain if Zoe even really was missing.

It was clear by the second day, though, that the conference was happening no matter what we said or did, and by that point it was probably time. We needed to get Zoe's face out there.

ANDREW FLOWERS:

Initially, I'd tried to defend Jai. We'd parted on bad terms but I still thought they had him wrong. I was being slowly undone on that front, though. They began reading me these messages that had been going back and forth between them, him and Zoe. *I've never felt this way before, can't wait to see you, same time same place*, etcetera, etcetera, painting him as some Lothario all of a sudden, a dangerous man. I think I said that Jai might have his secrets but that being dangerous wasn't one of them.

They said, 'We hear he's got a temper, a violent streak.' I was putting them right on that when they interrupted, asked how he'd acquired all those cuts and bruises. I told them about the abuse he'd been receiving, the beating that had followed, I told them that we'd reported it to the police. Surprise, surprise, though, Officer Shitforbrains had never filed a thing. I tried to recover and tell them the fight hadn't been Jai's fault, he'd been jumped while taking pictures. They just asked how I could know that for sure. I said, 'Why would he lie?' Then they told me that since Zoe's disappearance several people had come forward with stories about Jai being a negative presence on campus, being a whip-out man or peeping Tom. I said all that shit was just innuendo, the result of a poison poster campaign that had, in my opinion, originated with the same police officers we'd spoken to following the theft of Zoe's underwear.

SARAH MANNING:

I heard Andrew repeat this accusation at the time. All I can tell you is that I spoke to the officers involved and can say with some certainty that wasn't the case. A more disturbing scenario to me is that Zoe's stalker saw her relationship with Jai and was jealous of it. He took steps to neutralize a threat.

Think about it.

Someone started a campaign to keep Jai off campus. Someone apparently beat him up, apparently broke his camera. If you believe Jai's version of events, it seems likely he brushed up against the same obsessive mind that Zoe did.

ANDREW FLOWERS:

I said I'd never seen or heard anything violent from Jai myself so I wasn't going to speculate. They said, 'So you weren't at Fifth Avenue nightclub on such a date?' I shrugged, told them I didn't keep a diary but might have been. Then they went into the story of him being dragged out of there, wasted. I said, 'So what?' You know, in my mind we're all lying in the gutter, it's just that some of us are face down in our own sick. But no. Jai had been trying to rape some girl on the dancefloor in their version of events. I told them that he wasn't the type. Then they asked if perhaps his substance abuse might play a role? They asked me if I'd ever seen Jai swallowing pills.

HARRY FOWLES:

Look, everyone knew Jai was selling drugs.

SARAH MANNING:

Upon learning that Jai Mahmood was selling drugs on campus, I made my concerns for Alex Wilson very clear. She seemed vulnerable, and had been under the influence the first time that we met. It was easy to imagine someone might be preying on her.

HARRY FOWLES:

I'd seen Jai giving cash to this absolute *unit* of a guy in the Great Central, over the road from Owens Park, which I told the police. Next thing you know, I'm down the station going through mugshots, trying to pick him out.

ANDREW FLOWERS:

You have to remember I haven't slept in more than twenty-four hours by this point. Now Zoe and Jai are both missing, apparently shagging, and the police think I'm responsible. They left me alone in there a while, an hour or so, then came back and started belting me with pictures of tough guys, running their records down for me. Telling me this one killed a man, this one raped a girl, all of them dealers, motherfuckers, fatherfuckers, babyfuckers even. All possible known associates of Jai's. They're telling me that they suspect he's dealing drugs to vulnerable young women, that he's taking advantage of them. My head was like a merry-go-round, my face hurt, I felt sick. I didn't know him very well, but I'd thought he was a decent guy, it upended me. Finally, I said, 'Look, unless I'm under arrest, I want to talk to someone, I want to go home.'

They admitted there was no legal case to hold me so they sort of shrugged and said I was free to go. I didn't even know where I was, which station, what part of the sodding city I was in. I hadn't seen natural light in hours. So I went out into the corridor and called my father. It was the first time we'd spoken in six months. Afterwards I kind of walked out into the street, probably crying and pissing my pants, and saw Rob Nolan, Zoe's dad, heading straight for me.

SALLY NOLAN:

I was never anything to do with Rob's plan. When he told me what he was up to I didn't know where to look. I thought, *Who the hell are you? What the hell are you thinking?*

ROBERT NOLAN:

The press conference I'd organized was the next day, the first Monday after Zoe went missing. It was planned as an appeal for information, to get her face out there and make it clear that her family meant business. And I wanted the police to get that message, too. They'd been shit from the word go. Pure shit. Slow to take us serious or even *get* that Zoe wasn't the kind to just wander off without a word. So I was trying to pressurize them as much as anything, and it worked because they finally came up with a name for me and a kind of a strategy.

They asked if they could add an appeal for a young lad to come forward, a Jai Mahmood. There was stuff in the press after about racial profiling, but that was something of nothing. I don't see it, I don't care if you're black or white or green. I just said, 'Absolutely, fantastic, we're finally getting somewhere.' So a part of me did want Andrew – apparently Jai's best mate – to be up there with us. I thought maybe that'll bring this Jai out of the woodwork faster?

But I knew I had to play every side.

When I saw that lad Andrew's face, my girl's scratch marks in his skin, nothing could have convinced me he wasn't involved. Nothing. I thought other people might feel the same way, so I decided to put him on stage, scratch marks and all. I thought, *Let's let the world decide, then we'll see if he feels like talking.*

SARAH MANNING:

I wouldn't have been doing my job if I hadn't advised Rob and Andrew against going ahead with it. To Rob, I tried to make the case that he'd be turning his appeal into an entertainment, a zoo, but I think that appealed to him. It was his way of taking control of the narrative and showing that he was the man in charge.

With Andrew, I just showed him the picture of his face we'd taken at the station, asked him what he thought people might think when they saw it. Unfortunately, it didn't work, his mind was elsewhere. He was trying to act in the way he thought a normal person might. The problem is, for better or worse, Andrew Flowers is unusual. I don't say that judgementally but as a statement of fact. His background's unimaginable to anyone outside of the 1 per cent. Motorbikes for birthdays, ski trips for Christmas. That means when he tries to imitate normal behaviour patterns he massively over-shoots or undershoots because they're just alien to him. It's not that he's speaking a foreign language, he's doing an impersonation of someone speaking a foreign language. So he eventually said, 'Her family's asked me to help. How can I say no?' And I wanted to shout at him, 'You can say no because it's going to *ruin your life.*'

ANDREW FLOWERS:

I'd called my father but he didn't have time to talk, he just put me on to Lipson, the family lawyer. So when I left that station and walked into Rob Nolan I suppose I was quite emotional, I suppose I was quite stupid. I just saw a dad taking charge, doing everything he could for his child. When he put his hand out for me to shake, I took it. Looking back, I should have told him to stick it up his arse.

--13--

'Under Pressure'

On the third day of the investigation into Zoe's disappearance, the Nolan family's press conference forces them into the spotlight, with disastrous results.

ROBERT NOLAN:

You want to go in and start shouting. That's your first instinct. Fight the universe. Then you think you should talk to whoever it is that's done it, make a deal and reason with them. Say you don't have to involve the police at all, you can settle it quietly, they just need to let your kid go and all's right with the world.

SARAH MANNING:

We briefed the Nolan family not to make an emotional or aggressive appeal. Everything we know about these situations tells us not to point the finger, not to make any inflammatory or accusatory statements. We asked them to make it clear how much they loved their daughter, how painful it was to be apart from Zoe, perhaps even articulate the emotional weight of not knowing. The aim of the game is to humanize the missing person and humanize your family. We know that an individual who might take a young woman is likely someone who's become temporarily or permanently empathically disengaged, someone who's lost all sympathy. We're trying to communicate directly with them, to say, 'This is a person, be careful.' That's a complex enough message without playing games.

ROBERT NOLAN:

It goes against what you're thinking and feeling in the moment, because you know someone's done something, you know your kid hasn't just wandered off. All parents do in that situation, they can tell when something's wrong, and my heart goes out to them. It's the worst club in the world you can be a member of. So I got through it by telling myself it was a performance. I just learned my lines and recited them, but I made damn sure I was playing all sides.

ANDREW FLOWERS:

On the morning of the appeal, and with some sleep in me, I happened to look at the picture the police had taken of my face. Constable Manning had left me a copy, and I started to see what she was saying. I tried to broach the subject with Rob Nolan, to suggest it might be a distraction having me up there looking like something the cat had been at.

ROBERT NOLAN:

I said, 'You've got to be up there. If Zoe's watching and she's upset about this fight, it's important she sees you want her back, that she isn't in trouble.'

ANDREW FLOWERS:

When I sort of started to say I didn't think she'd feel particularly bad about the fight, Rob just interrupted, got loud, hammered me with questions he already knew the answers to. If all else failed, he'd lean on his age, his supposed life experience. A few times he even shouted me down. He reminded me of my own father in that respect. He expected to be listened to, his instructions followed. He told me it wasn't too much to ask. And besides, he said the police were requesting that I go up there now, he said they wanted me to appeal for Jai to come forward.

SARAH MANNING:

No one ever told Rob Nolan that Andrew's presence was required for Jai to come forward. Quite the opposite.

SALLY NOLAN:

Well, Andrew was reluctant, we could all see that, so Rob said, 'Don't you worry. If anyone says anything, I'll make it crystal clear those scratches are nothing to do with this. We think of you as part of the family – you're doing a brave thing. And you're doing it because my Zoe loved you and you loved her.'

ANDREW FLOWERS:

It didn't seem like the time to clarify that, 'Well, actually, I thought she was *all right* . . .'

ROBERT NOLAN:

If Sally tells you that's what I said, then we have to agree to disagree.

That day, that week and everything round it was madness, but I don't think I made any promises like that to Andrew. If it's not clear by now, I'll spell it out. I'm what they call a man of the old school – I say what I mean and I mean what I say.

KIMBERLY NOLAN:

The press conference was first thing Monday morning, so December 19th. It was the third day Zoe had been missing, and you couldn't help but wonder where she was, what she was going through. None of us had really stopped or slept or eaten in that time. We were all hollowed out and jumpy, not even really speaking because everything – *everything* – turned into an argument. We were all living on top of each other in Owens Park and every time the phone rang or someone walked into a room we all thought they'd found her. Sometimes you'd think it was bad news and sometimes you'd think it was good, but it didn't seem possible that it would be nothing, it didn't seem possible that there could be no news at all. But that's what it was, every single time.

LIU WAI:

So it's this exhausting roller coaster of constant ups and downs and disappointments, even when nothing's happening. And of course for the parents – I mean, I'm sure they couldn't help but wonder and worry about where she was. I'm saying this to kind of explain why they looked like a pretty ragtag bunch when it came to the appeal. Mrs Nolan had kind of *aged* with worry, she was just staring off into the distance like a fisherman's wife. Mr Nolan, Rob, looked like he was trying not to shout and scream, and his hair was all crazy and all over the place. Then you've got an extremely pale, thin and temporarily de-Gothed Kim – but still with her black brush cut. And bringing up the rear you had Andrew, looking like the world's least successful rapist, claw marks all down his face.

If I'd been watching it at home not knowing any of them, I'd probably have thought, *Wow, I think they can close this case.* Like, arrest everyone on camera.

FINTAN MURPHY:

Robert offered me a place on the appeal. He thought I might discuss Zoe's love of music, but I didn't quite think it was appropriate. To be honest, I thought that Kimberly would want to say something in that vein, something personal and touching, but she never even opened her mouth. There'd been some kind of blow-up between her and her parents, but still. Andrew was asking Jai to come forward, so I just helped Robert and Sally get their feelings down on paper so the statement wouldn't sound artificial.

ANDREW FLOWERS:

I knew immediately that I'd made a mistake. The appeal was filmed at Owens Park and the second we got in front of the cameras every eye in that room was on me. I mean, why wouldn't they be?

KIMBERLY NOLAN:

I couldn't have spoken even if I'd had something to say. When I see pictures from it now I think it looks more like a police line-up than an appeal. My parents did their bit: 'Zoe, we love you, please come home.' Andrew kind of stammered through his thing to Jai, 'You're not in trouble, mate, we just need to talk.' Then, when they went to questions from the press, you could see which way it was going.

ANDREW FLOWERS:

Of course, the first fucking question was, 'How did you get the scratches on your face, Mr Flowers?' I looked to Rob for his promised ride to the rescue, but he never saddled up. He didn't even look at me. My heart sank down to my stomach, and finally, I said something like, 'We're not here to talk about my face, we're here to talk about Zoe.'

SARAH MANNING:

The whole thing devolved into my worst-case scenario. The read-through was fine. You could maybe say Rob Nolan looked like he wanted to punch the camera while he recited his 'please come home' message, but who wouldn't? The words were neutral at least. What felt disastrous was how the focus landed on Andrew and stayed there.

The whole point of this conference, as we saw it, was to get Zoe's picture circulating and appeal for Jai Mahmood to come forward. The call history and texts on Zoe's phone, her unexplained absences from class – all of it pointed to a clandestine relationship that her friends hadn't known about. Jai, the person we needed to talk to about that, had fallen off the face of the earth and we needed him back. But the only questions were 'Who scratched your face, Mr Flowers?', 'Was it Zoe?' Then into stuff like 'Were you at the party that Zoe went missing from, Andrew? Can you account for your whereabouts from Saturday into Sunday?'

ANDREW FLOWERS:

I just stood there and took it. I didn't need to look at the newspapers the next day to know what the headlines would be, though. None of them could come out and explicitly say I was anything to do with Zoe's disappearance, but it was all there, written between the lines, written on my face in fucking scratch marks. I heard from my father quite quickly after that, believe you me.

SALLY NOLAN:

We argued. And in that stupid tiny flat with Liu Wai and Fintan and Kim. I thought Rob had been stupid. Playing games while Zoe was missing. There was no one he could kick or punch, so he did the next best thing. It wasn't about helping the search or doing what we had to, it was about proving he still had it, whatever *it* was. I didn't like Andrew – I took a dim view of him the day we met. Believe me, it's got dimmer since, but if he was involved then this was exactly the thing that could make him do something stupid, hurt our daughter, or worse. The one thing we'd been told not to do.

KIMBERLY NOLAN:

I remember Mum turning grey. She was holding my dad's arm afterwards, saying, 'What about this Jai Mahmood? What about this lead we were given by the police? The one name that's come up in connection with all this, from the professionals, as a result of talking to everyone involved?'

He just shrugged her off.

Most of the papers didn't even print Jai's picture, they all just went with Andrew. Some of them printed bigger pictures of Andrew than they did of Zoe. That scared me because, through all of it, the weirdness of that situation, I thought everyone at least agreed that they wanted to help, everyone at least agreed they wanted to get my sister back. When they printed Andrew's face instead of Jai's, I saw it all for what it was – a fucking game show.

ANDREW FLOWERS:
My father ordered me back to Surrey for Christmas. He had Lipson, his lawyer, speaking to the newspapers – he still had quite a lot of sway in those days. He said they'd change the tone of the stories, get my name and face out of it. You'll think I'm making this up, but he literally didn't ask me about Zoe. Not what had happened, not what she was like or how I was feeling. I was pissed off with Rob Nolan, he was a different stripe of bastard altogether, but at least I could see his logic. He thought I'd hurt his daughter so he acted accordingly, like a father.

So I told mine he could whistle and hung up. When I got a call back a few minutes later it was from Lipson, who said he'd been instructed to drop his pursuit of the editors and to let them have me. I hung up on him, too. Over the next few months – and over those first few weeks especially – the fuckers almost literally ate me alive. They ran interviews with disgruntled exes, room-mates from Harrow, even a few teachers who spoke quite eloquently about what a horrible little cunt I'd been in school. Everyone I'd ever wronged got their own back and made a bob or two. Some days I was scared to walk down the street.

KIMBERLY NOLAN:

There was a communication breakdown between me and Dad. Over the weekend, once he'd dealt with my arrest and my shock, he had to find out all these things that Zoe hadn't wanted him to, and he blamed me. Whenever he called us after we moved out, I'd say we were both fine, doing well, and Dad actually brought all that up, said I'd been lying to him, like I was supposed to have been spying on Zoe all that time. I was starting to see – well, I was starting to realize – that she'd needed to get away from him as much as I had.

ROBERT NOLAN:

Listen, I'm hearing stories about my daughter's clothes going missing, about boys on campus turning it into a bloody joke, then this other lad throwing her pants round at a party like confetti. I couldn't believe it. I couldn't believe my ears. So I didn't shout at Kim – I'm sure she'll say I brought the house down – but I was just trying to understand what she'd been thinking. I said, 'For Christ sake, you were here to look after her.'

KIMBERLY NOLAN:

Which was the big red button in my brain that said, 'Do Not Push'. I just exploded, and everything, all of it, came out. How I'd never been good enough, how he'd always preferred Zoe, how I knew for a fact he'd rather I'd gone missing than her.

SALLY NOLAN:

When Rob didn't say anything to that, when he just sat down and started reading through the papers, his precious coverage, I couldn't believe it. I couldn't believe what was happening to us. I remember holding both their hands, trying to join them together and show them we were all connected, we were all we had, but it didn't work. I don't think they ever touched each other or really talked again.

KIMBERLY NOLAN:

I was just trying to make a point to him and explain it as calmly as I could. In my mind it wasn't something to shout about or scream about, in my mind it was the most reasonable thing in the world. You know, 'I wasn't put on this planet to follow my fucking sister around, I was supposed to live, I was supposed to have my own life.' He didn't even listen, he couldn't hear me over himself.

ROBERT NOLAN:

The main thing that shocked me was that 'essay' on Zoe's computer. It froze my blood. They should have been on to the police the second they saw it. They would have been, if I'd known. I was worried about Jai, I thought he sounded sick in the head, a real pervert, but the essay was different.

See, that was written by a different kind of person, someone intelligent, someone who had access to Zoe's room and her life. It was written by someone who knew her. The police didn't seem to be taking it serious, they weren't seeing it for what it was – to me that essay was as good as a ransom note – and while the wider world didn't know about it, there was no one who could really hold them to account.

ANDREW FLOWERS:

When the essay leaked to the newspapers a couple of days after the appeal, my core really went into meltdown. The articles were presented in such a way, with my picture placed so prominently, that anyone would think I'd written the fucking thing. If you google me now it's still the first result that comes up. My face next to that psycho message, usually accompanied by the pull-out quote about wanting to walk around in her skin, to see out through her skull.

From: evelynidamitchell@gmail.com

Sent: 07/02/19 11:55

To: you

on Thu, Feb 07, 2019, Joseph Knox joeknoxxxx@gmail.com wrote:

Hey E, so I've just finished ch.13. Am I right in thinking Rob Nolan
leaked the essay from Zoe's laptop to the press?! Shocking if true.
Surely the police wanted that under wraps to weed out any
fantasists?

Jx

Hey, yes, you're reading it right. Rob was always playing by his own
rules and his behaviour only really got worse. Leaks were a big
problem, although in fairness so was the poor police response.

Bluntly, it seems like it was LOW priority for GMP. I've found it
impossible to get anyone other than Sarah on the record for two
reasons: one, yes, the case is nominally still open, but two: there
simply weren't that many people involved. Reading between the
lines, I think senior officers just wrote her off as some runaway early
on, then when they realized it was worse than that it was too late.
Anyway, Rob made a lot of bad calls – I can't say I particularly enjoy
talking to him.

And speaking of bad calls, I know I've had some weird ones in the last few days but my landline's been burning up lately. My agent sometimes gets me there and she's reading the early chapters right now, so I have to keep answering. Long story short, I'm picking up to man after man trying to arrange meetings with me. Once I start asking questions they tend to hang up, but one got as far as asking how much I charge for extras. I was like, 'Extra what buddy?' He said watersports(!) piss play(!!) scat(!!!) I told him it was probably more than he could afford and hung up, but the phone keeps on ringing.

E(urgh)x

PS. At least now I've got something to fall back on if the book gets rejected . . .

PPS. ██████████████████████████

eXXX

--14--

'Unnamed Sources'

With a burgeoning information problem for the authorities, and the press getting closer to some members of the Nolan family than others, a missing person finally resurfaces with revelations about Zoe's personal life.

SARAH MANNING:

The disarray of that press conference set the tone all wrong. The conclusions we allowed people to draw from it hindered our investigation from the off. It was like a starter's pistol for every exploitative reporter, every cowboy with a pet theory. Every dirty cop with a story to tell. Basically anyone and everyone with a mortgage to pay.

ANDREW FLOWERS:

They say everyone gets their fifteen minutes of fame. Mine were merciless. There had been the pictures, the insinuations made about me, but then came the unnamed sources. Someone from the police putting it out there that I had a criminal record for theft, even though I was a 'rich kid' and could apparently have anything I wanted. I know for a fact that one of my arresting officers from Surrey sold a story anonymously, one suggesting that I referred to the police as 'pot bellies'. I know it had to be him because I'd shouted words to that effect while he was handcuffing me six months before. A man spat at me in the street one day, women refused to serve me in shops. When I tried to walk away they shouted stuff like, 'Where's Zoe Nolan?'

SARAH MANNING:

Andrew has a particular way of speaking. One that immediately put the back up of every officer working on that case, myself included. I'd like to think I'd never let something like that cloud my judgement, but there was legitimate unease about his answers to some of the questions we put to him. James's team were dissatisfied with his responses on the so-called sex tape, that was certainly true. They thought he was hiding something, they were concerned about what Alex Wilson had said – about Zoe being scared of him that day – but to see those theories printed in newspapers, attributed to officers who 'wished to remain nameless', was a different thing. It incensed me. Frankly, it pissed me off, but there was a feeling in the team that keeping this kind of pressure on Andrew might yield results. At the same time, the family were reading all this unattributed stuff, some of it true, some of it gut instinct, some of it smoking-hot garbage, then thinking I was holding out on them.

No one who gave quotes to the press ever did it in a measured way. They never said, 'This kid's been through an emotionally demanding situation and acted strangely.' They never left any room for doubt because doubt doesn't sell newspapers. The quotes you'd see would say things like, 'Everyone in that room knew he was lying about the sex tape, he was the only person who could have leaked it.' Whether that was true or not, the place for those kinds of conversations was the incident room, not the national press.

KIMBERLY NOLAN:

I was surprised that was even allowed, to fabricate things or attribute them to anonymous sources. Stories ran about everyone, but especially about me, and about Andrew and Jai. The article would be in the paper one day, then the pensioners would write in from Wigan the next. All these poisonous fucking letters pages, all saying we 'looked' guilty or knew something more than we were letting on. They said we were in it together, we'd done something awful with Zoe's body. I tried not to let it get to me but I felt like I had to read it, I had to try and steel myself against it somehow. I ended up just memorizing it all, replaying it in my own head. They said I was 'dark' and 'troubled'. I'd cut my hair off and started wearing black because I worshipped the devil, because I hated beauty, because I hated my sister and didn't want to look anything like her. It was a crash course in how fast people fucking judge you. You start catching looks in the street, hearing whispers while you're in line at Aldi, but what can you do? You can't stop passers-by and swear your innocence, explain your life story, like, 'Wait, it's not true, I just wanted to try and look like myself,' so people judge you. At a certain point you see and hear so much shit it becomes like the voice in your head, you start judging yourself for them.

And I was losing my mind as it was.

Walking into rooms not remembering why I was there, leaving things on the hob or in the oven or whatever. Picking up cups of coffee I thought I'd made five minutes before and finding them stone cold. I got burn marks all over my hands and round my wrists from just not thinking in the kitchen, and then the fucking *Sun* printed a close-up of my arm when I'd been in a supermarket one day, saying I was self-harming. The worst one was my own fault, though. My favourite band at the time were these Danish punks called Iceage, they'd made this kind of new-wave-noise punk album, all dangerous and teenagers and smouldering and gorgeous. And stupidly, I went to see them about five days after Zoe went missing, right before Christmas.

I just needed to *feel* something good, hear something other than these horrible voices in my head. I needed to get my hair blasted back by music that I loved and forget who I was. All we'd been doing for days was sitting round watching the phone, watching stale sandwiches curl up at the corners like smirking fucking faces. We were just watching the news, waiting for a knock at the door, and the quiet and the stillness felt like it was *actually* killing me. You couldn't put a film or a song on, you couldn't pick up a book and even get to the end of the first sentence. So I went to see some live music and it was cathartic for me, life-affirming and life-saving. I threw myself around and I sweated and I screamed and I walked out of there remembering what life felt like, what it could be. I couldn't hear the pensioners in Wigan over the ringing in my ears, I shouted them all down, and that night I slept properly for the first time since Zoe went missing. Then Dad came into my room a couple of days later and threw a newspaper at me.

226

SMELLS LIKE TEEN SPIRIT

Kimberly Nolan made a boozy exit from a Manchester nightclub after partying alone on Wednesday night.

Kim, 19, the twin sister of tragic missing Zoe, let what's left of her hair down at a rock concert held in the city's Soup Kitchen nightclub.

The punk-rock student looked unrecognizable from her sister in a thigh-skimming black miniskirt, fishnet tights and Dr. Martens.

Sporting a shaved head and emo-style make-up, Kim rocked out with confrontational and controversial Danish punks Iceage, before staggering outside for air.

Iceage, who released their debut album this year, have been plagued by accusations of xenophobia, with reports of fans giving the *Sieg Heil* salute at their concerts.

Kim appeared to be refused re-entry into the nightclub following her breather and decided to call it a night.

Kim and Zoe's parents, who led an emotional appeal earlier this week, have urged anyone with information on their daughter's whereabouts to come forward.

THE SUN, Friday, 23 DEC 2011 - E.M.

KIMBERLY NOLAN:

Needless to say, the stuff about them being Nazis was bullshit.

JAI MAHMOOD:

Oh man, my mum called saying she'd seen my picture on the news, that the cops wanted to talk to me. I'd never heard her like that, crying so much she couldn't breathe. She said they thought I was jungled up with this girl who'd gone missing. That was the first time I realized what was going on, man. I was still keeping my head down at Tariq's, worrying about owing Vlad a grand. I got online and read the official story, which was bad, then I got on Facebook and read the real one, which was worse, all about the sex tape, the fight, the crazy appeal and stuff. That got me out of the house for the first time in days.

It actually scared me into going back to the tower.

So here's me thinking I'm walking into roadblocks and helicopters, dragnets and manhunts and shit. I'm thinking I'll be surrounded straight away, I'll tell them who I am and we'll be sorted. But Owens Park was a ghost town, everyone gone for Christmas. I know GMP came out years later, swearing up and down they did their best, but I'm telling you, yeah? Their number-one suspect walked right into their crime scene without passing a single high-vis jacket. And I guess it just downgraded it all in my mind. It sounds stupid now so much of Zoe's stuff's out in the open, but at the time, when I saw even the police weren't taking it seriously, I thought it must be innocent, she must be doing what I was.

She was making them all suffer, y'know?

She'd been fucked over by Andrew, just like me, and I thought she was probably planning to reappear once she got bored or thought he'd been punished enough. And in the meantime, I knew stuff about her no one else did, and I thought she probably wouldn't want her life to blow up while she was away. So I snuck in there and made some problems disappear. I went up to the roof, crouched under the police tape, removed evidence and tampered with the crime scene. And when I got in and out of the tower without anyone seeing me, without anyone saying anything, I just kept on going, man. It clearly wasn't as big a deal as I thought, and I didn't know anything special about her going missing, so who was I hurting?

ROBERT NOLAN:

There's no roadmap for this stuff. I was moving Heaven and Purgatory and Hell and Earth to try and keep the story alive. Either you hit the ground running or you splatter on the tarmac. So that meant talking to reporters, calling radio shows, going on TV – the lot. It meant stopping and talking to everyone who recognized me in the street, shaking hands and making time. And I know how that can look, but it was what I had, it was what I could do. Connect with people. Some of the things that have come out since, some of the things I've done, okay, I hold my hands up and I'm not proud of them. But to keep Zoe's name and face in the news? Yeah, I'd have done anything. Absolutely anything, and I couldn't give a toss how it might make me look.

SALLY NOLAN:

You just want to close the door, but there are reporters in the house with you and in the car with you and taking pictures, asking stupid questions.

'How does it make you feel?'

Well, God help us. Then you'd read about it the next day because you had to read everything, because who knows how or where or when you'll see something important? I learned more about Andrew and Jai from the newspapers than I ever did from the police. I found out more about our Kim, more about Zoe, even. But at the same time things never quite lined up, because I'd read stories about myself, things I'd been there for, and think, *That's not how it was.* Then I doubted myself and started doubting everyone else, too. For me it started to feel like there was no one real version of the truth.

Rob was the opposite.

He'd read something and it would rub out whatever the reality was, replace it. Newspapers were more real to him than his family, than life.

KIMBERLY NOLAN:

Feeding stories to the press is dangerous. And especially when you're someone who loves attention, because where's the line? How can you say for sure what you're doing for your daughter and what you're doing for yourself? I really think Dad got drunk off it. He started taking more care over his appearance, rehearsing soundbites in front of the mirror. There were reporters and photographers coming to town from London just for us, all staying as close as they could because Dad was trying to turn our family into the story. They were involving themselves in our lives, intruding everywhere they could, and at the end of the day they'd all go to the same pub where my parents ate dinner every night. They'd offer to pick up the cheque or buy them a drink, then another, then another. Mum started coming home on her own because she realized that they'd always be buying as long as Dad was talking, and he'd always be talking as long as they were buying. Then we'd find out what he'd told them in the news the next day.

That was how I found out he wanted to launch a charity, the Nolan Foundation. Zoe hadn't been gone two weeks when he started talking about it. And when stories started coming out about her, about me, personal things you wouldn't want anyone knowing, things that had nothing to do with my sister going missing, I just started to trust him less and less. I couldn't talk to him or to my mum, because I knew I'd be reading whatever I'd said the next day in the *Daily Mail*. I mean, my dad was the only person I ever told about going to see that band and look what happened there.

JAI MAHMOOD:

I guess I picked up to Andrew on the Wednesday or the Thursday, a few days after Zoe had gone missing, anyway. I knew something was up. He was treading too careful, sounded like he was at gunpoint on the other end of the phone.

SARAH MANNING:

We'd encouraged Andrew to keep trying Jai. He still seemed like our best bet of bringing him in voluntarily. I'd instructed him to make sure Jai was okay, then ask him to report to his nearest police station to give a statement. Of course, this being Andrew Flowers, he went wildly off-script.

ANDREW FLOWERS:

I'll only shoulder a certain ratio of responsibility for that. I'd been asked to get in touch with Jai, and I did. He sounded worn out and paranoid. I'm sure, to some extent, we both did, but it quickly became clear that this wouldn't be as simple as having him flag down a police car and say, 'Recognize me?'

He didn't seem to grasp the seriousness of the situation.

Not only was Zoe missing, but we were all on the spot for it, we'd all been unaccounted for at the crucial time. His speech was slurred – it sounded like he'd taken something – and I had what the police had said to me blasting through both ears. Namely that Jai's a junkie and he can't be trusted. I delicately broached the subject with him and he admitted he might need a day or so for stuff to pass through his system. I said that was fine and I could meet him the next day. I felt like a pretty solid friend until he said he'd rather not meet me alone, he wanted someone else to be there. Oh, and that he needed a fucking grand first.

KIMBERLY NOLAN:

When I saw Andrew was calling me I nearly didn't pick up. I probably shouldn't have. He asked how I'd been, but I could tell there was something else and at some point he blurted out that he knew where Jai was, he just needed my help in making him come forward. This was it, my one attempt to try and play the game. It was after the story had come out about me 'partying' in the wake of Zoe's disappearance. I let Andrew convince me that we could clean up our images and come out looking like the good guys, which, obviously, we didn't.

We went into town and met Jai in the Temple, this tiny underground toilet of a pub on Great Bridgewater Street. I'm sure you've seen the pictures, but he looked awful, like he really was guilty of something. Like I say, I tried not to, but I'd read every headline, every story, every radioactive comment section. I was at the point where I believed the bad things they said about *me*, so of course I could believe the worst of him as well. There were too many coincidences for them not to show in my face. The theft stuff, this suggestion that him and Zoe had been seeing each other on the sly, the fact that he'd been unaccounted for when she went missing and had turned up afterwards wanting money.

ANDREW FLOWERS:

I think, to some extent, both Kim and I felt like a stranger was walking through that door. He even looked different, although I could hardly mount my high horse on that front. My face was still fairly distinctive to say the least. I was wearing Kim's concealer over the scratches, essentially looking like a Bond villain on his day off. But I did hope that in coming and taking my money that Jai was letting me off the hook for how I'd acted. Instead, his first question was, 'Did you find your watch, then?' Like, really satirizing the importance I'd placed on it. I said, 'No, no one cares about the watch any more, mate.' He shrugged and said, 'Some of us never did.'

It didn't seem like there was much more to say so I gave him the cash – taken from my current account, I might add – then we went with him while he handed it to this sketchy guy, paying off his hangover. And we're talking ten minutes at the most. He met him in the McDonald's at the top of Oxford Road. It was Christmas week, so shit weather and last-minute shoppers everywhere, low visibility. We didn't realize we were being photographed the entire time. When we met Jai, when we handed him the money, when he met his Russian, the lot. We were fucking clueless. Afterwards, we did manage to take him to the police, afterwards, he did cooperate – but of course no fucker printed that.

FINTAN MURPHY:

I was with Robert and Sally when they read that story, about Kimberly and Andrew's dirty meeting with Jai, them handing thousands of pounds to this known drug dealer, this violent man. I never told Kim this, but Sally had a fall that morning. At the time I thought she'd had a heart attack or a stroke or something. It was one of the worst moments of my life. Rob stormed out afterwards and I had to spend the whole rest of the day caring for her in this poxy student flat. I thought, *What the hell have I got myself into?* I had my own mother on the phone, herself reading these terrible stories, begging me to come home. I kept saying I would, I'd be on the next flight out, but then I'd see a picture of Zoe and think, *Christ, what kind of friend am I?*

JAI MAHMOOD:

I didn't see the pictures at the time, but I knew they were bad. I felt like shit for Kim, whatever was going on, because I knew she was getting hurt and I had the same thing with my own family. They were seeing and hearing these bad things about me, thinking I'd changed. I couldn't pick up the phone and talk to them for a year after. That day, though, I was just in with the police. There was tinsel up in the interview room, man, I thought I was still high. I just got hammered with questions, started to feel like public enemy number fucking one.

ANDREW FLOWERS:

Not to get competitive, but I'd say we were in joint first place on that score.

JAI MAHMOOD:

They were asking me things I didn't know, about thongs and this threat on her computer, and then worse, about stuff I didn't think *they* knew. They wanted to know why Zoe and me had been texting each other, why we'd been meeting up. I think I said we were friends and tried to leave it at that, but they had all these statements from the others saying we weren't, that I never spoke to Zoe and she never mentioned me, that we must have been carrying on in secret.

In the end it all had to come out.

LIU WAI:

To this day, I refuse to believe that Zoe was using drugs. First of all, I lived in the next room, I would have known. Second, Zoe told me things, personal things, we were close. I thought at the time, and I still think now, that the so-called 'revelations' about her personal life were generated, leapt on and perpetuated by the police because they didn't know what they were doing or where to look. They just saw an attractive young woman and filled her with every kind of salaciousness they could dream up. But drugs? I'll accept that she was speaking to Jai, maybe he was preying on her, but I just can't believe the worst about people I love. In my opinion, he threw her under the bus to save his own skin.

KIMBERLY NOLAN:

My parents, Fintan and Liu, they all came down on Jai as a fantasist and a liar because it was too painful to consider that they didn't know Zoe, that none of us really had. Everyone seemed to agree that she'd been acting out of character, abrasively, going quite quickly up and down, but no one wanted to look at why that might have been. It made sense to me, though, I could see it. And I could see how she might feel more comfortable confiding in a stranger than in me. It hurt, but we'd been driven apart. I could definitely see it.

JAI MAHMOOD:

Zoe was depressed, man, that's what she told me, that's what was apparently so controversial. She was like a fucking submarine or something, pressure from all angles, mad stresses from her family and friends to try and be perfect. They had this dream that she was about to be famous or something and she'd lived under that for so long she'd started believing it herself. She'd been trained to believe she was this one-time talent, yeah, then realized in the last year that it was all bullshit. She said she used to watch *X Factor* and *Pop Idol*, all this reality TV, and just feel sorry for everyone involved, all these poor, deluded people. But by the time I was talking to her she saw herself as one of them.

I didn't think she was deluded or un-special, which is what I tried to say, like, 'We don't all need to be famous to be someone.' But they'd spent so long polishing her surface she was scared there was nothing underneath.

It started with her seeing me out on my rounds in Owens Park one day, asking me what I was doing. I said, 'Nothing much,' and she laughed and said that wasn't what she'd heard. I was surprised when she tried to buy but I was hardly the person to say, 'Maybe this isn't such a good idea.' So I just tried to respect her privacy, I tried to make it as easy on her and as safe as possible. For handovers I couldn't go to her place because they knew me there, she couldn't come to mine because of Andrew, so I thought about that first time I'd seen her up on the roof, and suggested we meet there when she wanted something. When she did, we'd talk, I'd get the inside track on why she was using in the first place.

One thing she did say, yeah. She thought someone was stalking her.

When I asked why she thought that she said she'd nearly caught him once or twice, that she had this sense of a shadow, always ducking away, moving out of her sightline at the last second. And, look, she was buying tiny amounts of stuff, too. Sometimes I thought she was paying for the talk as much as for the pills. She said she'd had an 'episode' sometime in the last year and was scared to have anything too serious lying around. I assumed 'episode' meant overdose or suicide attempt, so I never tried to upsell to her. It meant more visits than I'd usually make, people usually bought in bulk, but I didn't mind. I liked the tower and I liked Zoe. We'd meet on the roof, I'd sell and we'd talk, and that's all there ever was to us, whatever anyone else says.

SARAH MANNING:

It certainly illuminated some aspects of the case – Zoe's increasingly abrasive behaviour before her disappearance, for example – and it explained why she'd felt this sudden urge to visit the rooftop after her blow-up with Andrew. I have to say, I felt like we weren't getting the whole picture of Jai's drug use, or his distribution. I was worried about how much Alex Wilson had been slurring her words on the day Zoe went missing, for example. When I asked Liu, who was the most talkative of the group, she intimated that a guy Alex was seeing sometimes gave her drugs. I'd met Sam Limmond, and I was surprised by that, but Liu said no, Alex was seeing someone else as well. Unfortunately, she wasn't sure who this second guy was. For obvious reasons, I wish we'd tried harder to pursue that.

JAI MAHMOOD:
I never sold drugs to Alex. Ever. She asked me and I turned her down flat. I knew she could be quite manic and I didn't want to fuck with her head, that's never what I was about.

SARAH MANNING:
Look, Jai's statement tallied with what we already knew – Zoe's disappointment, her suicide attempt – so in some ways it was welcome. But it was just like Kim's arrest and it was just like Andrew's sex-tape denials. The explanations we got were the bare minimum. They left a lot to be desired.

JAI MAHMOOD:
They were asking me stuff I didn't know, so yeah, I was struggling. They wanted to know what Zoe and me did all day, and I'd say, 'We didn't spend that kind of time with each other.' We'd meet on the roof *some* evenings for five, ten, twenty minutes max, but they kept

on hammering, 'Where does she go during the day?' I was like, 'I don't know, I guess she goes to class?' They didn't believe I didn't know, but what could I tell them? I'm not psychic. Then came all the money stuff and my head just spun off my body.

KIMBERLY NOLAN:

The police search of Zoe's room in the tower was pathetic. I guess it might be different if they thought she'd been murdered, but they didn't even take stuff away, just told us not to touch it. One day while we were sitting round going stir-crazy, and probably because we were missing her as much as anything, we decided to go through her things anyway, just Mum and me. At a glance it all seemed normal, what you might expect from a teenage girl's room, then I found this brand-new laptop under her bed. I knew by then that she'd given her old one to Liu Wai, but I'd thought that was more to do with how she felt about the message that had been left on there, you know – it was soiled. We'd both arrived with the same model, second-hand Toshibas, but her replacement was top of the line, still in its box. I couldn't have afforded it with everything I had, and she hadn't even bothered to unpack it. And then there was more stacked up in the wardrobe. Bags from Harvey Nichols and perfume from Jo Malone. Dresses, coats, clothes – all stuffed away, most of it unopened, still labelled, untouched. We went through them and found receipts in the bags showing she'd paid for everything herself, on her own card. We just weren't that kind of family, we'd never had that sort of money. While I'd been looking for bar work in the weeks before Zoe went missing, she'd been spending *thousands* of pounds.

SARAH MANNING:

It's standard procedure to examine bank accounts for unusual activity. Up until this point in the investigation, that meant checking to see if Zoe's cards were being used to withdraw cash or make purchases after her disappearance, which they weren't. When Kim and Sally came to me with evidence of extravagant spending I passed it on to the team and they began a more detailed process of financial forensics. From experience, I thought we were probably dealing with credit-card fraud, or maybe some kind of ridiculous overdraft situation. Neither one uncommon for students, especially those coming from lower-income households. The banks throw so many cards, loans and overdrafts at them it's easy to amass some substantial debt. People in that situation cut and run all the time, then usually come home safe once they've calmed down. If anything, I thought it might be a positive thing, a simple solution. Instead, we found funds in excess of £77,000 in Zoe's current account.

JAI MAHMOOD:

And by this point, the trillionth time of asking, seeing how fucking furrow-browed everyone was, I told them about our system. There was this antique tin hidden on the roof, near the gutters, an old Twinings tea tin, and that's where Zoe left cash for me and I left Xans for her. We never handed stuff to each other. I'd arrive and she'd usually be leaning out over the ledge, looking down. I'd open the tin, take the cash, leave a pill. If she was there, then we'd talk. The only reason I told them about it was because I'd cleaned it out that day I snuck back into the tower, I'd already swallowed what had been left inside there, so I thought, what's the harm?

SARAH MANNING:

The tin was our first significant break in the case. When officers accessed the roof with Jai, he led them to it and they arranged for its recovery by forensics. This would have been Christmas Eve. There were no drugs inside, there was no money, either. There was just a photograph of a smartly dressed man in his forties.

JAI MAHMOOD:

They had to do prints and stuff so they didn't open it there and then. In my mind, it was just some empty tin, same as I'd left it. I only found out later when they dragged me back in for more questioning that something had changed. What spun me, right, what's still spinning me now, is I'd been back to the tower, like, *days* after Zoe's disappearance. Like I say, the cops were nowhere so I went through that tin and emptied everything inside into my pocket. It was a couple of pills and that was that. So I'm telling you, hand on heart, that when she went missing there was *no* picture in that tin. Someone planted it after and that should shit us all up, even the people who want it to be true.

Because it was like everything else the police were working off, and it was like everything else the papers were printing, it was just another anonymous source. Someone was way ahead of us, man, scattering breadcrumbs for people to follow. Only problem was, to my way of thinking, that trail took us right off the edge of a cliff.

on Fri, Feb 08, 2019, Joseph Knox joeknoxxxx@gmail.com wrote:

Ugh, that's really disturbing about the phone calls, but if you WILL go around writing your number on the walls of public toilets . . .

In all seriousness you should disconnect the phone for the night and maybe talk to your provider about going ex-directory (or even changing the number). Is it possible someone's playing a weird prank?

Just reading through ch.14. I'd love to know wtf happens to £77k when it's untraceable and in a missing person's bank account? I'd also be interested to see a copy of this picture they found on the roof.

One final rogue thought re: phone calls. Have you given your home number to any of the people you've been interviewing? Because if there's any element of danger here, you should consider stopping altogether. The story's not worth that.

Jx

Hey JK. SO. The cash is actually STILL in that account. I think you need to be missing seven years for the high court to rule death in settlement of an estate, so it's happening now. I'd imagine it'll go to Zoe's family.

You don't think it could have been a motive for them to get rid of her? Guess it would be playing a very long game if so . . .

Scan of rooftop picture from Sarah Manning here:

I wasn't going to say this, but I think I actually will: What do you mean that I should 'consider stopping'? Stop writing the book? And are you saying the story's not worth it because it's not interesting, or because I'm not presenting it in the way you would? Because it's worth it to me and that should be enough.

And on those phone calls, after the 50th one (only a *slight* exaggeration), I finally fucking googled my number. I found it's been listed on a personal ads site saying I can 'suck the freckles off a man's dick'.

Obv unpleasant to think about who might have put it there and why, but there's no chance I'm stopping now, whatever you might think about my story. ███████████████████████████████████
███████████████

One thing I've been meaning to ask, Joe – you haven't been sharing this with anyone, have you?

Ex(hausted)

--15--

'Heart Attack'

With new information finally emerging about Zoe's secret life, her family and friends are forced to confront some uncomfortable facts.

ROBERT NOLAN:
We spent Christmas Day in the tower. That's where the police came in with a picture, saying, 'Can you identify this man?'

ANDREW FLOWERS:
I'd gone from estrangement from my father to derangement of my father, to probable disinheritance. The press conference had been one thing, then there was the story in the *Mail* showing myself, Jai and Kim all engaged in the apparent act of buying narcotics. They implied some strange bond between us, a sex triangle that saw us harbouring Jai and plotting something, rather than just trying to take him in to talk to the police. Owens Park had been almost entirely cleared out for Christmas, it was just losers like us with nowhere to go. I'm sure I speak for everyone involved when I say that time of year's really lost its lustre for me. Someone should write

a Christmas song about what a lot of shit it can be – they'd be set for life. By this point, Owens Park was this cavernous, deserted student village which handily contained every known suspect in a young woman's disappearance. So after the drug pictures there was this constant snarling wolf pack of photographers camping out at the gate, waiting for anyone to go in or out.

I don't know why the Nolans didn't get a hotel – money, I suppose – but yes, it was certainly uncomfortable. Jai and I were avoiding the rest of them – they suspected us of everything you can think of – and we were trying to avoid each other for the same reason. There was the bad smell in the air from my trying to fight him at the party, accusing him of taking my Rolex, and at the same time he was trying to go straight or clean, or whatever they call it. I was still hiding my face while the scratches healed, still miffed that I'd paid off Jai's drug debts without so much as a thank you, so the atmosphere was certainly fraught. More so when the police arrived on Christmas Eve to take him back in for questioning.

SARAH MANNING:

I was wary of the photograph because it felt too good to be true. After spending time with the family, with Rob especially, I knew how it might get jumped on and interpreted as the answer to all our problems. And I'll admit I was concerned about how fast it might find its way into the press.

Evidence can't exist in a vacuum. You're talking about inanimate objects that become supercharged because of the context surrounding them – so much so that they might even change meaning on you sometimes. Yes, we had this picture of an unknown man found amongst the possessions of a missing woman. But it was also a glossy photograph, ripped out from a magazine or some kind of publication, and it had been found in what amounted to a communal space. We only had Jai's word for it that Zoe even used that tin. The entrance to the tower's roof was a service door, residents weren't supposed to go up there, but the lock was broken and they obviously did. Zoe and Jai went out there often enough, so why not others?

In fact, a few people did come forward saying they'd been on the roof themselves before Zoe's disappearance, smoking cigarettes or getting the view, some of them had even seen her up there. I just urged the team to find out everything they could before alerting the family and giving them false hope, especially at Christmas. I'd been on the scene and I'd spent a lot of time out at the tower by this point. I knew someone could have planted it there if they really wanted to.

JAI MAHMOOD:

They sat me down and started showing me picture after picture, but kept circling back to one of them again and again. Some city boy I'd never seen before, which is what I told them. They kept asking me about the roof, about me and Zoe, our arrangement, the tin. Did she keep anything else in there except for the pills? I said, 'Not as far as I know.' Then they told me that this picture had been found inside the tin and my brain started to bake, man.

Look, we were careful, we didn't want to get caught, we were meeting on the roof of a fucking tower block. So I'm shouting this one out for the cheap seats: *We were the only ones who knew about that tin.* Y'know, if she didn't tell her boyfriend, didn't tell her best friend and didn't tell her twin sister, who else was there? And, like I said, I'd gone back there a few days after the party. I swear on my family's life I looked in the thing and there was no picture. Someone put it there after she went missing, and the only person who'd know about that spot was the same nut who'd been stalking her.

SARAH MANNING:

One thing we *were* certain of was that the tin, the surrounding area, the bannister on the staircase and the door leading up on to the roof had all been spot-cleaned. Every surface wiped down with alcohol. Now, whether you believe that could have been a drug-addled Jai or not, it's certainly disturbing.

SALLY NOLAN:

They called ahead, said they had something to show us, this is Christmas Day. Course, every thought goes through your mind at once. She's dead and she's alive and she's on the other side of the world. She's being held hostage or she doesn't want to come back – everything. The detective, James, came in with Sarah and showed us a picture of a man, the one that had been found in Zoe's things. We passed it round, me, Rob, Fintan and Kim. Liu Wai had gone home for Christmas by then. Rob thought he knew him but couldn't say from where. Kim looked at the picture for the longest time, we all held our breath.

KIMBERLY NOLAN:

I thought I recognized him somehow, but Sarah stressed we shouldn't put all our faith in this one picture. It had been found in

Zoe's things but was cut out from a magazine – it might have been anything. I might know him from a film or an advert. It made the hairs stand up on the back of my neck, though. I couldn't help but wonder if this was the shadow man I'd seen standing outside our building the night before Halloween. I wondered if we'd met.

ROBERT NOLAN:

There was something about the face, I just couldn't place it. So to my way of thinking, the next step was to get the picture on the news. Let's get him out there, a wanted, dangerous man, let's warn people, but the way Manning and James looked at each other told me I'd have to fight for it.

SARAH MANNING:

You have to remember that all we had was a picture that looked like it had been cut out of a magazine. The chain of evidence didn't even lead conclusively back to Zoe.

FINTAN MURPHY:

We were all sitting in silence in one of those wretched tower communal spaces when I got a brainwave. Having spent more time online than was probably healthy, I asked if they knew of Google's reverse-image search and was surprised when they said that they didn't. Essentially, you upload a picture that you can't trace the provenance of and it finds identical ones online, usually taking you to the original source. We were in the tower so we went downstairs there and then to the computer lab, unfortunately to no avail. We uploaded the picture, but it didn't match any others online. To me that seemed to suggest that it wasn't an advert, this wasn't an actor or a singer or something.

LIU WAI:

I was contacted by Essex Police on Boxing Day? They came out to my mum's place with a copy of the picture so I could look at it. In spite of the circumstances, it was kind of thrilling and I was desperate to help. I'd felt guilty about leaving, but I didn't want to have Mum on her own for Christmas. So I stared at it for a long time, like, smoke coming out of my eyes and ears, brain on endless scroll, but I didn't know him. I have a pretty good memory and felt safe in saying I'd never met him before.

I suppose if one thing stood out to me, it was that he looked a little bit like Andrew Flowers? Kind of arrogant and rich and snobbish, but handsome in a way. I wondered if this was the *other* man she'd hinted she might be seeing when we were in the cab a few weeks before? Y'know, like, maybe Zoe had a type . . .

SALLY NOLAN:

That was that – they left and we went back to waiting, all except for Rob. Rob said he needed some fresh air, but I knew what he'd really be doing. Heading straight down to the Great Central to see if any of his press friends were still around, anyone he could drown his sorrows with. Some Christmas.

KIMBERLY NOLAN:

Afterwards, we were told to keep it between ourselves. Sarah really stressed that leaked information might harm or prejudice a case, but the lead was still right there in the newspapers the next day. The next *day* . . .

We weren't allowed to keep copies of the picture, which is probably the only reason it wasn't in there alongside the story.

SARAH MANNING:

The money in Zoe's bank account seemed like a more promising lead to me. The first aspect of discovery on that was to speak to the people in her life. We knew she'd been spending beyond her means, but the one person around her who would have immediately questioned that, Kim, had been shut out from her sister's life. To the rest of her friends, I suppose Zoe affected the air of someone who could walk out one day and come back with a new iPhone like it was no big deal.

LIU WAI:

When I'd asked Zoe, like, 'How can you afford all this?', she told me it was through her singing work. She'd saved the money she was making over the years and she still did private shows and things. I didn't know anything about the economics of live performance so I just assumed that was true?

ANDREW FLOWERS:

I'm sure Liu Wai can make herself believe in anything that benefits her. Look, to some extent, I was the same, but at least I can come out and say it. I didn't have so many questions about money back in those days because it was a fact of my life. I wish like fuck it still was. At the time, I'd always had it and so had everyone around me. I never thought to ask.

FINTAN MURPHY:

As I've said before, I'm not certain my friendship with Zoe was necessarily representative of the friendships she shared with others. When we were together, we walked, perhaps we got a coffee when we felt extravagant. I didn't have two cents to rub together so I'm sure Zoe would have felt it incongruous to flash the cash in front of me.

SARAH MANNING:

We knew the date that the money started to arrive in Zoe's bank. The first payment was a small amount, a couple of hundred pounds, likely a test, before the second payment of £15,000 reached her account on October 1st, so just a couple of weeks after she moved to Manchester. Certainly not singing money saved from down through the years.

ROBERT NOLAN:

Zoe had been picking up paid singing work since she was sixteen years old. We're talking cash in hand, though, fifty here, a hundred there. The biggest shows she did were with choirs and orchestras, concerts where she'd travel with a group of other musicians, usually by bus, but it was rare she stayed away – and that was really just for the experience more than the money. It wasn't about that for her.

SARAH MANNING:

We could also see where some of the money had gone. The largest purchase was an Apple Mac laptop, but there were plenty more. Frédéric Malle perfume, Moschino dresses, Chanel make-up. And then there were the more social expenses. Meals, cinema seats, gig tickets. Liu Wai and Zoe were due to go and see Bruno Mars, the cast of *Glee* and Beyoncé in the new year, all paid for on Zoe's card.

Frustratingly, none of the social expenditure went any way toward explaining the unaccounted-for times in Zoe's days. This is all a very long way of saying that we had to get right down into the nitty-gritty of her financial life, times, dates and places, because the source of the cash – what should have been the single biggest lead in the case – was untraceable. The analysts hit a brick wall.

MARTIN BLACKMORE, *Independent financial forensics analyst*:

In the normal course of things, each time you make a payment, your transaction will be recorded alongside your personal data. So, tracing the cash in a person's account is usually a matter of speaking to their bank manager for five minutes, supposing you can get authorization to do so. Of course, some payers are cleverer. As more cash and information gets exchanged digitally, so, too, the desire for anonymity increases. We're talking about behaviour that's widely discouraged by the authorities, but then, so's smoking and drinking. So's not paying your taxes.

As long as there's a demand for anonymity, someone out there will provide it. And where even one such service in the world exists, there's no real way to stop people from using it. As things stand, you've got various methods at your disposal, all of them providing greater or lesser degrees of security. You could set up a trust, for example, or a shell corporation, and send money from there. There's the mythical but still somewhat effective Swiss bank account, estate transfers, on and on. Cryptocurrency is thought of as a fairly recent example, but it was established in 2009, two years before Miss Nolan went missing, so it's certainly possible. Crypto brands itself as a decentralized digital currency with no central bank or administrator, something attached to no one nation or government. A cash transfer system so anonymous that no one even knows who really established it. I could set up a bitcoin account and be sending anonymous payments to anyone I pleased before you could clear security and leave this building. All I'd need to give them is an email address. And that's just one kind of cryptocurrency.

So that's the how of it, but what about the why? Why do people want to go to the trouble of sending payments anonymously? Well, let's look at the examples that might have been related to your case. The three Es. Espionage, extortion or extracurricular activities, by which I mean paying someone to do something illegal. You don't want to use your Lloyds online account to hire a contract killer, for example.

Espionage feels unlikely, the idea of the digital dead drop. From what you've told me, Zoe wasn't moving in any particularly grand circles, not travelling internationally as part of her work, and the sums are far too great for the spooks I've met. There are the unaccounted-for times and dates in her life where I suppose you could imagine her crawling through the air vents in Sellafield with a camera attached to her head or something, but I think it's a stretch.

Then you've got extortion, which feels like a more comfortable fit. By extortion in this instance I think we'd be talking about straight blackmail. Zoe acting as middleman for someone who could expose an individual or institutional vulnerability. Or perhaps she even initiated it, personally blackmailing a man who'd behaved inappropriately, for example. Seventy-seven grand seems a bit steep, price-wise, but there you go.

For me, the most intriguing E is probably extracurricular. I shouldn't think she's a hit-woman or a bank robber, but the people I encounter in my line of work who pay like this to youngsters with no discernible reason usually turn out to be criminals. Gun against my head, I'd say the most likely scenario is that Zoe was a money mule, a smurfer, for a criminal enterprise. Perhaps she didn't even know it. She was approached or seduced into the operation, promised a fee to allow this money to rest in her account for a while. She's someone who no authority on earth would suspect of hiding vast sums, so she'd be a good fit for a criminal to try and launder it through.

Unfortunately, there are strong arguments against all three. Her disappearance certainly fits espionage, but nothing else we know of her life suggests it. The cash suits extortion, but then why wasn't the money claimed after her disappearance? Why didn't anyone even try? And the same goes for being a mule. In fact, in that instance, you'd expect to see test payments in *and* out before they transferred any whopping great sums to her, and the payments out never happened, not even small ones. It seems unlikely that they'd keep pumping cash in without even attempting to move it on.

Given her background, her social standing, her youth, what I don't really see is any way your Zoe acquired this kind of money in anything other than illegal circumstances. I'd suggest that whatever the poor girl got wrapped up in, it was as serious as a heart attack.

From: evelynidamitchell@gmail.com
Sent: 13/02/19 22:17
To: you

Hey, Foxy Knoxy – are you not talking to me now?

Here's an icebreaker, then. Today I opened the door to a nervous guy asking if I was Evelyn. I said, 'Yeah, do I know you?' He said he was my five o'clock. I was like, 'My five o'clock what?' He was sweating by this point and it SUDDENLY dawned on me what he was there for. I said, 'Sorry bud, I think someone's playing a prank on us, can I ask where you got my address?'

He was nice enough, bit out of breath, but he did show me the site. It was ANOTHER personal ad, saying roughly the same thing as before, and that I'd undercut any other girl in the area. He'd messaged them to arrange a date and someone actually replied, setting one up, sending him to MY FLAT.

This guy got into the building because someone was leaving when he walked in, but my door's been buzzed THREE TIMES SINCE. I've contacted the site and had it taken down but wanted to say sorry for blowing up at you before. I know you were just worried.

I guess it's just hard to hear those kinds of doubts from one of the only people I feel like I can trust.

Anyway.

E(x)

--16--

'Unidentified Man'

As Christmas comes and goes with no contact from Zoe and no news on her whereabouts, the Nolan family are forced to explore new avenues to try and keep the story alive.

ROBERT NOLAN:

When I saw leads wouldn't just drop out of the sky, that the cash in her account and the man in the picture might somehow come to nothing, I started working on ways to keep Zoe's name and face out there. The students were coming back to Owens Park after the Christmas break, so Sal and me moved out and went back home. She'd wanted to go back before Christmas, we fought up and down about it, but in the end I had to admit nothing was doing. I still found myself driving back to Manchester most days.

SALLY NOLAN:

I couldn't live and breathe it like Rob, it was like scratching at the wound and reopening it, and I said that to him. He said, 'Well, I want to keep scratching at it, I want the wound to stay open, I want to rub people's faces in it.' So he took indefinite leave from work – he was still plumbing at the time – and that's what he did. He's never stopped rubbing faces in it since.

ROBERT NOLAN:

I had plenty to do. The police had set up a tip line, and as much as the press might have intruded on our lives, as long as they said, 'Anyone with information on the whereabouts of Zoe Nolan should contact the police,' at the bottom of each story, I didn't care. I'd been pushing for everything I could get, just day to day, always on the back foot, always reacting, but I saw I needed to start thinking strategically, short term, long term.

In the short term, I knew the best way to get visibility for Zoe would be on TV, a reconstruction of the night she went missing. Someone saw something, someone had to – I wanted to kick at the bushes and see what creatures came out.

SARAH MANNING:

Rob Nolan was talking about a reconstruction from the first week we met. At the time that seemed premature – there was still the chance of Zoe walking back into their lives any day. We didn't have the more troubling aspects of her history of self-harm and drug abuse, we didn't know about the money in her account or have this photograph of an unidentified man hanging over us.

Now, with all those loose threads in our hand and none of them leading anywhere, with no new developments and a stale tip line, it seemed like the moment to go wider. I contacted the BBC's *Crimewatch* on behalf of the Nolan family and set up a meeting on

January 15th. One of the producers came to Manchester to discuss the suitability of the case with us. That meeting was my first real warning sign. Where I'd expected to be representing the whole family, maybe even some of Zoe's friends, the only person who showed up was Rob. He hadn't told anyone else about it.

CARYS PARRY, *Former producer,* **Crimewatch:**

When we were exploring the possibility of a reconstruction, the duty of care to families and victims was always at the forefront of our minds. We never pursued a story without the consent and wider involvement of the police and the family. We never wanted to intrude without everyone's blessing, basically, but when I met with Mr Nolan I could see he was highly motivated for this to go forward. For my part, I felt the story sat comfortably within our purview. It seemed like exactly the kind of situation where we might be able to help.*

SARAH MANNING:

It was my first time liaising on anything like this, so my primary concern in that meeting was to establish what would be required of the Nolans and of me. Carys explained that it was important for her team to speak to everyone – of course the family – but mainly the people involved in the incident or incidents that we hoped to restage. For us, that meant the party on the fifteenth floor, the fall-out over Zoe's missing clothes, the revelation of an explicit video and her

---

* All interviews with Carys Parry were conducted by Joseph Knox and added to Evelyn's text in 2019.

subsequent argument with Andrew, ending with Zoe walking up to the roof alone. Essentially, they'd need to re-interview everyone.

CARYS PARRY:

While we tried to avoid insensitivity in what was usually a highly charged situation, we also needed to present as accurate a picture as possible. We needed to know what had happened before, during and after the event, and what the overall effect had been. We interviewed subjects, then wrote scripts based on what we found. We were a small team, so the scripts only really passed through us and our programme lawyers before they were ready to shoot. And we wanted our audience to connect as much as possible with victims, to encourage witnesses to come forward, to trigger memories that could prove vital, so the more detail, the better.

It wasn't unusual for some families to get protective or even demanding, I'd say that was their right, but Mr Nolan was forceful from the off, and he became insistent on two key points. First, he wanted some of Zoe's actual singing to appear in the reconstruction – that's exactly the kind of flavour that can make a personality stand out, so it was easy to agree to. Second, he wanted Zoe's twin sister, Kimberly, to portray her.

SARAH MANNING:

Carys resisted the idea of Kim portraying Zoe. She explained how traumatic a reconstruction can be. The production company encouraged some victims not to attend their reconstructions at all, to make sure they had someone they trusted with them if they decided to watch it. Rob seemed confused, frustrated by all this, he said something like, 'It was Zoe who went missing. Kim's not a victim of anything at all.'

KIMBERLY NOLAN:

I wasn't like Zoe, and definitely not like Dad, I wasn't a public kind of person. Dad thrived off the attention, but to me it was intrusive, so when he told me about the reconstruction I just shut down. People were already looking in on our lives but this felt like moving into a glass house. I hadn't left Manchester over Christmas, and I stayed on at university because it was the path of least resistance, on autopilot, not really doing anything. So I remember our talk about the reconstruction because Dad dropped into the tower unexpectedly, I didn't even know he was in town.

He sat on the edge of my bed and told me the producers would *only* go forward with it if I played Zoe. I'd lived my whole life as something like my sister's understudy, so it made some kind of sense. I don't think I even said anything, I think I just nodded and he left.

ROBERT NOLAN:

In my mind, Kim was enthusiastic. She saw like I did that she was the perfect person for the job. With the reconstruction finally walking on its own two feet, I turned to a more long-term media plan. It was too soon to establish a charity in Zoe's name, our Nolan Foundation, but I didn't want to be on the back foot if the time came, so I started making arrangements. I envisioned it mainly as a scholarship for gifted young women. I never went to college myself. A lack of opportunity more than a lack of talent, but it had been Zoe's dream to study music, and if I was about to find myself locked into this thing for years to come, I wanted to make sure other young women weren't having those dreams snuffed out.

FINTAN MURPHY:

I ended up staying in Manchester over Christmas, which was a difficult decision. My mother was in assisted living by this point. She had severe mental-health problems that had deteriorated as I got older. My father, Patrick, had been bedridden with depression when I was a boy. It gave expression to a feeling my mother had always nurtured, that I was weak in some sense, that I'd crumble and let her down one day as well. Perhaps she had some inkling about my sexuality even then, even before I did. So she initiated a programme geared towards toughening me up. All the old ways – sending me out to walk a mile in the rain, making me carry sacks of spuds back from town. Then she started trying to scare me. It started with me coming in and finding her collapsed on the floor one day. Except her eyes were wide open, and after the initial shock passed, I realized she was pretending to be dead. She could lie like that for hours, unnervingly still, never blinking, not responding. She wouldn't get up until I'd calmed down, then she'd emphasize the importance of the lesson, that one day I *would* find her dead and I had to be ready for it. Once I got used to that, she started to die in front of me all the time. She'd have heart attacks, brain aneurysms or strokes and fall down on the ground, sometimes she'd wet herself, even void herself, for the full effect.

It was just the two of us by my teens and there was something so self-evidently mad about her that I almost found it less disturbing than I should have. It's amazing what can seem normal when it's all you know. I spent my first five years dressed as the little girl she'd actually been expecting, which was confusing to say the least. Her issues grew worse as she started to drink more. I came home from school once, thinking she was out for the evening, then got woken up some hours later by the sound of screaming coming from under my bed. I mean, blood-curdling stuff. She'd been hiding there the whole time, just waiting for me to nod off. She'd hide behind curtains, under her own bed, in other rooms, and do the same thing. She was sectioned by one of my aunts before I went away, she was safe at least, but it made staying in town and trying to help the Nolans a difficult decision for me.

KIMBERLY NOLAN:
Maybe it was the way things were between us, maybe it was how I'd reacted to his suggestion I play Zoe in the reconstruction – not saying anything, just nodding along – but I was never asked by anyone to help with the charity. I was never involved in it at all. It's true I'd already left town by the time it got up and running, but they shut me out of those early conversations.

FINTAN MURPHY:
I'm not sure that's entirely true. I was in the room on several occasions when Robert tried to speak to Kimberly about it. With that said, it was amazing what you could miss at the time. I suppose it made more of an impression on me because the idea of two loving

parents was revelatory in my eyes. Even so, when Robert told me that Sally had suggested I help out with what went on to become the Nolan Foundation, I declined. Honestly, I felt like I was already putting my studies in jeopardy by dedicating so much time to them as it was, and I'd also started seeing someone, my flatmate Connor. It was early days, but he was my first real partner, and there just wasn't time for anything else. Then one day Robert broke down and said he didn't think he could do it without me. Sally was in too much pain, and his relationship with Kimberly was fraught, they weren't on the same wavelength at all. I thought if he pushed her they might end up in some huge fight again, so I agreed to help, not quite realizing how much work would be involved.

All I did that year was research.

Preliminary conversations, trying to work out what would be required – we were a long way from actually forming the foundation. But, well, suffice it to say that my relationship with Connor suffered as a result. I certainly sympathized with Kimberly a lot more afterwards. I got to see Robert's great skill close up. He can play people and make them feel like they don't really have a choice in things.

SALLY NOLAN:

Rob thought Kim and me couldn't take the strain of dealing with the foundation, so neither of us ever had much to do with it, even when it was still just an idea. I never suggested Fintan help out, it just wouldn't have occurred to me. I mean, it made sense – he was an old soul even then. But no doubt Rob was telling another one of his white lies to try and get his way.

ROBERT NOLAN:

The way I remember it is that Fintan did all the early legwork without my ever needing to ask. You could probably say there'd be no foundation without him. I didn't have that kind of patience, I was too hard-headed.

--17--

'Bad News'

As Alex's personal problems begin to spiral out of control, a figure steps out of the shadows, with tragic results.

SAM LIMMOND:
After Christmas, Alex was different, and especially with me. Distant, wasted. I knew she was upset about Zoe, she was struggling, but we started spending less and less time together. I still feel like shit about that now.

Drugs were something I just didn't understand. They were out of my realm. Then, being a teenage boy, thinking everything was about *me*, I took her behaviour as a rejection, instead of a cry for help.

LIU WAI:
I'd gone back early after the Christmas break, expecting to be at the centre of this big investigation, but it was like nothing had changed. I mean, nothing except the people, since everyone was acting different. I guess Kim was with her parents somewhere that night. Anyway, I called Sam because I didn't know what else to do? I was

in my room and I could hear Alex in hers, having what sounded like this *huge* argument with someone, laughing, swearing, the works. Sam was always quiet, always sweet, so I assumed she had to be with this infamous second boyfriend she had on the side. Except, when I happened to walk by her room, the door was open and it was obvious that she was alone . . .

She was really agitated, really stressed out, and her eyes were all red from where she'd been rubbing at them. She heard me coming and *launched* herself across the room, like, nails digging into my arm, saying, 'Can you see him? Can you see that man? Tell me you can see him?'

I was *terrified*.

My hairs were standing on end, it was like a film or something. I sort of stammered, I sort of said, 'Alex, sweetheart, there's no one there.' She looked at me like death, these red-raw eyes, then went back into her room and slammed the door.

SAM LIMMOND:

Liu called and I went running over there. I'd never seen anything like it. Between us, we eventually got into Al's room, got her calmed down. Liu could be nosey, a bit of a gossip, she could talk a Samaritan to death, but at least she tried. She always made an effort, she made time for people, and I'll never forget her being there for me that night. Bad as it got, she stuck by me. Al didn't know where she was, she barely knew *who* she was – she fully disassociated. I thought about doctors, calling her mum, but I knew how scared Al was of being sectioned. Plus, well, I found pills in her room. Like, illegal stuff. In the end it took us two hours to talk her down.

LIU WAI:

The second she was asleep, Sam went almost as crazy as she had. And, like, I was right there with him. Anyone who cared about that girl would have been angry. He wanted to know who she'd been with, who'd given her these pills. I just told him the truth, like, no one comes and talks to me about their drug use.

All I knew was that there was this *other* guy in her life. Well, Sam knew that but I still saw his heart, like, actually *breaking* as I said it. Then I got an idea where the drugs might have come from.

JAI MAHMOOD:

So I opened my door and got launched back into my room by that guy Alex was seeing, Sam, screaming at me about selling pills to her. I was like, 'Woah, mate, a hundred per cent no.'

SAM LIMMOND:

I was possessed that night, I think I actually had him by the throat. Jesus Christ. We went back and forth, me slowly calming down because I thought it sounded like he was telling the truth, he'd never sold to her. Then he remembered something, seeing Al around with some other guy he'd sold pills to a few times.

He said, 'Maybe he gave them to her?'

And look. Yeah, I knew Al was seeing someone else. It can't always be equal, sometimes you love someone more than they love you. I guess I'd known all along that whoever this guy was, he was bad news. I didn't dare make a big deal of it because I was scared she'd choose him over me. If I'm honest, I know she would have. But this was different. This wasn't Al cancelling plans or turning up at mine strung out or hung over, it was life or death. He'd given her this stuff that no one in her condition should have been taking, he used her, then walked off without a word to anyone while she was mid-breakdown. I wanted to know what kind of man could treat another human being like that.

JAI MAHMOOD:

I didn't know the guy's name, but I thought I had his number from a buy a couple of weeks before. Sam wasn't getting out of my face any time soon, so I called the guy up and asked if he'd be interested in some Xans, which is what he was into. He agreed to meet us at the Great Central so we went over there.

SAM LIMMOND:

Jai pointed him out to me through the window. A real prick, sitting at the bar reading a paperback, this smug look on his face, stupid floppy blond hair. I went in, grabbed him by both shoulders and headbutted him as hard as I could. It's the only time I've ever tried to hurt another person, and I wasn't proud of it, but if you'd seen Alex that night, you'd know. I had to do something, to try and pro-tect her – no one had done the same for Zoe and look what happened. He hit the floor, I saw blood all over his copy of *Fear and Loathing*, and I just about managed to tell him to stay away from Alex before the bouncers dragged me out.

JAI MAHMOOD:

I felt pretty bad about it for a second, man. I'd thought we were there to talk. I picked the guy up and helped him into the toilets, his nose was obviously broken, like, streaming with blood. He made me take a picture of him on my phone, then started demanding I send it to him, saying he was gonna sue Sam, sue Alex, all this shit. I laughed and put my phone away, like, 'Mate, to be honest, it sounds like you're getting off easy.' I told him to lose my fucking number then left. Never saw him again.

SAM LIMMOND:

No, I never saw him again either. It was the next day when I went round to check on her. Kim opened the door and we knocked on to Al's room. There was no answer, so we both looked inside. We just saw a piece of paper in the centre of the bed that had 'Sorry' written on it.

I called her about a hundred times that day but she never picked up.

'I'LL LOVE YOU UNTIL THE END OF THE WORLD'
Friends pay tribute to 'thoughtful, beautiful girl'

A young woman who tragically fell to her death from Stockport Viaduct has been named as Alex Wilson.

The 20-year-old plunged 110 feet from the Victorian structure and died at the scene of the tragedy, near to Manchester city centre, in the early hours of Tuesday morning.

Alex, who was studying psychology at the University of Manchester, was originally from Nottingham.

Her family released a statement via Greater Manchester Police.

It read: 'Alex was a thoughtful, beautiful girl. Our lives, our world, will never be the same without her. She will always be missed and loved by her friends and her family.'

Floral tributes and messages have been left at the scene.

One read: 'I'm so sorry I wasn't there for you. I'll love you until the end of the world.'

Another said: 'I can't believe this is happening.'

Alex was a room-mate of missing student Zoe Nolan, but Greater Manchester Police have moved to assure the public that the two incidents are unrelated.

Detective Inspector Gregory James, who is leading the investigation into Zoe's disappearance, urged people to allow the Wilson family to grieve in private.

MANCHESTER EVENING NEWS, WEDNESDAY, 11 JAN 2012 — E.M.

SARAH MANNING:

No, I'd never even heard that story before – Jai and Sam and this other man. Our investigation never overlapped with the inquest into Alex Wilson's death. Everyone acknowledged that Zoe's disappearance and the investigation itself were probably stress factors for her, but beyond that there was no suggestion of any link between our case and her death. From what I remember, there seemed to be no question that it was a suicide. Alex had a history of mental illness, of self-harm, one serious attempt in her early teens, and I know the blood tests came back negative for drink or drugs. With that said, if this other man was preying on her in the way that it sounds like he was, then we would have been extremely interested to talk to him.

SAM LIMMOND:

I know your book's about Zoe, but for me the defining tragedy of that time was what happened to Alex. I still don't understand it. It was only as the days, weeks and months went on that I really started to think about that guy, that fucking user. With everything that happened, with all the years that have passed since, you can't help but wonder, can you? Who was he? Where did he go? And what the fuck was his problem?

PUBLISHER'S NOTE

The following Facebook update was posted by Jai Mahmood after the original publication of *True Crime Story*. The information it contains was not made known to Evelyn Mitchell during the writing of the book, nor to Penguin Random House during the editorial process. We are pleased to include it for clarity in this second edition.

Like most here I read TCS. One part that sticks outs the stuff about Alex's 2nd boyfriend or whatever. Something was doing my head in and I realised its cos Ive actually SEEN the guy since the book came out. Went through my Facebook uploads and confirmed it.

I've tried to get in touch with him but he's TOTALLY REFUSED to talk, SO, for your viewing pleasure, I present the "Man" Sam Limmond nutted in early 2012. The "Man" who helped Alex overdose then left her high and dry. The same "Man" who went on to steal Evelyn's book from her: Hack writer JOSEPH KNOX.

MY QUESTIONS: How did he read those chapters and not own up to Evelyn? Does he know more about Alex's death? Does he know more about Zoe??? PLEASE SHARE THIS GUYS.

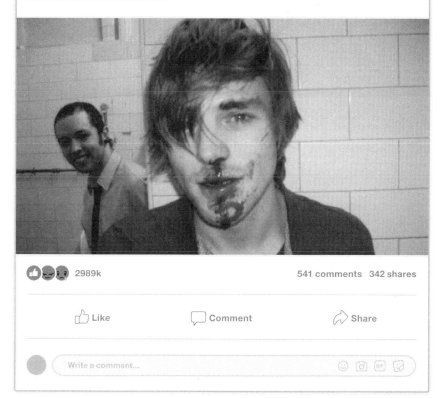

EDITOR'S NOTE

I am, in fact, very pleased for this opportunity to clarify my role in the events of *True Crime Story*. As I stated in my introduction, in 2011, I was twenty-five years old, and living in Manchester myself. In a city with a population approaching three million, I thought the chances that I had interacted with the participants in this book were vanishingly small. As a result, I failed to fully interrogate my own personal life, and I failed to fully guarantee my own objectivity. However, my failure to mention a relationship with Alex Wilson was never an attempt to deceive Evelyn or her readers, nor is it suggestive of any deeper involvement in the case on my part, or any manipulation of the facts.

It was simply a failure.

As I read Evelyn's chapters I did not recognize myself as the man described by Mr Limmond and Mr Mahmood as a 'user', although I do not dispute all elements of their recollection. I did not recognize Alex Wilson as the young woman – *Lexy* – who I saw a handful of times across late 2011 and early 2012. And I did not recognize the description of events which took place at the Great Central pub in Fallowfield, where, to the best of my recollection, I was punched rather than headbutted.

Neither Alex nor myself ever thought of our relationship in terms of boyfriend or girlfriend and, to my mind, we only ever met on four or five occasions – usually when one or both of us had been drinking. I don't recall being introduced to any of her friends or flat-mates, and I only visited her in the tower at Owens Park once. Perhaps most indicative of how casual our acquaintance was, she *never* spoke to me about Zoe Nolan or the events surrounding her disappearance.

After being assaulted and told in no uncertain terms to stay away from the girl I'd been seeing, I did just that. I never heard from or interacted with her again, and I only discovered that she had taken her own life when Mr Mahmood's Facebook post was brought to my attention some eight years after the fact. Although the inquest into Alex's death ruled it a suicide, and although I dispute the assertions from Liu, Jai and Sam that I supplied drugs to Alex, it's impossible for me not to feel at least partly responsible. I could have been better, and I should have been better.

As to Mr Mahmood's wider accusation that I in some way 'stole' Evelyn's work, this could not be further from the truth. Although it had previously been a private arrangement, all advances and royalty payments for *True Crime Story* have been split equally between myself and the Mitchell family. Further, following a period of reflection, I have decided to donate my share of all future earnings to the Nolan Foundation.

Although I know this episode will taint my involvement in the project for some, and that many readers may even be tempted to read the rest of the book differently as a result of this intervention, I would urge them not to do so. This statement describes my full involvement in the case. A brief affair with a troubled young woman, a much-deserved broken nose, and a failure of memory that has been deeply painful for both me and my family.

I was a friend of Alex Wilson's, I was a supporter of Evelyn Mitchell's, and I urge readers not to minimize the stories of two young women by searching for my shadow at the margins of this book. I can assure you that it is simply not there.

Jtmax, 2020

--18--

'Scream Mask'

Following Alex's funeral, interviews and pre-production for the reconstruction of Zoe's disappearance resume, taking place across mid- to late January 2012. A sudden break in the case arrives from an unexpected source.

DOT SHELDON, *Cleaner:*

Well, I'd read about this missing girl and I knew her face and everything, but aside from thinking, *How awful*, I hadn't given it much thought. I usually cleaned at the College of Music, the Royal Northern on Oxford Road, for a firm called Rise N Shine. Only, two of the girls had gone down with stomach bugs and they needed a volunteer for some nights at the new police station, out at Central Park. This is three or four weeks after Christmas and I needed the hours, so I took them. On my second or third night there I was going round a *wreck* of a room – if you think students are bad, you should see coppers – trying not to touch anything important, just sweeping, brushing, wiping, emptying bins. There's two blokes staring at a picture they've got pinned up, clearly wondering who it is. So I stop, dustbin in one hand, cloth in the other. One of them says, 'Can we help you, Mrs Mop?' *[Laughs]* I went, 'I don't know about that, but I think I can help you, PC Plod.'

SARAH MANNING:

Mrs Sheldon immediately identified the man in the picture. Professor Michael Anderson, a senior lecturer from the Royal Northern College of Music. She saw him almost every day while she was cleaning there.

KIMBERLY NOLAN:

Everything moved so fast. One minute, Dad was telling me about this idea of a reconstruction, the next we're sitting in a café with a woman from the BBC. The first few weeks of that year were like watching someone else's life on fast forward. I don't even remember Alex's funeral, I just know Mum put me in a car, drove me there, stood next to me then drove us back. It was insane, it was too much, and all the time Dad's in my ear, saying, 'I need you to be Zoe.'

On this day, the producer was taking us through the results of their interviews. We were on to Fintan, which was uncomfortable for me because he'd really zoned in on my drinking from the night of the party. He knew I'd have the transcript read back to me, that my parents would, and he did it anyway.

FINTAN MURPHY:

Ah, shite. So someone from that stupid party had said in their statement that they thought Kim was so wasted she must be doing drugs, just like Alex, Jai and Zoe were. I'd been with Sally when she saw that story in the press about Kim and Jai paying for drugs on Oxford

Road. She fell down, collapsed, I thought it almost killed her, so in my statement I just went to great pains to say Kim was drinking *and that's all*. I don't think it occurred to me how it might come across to her in isolation. It sincerely was not said to hurt her.

KIMBERLY NOLAN:

I was glad of the interruption when Sarah got a phone call and we all took a break. She went out for a minute then came back to tell us there'd been a development, that they'd identified the man in the picture. When she gave us the name I broke out in goose bumps.

ROBERT NOLAN:

Michael Anderson was head of the panel that failed Zoe in her Royal Northern College of Music audition, despite her being more than qualified to be there. And now we find out this picture she'd hidden was of him. I hit the fucking roof.

SARAH MANNING:

Anderson's face was about to start going out to the world as part of a press appeal. We had to share his identification with the family immediately so they wouldn't find out about it from someone else, but of course we were concerned about Robert's press relations.

KIMBERLY NOLAN:

Dad was just shouting, 'Is he under arrest?' Grabbing his keys and putting his jacket on, trying to get out the door like he could go and get him himself.

281

SARAH MANNING:

I was trying to explain that we didn't know what this information meant. It was still just a glossy picture cut out from a magazine. One found inside a tin that we suspect someone else might have tampered with. It was hardly a smoking gun.

KIMBERLY NOLAN:

In all the excitement, them shouting then trying to calm each other down, I just got up and left. We'd been talking to the producer in a coffee shop in Fallowfield and I started walking, then running back to Owens Park, because I'd finally remembered something. I went straight to the tower, up in the lift and down the hall. I unlocked the door to 15C, just sort of shaking and out of breath, double-locked it behind me and went into Zoe's room. Here's all this stuff the police had been through, all this stuff *we'd* been through, over and over again, and there in all her music books I found the prospectus for the Royal Northern College of Music. I remembered it because she'd left it lying open in our room for weeks when she was applying there. I turned to the page where I knew I'd seen this man's picture and found it had been ripped out, someone had taken it.

So . . .

I realized I was holding something really important, something vital, because whoever put that picture up on the roof *had* to have taken it from here. I was thinking of DNA, fingerprints, holding it by the edges, when I heard this rumbling sound from somewhere else in the flat, like someone banging, shouting, trapped inside the walls. I went out into the hall as fast as I could but heard this thud from somewhere behind me, then this thing like a scream. I was at the door with my hand on it when I had to stop and turn around, because I could hear someone breathing hard, like, struggling for air in the hallway behind me.

There was a man standing there, I think it was a man. He was wearing Andrew's Halloween costume, the *Scream* mask and black cloak, watching me, breathing like he'd just run up fifteen flights of stairs. He held out his hand but I put the prospectus behind my back, which was pressed against our front door. There was this energy in the air, like this ambient hate coming off him in waves, and I could tell that whoever it was knew me. You can't look at someone like that unless you know them. Whether he was the one I'd seen buzzing our door that night, the shadow, or someone else, I didn't know. But he took one step forward and punched me in the stomach so hard I fell down and threw up. He ripped the prospectus out of my hands then stepped over me, struggled with the door and left.

PROFESSOR MICHAEL ANDERSON:

My recollection of events is that I was only too happy to cooperate, to help the police in any way I could. Just as I'm only too happy to set the record straight with you today. I had absolutely nothing to hide and, in my mind at least, no connection whatsoever to this unfortunate young woman.

SARAH MANNING:

Michael Anderson lawyered up immediately, refused to answer anything but the most basic questions and threw up every road-block he could think of. 'Cooperative' is not the word. In that first interview he didn't make a single statement that wasn't delivered through his legal representative.

PROFESSOR MICHAEL ANDERSON:

I *believe* I was leading a workshop at the time, probably taking one or two students through the very basics of whatever their elective path was, be it composition or improvisation or so forth, when the police arrived. We moved into my office to talk more comfortably and they asked if the name Zoe Nolan meant anything to me. I had to confess that it didn't, so they showed me her picture. I took my time looking at it because so many young women passed through those doors each year, but she didn't seem familiar. I asked what it was all about and they told me that she was missing. I said I was sorry to hear it.

SARAH MANNING:

What struck the team as unusual was that, of course a lot of young women passed through Michael Anderson's offices, it made sense that he wouldn't remember one who hadn't progressed past the interview stage. But we already knew for a fact that wasn't where his relationship with the Nolan family ended.

ROBERT NOLAN:

I'd found his office number listed online after the Royal Northern rejected Zoe. This must have been about six months before she went missing. I called him the same day and asked respectfully, in that first instance at least, if there was anything we could do. If Zoe could prepare three more songs for another performance, or if he might take a second look at her scores. We spoke for five or ten minutes and I made him take me through the whole list, pull up the file, every reason he didn't think she was good enough, we discussed her in detail.

He said I should leave it with him.

SALLY NOLAN:

To Rob's way of thinking, he'd had so many doors closed on him because of his background, he didn't want to see the same happen to Zoe. It twisted him up in knots because he thought his accent or his lack of theory or a wrong word here and there had hurt her chances. So he called Anderson and tried to fix it. I was in the room with him for every one of those phone calls and they all got heated. We're talking five or six conversations over a couple of weeks, the last of them turning into a shouting match. Rob had called him at home, at night, and Anderson said it was getting too much, he'd failed Zoe and that was that. He said the next time Rob called he'd find himself talking to the police.

Now, I can believe *Professor* Michael Anderson might lead a much more interesting life than us, that he has thousands of teenage girls batting their eyes at him all day, but who'd forget something like that?

PROFESSOR MICHAEL ANDERSON:

Well, naturally I remembered her during the period when Mr Nolan was harassing me on the subject of her audition, she was fresh in my mind. Rejecting anyone for anything, particularly self-expression, is an extremely painful thing for me. I recall it all acutely for a few days and then it gets filed away at the back of my mind just so I can stay sane, it has to. In Zoe's case, I suppose she got a few more weeks' headspace because of her father's behaviour, but I'm afraid that's it. After that, I had a few hundred more students showing up on the doorstep who became my main focus. And I'd like to take this opportunity to stress that there has never, not once, been *any* suggestion of impropriety on my part across a teaching career of more than twenty years.

SARAH MANNING:

If Anderson had claimed not to know anything about the circumstances of the case, that might have been one thing, but he said he didn't recognize Zoe, didn't recollect her name. At the time, admittedly, we were in the eye of the storm, but I don't think anyone on the team could quite believe he'd have missed all that media coverage. You've got to remember that Zoe's name and face had been all over the local news for weeks by this point.

PROFESSOR MICHAEL ANDERSON:

Yes, well, I'd suggest I was reading a rather different *calibre* of newspaper to the rest of those involved. The *FT* doesn't tend to lead with missing blondes. I myself find stories of that kind quite grisly, and I really was incredibly busy.

SARAH MANNING:

The computers, phones and email addresses that Anderson handed over for examination were all brand new as well. Tech support at the RNCM told officers that Anderson's desktop PC had been damaged in an accident, water in the circuitry, sometime during Christmas week – so, almost immediately after Zoe's disappearance – and disposed of the same day.

According to Anderson, this was around the same time that his personal email was hacked, too. He said he'd been forced to delete the account and set up a fresh one. He purchased a brand-new laptop, a brand-new phone. As I recall, he told officers his old model had been handed over to shop staff for recycling, but the Vodafone store on Market Street had no record of it. His old laptop was apparently thrown out altogether. No back-up.

PROFESSOR MICHAEL ANDERSON:
One never quite fathomed what the suggestion really was in the first place. That I failed to progress Zoe and she fell in love with me in the same instant? I was given to understand that a photograph of me was found somewhere in her possession, a picture from a freely available and mass-produced prospectus that everyone seems to agree she owned a copy of. So I really fail to see what more there is to it? If there'd been a picture of Beyoncé on her bedroom wall, would they have hauled her in as well?

KIMBERLY NOLAN:
When I got back to the coffee shop I could hardly speak. Sarah saw something was wrong with me. She met me at the door and it all just flooded out.

SARAH MANNING:
Kim was wide-eyed, shaking, out of breath. I was trying to sit her

down but the words started tumbling out. She told me she'd remembered where she'd seen that picture, Professor Michael Anderson, and even found the prospectus it had been torn from, only to discover an intruder in the building who'd launched this terrifying physical assault. I called it in immediately. I asked if Kim would be okay there with her dad, then headed over to the tower myself to secure the scene. As I saw it, the fact she'd been attacked for the prospectus suggested that the culprit might not have been so careful with fingerprints there as they had on the roof.

KIMBERLY NOLAN:

We were double-locking the door, in and out, without fail. We were scared, it was all we could think of. So yes, I was sure. I double-locked that door when I went out to meet my dad and I double-locked it behind me when I went back for the prospectus. I knew the man hadn't followed me. He hadn't picked the lock or kicked the door down. He was already inside the fucking flat when I got there. He had to have been.

SARAH MANNING:

Kim insisted the door had been locked, that her attacker had already been inside. She'd heard a thud from one of the empty rooms, and when myself and two responding officers accessed the premises we saw definite signs of a disturbance. The wardrobe was open – the girls had been using the room for storage – and clothes were scattered everywhere. Then we saw the service hatch inside leading on to wiring and pipework. The vent covering the hatch was hanging off the wall. It seemed obvious to us that someone had used it to gain access to the room. That was a disturbing thought, given what we were dealing with. I was the smallest person there so I volunteered to climb inside and see where it went.

CARYS PARRY:

I'd been trying to speak to the Nolans about Kimberly's involvement in the reconstruction when she abruptly got up and ran out of the café. I asked Rob if we should take a break but he insisted we continue, which we did in fits and starts. After about half an hour Kimberly came back, clearly distraught about something, and spoke to DC Manning. Then she sat back down with us, white as a sheet. I asked if we should postpone our conversation but she didn't react. Rob insisted we carry on. I looked between them and said, 'Listen, I'm not sure Kimberly playing Zoe is the best idea.'

KIMBERLY NOLAN:

At which point my attention snapped back to where I was and what I was doing. I'd been told that me playing Zoe was one of the BBC's demands, that it was the only way they'd agree to the reconstruction. That was when I found out it was all bullshit. They thought it was as bad an idea as I did.

ROBERT NOLAN:

I never told Kim she *had* to do it. I did think she owed it to Zoe, to her twin sister, to try and find her, and I'm sure I said words to that effect, but I don't recall saying it was one of the BBC's conditions.

CARYS PARRY:

Mr Nolan said something like, 'If you couldn't give two fucks about her, then don't do it.' By this point we'd interviewed all the key players, created a production schedule, cast the parts. We were all but ready to shoot. I've cancelled whole productions on the day of filming where I've thought it could do more damage than good, though. I'd much rather our time and money went down the drain than did permanent harm to someone suffering the after-effects of a traumatic event. So I suggested we just press pause on everything for a while.

KIMBERLY NOLAN:

Dad launched himself up and nearly turned over the table. Coffee cups and cutlery went everywhere, everyone was staring at us. He gave me this look like he might spit in my face and walked out. Then me and the producer, whose name I forget, just sat there in silence. I hadn't even been able to tell him about what had just happened, the prospectus and the man who'd hit me.

SARAH MANNING:

I'm small, five foot four, fifty-five kilograms, and even I found moving inside that space like a living panic attack. It was cramped, pitch black, unbelievably hot. A lot of pipes ran through it, some of them ice cold and some of them scalding to the touch. I had a torch but I was keeping it low, trying to watch where my feet were going. I was acutely aware of being on the fifteenth floor of an old tower block. For all I knew, I might step on a hole in the ground and fall right the way down. So I'd walked sideways, carefully, for a few metres when I saw light at eye level.

It was a hole in the wall looking right through into Zoe's room. I could see her door, her desk, her bed. Even the mirror in the wardrobe that she would have dressed in front of. That unsettled me, but turned out to be the least of it.

Roughly six feet further to the right I came to an opening, a kind of cupboard-sized space of breathing room, which felt like a relief to me for a second. Then I moved the torch around and saw pictures pasted to the walls. Photographs of Zoe standing on the roof of the tower, at the edge of it, looking like she might jump. They looked candid, as though they'd been taken without her knowing. Then my foot brushed against something and I realized there was a body at my feet. I saw a flash of blonde hair, dropped the torch and heard it break, then I started banging around, trying to get away. I couldn't see anything or tell which direction I was going in, so I just pushed through and burned my arms on the pipes until I came back to the vent again. They pulled me out head first because I screamed at them to get me. It was only when we were all lying in a heap on the floor that I saw the blood on my hands. I didn't know if it was mine or someone else's, I didn't know what the hell I'd just seen.

From: evelynidamitchell@gmail.com
Sent: 14/02/19 13:35
To: you

on Thu, Feb 14, 2019, Joseph Knox joeknoxxxx@gmail.com wrote:

Hey – of course I'm still talking to you, don't be silly. I've actually tried calling a couple of times to no answer.

I've just reached the discovery of the crawlspace behind the wall, which I find really disturbing. What disturbs me more is the harassment that you're going through, though. If I misspoke it's only out of concern.

To be clear, I think this story AND your presentation of it is brilliant. It's just that it seems to be getting so much bigger in scope than you originally intended. Just don't be afraid to ask for help if you need it. I know I've been busy with my own projects, but if you wanted, I could help? I could edit or even come on board for example? Just a thought.

Something that's leapt out at me with the mention of all these pipes is that Rob Nolan apparently worked as a PLUMBER at the time? I'm not pointing the finger but, given some of the things we know about him now, I just wonder if he'd be better OUT of your life?

And wtf is going on with Anderson? Why did he even agree to talk? Does he have any idea how he comes across on the page?

Jx

Hey, ▓▓▓▓▓ happy valentines day. ▓▓▓▓▓▓▓▓▓▓▓▓▓▓▓▓▓▓▓▓▓▓▓▓▓▓

Thank you for your concern . . .

Can I ask what you mean by 'come on board'? Like, as a co-writer? I'm sure that comes from a good place, but don't you think it might undermine what I'm trying to do? Apologies if I'm getting the wrong end of the stick here.

I had NOT considered Rob's work as a plumber in the context of the piping. I'll look into it. You're thinking he could have worked inside the building at some stage???

Like I said, the tower was fully finished in '66 but only went up to 15 floors. Work started in '74 to ADD four floors on top of that BUT because it hadn't been part of the original plan, and because they didn't pay the original architect to come back, there were some 'quirks' of the construction. I haven't been able to speak to anyone who worked on it directly – best-case scenario they'd be in their 60s or 70s now – but I did speak to an architect who's been involved with adding floors to other tower blocks. He said it could throw up all kinds of strange spaces if the work was sloppy.

Basically, if the girls had been in ANY flat other than 15C, Lois wouldn't have been disturbed by those sounds (which may well have been someone moving through the crawlspace), and the intruder couldn't have spied on Zoe or gained such easy access to her life. Talk about the wrong place at the wrong time.

And I know, Anderson's an eel. When I first approached him he was unbelievably patronising and flat out refused to talk. Said he was still raw from being 'doxxed' at the time (one of his students published his address on Facebook after it emerged he'd been questioned). So I got in touch with some of his colleagues, and from there his ex-wife, and SUDDENLY he was on the phone, very eager to meet and speak. 'Don't want you getting the wrong side of the story, now, do I, darrrrrrling?'

I want EVERY side of the story, treacle.

Ex

PS – I'm surprised you're not more interested in Alex Wilson's suicide? Nothing to suggest it's connected but still a pretty big deal, right?

--19--

'Blood Red'

As a disturbing discovery is made in the fifteenth-floor apartment formerly shared by Kim, Zoe, Liu and Alex – Kim finds herself forced into a role that she has tried hard to avoid for her entire life.

LIU WAI:

Frankly, I thought that if I never saw Jai again it would be too soon. He'd got his horrible little druggy claws into *two* of my friends by this point. I was meeting Fintan for the first time just the two of us, and Jai was skulking around the lobby of the tower, looking absolutely shady as fuck. Then he was all over me.

JAI MAHMOOD:

Fuck that. That picture of the professor kept me up at night, man. Zoe must of been gone for about two months by that point, but Alex's death properly shook me. I wanted to help, I didn't want to be too late again. So I was thinking about who might have planted that picture. Someone was helping or someone was fucking with our heads. Either way, I knew I should make it known. I was done talking to the police, so Kim seemed like the right person. I went to the tower and buzzed her flat – I tried, I just got no answer. So I buzzed a few more times until someone let me in.

FINTAN MURPHY:

It was a few weeks after the Christmas break. I was supposed to be meeting Liu at the tower and found her in this heated debate with Jai. The last time I'd seen him had been at the party, when he produced Zoe's underwear from his pockets and got beat up, so I was understandably apprehensive. I didn't go over at first because him and Liu were going at it.

LIU WAI:

I don't remember what we were talking about.

FINTAN MURPHY:

Jai looked like a haunted man to me, like he'd seen something terrible, or perhaps just taken something terrible. He was talking far too fast, jumbling his words and getting ahead of himself, saying the second halves of his sentences before the first, rattling on about Kimberly, her parents, some kind of danger.

I cut in and gently started explaining that he should speak to the police if he knew something, when the lift doors opened and DC Manning emerged alongside two other officers. They were all stark white and slick with sweat. Manning had an open wound on her arm, she was bleeding, she was angry. I'd never seen her looking angry before. It felt like something huge had happened.

SARAH MANNING:

Given that there'd been a reported intruder, given what we'd just found behind the wall of Zoe's room, I found it *interesting*, to say the least, that Jai Mahmood was hanging around the lobby of the tower.

Red-eyed, agitated, forever in the wrong place at the wrong time.

I asked what he was doing there and he started to back off. One of the constables, Roberts, was the one who'd questioned Mahmood in late September about Zoe's missing underwear. He'd found candid photos of Zoe in Jai's possession, and they sounded similar to the ones I'd just seen in the crawlspace. Jai made a break for it but crashed into the lobby doors instead. We arrested him on the spot.

KIMBERLY NOLAN:

I'd left the TV woman and worked my way back to the tower, feeling weird. I was staring daggers into every man I passed, wondering if any of them could be the one who'd just hit me. I knew it wasn't safe for me to go back there, I just had to know what they'd found. Then when I arrived they were dragging Jai out in handcuffs. He saw me and started resisting them, shouting and trying to get to me.

JAI MAHMOOD:

I just wanted to talk.

LIU WAI:

None of us knew where to look, but it seemed so obvious to me. The police had finally put together the fact that Jai was fixated on Zoe, and now that fixation had shifted down a gear on to the next best thing, Kim.

SARAH MANNING:

When DI James arrived on the scene and I explained the intrusion – Kim's assault then, latterly, what we'd found on fifteenth, he sent in Forensics. They managed to get two people inside the crawlspace to swab, dust and print everything they could see. In the end they had to remove a part of the wall to gain full access. I left the scene for medical attention, I had cuts and burns on my arms, but I checked in from A&E. That was where I was when I found out everything in that space had been wiped down. 'Forensically cleaned,' I was told. Mine was the only blood found. No loose hairs, no fibres, no fingerprints. It was immaculate in that sense, just like the rooftop, and I always assumed the same person was responsible. They recovered one or two further items of Zoe's from behind the wall – some more clothes, some more jewellery, a set of keys belonging to Lois Best. The photographs I'd seen were quickly verified as Jai Mahmood's work.

The object I'd mistaken for a body was actually a mannequin. It had been messed with. Dressed in Zoe's underwear, amongst other things.

KIMBERLY NOLAN:

I never saw it, I never wanted to.

SALLY NOLAN:

I'd rather not talk about that.

ROBERT NOLAN:

It felt like some vindication for me, personally. Proof positive that a sicko had fixated himself on Zoe, she hadn't just run off.

ANDREW FLOWERS:

The brown-eyed girl? I only know about it because the police came asking if I'd kept any of Zoe's used 'feminine hygiene products'. I probably blinked at them eleven or twelve times in a row then said, 'That's an unusual question, may I ask why?' Then they showed me a photograph of this *thing* they'd found. It was like an old shop-window mannequin, maybe roughly Zoe's size and build, wearing a blonde wig and some of her underwear. Whoever put it there had apparently stolen two of her used tampons. They'd cut off the tips and attached them to the face as eyes. I guess they'd originally have been blood red, but by the time I saw them they were this terrible stale-brown colour.

SARAH MANNING:

The mannequin was grotesque, but no more so than what that space told us. That someone had been watching Zoe closely for a long time, and they'd been able to come and go from that apartment as they liked. There was a maintenance hatch on the stairwell that gave access, but it could only be opened with specialized tools. You'd have to know it was there and you'd have to know exactly what you were doing. It was awkwardly placed, an alcove, but you could just about access it without being seen from the lifts.

The strange thing was that it could only really get you behind the walls of 15C, suggesting to me that the intruder knew about the access panel *before* the girls moved in. But then, the theft of Zoe's personal items, especially the soiled feminine hygiene products, spoke to someone who was sexually obsessed with *her* specifically. We couldn't work out which order it went in. Did the intruder lie in wait behind those walls for just anyone? Or did he notice Zoe first and happen upon the panel afterwards? Wasn't that too much of a coincidence?

FINTAN MURPHY:

Liu and I started meeting most days after that. Awful as it sounds, we were energized by Alex's death, and Liu had this brainwave, one that turned out to be quite brilliant, actually. We'd been briefed, along with the family, about this mystery man, this picture found amongst Zoe's things. Of course, by this point the man had been identified as Professor Michael Anderson, but it seemed as though that had all ended in disappointment. Where we'd thought the police were charging off to arrest him, they'd simply asked if he knew Zoe and he'd simply said no. Speaking for myself, I remember Zoe and I walking, that first day we met, when she'd stopped cold at the sight of the Royal Northern. At the time I'd put it down to her being upset about not studying there, but I'd come to the conclusion that it had been more serious than that. She'd barely been able to speak, she'd been traumatized by something, and that place represented it to her. I was convinced that she was traumatized by Michael Anderson himself.

At the time I think we all felt the same way – useless, sick with worry and uncertainty – so when Liu suggested we try to find some kind of link between Zoe and Anderson, to *prove* that he might have known her outside of that audition, I leapt at the chance to help. What with my time spent assisting Zoe's parents and my attempts to actually study, that meant pretty much no sleep for a few weeks. As you may have noticed, I'm not so good at putting my own life first. What had been a promising relationship with my flatmate Connor unfortunately started to fall even further by the wayside.

LIU WAI:

I could see how run down Fintan was, I felt guilty because I *knew* he was incapable of saying no, but I couldn't think of who else to ask. Certainly not Kim, Andrew or Jai. And it was too big a job to do on my own. So much of Zoe's life was on Facebook. Nowadays, that kind of stuff would probably be a big lead for the police, but outside of a cursory glance, I wasn't sure they'd really taken that much interest in Zoe's life online? From what we could see, Michael Anderson didn't have an account, at least not under his own name, but there were *literally* thousands of pictures on Zoe's page that we could work our way through.

FINTAN MURPHY:

Everything. Every last thing. Everything Zoe had uploaded and everything that she'd been tagged in, just anything to find some link. It took us for ever.

LIU WAI:

If Zoe was tagged even once in an album, we went through every single picture, even ones that had nothing to do with her. It took us days and days because when we found albums that we couldn't access, usually because they belonged to other users who'd made them private, we'd message the people who'd uploaded them, explaining our situation, asking for their help. It all took time.

FINTAN MURPHY:
Alongside that work we were also going through Zoe's wall uploads as well, making note of any strange comments left by people we didn't know or any unusual posts made by Zoe herself. Anything mentioning secrets or men of course, but there was precious little like that. Zoe would mainly post links to music videos or quotes of song lyrics. The only thing that really stuck out to us in that regard was when we saw she'd posted one particular song several times. We collated each instance we could find and saw that it was always uploaded at the same time, midnight, on the first day of every month. It surprised us to see that she'd been doing this for years, twenty-something posts, with only one brief gap, the first few months following her RNCM audition.

We started scrolling back, looking for the original post, and the earliest we found was from August 2009, roughly two years before she went missing. It was a song by a Scottish band neither of us had heard of called Mogwai, not really Zoe's thing at all, and it was called 'R U Still in 2 It?' This kind of sad, dirty, strangely romantic love song. I can't go a day without thinking about it now.

LIU WAI:
It gave us a window to focus on. Pictures, albums, uploads from 2009. We wanted to find whatever had sparked off this weird

tradition. Zoe would have been fifteen or sixteen that year and had started doing a lot more music-related activities outside of school, judging from her Facebook activity. Travelling with busloads of kids to perform concerts in Birmingham or something, then all coming back again the same night. Seemingly everyone on those trips would take pictures and upload their own albums to Facebook, so you'd have the same night from twenty different angles. It was useful for us but, you know, *endless.*

FINTAN MURPHY:

It was literally the end of the day, a minute or two to midnight, when we found it. We'd been listening to a playlist that Liu and I had compiled of Zoe's favourite songs, which was about six or seven hours of music. It had run out and stopped playing ages before, which gives you some idea how long we'd been sitting there. This was probably our fifth or sixth day straight. I was standing up, stretching, getting ready to leave, when Liu started hitting my arm, pinching me. She couldn't even speak.

LIU WAI:

Because we got the fucker. Zoe and Michael Anderson in 2009. On stage. Together. Two years before her audition at the Royal Northern College of Music. Some choral performance in Manchester. There are, like, twenty-five people on stage and it's a rehearsal picture, but there they are. Not standing together, not looking at each other, but in the same place at the same time. It was soon afterwards that Zoe started posting the 'R U Still in 2 It?' song on her page. I thought, *Boom, scumbag.*

303

on Sun, Feb 17, 2019, Joseph Knox joeknoxxxx@gmail.com wrote:

Evening, E. Some thoughts on Ch.19:

1/ 'R U Still in 2 It?' as in, 'Are you still into it?' As in, the phone calls Zoe was getting as a kid? Kim said those calls stopped abruptly AFTER Zoe's failed audition. Is it possible she met Anderson on the road at 15, was coerced into an affair with him, then split when he knocked her back from the RNCM audition?

2/ This fucked-up menstrual thing with the mannequin. Sarah says it made her think of sexual obsession, but couldn't it equally be linked to fertility? Does Anderson have kids? Any history of difficulty conceiving? I know that's mad but so's everything.

3/ If what Sarah's saying about Zoe's living space is true, i.e. that it was uniquely suited to the kind of surveillance she was under, then it makes me wonder. Sarah said they couldn't work out if Zoe's stalker ever really targeted her, or if they just already knew about the crawlspace and waited to see who moved in. Did Anderson ever work or study at Manchester University? Could he have found out about the space that way?

My comment about coming on board with the writing was just a thought, but there are things you can't just power through.

I love the way you're handling it, but I guess it's still a story without an ending. A more experienced hand might be able to help you shape some kind of conclusion from all this material.

My worry is that unless you can say what happened to Zoe, you might not be able to find an ending or a publisher. I'm not saying my name opens doors exactly, but it might lean on them a bit . . .

███████████████████████████████████████

Jx

Hey – Some of these questions are answered in the next couple of chapters so I'll leave you hanging until you get to them, some we might need to come back to. I can confirm that Anderson has never studied or worked at Manchester Uni, though.

In terms of the Facebook discovery that Zoe and Anderson might have met in 2009, Sarah said it didn't make much of an impression on the case (which I found shocking). The team didn't buy that Zoe posting the Mogwai song was some secret message to Anderson, so as far as they were concerned, the photograph existed in a vacuum. It was just circumstantial evidence that said nothing for sure. Definitely makes my stomach turn, though.

I've finally got hold of the maintenance firm who go in and rebuild Owens Park/the tower every year after another few thousand students have been through and wrecked it. Fairfield Property Management. They confirmed from memory (and some photographs) that Rob Nolan has never done any work for them in any capacity, so you swung and missed there, champ. The owner, sadly, doesn't have a full list of everyone who worked maintenance at Owens Park in the 2011 summer before the Nolans arrived. I've asked if there's any way he can get one.

Unbelievably, he says Greater Manchester Police NEVER spoke to him at the time.

Also, he told me that he personally remembers passing through that crawlspace in the summer before the girls arrived. According to him, it was spotless. ALSO ALSO, after some uming and ahing he managed to produce an alibi for the night Zoe went missing. It turned out his firm had their Christmas party on the 17th, so almost all of them were with each other, out of town in Stretford. I've called around and that checks out.

Argh, but Zoe's stalker HAD to have found out about the hatch somehow. In my mind, we're either talking about a student, someone who worked for the university or some third party who visited, like a maintenance man. I don't see who else it could be?

And as to ending MY book, there's no need for you to be such a fucking Anderson about it, is there? Why don't you leave that problem to me?

E

--20--

'Playing Zoe'

KIMBERLY NOLAN:

After Jai was arrested and they removed part of the wall in our flat, I got moved down the hall, to an empty room with another group of girls. I spent that night on my own. And it didn't escape me, it never did, that this was what I'd been asking for all those years, to be rid of Zoe. I think I found myself wondering if I'd wanted it so much I might have made all this happen, like, if I'd forced it into existence somehow? I don't believe in that stuff, cosmic ordering or whatever, but I thought it couldn't hurt to try doing the opposite.

To really *want* her back and do anything it took . . .

So I thought about playing Zoe, in my life as much as the reconstruction, and I decided I'd do it. If the only way out of all this was to give myself away, then I'd do it. I thought about the night she went missing, when I went up on to the roof of the tower and leaned out over the edge looking for her. I'd backed off from it then, I'd pulled myself in and carried on, but I decided that next time something called out to me, something that felt like a sacrifice, I'd just give in to it and let go.

CARYS PARRY:

Kim called me quite late one night, not long after our scene at the café. I thought she'd either been crying or drinking, possibly both. She said she wanted to be a part of the reconstruction after all. She wanted to play Zoe. Honestly? I tried to talk her out of it, but she was adamant. I could hardly tell her she was wrong, even if I thought she was. We were due to film the following week but I'd already begun pre-production on an alternative story.

Bluntly, I didn't think it would happen.

I knew she was trying to do a brave thing, but, well. I'd seen enough of Mr Nolan by then, I knew he exerted his will through shame, guilt, persistent pressure. He wasn't above using the police, the press, even me, to make his family do just what he wanted them to. It had been a recurring theme across the interviews we'd conducted with Zoe's loved ones, his domineering brand of grief.

So I suggested Kim have an understudy. We'd had exploratory conversations with an actor who resembled Zoe closely enough. I said if Kim really wanted to do it, then of course she could, but my one condition would be that Chloe was onsite, ready to step in and replace her if it was all too much.

SARAH MANNING:

Jai Mahmood was held for a couple of days before we had to release him. He freely admitted to taking the pictures of Zoe we'd found inside the crawlspace, but claimed that his room had been burgled, that those pictures had, conveniently, been stolen from him. He couldn't prove that, of course. He hadn't reported it to campus security or to the police, and he said he hadn't even told anyone about the theft. It was made clear to him, you know, 'You took these pictures and self-developed them, Jai. You're telling us now that they were stolen, but with no one to back that up we have to assume that you were the one behind that wall.'

The circumstantial evidence against him was ridiculous. The pictures, the rooftop liaisons, the stolen underwear. His unwillingness to allow a police search of his own room, when even Andrew Flowers had consented to one. That's before we even talk about the drugs. No one felt comfortable about letting him go.

JAI MAHMOOD:

And all this is being listed off at me like my fucking obituary. I'm sitting in the hot seat here because I tried to help. Then my pictures, my own photography, starts getting thrown in my face. They said pictures of mine had been found inside this crawlspace behind Zoe's room. I was like, 'Bro, I don't even know what a fucking crawlspace is.' They showed me the snap and it was just one picture reprinted dozens of times. Then I remembered that one of the constables who came to mine and Andrew's had grabbed a photo out of my hand when he left. I knew Andrew had seen it happen.

ANDREW FLOWERS:

Oh, I was just trying to keep my nose clean by this point. I didn't want anything to do with Zoe or her family. I certainly didn't want anything to do with fucking Fintan or Liu Wai and, sadly, I didn't want anything to do with Jai, either.

Because, most of all, I didn't want anything further to do with the police or the press. They'd been doing me from both ends for weeks by this point – odd stories, endless shit, occasional working-class heroes out on the street, all of these fucking Kevs and Bevs banging into my shoulder, shouting at me as I walked by.

So when Lipson, my father's lawyer, turned up at my door I thought it was the turning of the tide, some cessation of hostilities with my own family at least. Lipson was essentially approaching me on the police's behalf. He'd spoken to them and worked out a deal where I'd sign a statement disputing Jai's version of events re: a photograph the police had taken from him. He explained that I needed the points, with my father as much as the police, and with the press perhaps more than anyone. I just had to fuck over my friend to earn them. So I let him hold my hand through it, essentially saying, 'Jai was lying, the officer never took that picture from him.' It's just that when it came to the crunch I couldn't sign it. I let Jai down the night Zoe went missing and it ate at me, I couldn't do it again. So I said I was sorry and ripped up the statement, and probably my life and future along with it.

SARAH MANNING:

It turned out that a police officer had broken the chain of evidence by removing a similar picture from Jai's possession during the investigation into Zoe's missing underwear. We had to let Jai go because we could no longer say with certainty that he'd placed the picture in the crawlspace. Incidentally, that officer *did* find the picture he'd taken some weeks later, while cleaning out his desk. It's slightly different from the reprints we found in the crawlspace, so its presence in the outside world never truly exonerated Jai.

My mind kept going back to that hole in the wall, this obsessive life we'd uncovered as a result. I'd been inside that space. I knew what it took to move through it. We were looking for someone who was prepared to edge their way through total darkness just to get a *glimpse* of Zoe. Of course we wondered who that could be. The problem was that our list of suspects were all friends and family, all people already in her life. Why would any of them be so desperate to see her? They could just knock on her door at any time. I thought it had to be someone *outside* of her social circle, that was the only way that clandestine kind of close observation made sense.

PROFESSOR MICHAEL ANDERSON:

I had questions being put to me about times and dates I couldn't possibly account for – mine is simply not that kind of job – and about enormous sums of money, and, well, it was laughable. Teaching – I should say lecturing – doesn't leave a lot left over to siphon away into the bank accounts of young women. Would that it did.

SARAH MANNING:

At the time it was impossible to definitively tie Anderson to the cash, and of course he was less than forthcoming about it himself. His salary was somewhere between £80,000 and £95,000 a year. Good money if you can get it, but clearly not enough to be moving sums like the seventy-seven grand found in Zoe's account. If it came from him, it certainly wasn't from his salary.

ALICE ELLIS *(formerly Alice Anderson)*:

I'll be very interested to hear what Michael's said, but you *bet* I can clear some things up. All that cash is simplest. Michael inherited a pile of money from his grandfather in 2009, and another fat wodge from his mother in 2010. His grandfather was Sir Christopher Michael Anderson, a property magnate, richer than God. It was never explained to me exactly what kind of sums we were talking about, which I assume made them substantial. We had no mortgage on either of the houses, though, no monthly budget, put it that way. Oh, and I met Michael when I was one of his students at the Royal Northern College of Music.

Just by the by.

There was a roughly twenty-year age gap between us, so when it came to our finances I was more like his child than his partner. And by 2011 we weren't talking finances at all because I'd asked Michael for a divorce. Why? Why not? I could always smell women on him, by which I mean *girls*. I could always see lies in his stupid red face. I could always feel my life passing me by. When I suggested we separate he became cold, distant, holding me at arm's length while he got his affairs in order, so to speak. I suspected at the time that he was moving his family money around so he wouldn't have to cut it in half when we got divorced. The 77,000 could easily have come from that.

PROFESSOR MICHAEL ANDERSON:

Alice? Well, as with all things Alice, the twenty-year age gap is a *slight* exaggeration in her favour. I think she's perhaps seventeen years my junior, but let's not allow the facts to get in the way of a good soundbite. And our relationship, such as it was, didn't begin until long after she'd been a student of mine. Outside of Louisa, our daughter, we don't have any kind of relationship today. That's probably why Alice has an axe to grind now. At the time, though, I'd agree with her own self-assessment. She was a very sad person. When it comes to motherhood, some women rise to the challenge and some simply shrink away from it. Alice, I'm sad to say, was the latter. She acted like she had post-partum depression *before* she got pregnant, so you can imagine what she was like after. I just couldn't believe how disappointed she seemed to have this tiny miracle, Louisa, in our lives all of a sudden. That's why I initiated the divorce.

ALICE ELLIS:

A consummate dick right down to the end, I just wish I could say he was a big one. I wasn't *ever* sad or disappointed with Louisa, she was my only reason to keep on living, in the face of everything else. Michael would literally sit there and say black was white to your face. So, nights he told me he'd be home late from college he might not come home at all. 'I told you.' No you fucking didn't, darling. When I was raising Louisa I'd never been more on my own, so I *noticed* when he came in seven or eight hours late. After we separated I learned that he'd isolated me from my family and my friends by design. He hung up on them when they called me, he deleted emails, he didn't pass on messages. He told my mother, who was struggling with a weight problem at the time, that she disgusted me. We didn't speak for seven months. I know he'd deny all of this if it was ever put to him, but that's Michael. The ultimate vocal coach, the ultimate performer. A master of mimicking voices and styles, without any real style of his own.

A born fucking liar.

And at the same time, what could I say? I would have been homeless without him. When I finally did leave for good, somewhere in early 2012, I had to go in the night when he was passed out, black-out drunk. As far as Zoe Nolan goes? He was seeing someone, he was moving money around and his days were largely wide open to do whatever he liked with, I can tell you that from when we first got together. Oh, and that song, 'R U Still in 2 It?', that Zoe apparently kept putting on her Facebook page? That's fairly close to his heart, too. I know because it was *our* song, I played it for him the first day we met. There's no doubt in my mind that they were having an affair.

JAI MAHMOOD:

They expelled me the day before the reconstruction started filming, not that I'd been invited to the shoot or anything. I had to be out of Owens Park by the end of that week. I'd made it four months into higher education. None of the others were speaking to me by this point, not my family either, so I didn't have anyone to tell. My last night on campus I knew I should stay away. Something just took me there, man. It was dusk, the magic hour, this mix of lit windows, some darkness and some colour still in the sky. For the first time in months I remember wishing I had a camera. I went through the lobby of the tower no problem, straight up the stairs. I wasn't interested in trying to help or talk to Kim any more, fuck all that. I knew everything that had come before was finished and whatever happened to me next would be brand new. Maybe better, maybe worse, but definitely different.

The door to the roof had police tape on it, but that had been ripped off and broken, and clearly people were still going in and out. Then I opened it and wondered for a second if I was seeing things, like, hallucinating. Because there was Zoe Nolan, standing right at the edge, right where I'd seen her before, dangling her leg out over nothing, weeks and weeks after she'd gone missing. And no, I wasn't high, I wasn't dreaming. I knew I wasn't because something felt different about it, like, totally wrong. I crossed the roof quiet as I could, not wanting to scare her. When I got within reach I grabbed her arms, proper tight. She struggled but I just pulled back and we both landed on the rooftop together.

I stared at her, like, 'Everyone's looking for you, where the fuck have you been?' She stared back like nothing had happened, said she'd lost track of time. Then she saw something in how I was looking at her and closed her eyes. Started to laugh. She said, 'I'm Kim,' and then I saw it. I never normally mixed them up, but she was wearing the clothes, the make-up and the wig they'd got in for the reconstruction. It was scary in a way, man, nearly flawless, except for one thing . . .

When I found Zoe on the roof that first time after all the fire alarms, she was out on the ledge like a dreamer. She was watching everything and absorbing it, in love with life. Kim could look like her sometimes, and especially that night, but the difference was she looked like she might actually jump. I stopped laughing when that occurred to me, when I asked myself why she'd been standing on the roof ledge on her own at night. Kim just carried on cracking up, even when she saw how scared I'd been and how serious I was. My heart was going like a cat in a bag. You know how sometimes your body gets the picture faster than your brain does? It was like that, man. My body sensed danger, my brain couldn't work it out. I remember looking down at my hands and they were shining under the moonlight, gleaming with sweat. Kim just kept on laughing.

From: evelynidamitchell@gmail.com

Sent: 25/02/19 18:19

To: you

on Sun, Feb 24, 2019, Joseph Knox joeknoxxxx@gmail.com wrote:

Hey – well, message received and understood – this is your baby.

I've almost reached the end of part two. Now feels like the time to say: I'm really troubled by the whole twin thing. This might sound stupid – but is there any chance at all that Kim and Zoe switched places? i.e. – is the girl we now know as Kim ACTUALLY Zoe? For example, could Zoe have swapped places with Kim on the night that she supposedly disappeared (or perhaps even before that, for unknown reasons)?

Another thing: Rob Nolan wanted to BE someone and his best bet was with Zoe. Once the RNCM thing failed, once even Zoe saw her ticket to fame as null and void, it's *interesting* that her disappearance opened the door to a different kind of celebrity for her dad . . .

Say Rob and Zoe were in it together: He could get rid of Kim, the daughter he 'had no time for' and still have Zoe in his life (but now passing as Kim). They'd both get the limelight. Possible?

Jx

Hey JK – thanks for understanding.

No – Put simply, this is a stupid thing to think. Twins aren't just two interchangeable versions of the same person. People would have noticed and known, especially given the amount of scrutiny at the time. Full disclosure though: ***cough***, *I-thought-exactly-the-same-thing*. I edged towards asking a few people in interviews, but they openly laughed at me. The silver bullet to the twin-swap theory is that twins (apparently) do NOT have matching fingerprints. Kim was printed on the night Zoe went missing. Sarah Manning said the police absolutely confirmed it was her and ruled out this theory at the time, using multiple items that only Kim or Zoe would have touched and comparing the two.

It doesn't discount Rob Nolan straight up making Zoe disappear for the fame, though. And of course, this isn't to say Kim never pretended to be Zoe, which is something you must be just getting to if you're at the end of part two. You're basically at the end of the main investigation. Shit's about to get weird, Knoxy.

Ex

--21--

'Dead End'

With the reconstruction looming and the investigation effectively stalled, Kim takes matters into her own hands with a reckless attempt to find out the truth.

CARYS PARRY:

Well, my day didn't start with that panicked phone call, but only because I'd been up since 4 a.m. I wouldn't necessarily be on set for every shoot, but given that this story had originated with me and I'd made various assurances to the Nolan family, it had become my baby. So I was in the van and on my way to Fallowfield when Rob Nolan called saying that no one could find Kim.

ROBERT NOLAN:

Sal and me had spent the night before in Manchester. Plan was that Kim would meet us in the lobby of the Travelodge, and we'd get breakfast, have a coffee. Course, she never turned up. We couldn't get her on the phone either.

SALLY NOLAN:

Well, I was worried so I called Liu Wai, but she hadn't seen her. She went to knock on the new flat Kim had been moved to, but she wasn't in her room. Her new flatmates hardly knew her, they weren't sure she'd even been back the night before.

CARYS PARRY:

I told Rob that the last thing I'd heard from Kim had been positive. She'd completed a wardrobe and make-up test the previous day and, according to everyone involved, she'd been fine, really looked the part. Rob said, 'What happens to the reconstruction if she doesn't turn up?'

CHLOE MATTHEWS, *Actor*:

I'd only recently graduated from the drama department of the University of Manchester. I was three years older than Zoe but we looked a lot like each other and our first names rhymed. When the story was at its height and she was all over the news I used to get quite a lot of sideways looks. The police even turned up at the coffee shop where I was working once, because someone thought I *was* Zoe.

Carys had already explained the situation when we first spoke about the role. That I was sort of there to be on hand in case Kim couldn't make it, which I totally understood. So I was going to be on set anyway, but Carys called that morning saying it was quite likely I'd need to step in and play the role.*

---

* All interviews with Chloe Matthews were conducted by Joseph Knox and added to Evelyn's text in 2019.

SALLY NOLAN:

As soon as they had the replacement, Rob was right as rain. I just stared at him until he saw me, until he noticed. I said, 'Don't you think we should cancel all this? Concern ourselves with finding our daughter?' He said, 'I am trying to find our daughter.' It turned into a flaming row at the taxi rank on Oxford Road.

ROBERT NOLAN:

My feeling, which turned out to be correct by the way, was that Kim had lost her nerve and let us down. I knew she wasn't in any kind of trouble. She's just someone who falls at the final hurdle. She's got a lot of good qualities, but she doesn't see things through. She always thought Zoe got too much attention and, at certain points, she'd try and take it back, usually in a childish way. I mean, getting herself arrested on the night Zoe went missing, watching a band the same week her sister's face was on the front page of every paper. She didn't have Zoe's gifts so she made these maddening bids for attention.

SARAH MANNING:

It had always been my contention that the reconstruction was too much for Kim, so I was incredibly concerned. My duties with the family prevented me from joining the search myself, but word went out immediately, all points.

CARYS PARRY:

I was sympathetic, but running a production like that doesn't leave much time to look over your shoulder. We were filming Jai's discovery of Zoe's stolen clothes, the revelation of a leaked intimate video,

Zoe's fight with her boyfriend and her walk up to the roof, as well as the fire-alarm evacuation of the tower. All that plus dozens of extras, *plus* Robert and Sally Nolan on set. A full day.

CHLOE MATTHEWS:

I thought the shoot went well. It's a strange kind of set to be on. To a lot of people it's just a job, but for others it's obviously incredibly painful. You have to stay mindful of that. The way they stage reconstructions is to have the events narrated in post, so you don't really have speaking lines. I met Mr Nolan, Zoe's dad, he came over to say how much I reminded him of Zoe, tears in his eyes and everything. I took it as a huge compliment at the time.

SALLY NOLAN:

Kim's phone was in her bedroom so there was no point calling it, but I wasn't about to stand around eating free sandwiches while she was still out there somewhere. I left and left Rob to it.

ROBERT NOLAN:

I was embarrassed. All these people are coming together to help find Zoe, and her own sister, her own mother, can't make the effort? I'm not saying it was easy for me, either. I just wasn't going to let it derail what could be a really positive day. Kim never did explain herself, we were all supposed to just forget about it.

KIMBERLY NOLAN:

Where was I that day? Where else would I have been? I went to Michael Anderson's house. I'd seen Jai up on the roof of the tower the night before, and I was wearing what they were putting me in for the reconstruction. There'd been a make-up test, and he thought for a second I was my sister. I could see he wanted to tell me something, but I interrupted him, I wanted to know what they'd been talking about, him and Zoe, all those times they'd met up there. So he sat on the ledge next to me and said Zoe had been scared of something.

JAI MAHMOOD:

Zoe was scared she was a failure, in music and in life, and that came up a lot when we'd talk, but her biggest fear as far as I could tell was that she was losing Kim. She saw Kim as this person she couldn't be, someone who never followed the herd and blazed her own trail, whatever anyone else said about it. She said Kim had this thing that she'd always lacked in life, this bravery to just be herself. Kim didn't say anything to that. It was like this blindingly obvious thing about their relationship had never occurred to her.

Then I remembered what I'd been trying to tell her before, how Anderson's picture hadn't been inside the tin when Zoe went missing. She asked me what it meant and I shrugged, like, 'Fuck knows,' then patted her on the arm and left. Like I say, that was my last night living there. I wanted to say goodbye, y'know, mark the occasion, but she had enough shit on her plate without mine as well.

KIMBERLY NOLAN:

I didn't know what to think. Did the picture mean someone was trying to help and point us in the right direction? Or did it mean Anderson was being framed? Maybe it meant nothing? I wasn't afraid of the reconstruction any more, I just didn't see what good it would do. I'd lost my sister, I'd lost Alex. None of the appeals so far had gotten through to anyone, so I decided to do something that might actually answer a question rather than raise new ones. Anderson's address got posted online, so I went there the next morning and knocked on the door.

I was still dressed as Zoe, and when he opened up I knew he knew me. Knew Zoe, I mean. He must have been about to leave for work because he was wearing a suit, holding a satchel. His mouth fell open, then he looked over my shoulder and pulled me inside. For a few seconds he just stared at me, holding me by both arms. I was afraid he'd see I wasn't her, so I kissed him, let his hands move on me. He kissed my neck and I pulled him into me as tight as he could go, just pushing up against him.

He said, 'Are you still into it?'

I looked back at him and said, 'Yes.' Then we broke apart and he led me upstairs to the bedroom. I remember following him, watching my hand in his like it was an out-of-body experience. I wasn't sure if Zoe knew this house or not and I didn't want to give anything away, so I kept my eyes low. Once we were on the bed everything was easier. He wasn't looking for reasons to stop or slow down and I kept on pushing because I didn't want him to stop or slow down, either. Between kisses he said he was relieved to see me, he asked me where I'd been. He said everyone was looking for me, so I whispered into his ear that he was the lucky one, he'd found me. I resisted everything he said, shushed him like it was all boring so he wouldn't work out who I was and why I was there. And I kept on kissing him because I was afraid of him looking into my eyes. His hands kept going to my neck, but I had to keep them moving because I didn't want him to touch my wig. I just whispered that he should be quiet, said I'd straighten it all out, I'd just needed some time to think. Anderson said they knew about the money, said they'd asked about him, about it. I put my fingers on his lips and said the money was fine. There was a second where we broke apart, where he just stared at me, starting to squint, so I nodded at the bathroom, told him to go in while I undressed.

As soon as he left the room, I got up, head spinning, and walked down the stairs, past all these pictures of him with his wife and kid, then right out the front door. I was sick in his geraniums, then realized I'd left the wig inside, upstairs on the bed. I thought that was all the explanation I really owed him and left.

I think I was in and out in less than five minutes, and I left feeling like I do now. Sure of some things, unsure of others. I'm sure there was something going on between him and Zoe, sure he was moving money round, like his wife said afterwards. I'm sure he was a scumbag. But at the same time, in my heart of hearts, I can't say I feel like he had anything to do with her disappearance. He wasn't surprised to see me at his door, he wasn't surprised to see Zoe alive. He didn't look at me like I was a mystery solved or someone who'd come back from the dead. He looked at me like his side-piece had come back to her rightful place after some kind of argument. Michael Anderson was the same thing to me as I'm sure he was to Zoe – a disappointment, a dead end.

PROFESSOR MICHAEL ANDERSON:

I'm speechless. [Laughs] I'm actually speechless. Needless to say, none of that actually happened. None of that *could* have happened because I didn't know Zoe Nolan. If a young woman resembling her had actually arrived at my front door, I'd have called the police. And where's my wife supposed to be in all this? Breastfeeding our baby in the spare room?

ALICE ELLIS:

I moved out in mid-January of that year. I'd say I was breastfeeding our baby somewhere around Cornwall, as Michael well knows. From what you've said, I'd be inclined to believe Kim. How else would she know about the pictures on the staircase? The en suite in our bedroom? Michael's fucking geraniums? As much of a cliché as he could be, though, I never saw him as a killer. He certainly wasn't violent. He did things that were easy, he screwed young girls who didn't know any better, then lost interest when it got complicated.

And I was with him the night Zoe Nolan went missing. Not for every second, and he came to bed a good hour after I did, but he couldn't possibly have gone to Owens Park and back in that time. Couldn't possibly have disposed of a body. I want the world to know precisely what kind of person he is. And that means I can't sit here and blame him for things I know he didn't do.

KIMBERLY NOLAN:

I knew I had to do something for Zoe, something meaningful, and I did. The reconstruction was just a performance, somewhere my dad could live out his dreams of being a man of action, show the world he was in charge when actually he was falling apart. After confronting Anderson and taking my Zoe wig off I felt a lot lighter. I left all those horrible voices from my head where they belonged, in a puddle of sick in some geraniums.

I thought the question of who'd planted Anderson's picture, if anyone even had, wasn't really mine to answer. It was just another mystery. For a second I thought about telling the police, eliminating him as a suspect or whatever, but then I thought, *Nah, let the fucker twist*. Mainly, I thought about what Jai had said. The way Zoe had been thinking about me all those years, not as a failure but as something good. So I decided I should go out and actually *earn* her respect, I should find the thing that Kimberly Nolan might want to do with her life and then do it. I dropped out that day, packed a bag and left Manchester for good.

CHLOE MATTHEWS:

One thing I never said at the time, even though I probably should have. Mr Nolan – he said to call him Rob – he came over and complimented me on looking so much like Zoe, like I said, and even played me a recording of her singing.

The way he put his arm around me, though . . .

It made me feel uncomfortable. I knew he was suffering so I didn't say anything then, but when he really started to grip me about the waist I think I laughed awkwardly and looked at him, like, *Please get the message.* He took it the wrong way, though, brushed the hair back from my face and kissed me full on the lips. And I don't mean in a fatherly way, although I was dressed up as his daughter. I mean his tongue pushed past my teeth. It was moving round inside my mouth before I could shake him off.

on Fri, Mar 01, 2019, Joseph Knox joeknoxxxx@gmail.com wrote:

Hey E – I've tried calling a few times – wagwan? I just finished part
two so I'm fully up to date. Kim confronting Anderson like that is
insane. Don't get any ideas. He's got some balls even talking to
you. Not to go back into it now, but whether she ruled him out or
not, please be careful around the guy. He sounds like slime.

Jx

Sorry, Joe, it's all been mad here and I've gone off the rails a bit.

I've been pulling all-nighters for months now. I'm broke and working
flat out, hanging on by the fucking rings around my eyes. So I was
really hoping that's why I've felt so rough lately. I decided to try and
take it easy for a week or so but I think I might actually feel worse. I
really don't want to think about getting sick again rn. I can't.

And yes, yes, I'll see a doctor. I would have gone already but
someone broke into my car last week and pissed all over the driver
seat. Just another day . . .

That plus the phone calls and personal ads have me convinced that someone doesn't want me to be doing this. So thank you for not getting into your reservations again. When I lash out it's only because I agree. All I have are reservations. I certainly don't have anyone red-handed, no dead body or smoking gun. I know the appeal for this story's limited without any kind of answer on Zoe's whereabouts or her potential attacker. Believe me, I heard that loud and clear from Annalise at Curtis Brown when she let me go as a client last week. (Yep.) So now I don't have an agent, either.

I was talking to Kim just yesterday, saying how run down I was and how hard it felt to keep facing all this rejection. She told me what she did next, all to do with the van stuff, a TRUE exclusive. It's in rough form – there are still people I need to find and talk to, but I'm sending it so I know there's a safe copy out there somewhere.

Onward and downward. ██████████████████████

Exxx

PART THREE
ZOE NOLAN WAS NEVER HERE

--22--

'Super Dark'

As months go by with no new leads, the main players in Zoe's life begin to disperse and the stalled investigation draws to an effective standstill.

SARAH MANNING:

The case went cold. Our reconstruction was well timed, well produced and aired to millions of people on primetime television. It also allowed us the chance to blitz newspapers and magazines with renewed appeals for information. Rob Nolan did the rounds everywhere that would have him – photo-ops, phone-ins, on-air interviews, usually with either Fintan or Liu somewhere in tow. And all this in tandem with a £10,000 reward for anyone with information that led to Zoe's whereabouts.

Calls were coming in at first, believe me.

Crackpot theories, sightings, tips, none of them leading anywhere. There was burgeoning resentment in the team for Rob Nolan and the press relations he'd employed. Namely, selling stories to the tabloids to try and keep pictures of Zoe in circulation. Roughly a third of the calls coming in to the tip line felt like a result of that. A lot of people just wanted to tell us that they thought Kim, Andrew or Jai Mahmood were responsible for Zoe's disappearance somehow. By this point hundreds of man-hours had gone into the case. The entire local area had been door-stepped, a three-mile radius, thousands of homes. Every Owens Park resident had been interviewed, some of them several times. Anderson was under surveillance, but with an alibi for the night of Zoe's disappearance – with no hard evidence against him – with really nothing but the picture to go on, even that was curtailed.

To put it simply, there was no way forward. The sad fact is you can't have all those highly trained people sitting around spinning their wheels. The case was downgraded. It remained officially open, but DI James was reassigned, his team were disbanded. I was given other duties alongside my work with the Nolans but, quite honestly, they took up less and less of my time.

There was just nothing left to say.

ROBERT NOLAN:

Your daughter going missing, people can just about grasp that, the phantom-limb idea. You're disfigured and, saving a miracle, you won't ever be whole again. But to feel the *case* going limp, to watch it curl up and die in my arms.

It was the one thing in life keeping me going.

Not for ever, but just day to day. It didn't thrill me or make me jump out of bed in the morning, but it was like a life-support machine or something. Just enough to get through the twenty-four hours that happened to be in front of me. When the tip line went dry, when there was no news – not even bad news – when the phone just stopped ringing, that was my lowest point. I'd been using any distraction I could to stay at one remove from reality, one step ahead of it, but that felt like a nearly lethal dose of the stuff. I couldn't take it, I freely admit.

The future I'd imagined was gone and, well. I've always been a fixer, a self-made man, so I set about building a new one. I turned everything to kick-starting the Nolan Foundation. I'd been on leave until then, but I handed in my notice at work and said to myself, this is my life from now on.

SALLY NOLAN:

We spent less and less time together after the reconstruction. It was the end of so many things. The investigation, my marriage, my family. Rob came to bed hours after I did, got up again before I was even awake. Sometimes he didn't come to bed at all. I was angry and he knew it, but he'd gone too far down that road to turn back. I couldn't help but think, you know, we lost Zoe against our will, but now it's like we're choosing to lose each other, to lose Kim.

We knew she'd left Manchester, and she texted us every week or so to say she was safe, but that was it. She wouldn't say where she was and I knew why. She thought Rob would pass on her whereabouts to the press, anything to keep the wheels spinning, and she was probably right – there was nothing he wouldn't have done.

LIU WAI:

I tried to help in any way I could. Obviously I'd never say this in front of the Nolans, but I found myself almost hoping for the worst? Like, give me bad news, give me *anything*. Just give me something definite that can pull us out of this spiral and end the story one way or another. I tried to help with the start-up of the foundation. Making and fielding phone calls, applying for grants and funding, but it was too much. Mr Nolan was very *particular* in his vision of the charity. Things had to be done in this certain order, a certain way, and if you stepped outside of that he could get livid and take it as a personal insult. I never held that against him, given the circumstances, but alongside my studies it was just too much? I had to remember that there was a reason I'd gone to Manchester in the first place, there were still things I wanted. Some days I saw Fintan literally out on his feet. Like, however much he had to give, Rob Nolan always took it.

FINTAN MURPHY:

Well, as I've probably mentioned before, I was drawn to the idea of an active parent, even one who could be as domineering as Robert. In a strange way, I think we each fulfilled a need that the other had. He became a father figure for me, and I suppose I became a kind of surrogate child for him. We kept each other going. It was trying, sometimes to the point of exhaustion, but at the end of the day at least we were doing some good. The division of labour made itself apparent quite quickly. I was working behind the scenes and Robert was out front as the spokesperson. That's not to say we didn't have our disagreements.

He was always more drawn to immediate rewards than the rigours of running what amounted to something like a small business. So where I might want to pool our resources and pour them into our originally stated goal of establishing a scholarship in Zoe's name, assisting young women from working-class backgrounds in getting an education, Robert wanted to release a charity single of his own composition, 'Zoe's Song', to put her image, rather than her spirit, at the forefront of our operations. Where I wanted to spearhead Zoe's Law, to make it illegal for teachers to engage in relationships with students, Robert was more drawn towards lobbying celebrities to join the appeal. You said that Sally told you Robert believed everything he read? I'm not sure that's quite fair, but I can see where she's coming from. The way I'd characterize him is to say that he realized a lot of *other* people believed everything they read.

Perhaps even the vast majority of them.

And so he was always gearing his message towards the largest populace he could. I'll admit now that I had some fear about his motives buried at the back of my mind. That probably helped me stick around through hard times when I might otherwise have walked away. It wasn't a huge deal, but I'd just gone through my first real break-up. Us weirdos from fucked-up homes are always so desperate to start families, to right the wrongs that have been done to us, and I guess I'd imagined adopting with Connor, or at least with someone, somewhere down the line. I knew if I stuck around the foundation that I'd be giving up that kind of future, at least for a time. The thing is, I worried that, unchecked, Robert might turn it into something garish. At first we each recognized that the other's response to the situation was valid. At first our two approaches complemented each other. But I suppose time isn't particularly kind to any type of relationship.

KIMBERLY NOLAN:

When I thought about what I loved, it came down to my greatest achievement, Chihiro, my bonsai tree, and the hikes I used to take in the back fields behind our house when we were kids. So when I left Manchester I tried to move towards those things. I got a job in Ambleside, in the Lake District, somewhere we'd gone a lot when we were kids. It's a beautiful grey town filled with English spaniels where it almost literally never stops raining. My job was with the National Trust. Conservation, a lot of outdoors work, gardening and learning simple repairs. How to be a handyman, basically. I didn't have any money and I lived in a tiny room above a pub at first. No one knew who I was, and when I went down to the bar on Sundays for my weekly pint I'd be so tired I could go whole minutes without thinking about things.

When you get a bit older you don't mind blending in so much, and I felt a lot older. When things did get oppressive I just went out walking. I had a mountain range – Helvellyn, Skiddaw, Red Screes and Scafell – on my doorstep. If I wanted to I could walk for ever, some days I nearly did. It was all those soaking hills and fields that saved me, because they reminded me that my problems weren't the end of the world. Those mountains had been there since before I was born, and they'd still be there when I was gone. They'd stayed standing through every tragedy I could think of, all the way right back through time, and for me that meant something. Maybe that beauty can't really be beaten, that good things endure somewhere. I hardly looked at my phone, and I didn't take a laptop or watch TV. At night I just read the yellowing bonkbusters that women left on the bookcase downstairs in the pub.

I never looked at the newspapers, and I didn't tell anyone where I was.

One night I came back from a walk, soaked through as always, and stoked the log-burner in my room. The barmaid had given me a tip for drying out. You screw up old newspapers and push them inside your boots in wads, then you put your boots by the fire. The newspaper absorbs all the moisture with the heat and then the next day they're good as new. Ambleside's a babe, a real beauty spot, a tourist trap because of all the walks, so the pub always had old newspapers lying around, some of them from all over the world. I always took the foreign ones when I could, to safeguard against seeing something I didn't want to. I was going through the motions one night, ripping out pages and screwing them up, when something caught my eye. It was a picture, half of Zoe's face, so I knew something must have happened. And I knew it had to be something big if it was in the foreign press. She'd been gone for four months by then. I couldn't do it, though, I couldn't look. So I screwed it up as tight as it would go and forced it into my boot.

JAI MAHMOOD:

Well, if you want to hit rock bottom, you start off by staying with friends, then friends of friends, then friends four times removed, until you look up one day and realize you're not staying with any kind of friend at all any more. Bedroom floors all over town, man, the box rooms of Hulme, every fold-out sofa in Salford. I did about ten thousand different shitty jobs, serving drinks, collecting glasses, wiping tables, cleaning toilets.

I was always working my way down.

I'd start front of house then get moved sideways, out of sight, then into the back, then out of the business. I got recognized every so often and it always caused trouble. People complained or asked me what I'd done with Zoe, where I'd put her body. I was washing dishes in a bar on Bridge Street for the longest, but I got fired when they found out I'd been filling my water bottle from the vodka optic. My boss picked up my Evian by mistake one night and chugged half of it down before he realized. Fired me on the spot. Then a week later the whole place burned down, faulty electrics, and all four of the kitchen staff burned with it.

By then that kind of stuff just seemed normal to me, though, man. All these near-misses and brushes with mortality. I was still using. I slept rough when I had to and I snorted everything in sight. Jai the Inhaler. The only person I ever saw from the old days was Fintan.

FINTAN MURPHY:
Well, I wouldn't say we stayed in touch, exactly. I was volunteering at a soup kitchen in Ancoats and saw a guy casing parked cars on my way in, clearly on the rob. As we came alongside each other he gave me this scary look, you know, the flash of the eyes that generally precedes a mugging. He didn't do anything, happily, and a few steps on I remembered where I knew him from. I glanced back and thought for a second I shouldn't get involved. Then I thought, *Now, Fintan, is that really what Zoe Nolan would have done?*

JAI MAHMOOD:
He got me something to eat.

FINTAN MURPHY:

I bought him some lunch in a greasy spoon. He couldn't keep his hands still, constantly tapping and twitching, looking over his shoulder. I asked if I could help get him into a programme or something, a place to stay, but he started crying and telling me he didn't think he deserved it. He said it would be time and money better spent on someone else, that his life was behind him. I found that incredibly hard to hear. Someone so young giving up on themselves. But I couldn't talk him round. In the end I just gave him what cash I had on me, my number as well. I said, 'Call me if you need anything.'

JAI MAHMOOD:

Yeah, I started sleeping in a storage lock-up, illegally, out in Hale, near the airport. To give you some idea of the place, there was another homeless guy staying there who told me a story. He said the garage I was in had belonged to this bloke who used to come out and visit it most days. He got done for speeding or drink-driving or something. Nothing serious, but enough to get him put away for a few weeks. Only it was high summer and this smell started coming out of the garage while he was away. When they broke the door down to get in they found this mentally ill girl he'd kidnapped and chained up in there. She starved to death because he never told anyone he had her. Look, I don't know if that's actually true, I hope to fuck not, but my point is, in that place it felt plausible.

KIMBERLY NOLAN:

The next day, when my boots were dry, I pulled out all the rolled-up newspaper and put it on the fire ready for that night. Then I went out to work and broke my back trying not to think about it. I came home ten hours later, showered and went down to the bar. I got drunk on whisky, which I never did, then went back up to my room with every intention of starting that fire. It was the first time the story had crossed my path since I'd left, so it felt like a test, and one my life might depend on passing. I built the logs up around the newspaper, got it going, then left the room.

ANDREW FLOWERS:

I received a fairly rude awakening that second term when the bursar got in touch with me about unpaid bills. My tuition and my rent cheques had both bounced, were both overdue, and I didn't have the cash in my account to cover them. I called my father but couldn't get him on the phone for a few days – nothing unusual there.

Finally, I got a tinkle back from Lipson, speaking on dear old Dad's behalf. He was apoplectic with me for not signing the statement the police had presented against Jai. As he saw it I was harbouring a criminal, keeping the story alive and associating his name with something unsavoury. And look, by that point I probably agreed with him. I'd put my balls in a vice for Jai and he'd screwed it shut. Then he'd pissed off a few days later without even saying goodbye. So I can't pretend I stood my ground as a principled man, I was quite ready to capitulate and sell out, I just didn't get the opportunity. Lipson said my father was cutting me off. I believe the precise phraseology was, 'If you want to be on your own, then so be it.'

KIMBERLY NOLAN:

I lasted about five seconds then went back in and pulled the ball of paper I'd seen Zoe's face on out of the fire. It was a bit burnt but basically readable. And just to get it over with I opened it up, saw it was from a French newspaper, *Le Monde*. Then I started laughing, and drunk-laughing with relief, because the girl in the picture wasn't Zoe at all. It was just some girl who looked like her, I mean, a lot like her, but it wasn't my sister.

My French went about as far as ordering a baguette, so I held on to the story, like, I was curious about it. I had to wait a week or something until I heard someone speak French in the pub so I could find out what it was all about. When I flattened the paper out on the table, the man I showed it to went 'Ah,' like it was big news over there and he already knew the case. I asked about it and he told me about this Jean Boivin, this millionaire who'd faked his own death in Paris. He'd burned his house down and upped sticks to Mexico, then got his wife to claim on the life insurance. What made it super-dark was that the house had burned down with three dead bodies inside. One that was originally thought to be him, one that was thought to be his son and one that was thought to be his nineteen-year-old daughter, Lucille. Lucille was the girl in the picture, the one who looked just like Zoe. They got rumbled, and the kids were both legally adults, so all three of them were in jail for it in France. It was the most news I'd had in months and basically blew my hair back a bit. I thanked the man and walked off with my shred of newspaper, then stopped and looked down at it. I saw that the house fire had been on December 24th, Christmas Eve, 2011. I mean, I could understand that much.

Roughly one week after Zoe had gone missing . . .

I went back and asked the man if they knew who the bodies belonged to, these ones that had burned up in the fire, if they'd been identified by anyone. He shook his head, said no, it was a tragedy, people thought they were probably vagrants who'd been kidnapped or tricked into it, people who'd been targeted because of their physical similarities to the family.

And like that I knew what had happened to me when I got grabbed outside Fifth Avenue. I knew why the men in that van went all weird when I told them about my fucked knee. They didn't care if I was in pain or found it hard to get around or even if I needed an amputation. They cared because I'd said I had a titanium screw in my leg and the girl they needed to replace didn't. I got this moment of lightness. People at the bar thought I'd fainted because I had to lean on something, but it was more like elation. I wasn't insane, I wasn't living in this mad world where anything could happen, where nothing meant anything or ever made sense. I felt light until I thought about the body that had actually been burned up in the fire, whoever it was they'd eventually used to replace Lucille. And then all of that lightness and elation went away, because like that I knew where my sister was.

--23--

'Hardcore Guys'

Kim travels to Paris, dead set on learning the truth about what happened to her on 8 November 2011, and about what might have happened to Zoe in the early hours of 17 December of the same year.

KIMBERLY NOLAN:

Those men must have wanted Zoe all along – that's all I could think about on the flight out there. She walked into Fifth Avenue wearing that bright red jacket, and I walked out in it. So when they picked me up, when they threw me outside of the van, when they pointed me at a hole in the ground and set me off to walk into it, when they said they'd fuck me and kill me if I told anyone . . .

They must have wanted Zoe all along.

At the time it felt typical. The defining moment of my life, and it hadn't even been about me. So I applied for a credit card, got it a week or so later and booked a flight to Paris. I wanted to go and make it about me, I wanted my fucking life back.

HENRI CARON, *Business associate of Jean Boivin*:

The first thing you must know about Jean Boivin is that this was no builder, this was no property tycoon, not as *La Croix* or *Les Echos* would have you believe. This was a *rock star*. A man who was able to live a life without limits, fearlessly and guided by his own principles. He said, *'Bien faire et laisser dire.'* *[Do well and let (them) speak.]* I know him first by reputation alone, as a man famous in Paris for growing roses from goat shit.

There was not the property, not the plot that he could not buy for nothing and sell for a ransom. Everywhere this image follows him like a chorus – the playboy, the beautiful woman on each arm, the yachts and the cars and the magnums of Krug. He is a celebrity, he marries one of the most beautiful women in all of France, Juliette Dupuis, an actress who was sleeping with François Truffaut at sixteen, a siren, a muse of Godard. The face a generation of schoolboys saw when they closed their eyes and clutched on to their pillows. And all of this, yes, while the rest of us go blind in sawdust, building and rebuilding, selling for fractionally more than we buy. We look at this man who succeeds without sweat and think we might just as well piss into our violins for all the good it does us.*

KIMBERLY NOLAN:

Reading up about Boivin felt like watching the bathwater go. Circling a drain, going round and round, getting lower and lower, but I couldn't stop myself. I joined the library in Ambleside, got online for

---

* All interviews with Henri Caron were conducted by Joseph Knox and added to Evelyn's text in 2019.

the first time in months and started reading everything I could find about him. I was running French articles through Google Translate so some things stuck better than others, but he was shady with a capital *shhh*. He'd been some real-estate guru, buying up all these old ruins in France for nothing, renovating them and then selling them on at a fat profit. From what I read, it sounded like he'd come from nowhere, just arrived on the scene as this fully formed success story. Everything he touched turned to gold, and it sounded like he spent most of the time touching himself.

HENRI CARON:

To buy low, to renovate cheaply and sell high, this cycle which possessed my every waking hour, Boivin accomplished in his sleep. When he triumphed against me at auction for a shit pile he then sold for three times his price of asking, I knew that my every waking hour was no longer enough. I drive out to this property to see, to sit at the feet of this master, to find out what I'm doing wrong. The problem is that from the driver's seat of my car, a shit heap the property remains. It is only then that I understand Jean Boivin. He is a man with two feet in one shoe, making two jobs appear as one. He is a man who makes black money bright again.

KIMBERLY NOLAN:

At the time I couldn't tell if it was the subtlety of the French press or my poor translation skills, but it felt like there was a story *underneath* the story, something the writers were hinting at but wouldn't or couldn't just come out and say. I read it like the suggestion that Boivin was involved with big organized crime on the Continent, and that's what it turned out to be. He was cleaning mafia cash through all these dodgy real-estate sales.

HENRI CARON:

Sometime later I even have course to meet the man and shake his hand, and I learn then that this Boivin is himself an illusion. He has been constructed like the façade of a building. He has been thrown together with plywood and paintwork, quickly and cheaply, like one of his own properties. He is playing the role of a tycoon designed by those who do not know such men. The outward appearance is close, but these walls, they are not load-bearing. There are no rough edges in his fingernails or in his speech, no callouses on his hands.

He is *fat* with easy life, with no interest in property, no knowledge of the market or passion for its nooks and crannies. He is a charlatan. I know then that nothing good will come from knowing this man, and when our brief talk turns to shared interests, joint ventures, you see, like this I decline. I go back to my sawdust and my clapboard and my minuscule percentages. I tell people that this Jean Boivin is a personification. He is a walking bubble, a talking boom. And when he goes bust and this bubble bursts, he will take everyone down with him. And so it is.

LT COL VICTOR BISSET, *Gendarme*:

Jean Boivin was arrested for tax evasion in March of 2011. This was a small charge, instigated to force his hand into three courses of action. The first, to cease his money-laundering activities and sever all ties with certain illegal business associates. The second, to allow the Gendarmerie greater scrutiny of his finances. And the third, to encourage him to work with us in a larger investigation into organized crime. It was surmised that Boivin had unique insights into black money, where it was being moved from and who it belonged to, and this proved to be the case. When his situation was made clear to him, the choice between a life in prison or cooperation with law enforcement, he decided that his loyalty to his former associates only stretched so far.

By agreeing to cooperate he was allowed a limited bail with assets frozen. We believe that this is when he initiated his plan to make use of the final item he had of value, his life-insurance policy. If he appeared to die and could somehow claim on this policy, he could be a rich man again, free of the police and his paymasters, free to disappear with five million euro and carte blanche. The only confoundment was that his staged death would have to be gruesomely convincing to prevent his former associates from getting suspicious. And so too would the deaths of anyone who wanted to join him in this next life, namely, his two children, Alex and Lucille.*

KIMBERLY NOLAN:

If Boivin wanted to fake his own death, the deaths of his two kids, then he needed three lookalikes, people who could believably replace them.

LT COL VICTOR BISSET:

On December the 24th of 2011, on Christmas Eve, a home invasion of extreme violence was staged at Boivin's St-Nom-la-Bretèche

---

* All interviews with Lt Col Victor Bisset were conducted by Joseph Knox and added to Evelyn's text in 2019.

residence. It was designed to appear as though a representative of Boivin's criminal past had broken in and executed the family before burning down the house with kerosene, all but incinerating the bodies. In fact, Boivin and his two children were already safely abroad, having travelled to Mexico City under false documentation. Post-mortems showed that each of the cadavers in the residence had received several high-calibre head wounds from a Remington 887, one of the most powerful shotguns in the world. This was likely done to obliterate as much identifiable dental work as possible.

As incredible fortune would have it, Boivin's wife, Juliette Dupuis, was spared. She was visiting her own extended family at precisely this time, and was therefore alive and well, able to claim against Boivin's life-insurance policy. A wonderful coincidence. Although she had made application to AG2R, it had not even been processed when a former business associate of Boivin's, Henri Caron, saw him and his children alive and well in Mexico and alerted Interpol. Boivin and family were arrested and transported back to France three months after the fire. Their plan was a costly, blood-soaked failure.

Jean Boivin was involved in a fatal stabbing on 11 April 2012 while in solitary confinement at Fleury-Mérogis Prison in the suburbs of Paris. A brief investigation found that the likely culprit was Jacques Moreau, a prison guard who was himself fatally injured in a car accident while leaving work that night. Authorities found that Moreau was likely speeding home to his wife, Ann Moreau, and mother, Mary Moreau, who were found bound and asphyxiated at his family home. Although no arrests have ever been made, one official speaking off the record said it was 'highly likely' that the deaths were related to Boivin's links with organized crime.

KIMBERLY NOLAN:

Boivin was dead by the time I got to Paris – this was September of 2012 – but he'd never really interested me, I just wanted to know how he'd gone about it and who he'd used. I wanted to know who'd pulled that fucking bag over my head. There was only one article I could find that touched on the actual mechanics of the triple-kidnap-murder plot. It referenced three English men, the Matthews brothers, who'd done casual work for Boivin in the good years. From what I could tell, they all lived in France and they'd all been arrested on charges of conspiracy to commit something, although exactly what was unclear. What got me on the plane was a story saying Gary, the eldest of the three, had been released on bail. And even that was strange because they said it was on the grounds that their family business, this dive bar in Paris, would go under without him.

Anyway, there was a picture of him walking out of court holding a jacket up over his head. You couldn't see him properly but there was a tattoo on his left hand, like a scowling, frowning face, like Tragedy. And it struck me that there was probably a smiling face representing Comedy on the other hand, just like the one I'd seen inside the van. A ghoulish, laughing clown face, a great big horrible grin.

RICKY PAYNE, *Property developer, acquaintance*
of the Matthews brothers:

Never saw one of those lads without a drink in his hand, I can tell you that. It's what they'd come out to France for in the first place, wasn't it? Bit of the easy life. I don't know, they'd had some cut-and-shut operation back home, doing up old houses so they looked good for the five minutes it took to sell them, then fell apart five minutes later. They made regular trips to the Continent, trying to make every pound coin spend twice, booze and blow runs, and that must be how they got it in their minds to move here. It would have been Gary's idea – everything was. Mike and Kev were always just along for the ride. They couldn't say a single swear word in French between the three of them, so their business on this side of the Channel never got far. [Laughs] Not even far enough off the ground to fall down and die again. They just limped. That's how they started working for Boivin. They weren't much cop and his standards were low. He didn't care if his properties got done up or not. He paid cash and he cut corners, so I suppose they all suited each other.

I knew them from the Green-eyed Monster, an Irish pub in Paris, a money pit the brothers were all mad enough to go in on. Can't say I was surprised when I heard they'd been arrested for something, although murder left a sour taste. After they went down I just assumed the Monster, the pub, would go down with them, then I walk by one day to see the lights are on and Gary's at the bar. I went in and saw he was blind drunk, all over the shop. I says, 'Gary, I thought you were serving time, not serving pints.' [Laughs] He said he was out on licence, extenuating circumstances, but I didn't know they ran to getting pissed. Rumour was he sold his brothers down the river for the home invasion and executions. Gave evidence against them and Boivin in exchange for his freedom. Like I said, he had the brains. [Laughs] If you could call them that.*

---

* All interviews with Ricky Payne were conducted by Joseph Knox and added to Evelyn's text in 2019.

KIMBERLY NOLAN:

All I knew about Gary was that he was out of prison and he owned this pub with his brothers in Jaurès, the Green-eyed Monster. I landed at Charles de Gaulle in the early evening and went straight there. I didn't have any real money but I was quite happy to burn up this credit card and hang around for as long as it took. When I got there I remember stopping dead in the street and laughing out loud. The fucking van they'd put me in was sitting outside the pub. The windscreen was covered in tickets, it didn't look like it could even run, but I'm sure it was the same one. There were even messages written in the grime on the back door, only now they were all in French. When I saw the pub I didn't even think it was open – the door was so dirty you wouldn't piss on it. And I mean, an Irish pub in Paris – you might as well build a golf course on the Great Barrier Reef – but it looked *extra* shit. I was surprised when I pushed the door and saw lights on inside. There were two or three terminal cases sitting in the corners, like, hardcore guys – blind, deaf and dumb drunk. No one was serving so I went over to the bar and waited. If the ceiling was as sticky as the floor was, you could have walked on it. I'd been there about five minutes when a man staggered into the room, and that was when I saw his face for the first time.

Gary Matthews.

He looked like one of those fat, inbred English bulldogs. Booze jowls, big red eyes and breathing difficulties. He nodded at me to order, but I wanted to hear his voice so I waited. I looked at him. I'd lost weight since they'd picked me up outside of Fifth, my hair was short and I was wearing black, he didn't recognize me. He sighed and said, *'What you want?'*

353

What I really wanted was to stick a pin in his face and see if it deflated, or take a blade to his belly and drain it for him, but in the end I settled for a beer. Maybe there was the slightest pause when he heard my voice, but not much more than that. I remember he had to turn in stages to pour my drink, like a fucking oil tanker or something, and I started laughing again. It was the kind of place where laughter really stuck out, so he scowled over his shoulder, but I couldn't help it. I thought, *This is the man you've been so scared of? This is the man who made you run away and put those bags under your eyes? He's a joke, he's pathetic, he probably hasn't seen his dick in as long as you haven't seen Zoe.* Then he set my beer down with his right hand, and there was a Comedy tattoo on it, the laughing face I'd seen inside the van.

And that was it, the way I looked at his hand.

When we looked at each other I could see he knew me. His whole face went red, then beetroot, then dickhead purple. Then all the skin I could see, his ears and neck and forearms. I'd have thought he was having a heart attack if I'd thought he had a heart. He broke eye contact. Turned round and muttered something about the drink being on him. I thought about the building site, him and his brothers pouring piss and vodka in my eyes. I said, 'Yeah, thanks, I think the last one was on me.' After that he disappeared while I sat there and drank the whole pint. Over the next half-hour one or two of the others tried to get his attention, they came up to the bar and called for him but he didn't come back. Once they'd all *sacré bleu*'d and stormed out I went behind the bar and made myself another drink, something expensive this time, from the brandies, then I followed Gary into the back. He was sitting on a stool, staring into space like some little boy whose mum had just bollocked him. I don't know if he was upset for me or for himself or for his brothers or his bar. To be fair, he looked like he was sorry for his whole stupid, shit life. I said, 'What did you do with Zoe?' and he looked up for a second. He didn't say anything, so I said, 'What did you do with my sister?' He just shook his head and wiped his face with a rag. He said, 'Dunno what you're on about.' Then he said, 'Get out, we're closed.'

RICKY PAYNE:

Right, yeah, then just the same way, I walked by one night and the lights were off again. I never knew what happened, whether he lost the business or lost his balls or what. I didn't see him for a long while after so I couldn't ask. I heard he'd left the area, though. There were sightings here and there of a man who looked like our Gary sleeping rough, begging on bad streets. He'd have done better in a mile radius of his bar – he'd stood enough of us drinks on *our* bad days – but I suppose he was ashamed or something. I still see him now from time to time, and I usually give him what change I've got on me.

Course, I don't condone anything he might have had a hand in. But then I'm not sure he remembers me or what he did. He's been drunk and outdoors for a good five years, so his freedom never did much for him. Funny thing, though, and I only noticed because it's the one he puts out for change, but he's burned the skin off the back of his right hand, that smiling face what used to be there. *[Laughs]* Probably no use for it any more.

Gary Matthews could not be reached for comment for this publication. His brothers, Michael and Kevin, declined to comment through their legal counsel. They are each serving life sentences in separate French correctional facilities for the murders which took place in Jean Boivin's home on 24 December 2011.

KIMBERLY NOLAN:

I stayed in a bed and breakfast as far away from the Green-eyed Monster as I could afford. I'd be surprised if I even rolled in my sleep, I went down so heavy. The next day I woke up clear-headed, had a croissant for breakfast and went to the nearest police station. I told them everything that had happened to me. It was the first time I'd ever said a lot of it out loud, and they listened, they cared, they offered me cigarettes. I didn't smoke, but I took them. I thought, when else will you be sitting in an interview room in Paris telling the police the story of your life? I spoke to a beautiful man called Victor Bisset. He had narrow policeman's eyes that went wider and wider the longer I talked. I think he couldn't believe that this crazy story, this wild case that had been going on over there, could possibly get stranger.

But there I was.

By then they'd identified two of the bodies from inside the house fire. The man who'd replaced Boivin was a Parisian vagrant, and they'd snatched some poor kid from Belgium to replace his son. The police thought the Matthews brothers had taken people from different places to try and leave less of a pattern, to make it less likely they'd be traced.

The one body they couldn't identify was the young woman's, the person who'd replaced Boivin's daughter, Lucille. When I'd finished speaking, once I'd showed them pictures of Zoe and told them what

356

had happened to me, they asked for a DNA sample, which I gave. After that Victor drove me back to the airport and suggested I call my parents. When I looked at him his eyes had gone narrow again, it sounded like an order, so I did it. I called Mum from France and we spoke for the first time in something like six months. It was just a few minutes but enough time to say how much I loved her and how much I missed her. That call meant a lot to both of us. I didn't say where I was or what I was doing but I hung up the phone thinking it was over. I remember breaking down in tears, happy tears, because I thought, I remember thinking, I'd done it, y'know? I'd solved all our problems, I'd saved us.

LT COL VICTOR BISSET:

Unfortunately, the DNA sample from Kimberly Nolan proved inconclusive. The young woman who had been used to replace Lucille Boivin was later identified as Elise Pelletier, a girl, a foster-care runaway from Brittany in France. Michael and Kevin both confessed to her kidnap and to her murder. Neither man has ever acknowledged a role in the attempted kidnap of Kimberly Nolan, but we do know several things with certainty. The first, that the brothers made a fortnightly drive from Paris to Calais, from there to England and to Manchester, a 'booze cruise' to a family pub in a town called Prestwich. The second, that they made such a drive on November 7th, returning one day after the attempt was made upon Kimberly. The third, that Boivin hired the Matthews brothers to find a suitable girl on November 5th. And the fourth, that Kevin, the youngest brother, had worked on the building site near to Canal Street. It seems highly likely that the brothers happened to be in this nightclub, noticed a resemblance between Kimberly and Lucille and made an unplanned, unsuccessful attempt to take her.

After she proved unsuitable because they believed she had a titanium screw inside her knee, they decided against taking a girl from England, making a separate and sadly successful attempt much closer to home. What we can say with 100 per cent certainty is that the girl executed and burned in Boivin's house was not Zoe Nolan. As far as we can tell, neither Boivin or the Matthews brothers ever even knew of her existence.

From: evelynidamitchell@gmail.com
Sent: 16/03/19 01:07
To: you

Just tried calling. I know ive missed msgs, sry things have been crazy and I mean not good crazy. Horrible horrible run in with Rob Nolan. Really bad, shouting, drunk, demanding to know where Kim was, but worse waass just.

I've been up late with my headphones on transcribing kims last tape. I thought I could hear something so I took them off and realized someone was buzing the door. I checked the time, this was only half an hour aho, half midnight, then went to the intercom and answered. There was no one there. So I forgot about it, put my headphones back on and then heard it go off AGAIN.

Went to the intercom, no one there. AND REPEAt. Thr third time I went down the hall, stairs, etc to the street entrance and opened it.

There was a MAN standing on the other side of the road watching me. I'm trawling back through the personal ads but can't see any more listings for me/my number/my address. This is something else. I'm fully fucking freaking out will you call me when you see this?

Exx

EDITOR'S NOTE

The final part of *True Crime Story* has, by sad necessity, been compiled from notes and recordings that Evelyn Mitchell left behind, but never got the chance to transcribe or arrange herself. According to her files, she made preliminary notes on this case starting in 2015, spoke to Robert Nolan in late 2017, then began interviewing Andrew Flowers, Fintan Murphy, Jai Mahmood, Kimberly Nolan and Liu Wai in early 2018.

By 25 March 2019, nine months after completing the first part of this book, and just over two months after sending me its prologue, Evelyn Mitchell was dead. Although the text that follows was not arranged by Evelyn, the transcriptions were largely taken from interviews she conducted in the last months of her life. These interviews represent her final work on the book and on the case, culminating in the breakthrough which revealed a killer.

Knox, 2019

PART FOUR

FRIENDS REUNITED

--24--

'After Life'

In late 2018, seven years after the events surrounding Zoe's disappearance, the Nolan Foundation, the charity established in her name, is rocked by press allegations of impropriety at the highest level. But as Fintan struggles to save the organization, an even bigger story lurks just around the corner.

SALLY NOLAN:

I was down in the garden when I heard a car. It's an old farm cottage at the end of a lane, so if you hear someone, they're usually there to see you. I walked round, but only in time to see a cloud of dust, something driving away. Then I went into the house and saw twenty messages flashing on the machine.

That's how I knew it was all starting again.

MARCUS LEE, *Former journalist,* **Mail on Sunday:**

In a story like this, you've got to do the work. It's not enough for you to just transcribe the he-said-she-said and press print, whatever people might think. So we were making a list and checking it twice, doing our due diligence. No one wakes up in the morning and thinks, 'I'd love to wreck so-and-so's life today,' and certainly not someone who might have done nothing wrong. With that said, when you've got something as spicy as this in the bag, you know someone might get burned. You do your subject the courtesy of a phone call and give them the chance to respond to the story, even to get out ahead of it.

Very often that's where some kind of arrangement's reached.

Say you've got the dirt on a celebrity and they don't want it coming out, they might offer you something instead – wedding snaps, an interview, dirt on someone else, whatever. The rule of thumb is, if you see someone famous giving a guided tour of their house, they probably got caught with their pants down. Point being, we weren't expecting anything like that in this case because he didn't really have anything left to barter with. By Friday, December 14th, we were crossing the *T*s and dotting the *I*s, and the relevance of that time of year was lost on no one.*

FINTAN MURPHY:

I've spent the last seven years working almost exclusively for the Nolan Foundation. We kicked off as a scrappy kind of start-up charity with two main objectives. To keep Zoe's name and face out there – ensure that coverage of the case wouldn't simply cease without new developments – *and* to try and enact some kind of public good.

And I think we're doing well on both fronts. Our profile's risen considerably in recent years due to our work around Zoe's Law, a

---

* All interviews with Marcus Lee were conducted by Joseph Knox in 2019.

sadly unsuccessful but nonetheless conversation-starting effort to criminalize all relationships between teachers and students. Most educational faculties have internal policies in place discouraging such relationships, but in cases where participants are of legal age, it's still largely advisory stuff. It was our feeling that although it may not have played a direct role in Zoe's disappearance, she *had* been in such a relationship. It may have been a factor in her feeling the need to keep secrets from her family, perhaps even in her suicide attempt of 2011.

We wanted a law in place that acknowledged not only the age of consent, but the skewed power dynamics inherent in such relationships. Unfortunately, the bill was rejected in 2017, not because it lacked merit, but because we couldn't point to any direct evidence that Zoe had been in a relationship with Michael Anderson. It was a disappointment, but it still led to our successful Never Forget campaign. Then in 2018, the September just gone, we saw our sixth generation of Zoe's Angels enrolled into higher education, and of course we'd made preparations to mark the seventh anniversary of Zoe's disappearance the following week. That was when I got the unwelcome phone call from Mr Lee.

ANDREW FLOWERS:

As soon as the Christmas lights start going up you know the anniversary's right around the corner, it comes quicker every year. You brace yourself for whatever's about to float to the surface – a memory, a feeling, a regret. I certainly wasn't bracing myself for major revelations, though, not some kind of eleventh-hour break in the case.

I was busy with work. To catch everyone up, my father cut me off, and although I'd failed my first year of university, subsequently dropping out altogether, I'd still managed to get a job at PC World in Manchester, selling electronic equipment for marginally more than a slave's wage. In the five years I'd been working at the branch in the Trafford Centre I'd leapt up the ranks – from lowly *Junior* Sales Assistant to exalted *Senior* Sales Assistant. Unfortunately, my rocket-fuelled ascent came during a time of belt-tightening and upheaval for the firm, and I'd been notified that my role was under consultation. That was a nail-biter for me because I lived month to month, and the prospect of being shit-canned from my shit job was keeping me up at night. So, no. I had no real sense of impending doom, but only because I was up to my tits in it already.

FINTAN MURPHY:

When you find yourself in a situation where years of good work might go down the drain because of some thoughtless, stupid actions, your first recourse can be to bargaining. At least, in this instance, my first recourse was to bargaining.

MARCUS LEE:

Murphy was hostile – don't let the charity show fool you, I had to hold that phone about a foot away from my ear when I called him. An expletive-filled rant about what I could and couldn't do, where I could and couldn't stick things, and a veiled threat of legal action. Like I say, you're basically giving them the FYI, so it's an eventuality you're always prepared for. For my part, I was just trying to explain that our story could be all to the good. Zoe Nolan might be the centre of his universe, but she's not the centre of anyone else's. Our reporting would be putting her back in the public eye, more than anything his precious foundation had managed. When he'd calmed down a bit he asked me for the name of the person who'd made a complaint, which of course I declined to give him, and then he asked me not to go to print, imploring me on the grounds it might 'hurt' Zoe.

FINTAN MURPHY:

Well, I suppose his recollection of events is probably more accurate than mine, and I'm sure I was being recorded so there's not much point disputing it. I would say that the man had a real way about him, though. He couldn't have been happier that this instance of human weakness had found its way to my door. So I'm not proud of that first response, but I don't think it was monstrous or irrational or outside of what anyone might say or do in similar circumstances, and I called him back a few minutes later for more details.

The second I got off that call, once I was convinced that what he'd told me was true, I began making arrangements to try and fix things. It wasn't the kind of awareness I wanted, and especially not so close to December 17th, but I'm not one of those people who buries their head in the sand and pretends the world's not out there.

KIMBERLY NOLAN:

They'd been quiet years for me – quiet, if not necessarily easy. I read an article about a man who'd lost his right hand in a climbing accident, and even though he knew it wasn't there any more, from time to time he'd find himself reaching for something with it. That was what my relationship with Zoe was like by then. I knew she was gone but I still found myself reaching for her. She moved in and out of my life in cycles. We shared a birthday, so that was always interesting. Hard to celebrate anything while you're wondering where your sister is. And of course there was September, a month that started with so much promise for us back then, rapidly followed by December, the anniversary of her disappearance . . .

They were all like open-ended questions, times for self-interrogation, self-flagellation, self-harm. You know, *What could I have done differently?* When I left France I'd felt sure it was over. I thought I could put my problems and my sister to rest, prove my worth to my parents and save my family, but that wasn't how it worked out. I brought some confidence back across the Channel by looking Gary Matthews in the mouth, seeing what a bloated joke he was and walking away. But I had to accept what Victor Bisset and the French authorities told me.

Zoe's wasn't the body burned up in that house.

There was no evidence she'd ever been a target. Everyone else they'd grabbed had been someone seen by chance, not much forethought or planning, just a pill in their drink and then thrown in the back of that van.

I always tried to make sure I was busy in December, working as much as possible, so last Christmas was no different. I was still with the National Trust, but at various other sites round the Lake District. I can't remember where I was – driving out to Wordsworth House or something – when I got a phone call from the office saying a *Mr Murphy* was trying to get hold of me. We'd never been close, we hadn't spoken in years, so I knew it must be something serious. It was raining like crazy and the reception was bad. I pulled into the side of the road and shouted, 'Fintan Murphy wants to speak to *me*? You're sure?'

ANDREW FLOWERS:

What do you call a group of teenagers who are let loose in the wild? A murder? A *bastard* of teens? Well, whatever it is, there was one in the shop that day, five or six of the fuckers, all dicking around, making the computer screens sticky, typing 'gay sex' into the search engines and being extremely amusing. When you have all that stuff on display, the gadgets and tablets, I suppose it's inevitable. My job was essentially to move the mouth-breathers along long enough to let an actual customer get a look in edgeways.

What was strange was that these kids were looking at me like I was their long-lost dad or something, and I don't mean lovingly. More like I'd left their mother with a fake phone number and a tear in her eye then never bothered to stump up for child support afterwards. It's a look I get occasionally. Whenever the story's in the news again or the foundation launches a new appeal, the picture of me with scratch marks on my face inevitably floats to the surface somewhere and I find myself on the receiving end of all these lingering hostile stares. That, coupled with all the Christmas decorations up in the shop, was making me pour a little heavier than usual when I got home. I think my liver was going grey faster than my hair.

KIMBERLY NOLAN:

When I got Fintan on the phone we both said hello, probably both felt the temperature drop a few degrees, then he got right down to business. He said I could probably expect some press enquiries over the next few days, that it might get rough and he wanted to offer me his full support. I said, 'Press enquiries about fucking what, Fintan?'

EMMY MOSS, *Zoe's Angels alumnus 2015–18:*

I was seventeen years old, so it would have been 2015. I didn't know much about Zoe Nolan but we – me and my mum – were struggling to work out how I'd pay for university. The course I was applying for was Structural Engineering. The fees alone were too much, and after that I'd still need somewhere to live. My tutor at sixth form suggested I apply for a grant from the Nolan Foundation, and I did, not really thinking much of it. A few weeks later I got an email from Fintan Murphy that felt like a miracle. He said they were prepared to pay my full fees for that first year in exchange for some nominal work for the charity. Once I'd read up about Zoe and the work they were doing, it sounded like a really good thing, something you'd want to be involved with anyway. I took a train to Manchester to meet Fintan, and Zoe's dad, Robert. They explained where they were coming from and what they could do for me. When they got some sense of how serious I was about my studies, it seemed perfect. Everything was agreed and they followed through on their end, absolutely.

But then Robert Nolan started texting me . . .

I knew I needed to show up to some functions, and I did, and they were usually fine. I met some of the other girls they'd helped – Zoe's Angels – and we all got along well, although it was weird. We all looked the same. All of us were blonde, we had similar builds, similar smiles and eyes, we all looked like Zoe. And then Robert started calling and texting me when there weren't even any events to go to, sometimes making things up that I had to attend. I'd get there and it would be just the two of us, sometimes in bars or restaurants, sometimes for whole evenings. And a part of me thought, *Well, if this is what he wants, some stake in your life, then what's the harm?* It just got a lot over that first year, and it got personal. He'd want to know where I was and who I was with. He was always warning me about drugs and 'bad guys'. He'd send me selfies and encourage me to reply the same way, saying, 'I just want to see where you are.' There was always this undercurrent, this constant suggestion and mention of money when I resisted. He'd say, 'Well, I really hope we can continue to help you, Emmy. I really hope we can support you into your second year, *LOL, smiley face, kiss, kiss, kiss,*' all this passive-aggressive, sweaty stuff. And Mum was so grateful to them I didn't know who to tell.*

MARCUS LEE:

Nolan was using a position of power at the head of his dead kid's charity to insinuate himself into the lives of these young women, and with varied results. I mean, look, at first I think he really was taking an interest, trying to help out, it's just that he started to feel entitled to something more, an emotional connection these kids couldn't really give him. The ones I've spoken to were all sweethearts, but they wanted good deeds under their belts, not fifty-five-year-old men.

So when Nolan couldn't get his paternal hugs and kisses, what was the next best thing? Well, spoiler alert, of the four girls that came forward, all had received overbearing, harassment-style overtures from him. Two had met with him alone, both reporting

---

* This interview was conducted by Joseph Knox in 2019.

inappropriate behaviour, one actually filing charges of sexual assault. We had sworn statements, times, dates, screenshots. We had a whole story ready to go. And all this a few days out from the anniversary of his daughter's disappearance. That was never part of the plan, really, just a happy accident. Nolan knew something was in the air because I called him in the first instance. He hung up then switched his phone off, went to ground and left Murphy holding the baby.

KIMBERLY NOLAN:

What can I say to those girls, except how sorry I am? When Fintan told me it made my vision go blurred. I had to sit in the lay-by for five minutes while I got my breath back.

ROBERT NOLAN:

Well, look. Look, I can say sorry until I'm blue in the face, I *have* said sorry until I'm blue in the face. And I can dispute some facts, some versions of events, but at the end of the day it's something I have to live with. I was given a kind of chance I'd always wanted, a platform, and I abused it. I didn't set out to hurt anyone, not knowingly, but I know how it looks and sounds. I found out the hard way I wasn't one of those people I'd always admired, I wasn't an artist, I wasn't Zoe, I couldn't handle it and I freely admit that.

And I'm ashamed, course I am.

But what I'd say to some of the people who've lined up to give me a kicking is that most of them won't ever be tested, not like I've been. Most people won't have to find out what they're really made of in front of the world. So I might be a monster, I might be a disgrace. I'd go along with both those statements now, to some extent. But I can also say I know myself, really and truly. It's ice-cold comfort some days, but I can say that at least. And after it all came out, I did what I could to limit the damage. Once I knew the story was running, I resigned my position as part of the board of the Nolan Foundation, I did the decent thing.

FINTAN MURPHY:

Did he now? See, in my recollection of events I called Robert roughly thirty-five times that day, but he never answered once. In the end I left a message advising him that we'd held an emergency meeting, that he was being *removed* from the board, effective immediately, and I told him I'd be briefing as such to the press. I knew I had to act fast if I was going to save everything we'd worked for.

He never called me back, incidentally.

We went from speaking almost every day during the course of those seven years to not exchanging a single word since, with one regrettable exception. I didn't have time to worry about it – it was more important to me that I make contact with the young women affected and offer them what compensation I could, as well as a plat-form to say whatever they wanted to, with absolutely no conditions or strings attached. They were all grateful, amenable, a wonderful group of young women and a credit to Zoe. None of them suggested I'd known about Robert's actions, and none of them wanted to see the foundation itself suffer. Once that was done, I notified Kimberly, left a message for Sally, then called a press conference to tell the world. This is all the same day I found out, so I really was doing everything I could.

MARCUS LEE:

It was Shakespearean, or at least, I assume that's the kind of thing they mean when they say that. A father's response to his daughter's disappearance ends up destroying him. Who wouldn't want to read about that? And after all, our readers were acquainted with Rob Nolan from years of stories, initiatives, quotes, interviews – they knew him inside out.

Full credit to Murphy, he staged a real response. He had a local press conference scheduled for 4 p.m. on the 14th, the same day I'd hit him with the allegations. It just turned out not to be the biggest fish in the deep-fat fryer. Soon as he walked in with his statement, the room, which had already been half empty, started emptying even more. Phones started ringing, local hacks started getting up and answering, walking out. I couldn't believe it. We were the only national newspaper there, and it looked like these smaller guys weren't even interested. For a second I thought I'd misjudged the public interest in Zoe after all these years. I thought, *What could be a bigger car crash than this?*

ANDREW FLOWERS:

It was something more than simple recognition – these teenage kids were openly laughing, pointing at me. By then I knew they weren't buying anything so I went over and asked them not to let the door hit them in their arses on the way out. I basically gave them both barrels and watched them disperse, still pissing their pants about something.

MARCUS LEE:

By the time poor Fintan hit that stage he was one of the only people left in the room. It was one of those moments you see more and more of now. News outlets being scooped by the internet. It was my first time being scooped by Pornhub, though.

ANDREW FLOWERS:

I saw what they'd been searching for on this tablet and it felt like my heart almost literally fucking stopped.

KIMBERLY NOLAN:

When I got home on Friday night there was one reporter *camping* outside my house, like, literally camping, in a tent. I'd never seen anything like that, not even at the height of Zoe's disappearance. There were two or three guys on the street I had to walk through to get to my door, and it seemed stupid to pretend, so I turned and said something like, 'Look, I don't know anything about my dad's personal life, we're not that close,' but they couldn't have cared less. One of them just shoved a camera in my face and shouted, 'Yeah, we know, but how close are you to Andrew Flowers?'

ANDREW FLOWERS:

The kids had typed my name into the search engine. My name followed by the letters *XXX*. The Net Nanny safety settings had prevented any results from popping up, but it gave me another bad feeling. I realized I was getting the same look from my colleagues that the kids had given me, then when I went into the break room a few minutes later I saw what they'd been searching for over my boss's shoulder. I realized I was watching the video, the so-called 'sex tape' that we'd recorded seven years before.

It had been leaked on to the internet.

I'd never seen a single frame since then, the night Zoe scratched my face off for it and went missing. My understanding was that it had never been uploaded anywhere, and besides, it was something like six seconds long. Then I realized that this was something different. This wasn't just those six seconds of me saying, 'Zoe, Zoe,' it was the full thing, more like sixteen minutes long.

MARCUS LEE:

I followed the locals out into the hallway to work out what was going on, and suddenly everyone around me's watching porn on their phones. I twigged it was the much-discussed Zoe–Andrew sex tape leaked in full and started walking back into the conference room for Murphy. He looked close to tears as it was. Then someone grabs my arm, like, 'No, Marcus, you're not understanding what we've got here. This is the fucking big one.'

Revelation sex tape reveals steamy bonk betrayal between Andrew Flowers, ex-boyfriend of tragic missing Zoe Nolan, and her troubled twin sister Kim.

In the video, which has already been viewed more than 88,000 times, a teenage Flowers, now 26, can be seen taking root in a young woman who he repeatedly calls 'Zoe'.

Although top cops knew about the tape in 2011, the *Sport* understands they had only seen a much shorter version of it, concluding that Flowers had indeed been sowing seeds with his then-girlfriend, Zoe Nolan.

But the 16-minute uncut revelation sex tape, which was uploaded to streaming sites anonymously on 14 December, clearly shows Kim, now 25, asking Flowers to call her by her sister's name.

In a budding romance which looks anything but garden variety, Flowers seems to struggle with thorny Kim's request until she firmly plants one on him.

Flowers kisses back, taking a leaf out of Kim's book and calling her Zoe, until both of them are coming up roses. Whoops-a-daisy!

It is not known how the footage was obtained or if the police have been contacted about the leak.

But their steamy fertilization will raise more questions for cops about missing Zoe Nolan, who fought tooth and nail with Flowers just minutes before disappearing from a Manchester house party in December 2011.

Zoe's best friend, senior human resources consultant Liu Wai, 25, said, 'Andrew Flowers and Kimberly Nolan owe the world an apology and an explanation.'

She said: 'The fact that they were carrying on behind Zoe's back, and that she had to find out about it shortly before she disappeared, breaks my heart.

'But clearly the two things aren't unrelated, and I really urge Andrew and Kim to take a look at themselves, rather than each other, and tell us what was really going on.'

Neither Flowers nor Nolan could be reached for comment.

Preparations for an anniversary celebration of Zoe's life, which had been organized by the charity founded in her name, were put on hold after allegations of 'impropriety' were levelled at Nolan Foundation founder Robert Nolan.

He has since stepped down from his position on the board.

WEEKEND SPORT, SATURDAY, 15 DEC 2018 — E. M.

377

--25--

'Full Stop'

LIU WAI:

Let's be real for a minute, shall we? I think we all worked out a few things on the spot when that story broke. I certainly got some insight into why my best friend had been so upset to see that video. I felt like I finally understood why she was so hurt, so betrayed, why she had to leave the party and walk up to the roof on her own and in tears. She'd just found out her boyfriend and her twin sister were playing some twisted sex game behind her back. She didn't know who she could trust. When the tape was uploaded I started to see why Zoe might have wanted to disappear full stop.

SARAH MANNING:

I'd already exited Greater Manchester Police when the tape leaked in full, so anything I say about how it might have affected the investigation is speculative. I *can* say that with Zoe still missing, her file remains open, even if inactive, and I'd think that a development of this kind would be enough to encourage detectives to take a second look.

Unfortunately for Andrew and Kim, an affair gives them the strongest motive we've seen yet to want Zoe out of the picture. We saw how she reacted when she found out, how seriously she took the news. And you could argue that they both benefitted from her disappearance because, seemingly, no one else discovered what they'd done, not until all this.

LIU WAI:

And even more worryingly than that, I started to see for the first time why Andrew and Kim might have wanted to hurt Zoe, how they'd always actually hated her. Andrew with his snobbish downward-looking boredom and Kim with her disapproval of everything her sister represented. I was shocked *literally* to my core. I remember that I started reading the story on my phone at work, then suddenly I was lying on the office floor, breathing into the brown paper bag I'd brought my Tesco Finest smoked-salmon sandwich in . . .

Because I started to see how much Andrew and Kim must have hated me, too, how personal it had always been. They let the whole world believe I might have had something to do with that tape leaking, when they knew all along that it was *never* on the laptop Zoe gave me, because *she* didn't film it, *she* wasn't even in it. *She* found out about it at exactly the same time I did.

SARAH MANNING:

That said, while I do think it might raise new questions for the investigation, and certainly point towards a possible motive, my first concern would be the provenance of that video. This is something that's lain dormant somewhere for seven years, which suggests someone's been holding on to it all that time. Our main suspect, our shadow man, was someone so obsessed with Zoe that he stole clothes and other objects belonging to her. He had access to that flat. I'd suggest that makes him the most likely culprit for this leak. So the question is, why now? Who does it benefit?

SALLY NOLAN:

Well, I'd listened to the first message on the machine, which was from Rob, telling me I might hear bad things about him, telling me not to believe them until he'd had a chance to explain. He didn't say much more than that, but I could tell by his voice it was serious, and of course the next message was from Fintan, who was more informative, more distraught.

Fintan had never had a strong father figure in his life, or a mother figure either, for that matter. He'd looked up to Rob in a lot of ways, and to me, too. I could always expect a call from him every few weeks. This wasn't that, of course, this was him calling to tell me that my ex-husband had been taking advantage of those poor girls from the charity. And obviously we were separated, but it still hurt. And I could tell how scared Fintan was, so I was calling him back when I heard a car outside. I hung up and went out to see Rob parking up. We didn't have plans, we hadn't properly spoken in years. He got out of the car looking like an old man and started shouting, 'There's something you need to know,' just like that, not even a hello. I told him I'd already heard, but he shook his head and said, 'No, this is important, about Zoe, a break in the case.' I told him to go home and sleep it off but he went on, some stupid story about that stupid tape. How it supposedly changed everything and now I had to do something for him. I started to walk back inside but he grabbed me – he'd never grabbed me before, he looked insane, I could smell drink – and he said if I couldn't do it for him, then I could do it for Zoe. He said no one would listen to him or take his calls because of the allegations, he said he'd been smeared, but I could still go to the press, to the police, and get the case moving. I said, 'Stop,' but he kept on so I said it again and again and again, until I was screaming in his face.

I said, 'You did this to us, Rob, all of it. You filled Zoe's head with your dreams, you made her hate herself for what she wasn't. You set her on the path to that pig Anderson, you turned her and her sister against each other and forced me to choose between them. If Zoe's got a killer, it's you.' He let go and I walked back inside and called Kim. I didn't look back, and I never have since. I heard the car start a few minutes later and I've never seen Rob again. I'm afraid I don't expect to.

SARAH MANNING:

Rob Nolan called me repeatedly, pressing me to use my contacts, to get the police to arrest Kim and Andrew. I told him I wasn't working for the police any more, and anyway, it wasn't that simple, but he wasn't listening. Once I got off the phone I thought about what I said to you before, about who benefits from all this. An affair gives Andrew and Kim a powerful motive to push Zoe aside, no doubt, but with the allegations against him in the press, it was Rob Nolan who really stood to gain from that video's release. I mean, put it this way, his bad behaviour wasn't the big story that day, was it?

CHLOE MATTHEWS:

When I saw the story about the girls from the Nolan Foundation it reminded me of that day on set of the reconstruction. Somehow, all the girls who came forward really resembled Zoe, and that day when Rob kissed me I'd been fully dressed up as her. Yeah. Unnerving. I felt like no one was really paying attention to that, though. It all got overshadowed by the video, Andrew and Kim.

KIMBERLY NOLAN:

Well, nothing I say about this is going to sound particularly impressive. I don't want to change minds or justify what I did. It wasn't good, I don't like myself for doing it and I don't forgive myself, either. All I can do is tell you the truth that, yes, I slept with Andrew while he was seeing Zoe, yes, I wore my sister's clothes, and yes, I asked him to call me by her name. And people should know that I was the one instigating, not him. I'd fallen for Andrew when we first met, I'd imagined a future, but I'd managed to put all that away and forget about it, before what happened to me inside the van. After it, though, I was a mess. We recorded the video, like, a week or so later. You can tell because I've still got blonde hair in it, I never have since. Zoe wasn't speaking to me. Now I know that's probably because Andrew said my name while they were together, and probably because she was busy spending another man's money, but at the time I didn't.

At the time I thought we'd lost each other.

Stupid as it sounds, I felt the same thing when those men let me go and I was thrown out of that van. I never go a day without feeling grateful, I was grateful then, but at the same time it was another rejection. It's fucked up but I convinced myself they'd wanted Zoe instead of me, just like everyone else. And afterwards, I felt like I'd almost died because I hadn't developed my own looks or personality. I started drinking too much, I stopped sleeping, and I just wanted to overwrite this shit thing inside my head with something I actually wanted. I *wanted* Andrew, I saw the way he looked at me, and I thought, *Why not? Why shouldn't I have something for myself for a change?* And somehow, in all of that, it became important that he call me Zoe. There was a part of me that had always wondered about being her: would things feel different, feel better? I thought if I could make myself look enough like her and sound enough like her and *be* enough like her, then it might feel like we weren't doing anything wrong. Maybe it would solve all my problems? Obviously it didn't. Afterwards I think we both felt horrible, Andrew and me. Then, as we were getting dressed, Alex walked in on us. She'd told me she was out for the day, the flat was meant to be empty, we froze.

SAM LIMMOND:

I didn't see the story when it broke but someone pointed it out to me a few days later. It made sense of what Al said at the time, about walking in on them doing something. She'd thought Zoe was acting strange and came away thinking that Andrew was abusing her or something. I guess it was actually just Kim shitting it, thinking they'd both been rumbled.

KIMBERLY NOLAN:

Andrew saved my life. He put his arm round my shoulder and pretended I was Zoe. I was dressed like her and just about held it together for a few minutes until we could get out of there. Alex was no idiot, she could see something was wrong. I was walking on eggshells for days after but either she never knew or she never said anything.

The final part of my confession is that I didn't tell Andrew I'd filmed us together. I knew it could never happen again so, if it worked, if it made me feel good, I wanted to be able to relive it. And I wanted to know once and for all if I really was so different from my sister or if it was all in my head. When I did watch the video back I hated the person on the screen, I hated myself, and it was probably the next day that I cut all my hair off and dyed it black. I realized I needed to let all this *second-best* shit go and become my own thing. In a fucked-up roundabout way it really helped me come through one of the worst times of my life.

And then I forgot about it – I mean, I actively *forced* myself to forget about it. Me and Andrew weren't making eyes at each other, we were never texting or meeting or passing notes. That video was just a file on my computer, one I sent to the recycle bin on the same day it was created. Then one night a month or something later, I walked back into the tower and found out someone had stolen it, leaked it. I never knew who, but when I heard Zoe had seen the tape and then stormed off to the roof I was terrified.

ANDREW FLOWERS:

How do I respond to Liu Wai essentially saying that this means we murdered Zoe? I don't know – how can you refute such well-argued points of view? Why is Liu Wai even involved with your book at this stage? Is this like the epilogue of an eighties movie where you show what happened to all the minor characters afterwards? Because I'm not sure anyone gives a shit. My response to Liu Wai is that I'm clearly not some master criminal in all this. The first thing I even knew about a recording was Zoe showing it to me then scratching my face off. I didn't know where it had come from, for a second I didn't even twig why she was so upset. And I couldn't even speak to Kim about it because everything went so rapidly to shit afterwards. The whole world was getting a good look at me one minute, then we were being evacuated from the building the next. Then they were telling me Zoe was on the roof, the building was burning down, Kim was running back inside, etcetera, etcetera. I couldn't even speak to her until she'd given a statement to the police.

She was standing in the dark, right at the edge of Owens Park, crying into her hands, saying it was all her fault. I tried to comfort her, told her that Zoe and I weren't that serious, we were on the outs. You know, I knew it wasn't ideal, but I was saying Zoe's tough, she'll bounce back from this. And that's when Kim broke down and told me about that night at Fifth, those disgusting fuckboys who'd forced her into a van against her will. She told me about where they'd dumped her, this building site, and that they must have thought she was Zoe, that they must have come back for the *right* twin. I said we should speak to the police, but one look at Kim told me she couldn't. So I suggested we just go out there and search for ourselves, set her mind to rest. I helped her get over the fence and waited while she was inside. Next thing I knew she was being carried out.

KIMBERLY NOLAN:

My worst fear from that moment on was that people would find out it was us in the recording, and I knew they would because of the state of Andrew's face. The only conclusion anyone could come to after seeing those scratch marks was that Zoe had attacked him for leaking it, that she'd meant to send *him* that message: *How could you do this to me?*

I knew people would think he was the reason she'd gone missing, and I knew he'd talk to save his own skin, because why wouldn't he? So once I was back in the tower the next morning, when I was going up in the lift with Fintan, I texted Andrew, telling him I'd go to the police.

ANDREW FLOWERS:

I'd just lost my own family, I knew what it felt like. I didn't want Kim to go through that. If telling the world would have made a difference, if I thought it would have helped find Zoe, I would have done it. As it was, the only thing we would have accomplished is making my life easier and ruining Kim's.

KIMBERLY NOLAN:

Andrew said he didn't think it was a good idea. He said we both knew we had nothing to do with her disappearance, so we'd just be distracting the police if we told them about us. He said his family would take care of him, he'd be fine, I should do whatever made my life easier. I was surprised that he came through for me like that, it wasn't really like him.

ANDREW FLOWERS:

Kim was someone who'd been sad and broken and momentarily reckless. Was that something worth destroying her life over? I decided that whatever came down the pike, I could bear it myself. It was probably the only decent thing I ever did in my life.

JAI MAHMOOD:

I don't know if it means anything, man, but I can say one thing about that. Andrew never told me anything about a tape or him and Kim having sex, but after Zoe went missing, when it was just me and him in that flat over Christmas, he asked if I remembered that night at Fifth when he took me home. Obviously I didn't, but that was when he told me about her being taken. The van, the men, the tattoo, all that.

LIU WAI:

It's very touching that Andrew managed to *bone* the PTSD out of Kim, but it's my opinion that *everything* should be re-examined in the light of what we now know. Clearly they were having an affair, obviously Zoe was a problem that got in their way, and clearly they solved that problem somehow.

Andrew always looked bad because he had no alibi for the night Zoe went missing, and neither did Kim. Now we know that they actually *did* have alibis. They were hand in hand, out at this abandoned building site a mile up the road. They never told anyone that because they knew the only thing worse than them being alone was them being together. *You* do the maths.

JAI MAHMOOD:

Liu Wai knew all this at the time. I told her in the lobby of the tower the day I got arrested. She wasn't pissed off about it then, not in all the years since, so why now?

LIU WAI:

Oh, Jai was out of his head that day, that's why he got arrested.

JAI MAHMOOD:

Liu was waiting for Fintan and started asking me if Andrew had said anything about where he was when Zoe went missing. I was pissed with him in that moment so I told her what Andrew had told me. He'd gone out to this building site looking for Zoe, with Kim. Liu asked why they'd think Zoe was at a building site and I told her. I shouldn't of, but I did.

LIU WAI:

We'll have to let your readers decide who seems more trustworthy.

JAI MAHMOOD:

Fuck that. When you interviewed us about the night Kim got grabbed outside Fifth, Liu was the one who told you Kim saw something inside the van, the tattoo on someone's hand, yeah? Kim didn't volunteer it. It wasn't in her interview with the *Mail*. So how else would Liu know? Kim told Andrew, Andrew told me, I told Liu. The only reason she's pissed at them now's because they had sex and she thinks they should have cleared her name on the laptop thing.

LIU WAI:

Well, so maybe Jai did tell me? My point still stands. On the night Zoe went missing, Kim and Andrew – who were having an affair behind her back – spent an unknown amount of time at an abandoned building site. It doesn't take a genius to work out what they were doing.

The building site at Canal Street was searched extensively by authorities after Kimberly's arrest on the night of Zoe's disappearance. Nothing suspicious was found at the time, nor during a subsequent three-year construction. After Kim's story about her ordeal appeared in the press, the Mail *funded a private ground-penetrating radar scan of the premises which was finally erected on the site in 2014. No disturbances or irregularities were discovered in the foundations.*

From: evelynidamitchell@gmail.com
Sent: 20/03/19 02:35
To: you

on Mon, Mar 18, 2019, Joseph Knox joeknoxxxx@gmail.com wrote:

Evelyn – How are you? I'm sure you're looking after yourself, but don't forget to check in. I've been thinking about Rob Nolan. There HAS to be something that links him to that crawlspace in the tower. In one of the early chapters somewhere in part one he said something about calling the university himself, asking for Kim and Zoe to be placed together . . .

Let's say that somehow he knew about the crawlspace in 15C before they arrived in Manchester. Could he have requested they get placed in that EXACT apartment so he could monitor them?? It must be worth asking if there's any record of his conversation with the housing department?

And I hate to hear about you feeling sick. Have you managed to see a doctor? As you say, you've been going flat-out and might just be run down. They might just be able to put your mind to rest?

Jx

Hey J

Re: Rob's tower request, I've spoken to student accommodation and it doesn't sound promising, especially if Rob just got on the phone and asked someone MAN TO MAN. We're talking about an informal call from seven years ago :/

I am gonna take another run at Fairfield Property Management, though. Someone found out about that crawlspace somehow, and I think I agree with Sarah. It only makes sense for it to have been someone who was OUTSIDE of Zoe's life. Her friends could go and see her any time they liked.

That, plus the harassment I've had, makes me think that someone I'VE interviewed must be on edge about all this. And who have I interviewed who was obsessed with Zoe AND shut out from her life? Rob Nolan.

I hear you on the doctor, I do. It's just that I know what happens next if it's bad news. Cancer could stop everything for me. Again. You've never had to go through that, you don't know what you're asking. I can't explain it, but I KNOW I'm close to something here. I just need a few more days before I can risk hearing the worst. It won't be longer than that because, honestly, I'm sick all the time atm. Anyway. Thanks Joe.

Ex

--26--

'Canal Street'

JAI MAHMOOD:

Oh man, you wouldn't believe how many times I woke up with no memory of the night before and a guy in scrubs standing over me saying, 'Son, you're lucky to be alive.' I thought, *Fuck me, if this is what luck feels like, curse me any time.* By then so many people I knew had died. Mickey Mouth, Bi George, Typhoid Mary. Some of them I called ambulances for, some of them just stopped coming round. They weren't like Zoe. There was never any mystery when one of them went missing. In a horrible way, you knew all about what happened.

I only made it to one funeral in that whole time, and that was my mum's. Wasn't even invited, and I was so broke I had to steal the suit I went in. After that it was bad. I called Fintan, crying, asking for help, but as soon as he said the word 'rehab' I hung up. I was doing the limbo, man. As long as I could still dance under that pole I didn't care how low down I got. Like, I was at that stage where you're down to one of everything. One pair of pants, one pair of socks, one pair of trousers. One pound in my pocket, one friend in the world, one-track mind. But because I was an addict, to me that was all I needed. I thought, *How can I stop now, when I've still got so much left to lose?* I was the real thing, a living, breathing oxy-moron. What I'm saying is, I wasn't sitting round thinking, like, *Where are they now?*

FINTAN MURPHY:

I'd hear from Jai every so often, sometimes in the middle of the night, sometimes with a call from someone he owed money to. More often than not from the police or the Royal Infirmary. I always tried to reach out, but he didn't make it easy. Maybe that's why I started steering the work of the Nolan Foundation more and more towards the problems of substance abuse. It was something Robert always resisted – I think he thought it unseemly – but it was the great problem of our time and place, and something it seemed likely Zoe had struggled with, too. Our work drifted naturally in that direction as Robert's attention drifted elsewhere. The foundation merged with a homeless shelter I'd worked at in Ancoats and then began expanding their programme. When four out of five people are walking through the door with addictions, it doesn't seem good enough to just give them a warm meal and send them on their way.

JAI MAHMOOD:

It was another year after the funeral before I ran out of things. Pants, socks, excuses. I got right down to my very last possession, right down to my soul, and I'd started to feel like even that had one foot in the grave. The limbo pole was set too low, man. I couldn't get under it any more. When I finally asked Fintan for help he never called me out on my shit. He never said, 'How many times am I gonna have to bail you out?' He stumped up and put me in rehab, probably he saved my life.

ANDREW FLOWERS:

Once the sex-tape story broke I got packed off home from work. My phone started ringing with strange offers and requests, and I got the whole sodding weekend to myself so I could really stew in it. Technology's come on leaps and bounds since the last time I waded through this sort of shit, and it was great to get a demonstration in how connected we are now, all the ways you can get called a liar, a cheater and a cunt without leaving the comfort of your own home. If you haven't received a death threat via LinkedIn, if there isn't a Twitter parody account with your picture attached – mine's called Andrew *De-Flowers* – then have you even really lived? One company called TripleXDirectory offered me money to produce an *actual* porn film, as long as I could get Kim involved. They sounded sincere, but I was probably live on Australian radio or something, I was probably speaking to a shock-jock or their prime minister, however it works over there. I told them the truth anyway, that it sounded a fuck-sight better than another Christmas in retail but, alas, I hadn't spoken to Kim in the worst part of a decade.

JAI MAHMOOD:

When you live a life like mine you don't get a lot of ideas about the future. I wasn't walking out of rehab with a five-year plan in my pocket. Fintan came through there, man. Food and lodging if I worked in the foundation centre in Ancoats. I'd been in often enough, always on the wrong side of the counter, but still. I knew the place, the people and what they were going through. And I wanted to help. I really did want to start giving back instead of taking all the time. I was doing maintenance, making sure people stayed fed and bedded, leading NA meetings – you name it. He said if Rob ever came round I should keep my head down, but he never did.

There've been about five million names, about five million people down through the years, and a lot of them I know I won't ever see again, so imagine my mug when I saw Vladimir, *Vlad the Inhaler*, my first connect from back in Owens Park days. He walked in wearing his rucksack and looking for something to eat. He'd shrunk down so much I nearly didn't know him. He'd been this great big guy before but everything had taken its toll, everything had sunk. You could have changed his name, too, just straight up called him Vlad the Impaler, because he'd graduated from snorting anything in sight to shooting it. When you saw his arms and legs they were like pin cushions, just war torn with sores and track marks, broken veins all over. I was surprised he was even alive. I could tell he had no interest in getting sober or asking for help. We were just somewhere he could sit indoors and get a bite to eat between binges – and listen, fair fucks, life's not for everyone.

He walked in mid-meeting that night. I couldn't stop and talk, but I was staring at him, assessing the damage, when I saw something I never thought I'd see again. I can't even remember the rest of the meeting. I just wanted to get it over with and talk to Vlad. With one thing and another, people coming up and stuff, I couldn't get to him in time. I might have spooked him, looked a second too long or something, but he left. When I ran down the road a few minutes later he was gone.

KIMBERLY NOLAN:

I emailed some of the websites streaming the video that weekend, I tried to get them to take it down but I don't think any replied. After what Dad had done I didn't feel like talking to him, and when Mum called I was too embarrassed to answer. So I called the one person who'd got in touch and offered me their help, I called Fintan.

FINTAN MURPHY:

I must say, I wasn't fully prepared for a phone call from Kimberly. Yes, I'd called earlier to put her in the picture about Robert, I felt I owed her that much – the foundation's full support when it came to the potential blowback from her father's actions, a small local scandal. But I'm afraid that all changed for me when ten or more journalists left a press conference I was hosting to watch a smut film she'd made with Andrew Flowers. I was dumbstruck.

Perhaps people who'd been around them more at the time were better equipped to deal with it than I was. Other people knew them better, perhaps they'd picked up on a certain kind of energy that was moving back and forth. But you have to remember that I only knew Zoe back then, Zoe, who spoke so highly of them both. And all the time they'd been having this sordid affair behind her back, taking her for a fool. Look, I've always been behind the curve when it comes to sex, I can come across as more conservative than I'd like, but it took my breath away that they didn't think it might be relevant in her disappearance. She went missing *minutes* after discovering their affair.

In my mind, their silence was either incredibly thoughtless or deeply suspect. I'm a man with a lot of sympathy, but for some reason I just couldn't extend it, it just wouldn't reach as far as the limb I felt like Kimberly was out on. I was still reeling from the revelations about Robert's proclivities, I'd almost lost everything I'd worked for, and I discovered the same day that Kimberly had done something at *least* as unforgivable, in my opinion perhaps more so. Andrew Flowers was a fly-by-night, a shallow, vain man without self-awareness, someone who you expect this sort of thing from. Kimberly was Zoe's *sister*.

KIMBERLY NOLAN:
He told me that I could, quote, 'Get fucked,' since that's clearly what I was so good at.

FINTAN MURPHY:
Yes, well, intellectually, I know you're right. It's not fair to compare them. Zoe and Kimberly are different people, vastly different interior lives. But, at the back of my mind, a part of me was thinking, *How dare you have that face? How dare you have that voice? Those eyes?* During the course of that conversation I came very close to saying, 'Perhaps, Kimberly, it's not a *feeling* of inadequacy you've always struggled with. Perhaps what we're looking at here is plain inadequacy, perhaps what we're staring in the face is the *fact* that you're not good enough, the *fact* that you don't even come close to Zoe.'

KIMBERLY NOLAN:

I hung up then looked out of my curtains at the hacks still standing in the street. You see people on the news and they're famous, there's a team around them. But for the rest of us, if your life turns into a story, there's no guide or help or person in your ear telling you what to do or where to go. So I just called into work and said I wouldn't be there the next day. If they had to fire me, then that was that, I wasn't going to have a photographer following me around while I dug up fucking flowerbeds. Then I packed a bag, went outside past this idiot in his tent and got in my car. Before I could even start up, my phone was ringing. I answered to a man asking for Kimberly Nolan. 'This is DI James calling from Greater Manchester Police. I think, in light of current events, we should probably have a talk, don't you?' He sounded bad, about a hundred years older, which at the time drove home how long it had been. I said, 'Okay, what do you want to know?' He said it would have to be in person, Monday afternoon. So that was it, I had a destination. I was going back to Manchester, seven years later.

ANDREW FLOWERS:

Yes, of course, amongst all the other horse shit, there was the not unexpected but still amazingly unwelcome phone call from the police. Detective Inspector James sounding like he wanted to reach through the phone and throttle me. 'Yes, sure, Monday, fine.'

JAI MAHMOOD:

So Vlad, man, he was as gay as the day is long. Like, *flame on*. That was why he bought me a drink that first time we met outside the

Great Central, he thought I was cute. He always called himself a 'large fruit smoothie', said that's why he'd had to leave Russia. Y'know, Putin's not into lads, is he? So after work I took a walk down to Canal Street, the gay quarter. From the state I'd seen him in he wouldn't be cruising any clubs, but I thought he might want to be around his people, y'know?

And there he was, sitting on the sidelines watching the boys go by. He didn't see me until I sat down on the street next to him, then he laughed. This fifty-year-old, ex-bare-knuckle-boxing, Russian, alcoholic shit-kicker with a slit nose, just laughing, throwing his wasted arm round me. I said it was good to see him and we caught up a bit. He'd been in and out of prison, made a break for the big time in London and had both his legs broken in response. He'd lived hard and crapped out, found himself out in the cold, back on the streets in Manchester. I told him where I'd been, explained all the gaps in my teeth and my memory. Then when we ran out of things to say I asked him, like, genuinely curious, 'So come on, impale me with it, Vlad. Where's a guy like you get an antique gold Rolex?'

--27--

'Showdown City'

JAI MAHMOOD:

Look, man, it didn't blow my brains out when I heard about Andrew and Kim – anyone with a pulse would have picked up on the tension there. I was probably a bit surprised to see Andrew was still in Manchester, that he was looking almost human. All I had to go on was the picture they'd printed of him in the paper. He was wearing a dark polo shirt from his job and the caption underneath said he worked in the Trafford Centre. I couldn't tell which shop from his uniform so I just went out there and walked round a bit. I don't know if you've been, but the Trafford Centre's basically laid out like a blind dictator's mansion, so it took me a minute.

ANDREW FLOWERS:

Well, of course we were coming up to Christmas again, somehow we always were. And of all the discount electronics-goods stores in all the towns in all the world, he walked into mine. I was in work early, waiting to find out if I still had a job. My consultation meeting with my boss, Keith, was scheduled for that morning, showdown city, except he said he wasn't quite ready for me yet. So I'd started the day as usual. Booting display devices, putting out the tills, recovering the shop floor. I wish I could say Jai was a welcome sight, or even a sight for sore eyes, but I'm afraid on that day he was just a sight. I went over, nodded and smiled, of course I did. He smiled back and I saw what a sad state his teeth were in, he looked like he had a lot more than just seven years on the clock.

And that was that.

Before either one of us could say anything Keith was at my shoulder, looking like he'd just swallowed shit, saying he could see me now. I asked Jai if he could give me a minute and followed Keith into the back, where he began my appraisal before I could even close the door. I interrupted and asked, 'Before I listen to all this, do I still have a job?' He smiled and said, no. He told me my conduct outside of the store had brought them into disrepute, my lifestyle was at odds with the 'values' of PC World. He had clippings, examples, the anecdote about teens trying to search for porn in the shop the week before. Then he smirked, nodded at the shop floor and said, 'Now you're bringing in bad sorts, too.' So I swept everything off the fucker's desk and left. I hadn't even sat down.

JAI MAHMOOD:

That's how a newly sober man and a freshly fired one ended up in the pub before eleven in the morning. Andrew bought two pints, decked his in one then pointed at mine and said, 'You drinking that?'

ANDREW FLOWERS:

When we started exchanging stories about the last seven years it turned out that neither one of us had exactly split the atom. I'd just lost my job more or less before his eyes so I didn't have much to shout about professionally. I still had most of my teeth, though, so it was one–nil there.

It was nice to see him.

It seemed in that moment like he'd swooped down out of the sky at my lowest point, potentially to pick me up. We were sitting in some awful chain pub listening to Christmas songs on a loop, always something I associate with Zoe. I felt like a lot of what had passed between us had washed under the bridge, it was just bittersweet that so much had washed away with it. We were both old men in our mid-twenties, coming in joint last position, just like always. And upon that realization, I think I went back to the bar.

KIMBERLY NOLAN:

I spent the weekend with Mum and got to my meeting with the police at Owens Park early, I didn't have much else to do that day. It was the 17th, the seventh anniversary of Zoe's disappearance, so I suppose I thought I should take a moment and pay my respects. I could see the tower from the street, but I knew it was empty. I'd heard it was scheduled to be demolished, which felt like the end of something. And I was nervous about talking to the police.

No one had ever asked me outright if it was Zoe in that video, but I knew I'd lied by omission and I assumed that was illegal. The detective, James, hadn't sounded happy on the phone. What worried me most was Owens Park, the main entrance, right on a busy road. I'd already had some odd looks, or at least I thought I had. My picture had been in a paper or two in the last few days, and of course the video was out there, so I didn't like the idea of being out in public. But I knew they had to have found something to arrange our meeting there . . .

JAI MAHMOOD:

When Andrew came back from the bar I wasn't sure how long he'd stay upright, so I got right down to it, the reason I was there. I said, 'That watch you had when we were living together, man, the Rolex . . .'

ANDREW FLOWERS:

I said, 'Yeah, what about it?'

JAI MAHMOOD:

'Did you ever find out what happened with that? Where it went? Who had it and why?'

ANDREW FLOWERS:

I probably looked at him a little more closely, a little more darkly, then answered carefully. 'No, and I assume it's gone for good.'

JAI MAHMOOD:

I said, 'What if I told you I knew where it was?' Andrew picked up his next pint and put a serious dent in it. Then he wiped his mouth and said, 'It's probably best left in the past.'

ANDREW FLOWERS:

Look, if he'd taken the damn thing I was trying hard to let him off the hook.

JAI MAHMOOD:

This thing that had been like life or fucking death for him seven years ago suddenly wasn't worth the time of day. He didn't have any curiosity about it. I said, 'Andrew, mate, I can get your grandad's watch back. How can you not care?'

ANDREW FLOWERS:

To which I said something like, 'Look, let's put our friendship above all that stuff. I don't want to know how you got it. My heart can't take it right now, okay? I don't want to think of you like that.' Then he started to get angry, asking if I was accusing him of stealing the watch, the very argument I was trying to avoid. He pushed his chair back and bared his gums, said he was clean, he was working for the Nolan Foundation, and anyway, he didn't have it, he just knew how I could get it. I said, 'Oh, let me guess. For a price?'

JAI MAHMOOD:

And, well, yeah. Look, man, I don't like the idea of someone paying to get their shit back, but I guess I'd gone there thinking, somehow, he still had money, he still cared. But neither of those things was true. Vlad had come straight out and said it, he'd stolen the watch, but not from Owens Park, and not from back then.

He said he'd give it up for a grand, way less than what it was worth, whatever state it was in. I tried to tell this to Andrew, but he wouldn't listen, he started to leave. I was like, 'So let me get this straight, you don't want your watch back?'

ANDREW FLOWERS:

I said, 'No, you can keep it. And I need to be somewhere, so I'll see you in another seven years.'

KIMBERLY NOLAN:

I'd been waiting there for the best part of an hour by this point. I was just about to call the police and make sure I had the right time when I heard someone behind me say, 'Kim?'

ANDREW FLOWERS:

Detective James had called me the night before for a light bollocking about the video. He said I needed to meet him at Owens Park to discuss the potential fallout of my not mentioning when questioned, *yada yada yada*. What with work and Jai and one thing and another, I was late. When I got there I couldn't see the police, just a woman with a duffel coat drawn up so high about her head I could hardly make out her face. I'd know that scowl anywhere, though.

KIMBERLY NOLAN:

I said, 'Andrew?' We laughed, I mean, just awkwardly, but still. And we hugged. I think we said hello in there somewhere, asked each other what we were doing. Andrew said he was meeting the police but he was so late he thought they'd probably left. I told him I'd been there for an hour and they'd never shown. I just remember the smile

fading off his face when he said, 'Why would they ask us both here?'
Then I think my smile faded, too.

I tried the number James had called from, but it just went to
answerphone. Then we both tried the police, we got passed around
a bit and finally Andrew got put through.

ANDREW FLOWERS:

Except DI James sounded distinctly different from the man I'd
spoken to the previous evening. What's more, he had no memory
of asking either one of us to meet him anywhere. He wasn't even
assigned to Zoe's case any more. I got off the phone and Kim said,
'But why would someone set us up to be here?' when I spotted a
man over the road taking pictures. A man who'd clearly been standing there the entire time. I walked straight through the traffic, threw
his fucking camera into a tree and grabbed him by his fat throat.

KIMBERLY NOLAN:

Andrew was lifting him off the ground by his neck, demanding to
know how he knew we'd both be there. The guy said his newspaper
got an anonymous tip, they'd sent him out to take pictures, then he
looked at me like I'd cool things down. I told Andrew to squeeze
harder. The guy was shouting at us that it was assault, which was
true, but I got in his face and explained to him that we were in a
unique situation.

ANDREW FLOWERS:

I was too furious to see straight, much less speak, my piss was at
boiling point. Kim said what I couldn't. Neither one of us wanted to

be pictured outside Owens Park on the seventh anniversary of Zoe's disappearance, and especially not smiling, especially not three days after that ridiculous video leaked.

But what incensed us was the suggestion of an anonymous tip. We'd both fallen foul of that game over the years, and I think after this last run-in especially, we were both coming to the conclusion that someone was behind it. These weren't isolated incidents, each represented one part in a sustained campaign of hate. Kim explained all this to the newspaper man, but when Clarke Kunt still couldn't grasp things she put them more bluntly.

KIMBERLY NOLAN:

I said I thought the video of me and Andrew had been leaked by the person responsible for taking my sister. I said we'd both been lured there by someone impersonating a police officer, and that his news-paper had been notified of our meeting before *we'd* even known about it. I was stressing that whoever set this photoshoot up could well be Zoe's stalker or kidnapper, her killer even.

MARCUS LEE:

Yeah, Lionel called, shitting it down the phone. These guys can take a choking, believe me, but from the sounds of it Flowers still had him by the throat. He put it to me, what they'd said, and I thought it sounded interesting. Then Kim got on the line and made me an offer I couldn't refuse.

KIMBERLY NOLAN:

I'd had requests for years to tell my side of the story, to do an interview or a photoshoot at the tower. I'd always said no – the idea repulsed me – but I thought, right there and then in that moment, let's cash it all in. I told him if he killed the story of me and Andrew, and if he had the number the tip came in from, I'd give him a full interview.

MARCUS LEE:

We were fresh off the reporting we'd done around her dad's alleged abuses of power, and still reeling from the leaked sex tape, so there'd be plenty for us to talk about before we even got on to Zoe. There was also the inevitable blowback an article like that might have. Bad news for Kim, but good news for us – it could run and run.

KIMBERLY NOLAN:

Me and Andrew were still standing in the street. I looked around and said I'd need somewhere to stay. Marcus suggested putting me in the Hilton, the skyscraper in Manchester. I was about to tell him he had a deal when Andrew took the phone out of my hand.

ANDREW FLOWERS:

I said, 'Marcus, hi. Here's how it's gonna be. You get Kim, you get a photoshoot, you get her signature today, but the price is ten grand, no ifs and no buts. Her minibar had better stay stocked as well. Call me back when you want to say yes.' Then I hung up. Kim started to give me an angry look but the phone was vibrating before she'd even fully frowned. Take it from me, if you're selling your soul, don't do it cheap.

MARCUS LEE:

I didn't even blink before I called back and said yes – it was a steal.

My one condition was that I wouldn't give her the number this tip came in from until the article had run, I didn't want her backing out. I took the train up there that day, checked in and spent the 17th, 18th and 19th interviewing her and writing the piece. What we got – the story about her being kidnapped from outside Fifth Avenue – was a blinder. It ran on the 20th, a tight turnaround, but nice for the anniversary.

KIMBERLY NOLAN:

Marcus brought the paper to my room that morning before he checked out. I wasn't interested, I never read it, I just wanted the number that the tip about me and Andrew at Owens Park had come from. He kept his word, said I should let him know if it gave me more to say. When I saw the number I knew it was familiar, but I had to go back through my phone to work out why. Then I saw it was the same one Fintan Murphy had called me from six days before, when he broke the news about what Dad had done.

on Fri, Mar 22, 2019, Joseph Knox joeknoxxxx@gmail.com wrote:

Hey – sorry – it was a little bit awkward when you called. ██████████

██████████████████████ Also on deadline but can

maybe squeeze in ten mins later tonight? Found it hard to follow

what you were saying without seeing a transcript but were you ever

able to follow up on Fintan's alibi? His flatmate/lover Connor

Sullivan??

Really glad to hear you finally saw a doctor. I've got everything

crossed for you, E.

Jx

It's okay. ███████████████████████████████

Yes – I called Connor a couple of weeks back. He confirmed Fintan's

alibi from the night Zoe went missing. Said Fintan got home late

(12–1am) and went to bed. He and Fintan went back to Owens Park

the next morning to pack up the speakers Connor had rented out for

the party. Connor didn't know the rest of them, he was a few years

older, but he said Fintan turned green when he heard Zoe was

missing. He left Connor to it while he went to join the search.

Sounds like that was the story of their life, like, Zoe kind of came between them. He's married now but started asking how Fintan was, if he'd ever managed to have kids, etc. Apparently that was the big dream back in the day. I'm starting to feel like this might be the book of lost dreams . . .

My guy from Fairfield Property Management's been back in touch. I asked before if there was any way he could build me a list of people who worked at the site in the summer of 2011, just before the students arrived. At the time he didn't think so, but his wife's been in the attic and thinks she might have some old time cards(!) She's wading through them now.

Yeah, I'm glad I saw the doctor too. She says she'll be in touch. I was expecting to lie awake all night worrying but I can hardly keep my eyes open. Don't worry about calling me back, I know you have other priorities.

E

--28--

'Being Wrong'

FINTAN MURPHY:

It was a rough few days. The revelations about Robert's personal life on the 14th, followed by the leak of the Andrew–Kim video and then the anniversary of Zoe's disappearance on the 17th. So when I wake up to two phones ringing on the 20th, messages coming at me from all angles, I thought, what now? Of course it was the world spinning off its axis in response to Kimberly's *Mail* interview.

I was furious, as you know.

It felt to me like she was taking oxygen away from Zoe. That's why I spent that week talking to you about it, ranting it all off my chest. When I got messages from the office in the wake of the news saying that Kimberly had called, that she was trying to get in touch, I ignored them. I knew you were interviewing her, though. And I knew her kidnap story would make for a good chapter in the book, so I think I started using you as a go-between, saying cruel things knowing they'd get back to her. Christmas week went by like that, both of us meeting you at different times to trash each other. At a certain point I just thought, *Who's this helping?* You know, I wanted a fresh start, to draw a line under it all.

I went into the office on New Year's Day, hoping to leave it behind. Then I'm in the middle of a meeting when Andrew Flowers storms into the room *demanding* to speak with me. I haven't seen him in seven years, I haven't even thought of him until this business with the video, and more to the point, I haven't wanted to. I start to say, 'Look, whatever this is, you'll just have to wait,' when I see Kimberly standing behind him in the doorway.

KIMBERLY NOLAN:

I'd never been there before, the Nolan Foundation. To be honest, I didn't think about it until I was actually in the building, but I was stunned. It wasn't some pant-wetting feel-goodery set up to absorb middle-class guilt. We walked in through actual *work*. I mean, the office is above the outreach centre in Ancoats. There were people in the doorway who relied on the place, who loved it. There were people inside getting meals and winter coats. There was a whole warehouse of household items to try and help the less well-off get back on their feet. I don't know why it surprised me to see that it was such a good thing, but it did, and in the best possible way. I couldn't stay angry once I walked through that door.

ANDREW FLOWERS:

We'd been trying to get hold of Fintan for over a week, but he was dodging us, so we decided to go down to the foundation. I asked him to explain how his fucking phone number had been used to call in a tip about our location to the *Mail*. He started stammering, 'My number? The *Mail*? What?' I told him we knew he'd set us up and the sooner he explained why, the sooner we could get the police involved.

FINTAN MURPHY:

I think I just sat down, it all just made me tired. I told them that obviously I had nothing to do with anything like that. I told them the truth, you know, 'For starters, I didn't even know either of you were in town until Kimberly's tell-all interview. For seconds, why on earth would I do something like that?' I sort of gestured to our surroundings to say, 'Is that really the kind of man I strike you as?'

That seemed to give them both something to think about because, look, I'm no saint, but I spend every waking minute trying to help other people. I asked who'd told them this and they admitted it had been Marcus Lee from the *Mail*. I said, 'Oh, right, that'll be the same sleazebag who broke the story about Robert, then. I wonder why he'd want us all fighting each other?' Andrew demanded to see my phone, but I had to ask him which one. My mobile? My desk phone? My home phone? What? Kimberly found the number and read it out. So I got up and told them to follow me.

KIMBERLY NOLAN:

We went down the stairs into the main building, then into the warehouse, which was amazing. Washing machines, dishwashers, sofas, wardrobes, kitchen furnishings – everything you'd need to make a home, all of it stacked up as far as the eye could see. Fintan took us to a corner office, opened the door and held out his arm. And there was Jai sitting at the desk.

ANDREW FLOWERS:

I walked in there still steaming. Fintan wasn't someone I'd ever really had dealings with back in the day, but he got under my skin like fucking scabies.

JAI MAHMOOD:

I said hi to them both, man, smiled at Kim, it was good to see her. Then Andrew said, 'Oh, Jai. Why did you do it?' I said, 'Why did I do what?'

FINTAN MURPHY:

Before everything got too far out of hand, I explained the situation as I understood it, that Andrew and Kim had both been set up outside Owens Park for a photo op. The tip to the newspaper had apparently come from the phone in *our* office. Of course, Andrew had to turn every dial up as high as it would go . . .

ANDREW FLOWERS:

I told Kim and Fintan that Jai had been into my place of work a week or so before asking me for money, that I'd knocked him back. It had happened on the same day that someone set us up with the press.

JAI MAHMOOD:

Fintan and Kim looked at me, like, 'Is this true?' And I said what Andrew hadn't let me say before. That a homeless guy had walked through the door a couple of weeks back wearing his fucking grandad's Rolex. I'd tried to get it back for him but the guy knew what it was worth and he wasn't letting it go for less than a grand. If Flowers didn't want it, that was fine by me, but I wasn't looking to make money off him.

ANDREW FLOWERS:

I started to say, 'Okay, so if you didn't call in the tip, who did?' At which point we all turn to see the villain of the piece, Mr Rob Nolan, falling through the door.

FINTAN MURPHY:

I was livid to see him there. Not only had he dropped me in the shit, but he'd run Zoe's name through it, too. More to the point, he hadn't bothered to answer the hundred and one phone calls I'd tried to place to him the day those stories broke. I said, 'You've got some nerve showing up here, Robert.' I'd never talked to him like that, but in that moment I think I could have killed. He didn't say anything so I asked him, 'What are you doing here?'

KIMBERLY NOLAN:

He stared at me, obviously drunk, and said, 'I'm here to see my second-favourite daughter.' I hadn't seen him since I left Manchester in 2012, I hadn't talked to him much, but you're not supposed to hear things like that from your own dad. It felt like being slapped. But the fucking thing is, right, I'd gotten stronger since then, he'd just crumpled in on himself.

ANDREW FLOWERS:

Time had taken a running jump at him, he looked and sounded twice his age, but I recognized his voice from the phone, the man impersonating a police officer. He'd been trying to truly wreck his one remaining daughter's life. I thought, *Fuck me, at least my father just pretends I don't exist.*

FINTAN MURPHY:

I apologized to Kimberly there and then. To Andrew as well. I told them that, as far as I was concerned, Robert and I were nothing to do with each other any more, I had no idea he was still coming and going from the premises.

ROBERT NOLAN:

All I saw was a room full of people who'd betrayed my daughter and betrayed me. I said I should burn the place down for all the good it had done.

FINTAN MURPHY:

He's screaming, blind drunk, ranting and raving. He says, 'For all the good this place has done, I should torch it.' For all the *good* it had done. Feeding hundreds of unfortunate people a week, improving the lives of thousands. It was nothing to him if he didn't get to stand on stage taking credit for it. I said, 'You're right, Robert. Frankly, I'm not sure there even *is* a Nolan Foundation without someone from the Nolan family involved. Certainly not one I'd want to be a part of.'

ANDREW FLOWERS:

Rob said that if that was the way Fintan felt, then he accepted his resignation.

FINTAN MURPHY:

I told him that wasn't what I was getting at. I asked Kimberly, right there and then, if she'd want to be involved with the foundation.

KIMBERLY NOLAN:

And I don't know if it was the madness of that week or how impressed I was with the place. I don't know if it was just to get back at my dad or what, but I accepted. Dad looked at me for a long time, then eventually just staggered out. I said, 'Okay,' like, trying to get my breath back and stop my hands from shaking. I looked at Jai and said, 'So what's this about Andrew's watch?'

--29--

'Bombshell'

JAI MAHMOOD:

Yeah, I told them what I knew about the watch, man. I said where I'd seen it, who had it and what he wanted for the thing.

KIMBERLY NOLAN:

All I wanted to know was where it had come from. Jai was adamant that this guy, this Vlad, hadn't taken it from Owens Park. He said he wouldn't even have gotten through the gate. That was interesting to me because I wondered if he'd stolen it from the person who'd *originally* stolen it. Jai said we'd need cash to get it back and I told him that was no problem, I had my *Mail* money.

ANDREW FLOWERS:

I didn't like that idea and I said so. I just wanted to leave the past where it was. It hadn't done us any favours when it was the present, so why go over it again? I didn't want the fucking watch back.

KIMBERLY NOLAN:

I didn't have time for whatever was going on with Andrew. I walked past him, back into Fintan and Jai in the office and said, 'How soon can we get it?'

JAI MAHMOOD:

I said if she got the cash, I'd get Vlad, but, you know, 'The guy's not exactly a safe-deposit box, I need to go looking for him.' Andrew was standing in the door, staring daggers into me so hard I thought they might break the fucking skin.

I thought again how weird it was that he didn't want the watch back. Then Kim went back out and I heard them fight about it outside. He was saying she shouldn't spend the money, she should keep it. She was saying, 'Don't you want to know who took your watch?' At this point I break in, like, 'Hey, guys, look, I'm not sure the information's for sale.' Kim said, 'I've got ten grand, Jai. If I want his fucking fingerprints, I'm getting them.'

KIMBERLY NOLAN:

I was charged up. It had been an intense few days but I felt like something had finally cracked. I got this sense that the truth was out there for the taking, I just couldn't lose my nerve. Andrew was being off-the-wall weird. Saying it was a bad idea, that we weren't allowed to do it if he didn't want us to, that he wouldn't be involved, all this. I sort of shrugged and said, 'Fine, don't be involved.'

FINTAN MURPHY:

Andrew stormed off. Jai left to find his friend and, for the first time,

Kimberly and I actually talked. Just five or ten minutes, but with some much-needed candour. I told her that the process of being interviewed for your book had made me reconsider my position on certain things. That I hadn't always felt good about what was coming out of my mouth. I don't know if she felt exactly the same way, but she said she'd been rethinking things, too.

It was a nice moment, but before I could let her leave there was something I had to know. I asked if she'd spent much time with Andrew in the intervening years. She said no, they hadn't spoken since all that. And then, with great difficulty, because I'm not good at these things, I asked if she was sure that she could trust him? She started to nod but I said, 'Think about it. The video, all these years, why did you keep it a secret?'

KIMBERLY NOLAN:

I said, 'It wasn't like you think. It was messy, we both just decided in the moment it was for the best.'

FINTAN MURPHY:

Well, that was my point entirely. I said, 'No, it wasn't for the best. Not for Andrew. For you, yes, had the tape come out, it would have made things difficult with your parents. For Andrew, though, it would have explained why his girlfriend ripped his face off, it would have exonerated him from the text message, from scaring her, from so many things. Why wouldn't he have just told the truth?'

KIMBERLY NOLAN:

So I just said what Andrew had told me at the time, about wanting to protect me. Somehow it didn't sound quite as romantic in the here and now.

FINTAN MURPHY:

I said that was laudable if true, but it didn't really sound like him. I just wondered out loud if there was an alternative explanation? Kim said, 'Like what?' I said, 'Maybe he wanted to stay in the frame for some reason? Maybe he wanted to stay close to the case? Maybe he liked having this secret over you?' You know, why *wouldn't* he want us to find out who stole his watch, who was behind all this? We said goodnight, agreed to meet the next morning, but of course we were both woken up by the bombshell instead.

JAI MAHMOOD:

So the first place I tried when I was looking for Vlad was Canal Street, where I'd seen him before, but he wasn't around so I went into town, trying to remember old haunts. When I went back by Canal Street in the a.m., the whole thing was cordoned off. If you don't know, it's nightlife central, and cordoning-off just doesn't happen there. So I was asking round, trying to find out what was going on, getting a bad vibe, when I saw them turn the floodlights on to the canal. There was a body in there. It wasn't until the next day that we found out it was Vladimir. They said he'd been stabbed through the back and pushed in the water. No one ever found Andrew's watch.

From: evelynidamitchell@gmail.com
Sent: 25/03/19 05:45
To: you

Hey, hey, HEY! Brace yourself for some insanely exciting news. I know I can't call you and it's too early for any sane person to be awake, but Den's wife from Fairfield Property Management came through with those time cards. I've been on the phone with them all night, he was reading them out to me as she was finding them, telling me what he remembered about each member of his crew that year. The full list of everyone on site's huge, some of them had been with him for ever, most were at their Christmas do on the night Zoe went missing, but they hired five casual hands to help out in summer 2011.

Here are the names – anyone look familiar???

Coulter, Stuart
Johansen, Andrew
Smith, Martin
Sullivan, Connor
Todd, Edward

Connor fucking Sullivan. A certain someone's alibi. I'm shaking writing this, going over there now. Next time we talk I'll have a tape so hot it might burn the house down.

I THINK I might finally have my ending.

And that isn't even my big news. Dr Lloyd called back about my tests. Guess who isn't sick again after all? Guess who's 7 weeks PREGNANT?

Exxx

In the early hours of 25 March 2019 Evelyn Mitchell was found unresponsive behind the wheel of her car on a residential street in Hulme, three miles outside of Manchester city centre. She was pronounced dead at the scene, with a post-mortem report later determining the cause of death to be blunt-force trauma to the head. The coroner noted that her skull had been broken with such ferocity that brain tissue was visible to the naked eye. That she walked the 27 feet from the home of her attacker to the relative safety of her vehicle is hardly surprising. Evelyn's strength could be incredible, at times almost unrealistic, and it endured, dynamically, until the very end. Had it not, perhaps her story would close like that of so many others, like the Zoe Nolans of the world. Young women filled with promise who vanish from the face of the earth through no fault of their own. Evelyn's bloody-minded determination meant that she left a trail leading from her car to the front door of her attacker.

Her final email to me left a similar trail.

It contained the name Connor Sullivan, listing him as one of five casual labourers employed by a maintenance firm working in Owens Park during the pre-term summer of 2011. As Evelyn must have immediately seen, it was also the name given by Fintan Murphy as his alibi for 17 December 2011, the day that Zoe Nolan disappeared. Far from being an alias or the invention of a fevered mind, Connor Sullivan was Fintan Murphy's birth name. According to Greater Manchester Police, the alibi Sullivan gave for Murphy *was* corroborated by officers in 2011. Unfortunately, neither one of the constables taking the statement at Sullivan's home had been involved in the search of Owens Park. They could have no idea that Sullivan and Murphy were one and the same, not least because Sullivan was able to provide two items of legal identification and spoke with a broad Mancunian accent. Because Connor Sullivan – Fintan Murphy – was born in Stretford, England, and was some six years older than he claimed to be, an old soul, as so many people went on to describe him. He had never so much as travelled to Ireland. Most disturbingly, despite his many claims to the contrary, authorities have been unable to find any evidence that he ever met Zoe Nolan, much less that he was her treasured friend.

Sullivan changed his name to Fintan Murphy in 2009, after being convicted of the 2008 assault of a Manchester Metropolitan University student. The young woman, who has asked not to be identified, discovered him hiding beneath her bed in the early hours of the morning, clutching a bag filled with her personal possessions. He had twice been cautioned for stealing clothes from young women, although authorities concluded at the time that these crimes were not sexual in nature. Sullivan's sexual preference was for men, and while he showed no interest in transitioning into a woman, he admitted to an obsession around certain objects, considering them to be talismans that would aid his fertility. Searching his home in

2008, authorities found a large collection of stolen clothing, hair-brushes and used tampons.

Sullivan often talked about wanting children, starting a family, 'righting the wrongs' that had been done to him. It seems, in spite of his temperamental dishonesty, that there was some sad truth in the back story he wove for Fintan Murphy. His mother really had struggled with profound mental-health problems, resulting in a diagnosis of paranoid schizophrenia, and Sullivan's placement into foster care at the age of thirteen.

Registrars at Manchester University confirmed that no persons giving the names of Connor Sullivan or Fintan Murphy were ever enrolled in any course during the 2011–12 term, nor at any time prior. It seems that a man matching Sullivan's description *was* asked to leave the first meeting of the Choir and Orchestra Society held at St Chrysostom's Church that term. While it's tempting to believe that this is where he saw Zoe for the first time, the truth is likely far more sinister. The professional working theory is that Sullivan discovered the crawlspace unique to apartment 15C while performing maintenance in Tower Block, working for Fairfield Property Management under his birth name, some months before Zoe even arrived in Manchester. The odds of him going on to meet or become infatuated with a young woman who happened to live there seem small. More likely, Sullivan positioned himself inside the apartment – was already inside the walls – when Alex, Kimberly, Liu, Lois and Zoe arrived on the week commencing 24 September 2011.

After that, he fixated on Zoe.

His presence accounts for Zoe's missing underwear, Liu's sense that a man had been inside the flat, the voices Lois heard at night and perhaps even the ghost that Alex claimed as her room-mate. His presence accounts for the vicious essay left on Zoe's computer, the theft of a personal recording made by Andrew and Kimberly, and the assault which took place on 30 January 2012 in which a prospectus was taken by force from Kimberly's hands. Evidence recovered from Sullivan's home suggests that he studied the personal texts, direct messages and emails of Zoe, his easy access to her room giving him ample opportunity to do so. He discovered that she was in a clandestine relationship with Professor Michael Anderson, who she had met as a fifteen-year-old music student. It's impossible to say whether Sullivan led the investigation in Anderson's direction out of a desire to help expose an abuser, or out of a desire to provide a promising suspect. It's impossible to say if the apparent rift between Anderson and Zoe – her aggressive spending of what was likely his money – was a result of Sullivan's interference or not. It's impossible to say whether Sullivan followed Andrew and Jai to Tree Court, whether he stole their flatmate Harry Fowles's keys and was also responsible for the thefts which took place there.

It's impossible to say, because Connor Sullivan – Fintan Murphy – took his own life on 25 March, as well as the life of Evelyn Mitchell. Greater Manchester Police discovered a so-called 'suicide kit' in Sullivan's home, suggesting he had been long prepared for his eventual outing.

Frustratingly, no evidence of Zoe's whereabouts was found.

On the evening of 16 December 2011, with advance knowledge of the Christmas party taking place at the tower, Sullivan moved freely through the building, using the name Fintan Murphy and affecting to be an invited guest. Such was his boldness that he even introduced himself to Kimberly as a close friend of Zoe's. Although he claimed to have left the building following Andrew and Jai's physical altercation, Mahmood has never been able to recollect being escorted outside. The most likely scenario would see Sullivan stealing the sex-tape recording from Kimberly's laptop in the days leading up to the party, then leaking it in an attempt to isolate Zoe from her friends. Knowing of Zoe's burgeoning reliance on pills, Sullivan would have had a chance to attack or subdue her on the roof, creating a diversion with the smoke alarm (or perhaps just taking advantage of a real emergency), before storing her body, dead or alive, inside the crawlspace beside her own bedroom. A crawlspace he had already remade as a shrine to her, decorating the walls with photographs stolen from Jai and dressing a mannequin in clothes taken from Zoe's room.

Perhaps Sullivan intended to hurt Zoe and perhaps he didn't.

Perhaps, having grown so obsessed, he simply could not bear the thought of her leaving for the Christmas holidays. DNA evidence showed no traces of Zoe's blood behind the wall, but police noted at the time that the space had been 'forensically' cleaned. Had he stowed Zoe's body there, his options for removing her would have been ample, with fully forty-three days passing between her disappearance and Sarah Manning's discovery of the crawlspace. With that said, Sullivan's best opportunity to remove evidence came on the morning of Zoe's disappearance, when around a thousand students moved their belongings out of Tower Block for the Christmas break, unimpeded by the police. Under his birth name, Sullivan made money by renting out speakers and DJ equipment. A young woman who hired speakers for the party on the fifteenth floor has since identified the man who delivered them as Connor Sullivan. Although she did not remember seeing him collect the speakers the following day, she claimed that both the equipment and the flight case it had arrived in were gone when she woke up on the morning of the 17th.

That Sullivan went on to so convincingly present himself as Zoe's friend likely comes from his close reading of her personal messages, and from the secrecy Zoe felt forced to live her life by. The lies, fabrications and falsehoods he went on to employ are almost too numerous to name. He stole Zoe's red jacket from Kimberly's room after she was assaulted outside of Fifth Avenue nightclub, later he lied about reviewing CCTV footage from the night in question to cast doubts on her. He planted evidence incriminating Michael Anderson. He stole a Rolex watch belonging to Andrew Flowers. He made anonymous tips to newspapers, listing the locations of Andrew, Jai and Kimberly. He became the head of a charitable organization under false auspices. He turned a blind eye to Robert Nolan's behaviour. He leaked the full video of Andrew and Kimberly to divert damaging attention away from the foundation, and he very likely murdered Igor Turgenev, otherwise known as Vlad the Inhaler, who is assumed to have stolen Andrew's Rolex from Sullivan's home. Whether Turgenev stole the watch after meeting Sullivan through the foundation, or whether they had some deeper relationship, is impossible now to determine. There are many such question marks still hanging over Sullivan. I find myself thinking about the young woman who hanged herself in Alex Wilson's room in 15C, two years before Alex arrived to live with Zoe and Kim. I find myself thinking of Alex herself, who went on to take her own life. We will likely never know if Connor Sullivan had some part to play in this.

Although no evidence of Zoe's whereabouts was discovered in Sullivan's home, her DNA was found across scores of stolen personal items – clothes, hairbrushes, hygiene products – that had been lovingly preserved for eight years. She remains a mystery to us now, unknowable in death as in life, with reported sightings still coming in from places as far afield as Africa, Australia and Havana. On dark days, when black clouds start ganging up and threatening the sun, I sometimes choose to believe these sightings, imagining her happy, laughing, under her own power and abroad for her own reasons. At such times I remember why fiction is so often preferable to fact.

Evelyn Mitchell had been working on versions of this book for several years, poring through information readily available to the public, but it only began to cohere when she started speaking to Zoe's friends and family. She had been collating interviews for some time before Turgenev's murder, and continued to do so for some time afterwards. She became close to the people who had been in Zoe's life, including Sullivan, and suffered a terrifying and anonymous ordeal as a result. She never chose to let this ordeal define her, always dealing with it through humour, resolve and bloody-minded determination. Her work revealed a monster, and when she confronted him with the truth he killed her for it.

Whatever happened inside that house, Evelyn got up and walked away, determined that Connor Sullivan would never make her his victim. He never did.

J. Knox, 2019

ADDENDUM

In their close analysis of the first edition of *True Crime Story*, it appears that some readers have come away with the misapprehension that I, Joseph Knox, was the father of Evelyn's child. They point towards the brief redactions I chose to make throughout our correspondence, to so-called 'missing emails' and to Evelyn's claim, in her final message to me, that she was seven weeks pregnant. This apparently would put conception in early February, when, according to the emails presented in this book, we both referenced meeting for drinks.

All I can say in response is that this is simply not true, and the idea that my interest in Evelyn went beyond her brilliant mind and her brilliant work should be considered a grave insult against her memory. The redactions, as I stated early on in these pages, were made to protect Evelyn's personal information. The so-called 'missing emails' were simply mundane exchanges with no bearing on the matter at hand. While it's true that a subsequent systems error led to my losing almost all of the original messages we exchanged, this is less a sign of my duplicity than it is of my disorganization. It should go without saying that the dissolution of my marriage following the publication of this book was an unrelated personal matter, and that neither my ex-wife nor I will be commenting further on the circumstances.

I have cherished and taken seriously my role in keeping Evelyn's spirit alive. Contrary to popular belief, it brings me great joy to see that *True Crime Story* has eclipsed my own work, both critically and commercially. My one regret is that Evelyn isn't here to enjoy the success that she worked so hard for. And also, that in the whirlwind of the book's original publication, I failed to properly thank her father, without whom none of this would have been possible. I have absolutely no problem in doing so now.

Jim Max, 2020

Robert Nolan remains committed to finding his daughter, Zoe, and still performs music around the Stoke-on-Trent area.

Sally Nolan is retired and entirely dedicated to her garden, her daughter and her closest friends. She is excited by the prospect of grandchildren.

Liu Wai was promoted internally by human resources consulting firm Mercer UK in early 2019, and used this momentum to showcase her talents externally, accepting a higher-paying role with The People People later that year. She loves to travel.

Jai Mahmood is now a professional drugs counsellor and amateur photographer. His work has been exhibited across London, Manchester and Paris. At the time of writing, he is stone-cold sober.

Andrew Flowers was tempted away from consumer electronics and into charitable work. During the course of his life he has lost a fortune but gained a loving partner. He feels incredibly lucky for this but, at the time of writing, is admittedly drunk.

Kimberly Nolan now lives in Manchester but makes frequent weekend trips back to Ambleside. She enjoys great relationships with her mother, Sally, and with her partner, Andrew. As the head of the Nolan Foundation, and as an expectant mother, she has broken the habit of a lifetime by working out exactly who and what she is. She is Zoe Nolan's sister – and she could not possibly be more proud of that.

ABOUT THE AUTHOR

Joseph Knox was born and raised in and around Stoke and Manchester, where he worked in bars and bookshops before moving to London. His debut novel, *Sirens*, the first part of the Aidan Waits series, was a bestseller and has been translated into eighteen languages. *True Crime Story* is his first stand-alone novel.

For more information on Joseph and his books, see his website at www.josephknox.co.uk or follow him on Twitter @josephknox__